# LIMITED EDITION: A POACHER'S ENDGAME

# Limited Edition: A Poacher's Endgame

## By
## Prakash Dighé

Progressive
RISING PHOENIX PRESS

Text Copyright © 2017 Prakash Dighé


All rights reserved.
Published 2017 by
Progressive Rising Phoenix Press, LLC
www.progressiverisingphoenix.com

ISBN: 978-1-946329-46-2


Printed in the U.S.A.
1st Printing


Edited by: Jody Amato

Cover photograph: "Sunset Over Acacia Tree and African Elephant," Big Stock Photography, Stock Photo ID: 170105591, Copyright © Artush

Book and Cover design by William Speir
Visit: http://www.williamspeir.com

# Acknowledgments

The journey to bring this book to fruition has been long and arduous and could never have been accomplished without the help and support of friends, fellow authors, and family members.

I am indebted to the proficient members of the Writers Guild of Texas in Dallas. The feedback and encouragement from those in their critique groups have been invaluable and I'm particularly grateful to my beta reader, Michael Risden, who provided me with vital input. The Guild invites distinguished speakers to their monthly meetings and organizes periodic workshops, which have helped me improve my writing skills.

Special thanks to Joe Black for his words of encouragement and suggestions on maintaining a brisk pace of the narration. My editor, Jody Amato, has done a remarkable job of polishing my shoddy manuscript. But above all, I am grateful to my publisher, Progressive Rising Phoenix Press – Amanda Thrasher and her team – without whom the book would not have seen the light of the day.

Lastly, my family—my wife, children, and their families—for their patience while I struggled through the manuscript and for the feedback and encouragement I received from them.

# Author's Note

Kenya, a country blessed with abundant wildlife and where dwell some of the warmest and friendliest people, forms the setting for this novel. Sadly, the menace of poaching impinges upon the peace and calm of the game reserves and it is to those brave souls who combat this scourge that I wish to dedicate this book.

The book is a work of fiction and all characters are fictional. The story is woven around events that occurred during the late 1980s and 1990s. They serve only to form a backdrop to the plot and neither the details nor the outcomes are based on actual events. The mutilated body of a young British tourist was indeed found in the Masaai Mara and her father did not accept the outcome of the official investigation. But the similarity with the incident in my plot ends there.

# Main Characters

| | |
|---|---|
| **Protagonists:** | Vijay "Jay" Gupté and his wife, Heidi |
| **Their friends:** | Richard and Anne Collins<br>Ravi and Meena Karnik |
| **The poachers:** | Jonathan Kiilu<br>("Tusker" John)<br>Koinet Olekorinko<br>*(Ndovu* Don) |

## The Police:

| | |
|---|---|
| **Commissioner:** | Michael Karanja |
| **Deputy Commissioner:** | Gideon Odhiambo |
| **Inspectors:** | Julius Wachira<br>*(Jay's contact)*<br>Boniface "Bono" Njoroge<br>*(Tusker John's contact)*<br>Wycliffe "Bic" Okello<br>*(Ndovu Don's contact)*<br>Peter Otieno<br>*(liaison with Nick)* |
| **Deputy Inspector:** | Titus "Toto" Kilonzo |
| **Others:** | Elizabeth—Secretary<br>Phyllis—Assistant |

| | |
|---|---|
| **British Tourist:** | Mary Wilson |
| **Her father:** | Barry Wilson |
| **Scotland Yard Detective:** | Nicholas "Nick" Cunningham |
| **The Minister:** | George K. |
| **The Parsee visitor:** | Bomy Daruwala |
| **Managing Director, Tea Authority:** | James Maina |
| **Manager of campsite:** | Paul Oloitokitok |
| **Russians:** | Mikhail and Olga Smirnoff<br>Daughter: Tanya |
| **Heidi's family (Germany):** | Father: Wolfgang Schlemming<br>Mother: Gisela<br>Brother: Kurt |

# Chapter 1

## *Friday*

It was late afternoon when "Tusker" John Kiilu stepped out of a *matatu*, one of the private mini-buses that hurtled through the bustling streets of Nairobi, Kenya, in East Africa. Despite the mild weather, beads of perspiration dripped from Tusker's eyebrows, and the twitch in his left eye intensified, much like the scowl on his face. The brazen operation he planned to execute in a few hours weighed on his mind while he trudged toward the city center to link up with his gang.

"Who does that man think he is?" he cursed, startling two young women as they walked across. "Just because he's a Minister, he thinks he can treat me like a mongrel? I'll teach him a lesson tonight."

In a region where game reserves bristled with wildlife, Tusker had ventured into poaching elephants for ivory, despite the risks and dangers involved. Steadily building up his territory in one of the largest game parks in Kenya, his reputation soon reached the ears of a senior Minister, who used his position to control the bulk of this illegal trade. Three years earlier, Tusker had started operating under the Minister's protection. There were a few close calls with game park wardens, but he always managed to slip away.

Just when he finally felt confident of a long-term working relationship with the Minister, an operation undertaken a few weeks earlier did not end well. Some days later, the Minister sent an intermediary to tell Tusker of his decision to end their relationship. Stung by this rebuke, Tusker hollered, "Tell your boss he can't do this to me!" and threatened retaliation. But the Minister did not relent and Tusker was furious that he had been dumped on account of one mishap. In any hazardous business, he reasoned, an occasional hiccup could occur and it was inexcusable for the Minister to take such drastic action. Fuming with rage, he vowed to drum up a plot to make the Minister yield.

From the emissary, Tusker gathered that the Minister would be working with an upcoming rival, who went by the name of *Ndovu* Don. "That stick-like man, who calls himself *Ndovu* (elephant), will run for his life with his tail between his legs when a real elephant comes charging along," Tusker sniggered to his men.

One of Tusker's men had a contact in Don's gang, from whom he gathered that a large sum of money was about to be handed over to the Minister. This was the sort of information that Tusker needed—he would snatch the money and hold it until the Minister relented and reinstated him to his cherished position.

"You want to know why people in my business call me Tusker, *Bwana* (Mr.) Minister? They do it out of respect and you will soon find that out," he had spat out with vehemence, as he sat with his group at the Uhuru Park the previous evening.

He hailed from the town of Muranga in Central Kenya. Bulkily built with huge shoulders, his very presence invoked fear among those around him. He had a distinctive large, round, balding head, with equally distinctive large eyes that protruded almost out of their sockets. His left eye twitched occasionally, more pronounced when he was agitated, a state he appeared to be in the better part of his waking hours.

In a business that was not for the faint at heart, John was a bully and could be ruthless—in fact, brutally so. He was a force to reckon with, which was how he had acquired the nickname "Tusker," a title that satisfied his ego immensely. A tusker—a male elephant with large tusks—is the acknowledged head of the herd.

Tusker's informant in his rival's camp had conveyed that they had recently slaughtered two elephants. The ivory was to be handed over today by Don to the smuggler in exchange for the payment. Since the Minister did not wish to be seen with the smuggler, he had asked Don to take possession of the money and pass it on to him immediately.

"Ha, now I'm going to teach them a lesson," Tusker announced to his cronies on receiving this information. He set in motion his plot, which had begun to raise his stress levels. The preparations for its execution had so far proceeded as planned—well, almost.

To carry out this heist, Tusker needed a new face—someone not known to Don. And he needed a fast getaway car. He had succeeded in getting both, but did not appear fully satisfied. One of his assistants, Daniel, had stolen a shiny Nissan—bright yellow in color.

"Now, you, Daniel, why this car with such a bright color?" Tusker asked in a gruff tone.

"Boss, this one has a turbocharged engine," an elated Daniel replied. "I can drive away fast; it's a very good getaway car."

But Tusker shook his head. "Why a car that will catch everyone's attention? Even the poor-sighted rhino will chase this car if you went near him."

"With the turbocharged engine, I can speed away from not just a rhino, but even a cheetah," Daniel bragged.

Tusker grunted quietly. Daniel was an expert in stealing parked vehicles. He was also an outstanding driver. With his aggressive driving, he had outwitted game park wardens while being chased—a skill that had earned him the nickname of "Daredevil" Daniel.

To snatch the money, Tusker had recruited a young man recommended by his cousin. The man's name was Fred and he was told to dress "smartly" in a suit or a jacket so that he wouldn't stand out among the well-dressed clientele in the restaurant where the money was to be handed over. Fred came dressed in a smart jacket—but again, Tusker was not happy with his choice.

"Why are you not wearing a simple jacket?" he asked, glaring at Fred's colorful attire with purple and black checks.

"I bought this special jacket because you wanted me smartly dressed," replied Fred. After all, he had spent the morning at the Gikomba flea market, known for "second-hand" clothes—old and used clothing, donated or discarded by the Western countries, and imported by the container loads into third-world countries.

"I watched CNN last night," Tusker remarked, "and one of the school bands, marching in a parade in the US, wore such jackets."

But there was little that Tusker could now do but shake his large, round head as the minutes ticked away and the countdown began.

***

A few miles away, in the Westlands neighborhood of Nairobi, a cool evening breeze brushed his face as Jay Gupté stepped into his garden. The month was August—winter in Nairobi, the "Green City under the Sun," which lies just south of the equator. Blessed with near-perfect weather all through the year, the mile-high capital of Kenya has beckoned visitors and settlers from far and wide, ever since the British discovered it at the turn of the nineteenth century. They had ruled this country for more than a hundred years, until it gained independence in 1963.

"We must be on our way, *liebchen*," Jay called out to his wife, Heidi, fondly addressing her in German. She was taking her time getting dressed after having attended her karate class that afternoon. She had been pursuing the martial arts the last few years and had earned a brown belt. "Never know when it could come in handy," she'd say.

Jay, an engineer by profession from India, and Heidi, along with their two children, had been living in this picturesque city for nearly a decade. He was the chief engineer of an engineering company, while she taught in a school serving mainly the children of expatriates. Their two children had traveled the previous evening on a vacation to Heidi's parents in Germany.

She stepped out of the house and locked the front door. Tall and slim, with blond hair and blue eyes, she flashed a dazzling smile at Jay as she stepped into the car, while he stared at her with a boyish grin on his face before turning to start the car. They were to spend the evening with their friends, Anne and Richard Collins. Once every fortnight, the two couples met at each other's homes, by turn, to play their favorite card game of bridge. After a short drive, Jay and Heidi reached the upscale Lavington neighborhood where the Collins had settled down after Richard retired from the local brewery. Jay turned off the main street onto a dirt road and drove past a few houses before pulling up outside the Collins' residence. The *askari* (security guard) peeped through the holes in the metal gate and, upon recognizing Jay's car, opened the gate and greeted him, *"Habari gani, Mzee* (How are you doing, sir)?"

*"Mzuri sana, na wewe* (Very well, and you)?" replied Jay.

*"Salama* (Blessed)," responded the *askari*, raising his arms toward heaven.

As Jay's car pulled up at the end of the driveway, Richard Collins stepped out of the front door and called out, "Hello there." In his late sixties, with a cheerful round face and gray balding hair, Richard addressed Heidi, "So, the kids are off to your parents, are they? The grandparents must be excited having their grandchildren to themselves."

"Yah," replied Heidi, "it's been a long time since they were all together. We spoke on the phone this morning. The weather there is fine and they're getting along quite well with their German."

"Oh, I can well imagine your parents doting on your lovely kids," said Anne, stepping out of the kitchen and welcoming Heidi and Jay with a warm hug and a peck on the cheeks.

They moved into the living room and Richard started to prepare drinks. "There's been an interesting development in the Mary Wilson case," he said.

"Really? We heard that our President has agreed to a joint investigation," Heidi responded. "But what's the latest, Richard?"

Seldom did a social conversation in Nairobi begin on any other subject since the body of Mary Wilson, a young British tourist, was found in gruesome condition at the famous Maasai Mara Game Park a few weeks earlier. She had been traveling alone in a rented vehicle, staying in campsites in the game park, and her partially burned body—with some parts of it apparently cut off—was found a day after she was reported missing.

The police said they did not suspect foul play; they determined that Mary was mauled to death by wild animals and the burns were attributed to a brush fire. Not too many Kenyans or British believed this version, not the least her parents in England. Her father, Barry Wilson, had immediately flown in and sought the assistance of the British High Commission. Through the press, he made it known, in no uncertain terms, that he did not accept the results of the investigation. He persuaded the British High Commissioner to put pressure on the Kenyan government to involve Britain's Scotland Yard in opening up a fresh investigation.

"Looks like Mary's father is one tough guy, since it appears he's gotten what he wanted, despite our government's resistance," Richard added.

The Kenyan police had understandably balked at the suggestion of involving Scotland Yard, as did the Kenyan government. But tourism was a vital sector of the Kenyan economy, with thousands of tourists coming from all over the world to visit the richly endowed wild-life game parks and the attractive beaches. Tourism brought in much-needed hard currency to the country's cash-strapped exchequer. Already, many Western countries were threatening to issue travel advisories that would affect tourism as a result of this incident—something that Kenya could ill afford. Meanwhile, the British government expressed strong displeasure at the outcome of the official investigation.

"What else could our President do under all that pressure?" asked Anne.

"Yeah," said Richard, "he has agreed to allow Scotland Yard to depute one of their detectives for a joint investigation. Now comes the interesting part." He paused, lowering his tone before continuing. "Through one of the officials at the British High Commission, I've gathered that Scotland Yard is unable to depute any of their regular detectives and is assigning someone who has recently retired: Nicholas Cunningham." And turning to his wife, he added, "It so happens he's related to Anne."

"I haven't seen him in years," she said, "but he knows we're here. I'm sure he'll look us up when he gets here."

"Fine old chap, this Nick, and a darned good detective, too," continued Richard. "I'm sure he'll find out what really happened to the poor girl and put an end to the cock-and-bull story that the cops out here would have us believe. You know, the British government spent more than half a million quid training Kenyan police detectives, and yet these guys here claim they have come up with a credible crime report. How preposterous!"

"Oh, stop ridiculing them, Richard," Anne chided him, "but I do shudder to think of what that poor girl must have gone through."

"What sort of a monster could have committed this hideous crime?" Heidi wondered.

"Well, we certainly hope the investigation will reveal who the real culprits are and they will be brought to justice," remarked Jay. "Our country needs to put this tragic incident behind us and restore its image as a unique tourist destination."

They settled down at the card table and the rest of the evening followed the usual routine: plenty of bridge, interspersed with drinks, a break for dinner, coffee, tea, and snacks. And the snide comments about their partners' mistakes—mainly from Jay and Richard.

\*\*\*

While the foursome enjoyed their game of bridge, sinister events were unfolding in the city center. From their vantage point, the ruthless poacher Tusker and his assistants kept an eye on the restaurant across the street and on their rival Don, who sauntered impatiently outside on the pavement. They perked up when the ivory dealer, a Somali, with a briefcase in hand and his assistant alongside, emerged at the far end and walked toward Don. The Minister was seated inside the restaurant, keeping a watchful eye on what was happening outside.

The snatch was perfectly executed. As the Somali and his mate made their way toward Don, a man in a dapper jacket walked past them. When the Somali reached out to hand over the briefcase, the stranger swung past them and, in a flash, snatched the bag from the startled Don. The man sprinted toward the road, where a bright yellow car drove up to him. The rear door swung open and he sprang into the rear seat, with the car speeding away before the Somali or Don could react.

Inside the restaurant, the Minister gasped in mid-conversation, not believing his eyes, as he witnessed the drama outside. Swiftly rising from his seat, he walked briskly toward the exit and asked his assistant, "Who were those guys?"

With the assistant unable to shed any light on the matter, the Minister retreated to a corner, pulled out his cell phone, and barked out instructions.

The yellow car sped off, with the man at the wheel deftly handling the powerful turbocharged engine. The mood inside the vehicle was ecstatic.

"We did it, boss!" crowed Daniel. "We did it."

"*Ndio* (Yes)," nodded Tusker, who was seated in the front next to Daniel. The dark scowl on his forehead had vanished and, to the extent possible, his face appeared aglow. "I wish I could see the looks on Don's and the Minister's faces. Anyway, Fred, you did a good job. When we break up, I'll take good care of you. And get rid of that jacket."

"Sure, boss," Fred said. "See, my uncle promised you that I could do a good job."

"That was good, man—that was very good," said Adam, Tusker's loyal lieutenant. He was seated in the rear next to Fred and had taken possession of the brief-case. "And just look at the briefcase! Me, I think it's made from genuine Italian leather. See the tag here? It says 'Limited Edition.' I would like to keep it if the Big Boss would give it to me. This Somali—he has good taste, getting such a nice briefcase."

"Stop your nonsense and give it to me," barked Tusker. Turning to the driver, he said, "And you keep your eyes on the road, Daniel. Don't go on the main roads—I don't want people to spot this car."

Before Tusker could take the briefcase from Adam, the siren of a police car drowned out the conversation and the mood in the Nissan suddenly turned foul.

***

It was almost midnight when Heidi and Jay bade good-bye to the Collins and the *askari* shut the gate behind them. Wary of the dangers of driving late at night in a deserted neighborhood in Nairobi, Jay surveyed the curving, dirt track, which led to the main road a short distance ahead.

He had barely covered a few yards when he heard the roar of a fast-moving car, followed by the screeching of brakes, and watched aghast as the car swerved onto the road he was on. A speeding vehicle at that hour meant trouble, with thugs almost certainly at the wheel. Attempting to get out of harm's way, he braked and swerved into a short-approach road that led to a gate, two houses away from the Collins' home. He turned off the car's lights, hoping that the occupants in the approaching vehicle might not spot his dark-colored Honda, hidden behind a shrub on the short-approach road.

However, the driver of the approaching car, a yellow Nissan sedan, sharply braked a short distance away from where Jay was parked and expertly swerved his vehicle a half-circle so that he now faced the direction of the main road. The lights of the Nissan had been turned off and Jay craned his neck around to see what was happening.

Another vehicle could now be heard with its siren blaring—obviously the police, hot in pursuit. Heidi gripped Jay's arm as they watched with angst the oncoming police Land Rover swerve into the dirt road and drive up with its headlights shining on the Nissan. The driver slowed the vehicle upon seeing the Nissan blocking his way.

Then, as Jay held his breath, there was a burst of action. The Nissan roared back to life and jerked forward toward the oncoming Land Rover. Jay was distracted by the sight of an object sailing out from the Nissan's rear window. It looked like a bag and he watched it fall on the road, away from the view of the police vehicle.

Meanwhile, the Nissan accelerated toward the Land Rover, forcing its driver to turn to one side. Swerving the other way, the Nissan driver found a gap to deftly navigate past the other vehicle. Gunshots rang out from the Land Rover as the police took aim at the fleeing thugs and it was now the turn of the police driver to swing his vehicle around. This he did rather clumsily, and by the time he completed the maneuver, the Nissan had sped away. More shots were fired by the police as they struggled to pursue the Nissan.

Jay and Heidi ducked for cover in their car as gunshots rang out barely fifty yards away. The stillness of the quiet neighborhood was shattered by the reverberations of gunshots and the roar of turbocharged engines, while the air was consumed with exhaust fumes amid swirls of dust. As the two vehicles drove away, a badly shaken Jay gathered his wits and consoled a near-hysterical Heidi.

"Let's get the hell out of here," he cried as he started the car and backed up. Turning on the lights, he started to drive along the dirt road when he abruptly stopped. The lights' beams shone on the bag as it glistened in the dark. It lay along the edge of the road on Jay's side. He would later wonder what made him stop— was it possible he sensed the bag contained plenty of cash? Enough to pay off his debts—and no one would know? Focusing his eyes, he could discern that it was a briefcase. He could barely take his eyes off what was clearly a stylish, expensive piece. It was lying undamaged on the road—how could he just leave it lying around and drive away? Heidi, meanwhile, who hadn't seen the bag, looked nervously at Jay, wondering why he had stopped.

Without further thought and unmindful of the consequences, Jay did what he believed destiny had cast him to do. He turned off the car's lights so that no one else could see what he had spotted. He looked around to ensure none of the *askaris* had ventured out of their gates—he was confident, though, that they were still crouching behind the gates after the shootout. Glancing once more in the direction of the beckoning briefcase, he drove slowly toward it.

Heidi sounded puzzled and asked, "What?"

It was too late. She had often berated Jay for acting on impulse. But he loved challenges and he now felt a surge of adrenaline course through him as he thought of what he was about to do. As the vehicle inched forward, Jay heard a voice within him ask if he really believed he could get away with it. But, as in the past, he paid no heed to that little voice.

Pulling up his car alongside the briefcase, he opened the door and leaned out to pick it up. For a split second, he wondered if it contained drugs or explosives, and he sniffed it. Despite the lingering odor of exhaust fumes and dust, the rich smell of pure leather was overpowering. Swiftly depositing the briefcase on the floor of the rear seat, he shut the door and drove off before Heidi realized what was going on.

He took a large swig from the water bottle in his car, tried to regain his composure while gently comforting Heidi, and called Richard Collins from his cell phone. He told him they were safe and had narrowly missed being caught in the crossfire that Richard would surely have heard.

Jay drove with one hand, the other arm around Heidi. She rested her head on his shoulder and said quietly, "Jay, I think I peed in my pants..."

***

All hell broke loose inside the Nissan.

"Boss, he threw the briefcase away!" cried Adam from the rear seat.

"What do you mean, he threw it away?" roared Tusker from the front. He swung around to glare at Fred.

"I thought... I thought..." stammered Fred. "I thought we were blocked by the police and there would be big trouble when they found out we had the briefcase."

"What have you done?" bawled Tusker, gasping for breath. "You've ruined me, you bloody fool!" He held his head in anguish.

"Boss, I think this man is very inexperienced in *magendo* (illegal) business," suggested Adam. "Why else would a person start pissing in his pants just because the police are chasing him? He needs more experience in such matters."

"I was hired only to snatch a briefcase," asserted Fred. "I didn't sign up to be taken around in a car being chased by the police and then to be stopped and shot by them."

"Did you hear this buffoon?" Tusker asked his assistants. "My cousin didn't tell me this guy was an idiot."

"I'm not an idiot," said Fred, sounding offended. "You know I did my job very well. Someone must have put the police on our tails and they came and chased us."

Tusker swung his fist to punch Fred, who ducked. He then cursed Adam for not holding on to the briefcase.

"I put my head down when the police started shooting," admitted Adam. "It was at that time that he snatched the briefcase and threw it out."

While they argued among themselves, the blare of sirens drowned out their conversation and another police car drove in from an intersection.

"What the hell's going on?" asked Daniel as he stepped on the gas pedal. "Don't the police have anyone else to catch today?"

"I'm going to skin this cockroach alive when we get done." Tusker glared at Fred.

"I wish I could have at least kept the briefcase," mourned Adam. "It was so stylish."

"Shut up!" bellowed Tusker. "Let's figure out how we can go back for the briefcase."

By now, Daniel had outmaneuvered the second police car.

"What do those fools think?" he said. "They can catch 'Daredevil' Daniel with those pathetic vehicles? I told you, boss, why I chose this car—it won't let us down."

And then suddenly, yet another police vehicle darted in from an intersection with its siren blaring and took up the chase.

"Boss, I don't know what's going on," Daniel shook his head. "It seems someone big is after us. We've stolen only a briefcase—we haven't hurt or killed anyone. And still, it seems that all the police cars in Nairobi are chasing us."

"That Don has poisoned the Minister's mind and they are creating too many problems for us," Tusker said. "And you, Daniel, made it easy for them to spot us because of this car's color. But we must now go back to the place where this idiot threw away the briefcase."

"I think it's dangerous, boss—the police must be there," replied Daniel.

"Hmm," said Tusker. "That means we have to ditch this car. Now, find a place quickly."

Daniel peered outside in the darkness. "We're near Lower Kabete. Okay, I know a quiet spot nearby. But first the police."

He niftily maneuvered the vehicle in and out of the side and main streets and soon the police cars were nowhere near. Slowing down, he turned off onto a dirt road that led to a few independent homes. A ridge lay at the end, beyond which was the dry bed of a stream. On the other side, a dirt road curved around to meet the main Lower Kabete road. Daniel found a small clearing, where he pulled up the vehicle. Shutting down the roar of the engine, he said, "It's going to be a long walk home from here."

"No one's going home," came Tusker's stern response. "We're going back to recover the briefcase. Now, if we don't find the money, we're all going to be cut up into pieces and thrown into the Nairobi River for the crocodiles to eat." He glared at the three of them. "So let's pray that the money is still there."

"We'll be able to spot the briefcase from far away," said Adam. "Me, I hope it isn't damaged."

Livid with anger, Tusker stormed out of the car, yanked Fred out from the rear seat, and hurled him to the ground. Mercilessly kicking him in the stomach and groin, Tusker cursed him, his mother, and his forefathers.

"Get me a rod from the car so that I can beat this pest to a pulp!" he ordered Daniel. Tusker was not concerned about the *askaris* in the nearby houses—he knew they would be too scared to come out and inquire.

From the Nissan's boot, Daniel brought out a wrench and a steel rod. Tusker grabbed the tools and landed a few blows with the wrench on Fred's back and arms as he cried out in pain. His new jacket was a mess.

"Boss, a car is coming," alerted Adam. The others looked up to see the lights of a car that had turned onto the road they were on. "Quick, we must leave."

Quivering with rage, Tusker struck heavy blows on Fred's back with the metal bar. Adam and Daniel winced as they watched the final blow land on the back of Fred's skull, followed by the sickening sound of a crack. Leaving Fred prostrate on the ground, the three quickly disappeared into the dry riverbed before the beams of the approaching car could spot them.

\*\*\*

"Careful, Mishka," Olga cautioned. "I saw someone there." She had caught a fleeting glimpse of the fleeing men when her husband, Mikhail Smirnoff, turned the car onto the dirt road on which they lived. He drove cautiously toward their house at the end of the road. When he reached their gate, the gleam of a vehicle near the edge of the ridge caught his attention. The *askari* checked through the peepholes before opening the gate to allow the car in.

"Yes, Njiru, what's going on out there?" Mikhail asked his *askari*.

"*Mzee*, I think some thugs were outside. They drove very fast in that car and stopped there. Afterward, I heard them step out and start to beat a man very badly. I didn't go outside because they sounded dangerous. Me, I think they ran away when they saw your car coming. But the man they were beating is still lying there, I think."

Mikhail had served in the former Soviet Army for ten years. He had faced several life-threatening situations and was not afraid to investigate what had just taken place outside. He dropped Olga off, asking her to lock herself safely inside the house. Pulling out a pistol, which he carried in his car, he drove out and turned toward the ridge.

Turning on the full beam of his car's lights, he drove with caution toward the yellow vehicle and spotted a man lying on the ground by the side. Blood oozed from the man's head and he wore what appeared to be a colorful jacket, now stained with blood and mud.

"*Kurva!*" muttered Mikhail and looked around and across the ridge, where Olga had observed some movement. There was no one around—the thugs had apparently abandoned the vehicle, crossed the ridge, and fled.

Mikhail lowered his car window and looked down at the man outside. "Hello, *rafiki* (friend)," he called out. The man continued lying still.

Mikhail picked up the flashlight in his car and shone it on the man's face. "Hello," he called out again. The man appeared to breathe with difficulty, but otherwise lay motionless.

Mikhail left the car's lights on, pulled out his pistol, and stepped out. He swung the flashlight and looked around. Calling out one more time, he kneeled down to take a closer look; the man needed urgent medical attention. Mikhail knew he had to handle the situation with caution, since this man was probably involved in a crime. He found a blanket in the car, which he used to cover the stricken man. He also fetched a water bottle that he opened and placed near the man's face so he could reach for it when he regained consciousness.

There was not much else that he could do, and Mikhail drove back home. He telephoned the police and reported the scene of the incident and the urgent need for medical attention for the seriously injured man lying near an abandoned vehicle. Satisfied that he had done his best, Mikhail retired for the night.

***

After the incident, the Minister left the restaurant in a huff, without addressing either the Somali or Don. He phoned them later to give them a piece of his mind.

The Somali made it clear that Don, not he, was to blame for allowing the briefcase to be stolen. In the past, the Minister never had problems collecting cash from the Somali. Why had he changed the procedure this time and brought in a new person? The Minister could surely not blame the Somali—as required, he had handed over the money to Don.

Don was forced to listen patiently when the Minster called him later to vent his frustrations. In no uncertain terms was it conveyed to Don that he was responsible for recovering the stolen cash. Don spent a listless night cursing Tusker, who, he was certain, had carried out the heist, and must now be gloating over what he had pulled off.

# Chapter 2

## *Saturday Morning*

The morning air was crisp and clear after light showers when Jay stepped out of the house and clambered into his car. With only a few hours of sleep, he had struggled to haul himself out of bed to head to the engineering plant, which operated, like other manufacturing units, half days on Saturdays.

As he drove in the light traffic, his thoughts kept drifting to his impulsive act the previous night. *Why did I do it... why did I do it?* he kept asking himself—though, of course, he knew the answer. How many noble souls could resist picking up a briefcase that one stumbled upon in the middle of the night on a lonely road—particularly when one has a large debt to clear?

When he had first arrived with his family in Kenya, Jay's employer had housed them in a large, furnished apartment. Two years earlier, he and Heidi had decided to buy their own house, with plans to settle down in Nairobi. As it turned out, they could not have chosen a worse time; the housing market was at an all-time high and the transaction turned out to be an expensive proposition. Interest rates kept rising, and the burden of the mortgage strained their finances. And now there was the additional burden of air tickets for the two children for their trip to Germany, which meant they would be strapped for cash the next several months.

While he waited for a traffic signal, Jay brooded about Heidi's delayed reaction on their way home last night. It had taken her several minutes to gather her wits after the shootout that had taken place barely fifty yards away. Fortuitously for Jay, they were almost home by the time Heidi found her voice to blast him in German, "*Scheisse Mensch! Was ist los mit Dir?* (What's wrong with you?). Darned smart of you, wasn't it, and expecting to get away with it? One hell of a shit you're going to be in, with the thugs, the police, all going after you."

Maintaining his cool, Jay attempted to calm her down. "You know, *liebchen,* no one could have seen us pick up the briefcase. At the very least, I prevented the thugs from laying their hands on it when they surely must have come back to pick it up. Wouldn't it be far better if we could now return it to the owner?"

"And the police? You think they won't be looking for it?"

He had tried to convey there was no assurance the police would return the full amount to the victim; at best, only a small portion might trickle back. But she was in no mood to listen and continued, "I know exactly what you were thinking—that there's lots of cash in there, right? Don't even think of using any of it—to pay off the loan or for anything else."

Jay knew she had a point. The police would ask all banks to alert them of large cash deposits, and they would comply—not due to statutory requirements, but to avoid being in the bad books of the police. Ruefully, he had to admit there was no way he could use large amounts of money without attracting attention.

"Now look," Heidi had said with finality, "I don't want to have anything to do with it. I've not seen it and don't want to know what's in it. As far as you're concerned, I don't even know that it's with you, okay? And you'd better turn it over to the police right away." With that, she had stepped out, slammed the car door shut, and stomped toward their house.

Jay had remained seated in the car, pondering whether or not he should drive straight to the police. While he knew it would have been the right thing to do, it would also mean his spending the better part of the night at the police station. From what he'd been told, they would question him about if he was in some way involved in the theft, and the onus would be on him to prove his innocence. No, he had decided, he was not going to follow that route tonight.

Picking up the briefcase from the car, he had proceeded to the guest bedroom where, in solitude, he planned to examine its contents. Taking abundant precautions, he spread old newspapers on the bed and donned a pair of gloves. After doubly ensuring that the door was locked and the window blinds were drawn, he placed the briefcase on the bed and rubbed his hands. *"Yes, I'm going to do it—yes I am going to open it,"* he mumbled to steady his nerves. The briefcase was not locked and on opening it, his first glimpse was of pink wrapping paper used as a protective layer. Pulling out the paper, he was greeted by the sight of more paper—old newspaper sheets. His heart sank—*gosh, was this all the bag contained?* He paused to take a deep breath and then, with one swift swipe, removed the remaining scraps of paper—to discover bundles of currency notes. There were plenty of them, and he settled down to count, blowing a soft whistle when he was done—fifteen million shillings, all in cash (about US $200,000).

He noted that the bills were not freshly printed and were not arranged in sequence—which one could expect if they were marked bills belonging to a bank or a government agency. There was little chance they would be detected if he were to deposit them in a bank, but he promptly banished that thought. He carefully jotted down on a sheet of paper the amounts in each denomination and pulled out a backpack from the closet. He couldn't help caressing the currency bills before placing them in the bag. A section in the closet contained old linens and he stashed the bag between old sheets.

He then had settled down in an easy chair, closed his eyes and, despite his assurances to Heidi, decided to make a cool assessment of his situation. Making a mental checklist of who could possibly have witnessed his deed, he had crossed out:

- The *askaris*: The gunfire would have spooked the unarmed guards in the neighboring houses, who sought shelter behind the gates. No way could they have been watching his movements.
- The police: They were blindsided when the briefcase was tossed out of the thugs' car, nor could they have seen it later, with all the action going on.
- The thugs: They had not seen his vehicle, hidden behind the shrubs. If they'd come later looking for the briefcase, they wouldn't be able to trace him, since he didn't live there.

Continuing to sit and ponder, he admitted he had not bargained for this large an amount—it would pay off not just the overdue interest, but also the outstanding principal loan amount. *And to think I did all this without being able to use any of the money*, he had lamented.

An important question had cropped up in his mind: whom did the money belong to? Only individuals normally carried money in a briefcase; large establishments kept their cash in boxes or trunks. Such a large amount could also not have been sitting in the home of an honest, hard-working individual. In all likelihood, this cash was to be used for conducting any of the illegal businesses that were being increasingly reported. If the money was unaccounted for, it was unlikely that anyone would come forward to report this theft. Rather than turning over the money to the police right away, why not wait until the next day to see whether the theft is reported? He decided to hold on to the money for now. Dealing with Heidi would be a problem that he would have to think through.

The last chore for the night was to get rid of the briefcase. He had leaned over to take a proper look at it—and recalled why it had caught his attention in the first place. It was made of pure leather and one of the metal tags stated that it was made in Italy. Another polished tag read "Limited Edition." Its sleek design, with curved contours, all finished in a pleasing light brown color, imparted it with a sensuous appearance. Its glossy finish had such a soft, seductive feel that his hands wandered all over the exposed surfaces, and the hidden ones as well. Oblivious to the late hour, he caressed the briefcase for a while until, with a shock and a sense of guilt, he realized he was being inexplicably aroused and he had yanked his hand away.

How could he even contemplate getting rid of such an exquisite item? But he knew he could not keep it in the house without attracting Heidi's ire. He decided to take it to his office the next morning and placed it in a shopping bag. His office desk had a hidden compartment, which was used at times to store the company's petty cash overnight. He would keep the briefcase hidden there, while he decided on his next move.

As his car approached the gate to the factory, Jay glanced toward the shopping bag that lay on the passenger seat beside him, wondering if he would get one more glimpse of the briefcase, while he reminisced about the moments that he spent the previous night examining it.

*** 

The soothing fragrance of lilies and roses in his garden wafted in the cool morning air as Mikhail Smirnoff stepped out of his house and strode along the wet pathway toward his car. A light sweater was all he needed in the mild Nairobi winter. Folks back in St. Petersburg, his hometown in Russia, had to bundle up in heavy woolens during the harsh winters, he smugly mused.

He was making a quick visit to his office, mainly to check for messages from his clients. There were no off days for them, and their only means of written communications was the fax machine. Dealing with warlords in the region was a lucrative business and, for Mikhail, spending a few hours on a Saturday morning in his office was well worth the trouble.

"I couldn't sleep until late last night," his wife, Olga, had mentioned earlier at the breakfast table. "I heard the police coming outside about an hour after you phoned them. I'm sure they'll come by to question you; I'll tell them to come later in the day."

As he turned on the car's ignition, he paused to reflect if it had been prudent of him to have driven out last night to the scene of the abandoned car—he should just have phoned the police. But given his background as an ex-army officer, he had no qualms about stepping out in the middle of the night to inspect a potentially unsafe situation and possibly help a victim. *Now, Mikhail,* he told himself, *remember, you must always maintain a low profile.* He would have to be cautious when the police came to question him.

His *askari* at the gate informed him that the police had carried the semi-conscious man away in their vehicle last night. Before driving off, Mikhail cast a glance toward the ridge. The Nissan had not been towed away and a policeman, who stood guard, waved to him.

*\*\*\**

At nine o'clock sharp, Michael Karanja convened his senior officials to discuss the case of the stolen briefcase. As the Police Commissioner for all of Kenya, he occupied a position in the upper echelons of power. But it came at a high price—political affiliations, one's tribe, and deftness in pleasing several bosses in power were some of the attributes required to occupy this position. Karanja had achieved a fair measure of success during his four-year tenure.

He was due to retire in six months, but he was finding it increasingly difficult to maneuver an ever-changing political landscape and the shifts in power. His recipe for holding on to his position was to play it safe.

He accepted orders from ministers and senior officials and carried them out as best as he could. His capabilities were mediocre, but that perhaps stood him in good stead—voicing one's personal opinion or being unduly assertive could mean treading on delicate toes.

First to seat himself at the large conference table was Deputy Commissioner Gideon Odhiambo. Tall and lean, with a slight stoop and a scholarly look, and dark-framed glasses sitting atop his long face, Odhiambo was systematic in his approach and a stickler for rules and procedures.

Three police inspectors, Boniface Njoroge, Wycliffe Okello, and Julius Wachira, soon followed. The mood was somber.

Karanja began with an admonition. "We were out-smarted last night by the thugs in the yellow car. Why did we give up the chase, Gideon?"

"Sir, all the three vehicles that are in working condition were pressed into action," his deputy responded. "But the thugs were driving a turbocharged vehicle that was too fast for us. Now, I've been suggesting for a long time that our department needs to procure turbocharged vehicles."

"You know that would be turned down—budgetary constraints, as usual."

"Our department needs to come up to the standards of the Western countries. You see in the Hollywood movies how police cars chase the crooks to arrest them," said Gideon. "I'm sure they drive turbocharged vehicles."

"Actually, it's the hero who drives a turbocharged vehicle and corners the villains in those movies," commented Wycliffe Okello. "The police cars always end up being wrecked by the villains."

There was a subdued titter in the room. The Commissioner, too, could not suppress a smile as he looked toward the speaker and nodded. Okello was the youngest of the officers, and one of the smartest, with a tall, willowy physique and almond-shaped face, adorned with a set of dazzling white teeth. His father was the largest distributor of "Bic" ballpoint pens in his hometown in Western Kenya. Wycliffe's physical resemblance to the ubiquitous pen prompted his school pals to nickname him "Bic." That name continued to be used in preference to his given name, even among colleagues.

The Commissioner responded, "The cops are made to look incompetent—no, actually like idiots—in all the books and movies, whether in New York, Los Angeles, London, or Paris. But you're right, Bic. It's always the hero who chases the villains in a fast car. Have you seen the movie *Bullitt*? I still recall Steve McQueen's superb driving in that film."

The younger officers had neither heard of this movie nor the actor, but were accustomed to the boss reminiscing about events and personalities popular long before their time.

Karanja paused for a moment before continuing, "Now, coming back to last night's incident, the driver of the Nissan was too smart for us—how could he dodge us every time? I think it must have been 'Daredevil' Daniel."

"In which case 'Tusker' John must have masterminded the heist," said Julius Wachira. Diminutive in appearance and somber in temperament, the reticent Julius had an analytical mind and invariably came forth with valuable suggestions.

"We don't know that as yet," cautioned the Commissioner. "Nor do we know the identity of the man who snatched the briefcase. But we might come to know more about the Nissan."

His deputy, Gideon, followed through with the latest developments. "The Nissan was found abandoned in Lower Kabete, near the house of a Russian. He reported it late last night. The man in the colorful jacket was lying nearby with severe head injuries. We took him to the Kenyatta hospital—he's still unconscious and the medics aren't sure if he'll survive."

"Is anyone from our department there with him?" asked Bic.

"Yes, Deputy Inspector Kilonzo is with him now. But I suggest, Bic, you go to the hospital to question that man. Hopefully, he comes around and reveals who's behind this whole thing," said Gideon.

"Yes, I can proceed right away. But I'd also like to question the Russian."

"Yes, of course, Bic," agreed Karanja.

Gideon Odhiambo adjusted his glasses. "The place in Lavington where the yellow car made the first stop and where our vehicle failed to corner them—maybe the thugs stopped there because they'd planned to pass on the goods to someone. We should check the area—the *askaris* there might have witnessed something. We also need to check along the route they traveled."

"Good point, Gideon," commented Karanja. "I think Njoroge should take that up."

"Yes, sir," came the response from the third inspector, Boniface Njoroge, who had remained silent until then. He was called "Bono" for short (pronounced *bawno*).

Julius Wachira posed a question. "Boss, we need more details on what exactly happened and what went wrong. Who is the victim, and what was stolen?"

Karanja did not wish to divulge who had called him the previous night. All he could tell them was that he had received instructions from "higher-ups." Rarely did he question what he was asked to do by his superiors, preferring a safe approach by faithfully carrying out their instructions. At times, this style put him in a tough spot with his subordinates, but eventually they assumed this was how things worked and started to follow their boss's orders.

"We've been instructed to recover a stolen brief-case," said Karanja. "We have the vehicle that was used to flee with it. We also have the man who, we're told, snatched the briefcase. Our task now is to hunt down the other men who were involved and recover the goods. Each one of us should use our contacts to find out who's behind all this."

"Are we looking only for a briefcase?" queried Julius. "Boss, we can't have so many officers looking just for a briefcase. We need to know what's in it."

The Commissioner squirmed in his seat. "Obviously, the briefcase wasn't empty—there had to be something precious in it that the complainant doesn't want too many people to know about."

"Could we have its description?" Julius persisted.

Karanja sighed. "Okay, Julius, I can see you won't be giving up. I'll find out and let all of you know. Now, I know you're working on that export fraud case, so I'm not giving you any specific assignments on this case. But get in touch with your contacts to find out whatever information you can. And I'd like you to attend our meetings—the more ideas we come up with, the better."

Karanja brought the meeting to an end. Later, he would let them know that the stolen briefcase was made from pure leather and had two metal tags: one of them read "Made in Italy" and the one at the bottom read "Limited Edition." And the color of the briefcase was—he had difficulty pronouncing the word, so he spelled it for them— "b-e-i-g-e."

***

Gazing through the window of the study in his home on the outskirts of Nairobi stood George K., as he was popularly called by his colleagues, or the Minister by others. After a disturbed night's sleep, his mood was foul and even though it was still mid-morning, he felt the urge for a beer. He asked his servant to bring him a bottle, warm—the way he liked it—and took a large sip as the frown on his forehead deepened.

His family owned vast properties, which helped him wield considerable influence within his tribe and enjoy the patronage of the country's political heavyweights. He had been a minister for nearly ten years, with privileged ties to the President. He was one of the senior-most ministers in the cabinet, and even though he headed a relatively unimportant ministry, he wielded hefty clout within the administration.

Haunted by the disaster of the previous night, he took another sip as the shrill ringtone of his cell phone interrupted his thoughts. He snatched it on the first ring and bellowed, "Hello!" It was Commissioner Karanja.

"Sir, the yellow car was found abandoned in Lower Kabete. A man was found beaten up and lying unconscious near the car. He's in poor condition and has been admitted to the Kenyatta Hospital. When he comes round, we'll question him."

"And have you recovered the stolen goods?"

"No, sir, we have no news on it. Those guys were smart—the one who drove the stolen car managed to dodge us."

"Why didn't you put in more cars to chase them?"

"Only three cars are in working condition and we used them all."

"And still the thugs managed to get away? Very poor, *Bwana* Commissioner. Now make sure all your men are on that job so we get back the briefcase without further delay. Are we clear on this?"

"Yes, Mr. Minister," answered Karanja. "Our men are on the job."

***

Less than a mile away from Nairobi's city center sat the sprawling Kenyatta Hospital, funded largely by the government. Throngs of patients from across the country crowded the hospital, resulting in a chronic shortage of medicines, beds, and trained staff.

Victims of street violence, or those left abandoned at crime scenes, were brought to this hospital by the police for recovery and eventual questioning. The latest casualty was the young man in the blood-soaked, colorful jacket. Luckily a bed was available, where he now lay in an unconscious state, with a police constable standing guard nearby.

Around nine in the morning, a young police officer made his way through the hordes of people into the ward and to the man's bed. The constable greeted him with a salute. Pointing to the unconscious man, Deputy Inspector Titus Kilonzo asked, "Is he our man?"

"Yes, sir."

"And do we know who he is?"

"No, sir."

The young officer walked over to the bed, eyeing the patient from head to toe. He wrinkled his nose as a mix of unpleasant odors in the crowded hospital ward overpowered the fragrance of aftershave lotion on his cheeks.

"Is that his jacket?" he asked, pointing to the one that hung on a hook near the bed. The constable nodded and the officer examined the pockets of the jacket. Not surprisingly, he found no identity papers—criminals do not normally carry them when on a mission. But he found scraps of papers, including part of a letter that suggested the victim's name was Fred.

Titus spoke to the doctor and the nurse on duty, who said the patient was in critical condition. His head injury had resulted in an excessive loss of blood, and unless he was given a transfusion, his chances of survival were slim.

"Can the hospital provide blood for this purpose?" Titus asked.

The nurse evaded a direct reply and said, "Patients who require a transfusion have to make their own arrangements for blood. Normally, relatives or friends donate the required quantity. Doesn't he have any relatives?"

"We still have to establish his identity," Titus responded.

Turning to the doctor, the officer asked if there was some way the hospital could arrange for blood to meet this patient's requirements. The doctor admitted the hospital had a small quantity of blood that was available for transfusion in very special cases. But saving the life of an ordinary thief would not be one such case.

There was little else for Titus to do. His supervisor had instructed him to proceed to the hospital and wait for one of the senior officers, who would come to interrogate the patient. He settled down in a chair and told the constable to take a break. Making himself comfortable, he looked around at the mid-morning activity in the casualty ward.

Titus was barely twenty years of age and hailed from a wealthy family. Bright and intelligent, he had recently graduated with a Bachelor's degree and joined the Kenya Police in the rank of a Deputy Inspector, while still undergoing training.

Life then was good—in fact, very good—for Titus, and there should have been little for him to complain about.

But complain he did.

And his biggest grouse was that he was not being treated like an adult.

Endowed with a cherubic face and a plump physique, he looked younger than his age. In school and college, he received affectionate glances from girls, teachers, and female staff, some of whom hugged him and treated him like a small, loveable kid. And to add insult to injury, his friends started to call him "Toto"—meaning a small boy—and that became his nickname.

He had expected that to change after he donned a smart police uniform. But it made little difference in the way people treated him. That was what bugged Titus Kilonzo.

Adding to his discomfort, he missed the hugs from all the women that he had received before. The pressure of their bosoms and bottoms would trigger tingling sensations in the lower part of his body that would often result in troublesome, but pleasurable, nights.

A loud male voice interrupted his thoughts. "Why are you taking so long to come clean me?" Toto looked at a patient with a scruffy appearance lying in one of the beds, rudely addressing a young nurse. She turned to face the patient and took a few measured steps toward him, swaying her hips. It was this part of her anatomy that attracted Toto's attention—the part he fondly referred to as "booty."

The conversation between the patient and the nurse ceased to interest him and receded into the background. He stretched back in his chair to relax and his eyes drowsily wandered from the nurse's bosom to her booty as she continued with her chores. Soon his mind started to drift and, as he was often inclined to in these situations, he started to fantasize.

The nurse had walked up close to where he sat. She put her arms around him and pressed his head against her bosom while he put his hand around her booty. Tingling sensations surged through the lower part of his body when he heard a voice in the distance calling out his name. Despite the interruption, Toto continued to be in a blissful state with his head in her bosom, when he heard the voice again. Finally, with a great deal of reluctance, he let go of the moment to heed the other voice.

"Kilonzo, Inspector Okello is here."

With a start, Toto came out of his reverie and looked up to see the constable near him and the inspector standing some distance away.

Toto stood up awkwardly with a "Yes, sir." He dared not straighten up because of the bulge in his trousers, and he shuffled his feet around to somehow get behind the chair. Standing behind its back to conceal his arousal, he said, "Sir, the man is still unconscious. I've checked his pockets—he's not carrying any identification papers, but I believe his name is Fred."

Inspector Bic Okello smirked as he wondered what the young Toto was up to. "Okay, Toto, time to interrogate."

\*\*\*

Fred stirred in his bed and struggled to open his eyes, sensing that he lay in unfamiliar surroundings. He had a splitting headache and bone-crunching pain in more than one part of his body. He tried again to open his eyes, but the effort was too much and, as he started to recall some of the previous night's events, he drifted into a state of unconsciousness.

Random thoughts floated through his mind. He recalled the face of a European man beaming a flashlight on him and offering water before covering him with a blanket. Despite the agonizing pain, he started to recall some of the action after he had deftly snatched the briefcase and jumped into the getaway car. Particularly the exhilarating mood that prevailed in the car until they found they were cornered by a police vehicle on a dirt road.

Befuddled thoughts crossed his mind, back and forth. When he had agreed to take up this job, all he had been told was to snatch a bag from someone named Don, after which he would be dropped off. Later, he had gathered from Tusker's conversation that they were involved in something big, and it was to "teach that mongoose a lesson." He was not told to prepare for a high-speed car chase through the streets of Nairobi, and for it to end with him being a sitting duck in a car, cornered by the police. He was a pickpocket and a petty thief, and all he had experienced so far was when the police picked him up and locked him in the slammer—no guns and no shootings. He had seen serious trouble ahead if he did nothing: a bullet in his chest or a long-term prison sentence. He had to do something quickly to save his skin.

*The briefcase!* he'd thought. *The briefcase!* The only wrong thing he had done that night was to have snatched the briefcase in the first place. If he got rid of it quick, before the police got him, they would have no proof he was involved.

After another groggy spell, his mind started to clear. The briefcase had been placed next to him in the rear seat. Without attracting attention, he had rolled down the window and grabbed the case. Suddenly, the car lurched forward as Daniel began his maneuver. Fred had been convinced there was no way their car would get past the police Land Rover. That was the moment. He had tossed the briefcase out the window as the Nissan swerved and accelerated. He had struggled to roll up the window before the others could realize what he'd done. But Good Lord! Daniel had managed to get past the police, and they were speeding away again.

But the respite had been brief. Thereafter, he could recall loud curses, punches to his face and body, and a sharp blow to the back of his head. And later, the European with a flashlight.

Fred opened his eyes to see a nurse looking down at him. "Where am I?" he mumbled.

"In the hospital. How are you feeling?"

"Terrible."

After observing him for a moment, she walked away. Fred heard her speak to someone in a low voice, and when he opened his eyes again, he was looking up at a police officer.

\*\*\*

"You feeling better?" Inspector Bic Okello inquired. Fred groaned in pain.

The nurse came up and gave the patient an injection through his IV. The inspector waited for one full minute, after which he shook the patient until Fred opened his eyes. "You've been up to a lot of mischief last night, haven't you, *rafiki* (friend)? Look at the mess you've got yourself into." In a firmer tone, Bic continued, "Now tell me what exactly happened, and who are you working for?"

Drowsily opening his eyes, Fred mumbled, "They beat me up."

"Who beat you up and for whom are you working?"

"Tusker."

The nurse heard the response and walked away.

"And from whom did you snatch the briefcase?" Bic asked.

With some effort, Fred whispered, "Don."

"Where is the briefcase?"

The patient shook his head, "Gone."

Suddenly Fred's face turned pale and his head fell to the side. The nurse came back and stood next to Bic. In a low tone, she explained that the booster dose that had been administered at Bic's behest had raised Fred's energy level temporarily, but nothing else could now be done.

Bic shook Fred and asked, "What do you mean, the briefcase is gone?"

Fred slowly opened his mouth. Bic bent and heard him mumble, "*Mzungu* (a European)... a *Mzungu*..."

Bic turned to the nurse. "Do you think he'll come around?"

She felt the patient's pulse and shook her head. Turning to Bic, she asked, "Did he say 'Tusker'?"

Bic nodded. "The fool can think only of Tusker beer, even on his death bed."

The nurse believed him. Tusker was a popular brand of a local beer. When she later filled out the medical sheet, she entered Fred's words as, "Patient asked for Tusker beer."

Inspector Okello was content to leave the nurse with that impression. He did not wish for the hospital staff or anyone else who might come snooping around to know that Fred mentioned "Tusker" John as the one who had hired him to snatch the briefcase.

***

Sulking as he sat outside a kiosk, Don bit into a piece of roasted *cassava*—a variety of yam. His mood was understandably dark after the previous night's debacle.

He belonged to the Maasai tribe, the semi-nomadic pastoral herdsmen and long the inhabitants of the savannah plains that were now split up, forming part of the two East African nations of Kenya and Tanzania. The Maasai know no national borders and traveled freely between the two countries, seeking pastures for their cattle.

He was named Koinet Olekorinko, the first name meaning "the tall one." "You'll grow up to be tall like your grandfather," his grandmother had often told him.

As was customary in their tribe, his earlobes were pierced when he was young and conical earrings, carved from animal bones, were inserted in the ear holes. As he grew older, the earrings were replaced with wider, heavier ones and the lobes continued to stretch. By the time a Maasai was fully grown, he ended up with long, hanging earlobes.

"This is our tribe's proud tradition," his father had explained. "It gives us a distinctive identity that sets us apart from the other tribes."

As a youth, Koinet had suffered a gash across his right cheek that left a permanent scar. When he took up elephant poaching, his adversaries taunted him, and one went so far as to sketch a caricature that showed his right profile resembling an elephant, with a snide caption at the bottom, "Whoever took *my* tusk away?"

For a long time, he had felt the need to take on a more recognizable name. After watching the movie *Godfather*, he opted to be called Don. Soon after he became a poacher, his friends started to call him *Ndovu*, pronounced with a silent "N," which means "elephant." It was then that he was stuck with the nickname *Ndovu* Don.

"Don't go into this business, Koinet!" his mother had pleaded with him. "We are herdsmen, not hunters. We hunt animals only when they kill our cattle." But her plea fell on deaf ears, and thereafter his family treated him like an outcast.

A man of few words, Don was cold, calculating, and determined, and his small steely eyes made it difficult to read what was going through his mind.

He made steady progress in building up his reputation as a poacher. Small-time poachers without the right connections risked being tracked down by the game park rangers. These officials were equipped with high-caliber weapons and sophisticated tracking devices, generously provided by donor countries. Bribing the officials helped, but only to some extent.

The rules were different for those working under the tutelage of a powerful official. For them, the tracking and monitoring devices remained ominously inactive while they moved around the game parks. In Don's case, he felt he was fortunate when the official, known as the Minister, decided to try him out in place of "Tusker" John, who was said to have become difficult to work with.

"You're lucky, brother, you've been given a chance," commented one of his tribesmen, who worked in a lodge in the game park. "I hear Tusker has messed up real bad."

He had carried out his first hunt under this arrangement a few days prior, which yielded several tusks. Don was aware they would be worth a fortune on the black market, but that was not his domain. His task was to hunt down the elephants, strip them of their tusks, ferry the trophies out of the game park reserves, and hand them over to an ivory trader, who in this instance was the notorious Somali. He, in turn, would arrange for the goods to be transported over the porous borders into Somalia, from whence the ivory was eventually sold on the international market.

While munching on the *cassava*, Don reflected on those fateful seconds the previous night, after the Somali had handed over the cash, meant for the Minister. *"Damn it—hog shit—what was wrong with me?"* he cursed himself. *"Why the heck did I get distracted?"* What was so unique, he wondered, about the briefcase that he couldn't resist taking a look at one of the shiny metal tags that read "Limited Edition"? That was when he felt a sharp tug on his wrist and the briefcase was gone! Right in front of his eyes, while he stood transfixed, the thief had sprinted and jumped into a waiting car that sped away!

For all practical purposes, the Somali had handed over the briefcase to him and Don could do little to defend himself when the Minister later lambasted him. Don shuddered to think of the consequences.

His three assistants, Paul, Francis, and Mike, joined him and inquired about the latest developments. A grim Don responded that he had none. His lieutenant, Paul, asked, "Your friend in the police is back from leave, isn't he? Have you been in touch with him?"

He was referring to Don's relationship with Police Inspector Bic Okello. They had recently been introduced by a cousin during Don's visit to Nairobi. They had remained in touch, with Bic briefing Don on the latest developments in the government's efforts to curb poaching. Bic had returned a few days earlier, after being away to attend his mother's funeral.

Don responded, "No, I haven't been in touch. But I've information from another contact that the thief was beaten up by Tusker and left for dead on a lonely road. I don't know what's happened to the briefcase. Now, this is what we'll do—we track down Tusker's hideouts. We have to hunt him and his men till we get back the cash."

He looked around and added, "There's no time to be lost. Don't forget—if we don't recover the cash, I'll be dead meat. And I'll make sure the same happens to you, as well."

He ordered *chai* as they sat down to discuss his plan.

***

"We've had good production figures the last two days. At this rate, we should have no problems executing the order from the Tea Authority on schedule," said Zach Omollo, the production engineer, as he stepped into Jay's office.

"That sounds great, Zach," Jay responded, as he prepared to wind down for the weekend. "We must keep up this pace—I'll make sure you get all the raw materials on time. You have a great weekend."

Jay started to clear the pending papers on his desk when he recalled that Heidi had phoned a little earlier to remind him to turn the briefcase over to the police. After a moment's deliberation, Jay decided to phone one of the officials.

A few months earlier, the police were called to investigate a break-in at Jay's plant and he'd been impressed with the officer in charge, Inspector Julius Wachira. After the investigation, the inspector had handed over his card and said he could be contacted if Jay needed the department's help. Jay had felt that Julius was the type of contact in the police that a person needed when living in a country where security is a major concern.

Julius also conveyed that one of his nephews needed a job and asked if Jay's company could provide him with one, even on a temporary basis. Jay had dealt with several such requests in the past, since virtually every government official made similar requests, but it was not possible to accommodate them all.

In the case of Julius Wachira, his request came at a time when Jay's company had received a large order from the Tea Authority, and thus he could oblige Julius. Now, Jay decided to take up Julius's offer and see how the inspector could help.

He called Julius and came up with a story: his close friends, living in Lavington, had heard gunshots near their house the previous night and police detectives had come around their neighborhood, questioning the *askaris* about a missing briefcase.

Unbeknownst to Jay, Julius had been one of the officers present at the meeting with the Police Commissioner that morning. Julius shared the information that his department was investigating the report of a stolen yellow car that was found abandoned in Lower Kabete. It was suspected to have been involved in a robbery and used in a police chase that covered several parts of Nairobi, including Lavington.

Jay's heart started to race; the abandoned vehicle had to be the same one that he had encountered. Desisting from revealing his curiosity, he asked, "You said there was a robbery? What was stolen?"

"We haven't yet been provided with details," came the response, with the astute police officer not wanting to divulge what little he knew about the briefcase. "But your friends can relax—we're on the job."

"This probably means the stolen goods haven't yet been recovered," probed Jay. After a pause, he continued, "When you have more information, could you please give me a call? I'm sure my friends would be keen to know."

Jay wasn't sure if the official would part with the information he sought. But Julius said he'd get back if there were any developments.

On his way home, Jay tuned into the local news on the car radio. There were no reports of a major robbery the previous night. On reaching home, he informed Heidi about his conversation with the police officer. Afterward, he said he'd find it hard to come up with a satisfactory explanation if he were to approach the police to hand over the money.

But Heidi was hopping mad. "However could you come up with such a dumb story?" she fumed, banging her hand on the kitchen counter. "You know you did something stupid last night and now you're making matters worse. Do you realize how dangerous this could be for us?"

Jay remained calm, aware that it would take a few minutes for her simmering temper to cool off. From the fridge, he pulled out a bottle of beer and poured the contents into two glasses, proffering her one. He took a large swig from his glass, while she continued to glare at him and ignored the beer. In a soothing and persuasive tone, he said, "You're right when you say that I did something dumb last night—I'd have felt the same if I were in your place. But what I did is now a *fait accompli*—a done deed. Let's consider the best way forward."

He took another sip and moved around the kitchen counter to her side. Tenderly putting his arm around her, he picked up her glass and raised it to her lips. "Just a sip," he coaxed. She turned to look at him and, after what to Jay seemed an eternity, took a sip.

He continued his case. "I now have a contact in the police—let's not underestimate its importance. There are still no reports on the TV about the burglary—suggesting that the money was probably being used for something illegal. And we also know that the police are on the job."

He paused for Heidi to dwell on what he'd stated, before continuing. "Now, *liebchen*, I shall be in touch with this officer so that I remain abreast of what's going on. Is there, then, a real urgency for us to turn the money over to the police?"

"Oh, Jay, you're creating so much confusion in my mind!" Heidi spoke in anguish. "Keep me out of all this and you better make sure you stay of trouble!"

Gulping down the beer, she stormed out of the kitchen, leaving Jay to warm up his lunch.

# Chapter 3

## Saturday Afternoon

*One more case solved to the satisfaction of my bosses,* mused Commissioner Michael Karanja, as he penned his signature on a file to close a successful investigation. Sipping his fourth cup of tea for the day, he recalled his apprehension when he first took this position, about his ability to please more than one boss. Looking back, he believed he had met the performance bar. He had solved or "resolved" all the cases he had dealt with, even if the methods or the outcomes did not quite measure up to judicial requirements. But the judiciary was weak and, in the name of law and order, Karanja and his team had, at times, resorted to drastic measures to resolve particularly sensitive cases.

He had not anticipated problems in recovering the stolen briefcase, the latest case to land on his desk. The theft had been reported to him the previous night soon after it took place, when he was at home watching television with his wife. They were interrupted by the loud ring of the telephone and on the line, in a very agitated state, was the Minister. Briefly reporting the theft, he asked the commissioner to immediately arrange to give chase to the thugs driving a yellow car. Within minutes, Karanja had organized that, even though the Minister had parted with minimal information. He now sat, disappointed that there was no sign of the stolen goods, despite his prompt action.

A knock on his door interrupted his thoughts and he looked up as Inspector Bic Okello walked in—one of the officers assigned to carry out this investigation. He had been away on leave for more than a week and had resumed duty the day before. Earlier that morning, he'd been asked to visit the Kenyatta Hospital from where he had presumably returned.

"So, Bic, were you able to question the thief?"

"Sir, that guy didn't pull through. I did my best to get some information from him, but he spoke very little. We gather his name was Fred and he admitted that he carried out the job for that notorious poacher Tusker, as we suspected. He snatched the briefcase from another poacher, Don. He also muttered something about a *Mzungu* (European). That must be the Russian who lives nearby—I suspect he's involved in some way with the theft." After a pause, he added, "But Fred said the briefcase is missing."

The Commissioner sat bolt upright in his chair. "Missing? What did he mean by that?"

"I don't know. Actually, he said the briefcase is gone. He seems to have lost it after all."

"What?" asked Karanja incredulously. "The briefcase that he stole has again been stolen? Where do we look for it now? You think the Russian is involved?"

Bic settled back in his chair and said, "Let's consider this scenario: after snatching the briefcase, the thief rode in the car with Tusker's gang. During the chase, did he somehow manage to hide the briefcase someplace? After the vehicle parked near the Russian's house, his *askari* reported he heard the thugs beat up Fred—probably to find out what he'd done with the goods? After they fled, the Russian, who had returned home, went out alone toward the car. He could've picked up the briefcase from where it was kept hidden by Fred, and brought it to his house, without the guard noticing it."

After a moment's reflection, Karanja said, "That's hard to say from what little we know—but in that case, why would the Russian call to inform us?"

"So that no one suspects him. I need to talk to him and find out more."

"Hmm—and we know nothing about the thief who's dead and has left us with very little information," lamented Karanja. "You realize he was the only one who could've told us under oath who the other men were? At this stage, we don't seem to have any other clues to work with. That's not good, Bic. We've got to get more details—who that damned thief was—and find the stolen goods."

"First, let me go over and question the Russian and take it from there."

The commissioner sat quietly, lost deep in thought. Bic did not rise to leave, as expected, but after a pause, said, "I was away for a short time, sir, and am surprised at the turn of events in the Mary Wilson case."

Karanja had sensed this was coming and braced himself for a long conversation—after all, significant developments had taken place during Bic's absence. The inspector had taken up this high-profile case with earnestness, Karanja recalled, when it was assigned to him several weeks previously. Ensuring the safety of the multitude of tourists who visited the country and who played a major role in sustaining the economy was a top priority with law enforcement officials. The discovery of Wilson's body had led to a widespread uproar in the media about inadequate security in tourist destinations. Investigations by Karanja's team had been hampered by interference from "higher ups," as he referred to them. The report of his department's findings that he eventually released received scathing criticism from the media and the public. Despite pressure to provide further details, Karanja and his men maintained a stoic silence.

Soon after being given the assignment, Bic had complained to the commissioner, "Sir, there are too many people poking their noses at the crime scene. Dozens of reporters from all over have been camping at the lodges and hounding the staff at the tent camp where Mary had lodged. They've been asking too many awkward questions and trying to find fault with our findings. You must bring a court order barring all these guys from the scene, like we did some years back when that woman was found dead."

Karanja had spent time reasoning with Bic. "The case of the woman was different—she might have been of Asian descent, but she was a Kenyan citizen. No foreign government could poke their noses into our affairs. And remember who the Chief Justice was at that time? It was much easier to get court orders then. But now the Brits are involved. Their High Commissioner is very pushy, and Mary's father is creating all sorts of problems. No, Bic, don't you see, this time it's different? Do you think our Chief Justice will allow a court order to be released that easily? No, this time we have a lot of hard work to do, or else *Mzee* (a title used to address patriarchs, in this case, the country's President) is bound to send me packing."

But Bic had continued passionately, "I hear the girl's father is talking about bringing in a detective from Scotland Yard. Now that's something we can not allow."

"Of course, we don't want those guys telling us what we should be doing. No, we'll not allow that," Karanja had assured Bic.

But that status had changed while Bic was away, and this was precisely what Bic now took up with his boss. "Sir, the President has agreed to allow a detective from Scotland Yard to reexamine the case. You had assured me this wouldn't happen."

Karanja shrugged his shoulders. "There was too much political pressure on *Mzee*. The British government threatened to reduce their development aid if we didn't agree. You know how badly our country needs that aid—the President finally had little choice but to give in."

Bic shook his head. "How do we make sure their man doesn't challenge our report?"

"You've been away too long, Bic. I worked with our guys to see how we could take care of that. We have also assigned Peter Otieno to be present alongside the detective throughout his visit. You know Peter. We briefed him yesterday that he must keep jabbering away as he normally does and keep the Brit distracted, so that he doesn't get to the root of the problem. Peter said he looked forward to the assignment. But you know him—he brags too much. I think he'll keep the Brit distracted to some extent, but all of us have to be on guard—we need to part with minimal information when the Brit asks for it."

"Okay, I'll do my best. But I'm not happy about this, boss. We don't want any foreigners snooping around, telling us how we should be doing our jobs. I'm not happy,"

Bic repeated for good measure, expressing his displeasure as he stood up to leave.

There was a knock on the door and Inspector Bono Njoroge walked in. Gesturing to Bic to remain seated, Karanja asked Bono to take a seat. Bono reported, "I've spoken to the drivers of our vehicles involved in the chase last night. Only one of them came face-to-face with the yellow car." He narrated the driver's description of how the thugs managed to drive away.

Karanja interrupted, "You said the thugs had stopped on a side road, where our vehicle tried to block them? What were they doing there? Maybe that's where they dropped off the stolen goods for hiding—or they handed them over to someone there. Bono, you should go there and check it out. Also, find out if there were any eyewitnesses."

"Yes, sir."

"Meanwhile, what have we found out about the stolen car?"

"It belongs to a Japanese executive—he says it was stolen from a parking lot outside a restaurant. Our forensics department is checking for evidence before we return it to him."

"Fine," said Karanja. "Now, Bic was at the hospital to interrogate the thief, but he soon died. The only information Bic could gather from him was that he worked for Tusker and stole the briefcase from Don."

Bic added, "He also said something about a *Mzungu*—I'm sure that must be the Russian who lives nearby. I'll be checking him out, but the briefcase is missing."

"Missing?" asked Bono, turning to look at the Commissioner. "What does that mean?"

"I'm not sure, but I know this complicates the situation and we don't have much to work with. Let's get whatever information we can from our contacts."

The two inspectors left the room. Karanja hunched forward on the table, holding his face in his hands as he gently rubbed his eyes with his fingers. *Why was this case getting so complicated?*

\*\*\*

With a loud burp, Tusker finished his meal of *Ugali* (cornmeal porridge) and *sukuma wiki* (sautéed collard greens). He sat under a tarpaulin sheet that passed as a roof, abutting a kiosk that served low-cost snacks and meals. Tucked away at the far end, off the main road, it catered mainly to the staff employed in the large homes in the upscale neighborhood of Lavington.

Tusker had been striking up conversations with security guards, gardeners, drivers, butlers, and servants in an attempt to find out if they had seen or heard anything of interest concerning the gunshots in their neighborhood the previous night. But none had any specific information. He was aware that he would raise suspicion if he were to meet them at their workplace—the residents would certainly report him to the police. So he continued discreetly talking with those visiting the kiosk, hoping that he might get to meet the night-shift *askaris* who worked near the spot where the confrontation with the police had taken place. It was a tedious task, since not all the guards visited this kiosk.

He had considered calling his contact in the police department, Inspector Bono Njoroge. But he reasoned that the police might not yet be aware of his involvement in the theft. The getaway car was stolen and Fred was not known to work for him. As long as Fred did not speak up, the police had no evidence of his involvement. Tusker was not aware of the present condition of Fred; he certainly had not been in a position to speak when they had left him the night before. Besides, the loss of the briefcase with money did not really affect Tusker. The money was not his; he had meant to use it as leverage against the Minister. The loss was the Minister's, though Tusker was aware that the Minister and his men would desperately be looking for the money. He knew he had to recover it quickly, as his involvement could not remain unknown for long and then, like hyenas, they would be at his throat. He had walked back with his men late the previous night to this area, but there was no trace of the briefcase.

He stood up and, with rising frustration, walked away from the kiosk. Seeking clues that might divulge where the money was, he looked around, his large, protruding eyes ablaze. His palms and fingers twitched as he mentally squeezed the neck of Fred and anyone else who was holding on to what he had worked hard to possess. The money was his and he would do whatever it took to recover it.

***

At three in the afternoon, a police vehicle bearing Inspector Bic Okello pulled up at Mikhail Smirnoff's residence. He was ushered in by the housemaid, who directed him to the living room, but he proceeded leisurely, surveying the house layout and taking in salient details along the way.

Soon Bic heard footsteps and turned to face the Russian, but wasn't pleased with what he beheld. The tall, burly man who towered above him had a heavy, muscular physique, rugged features, and a big, round neck. Bic found the man's bear-like appearance unsettling and it served to reconfirm his suspicions that the man was involved in business of a dubious nature. But he proceeded with the formalities.

"Good afternoon, sir. My name is Wycliffe Okello, an inspector with Kenya Police. I wish to have the details of what you witnessed last night when you called to report the vehicle that was abandoned outside on the road."

Bic made notes as Mikhail described what he witnessed and then inquired if the injured man had said anything, particularly about a briefcase. The Russian said the victim was in no condition to speak and had not uttered a word. He had neither sighted the thugs when they fled, nor was he aware of a briefcase.

"How is the injured man?" asked Mikhail.

"He passed away this morning."

"Oh, I'm sorry. Did he give any information about the car and how they got here?"

"No, and that's the problem. We know he was involved in a burglary, but we have not been able to establish his identity. We'd hoped you might provide us with some details."

"I've told you everything I know," replied Mikhail.

When asked for his personal details, Mikhail handed over his business card.

"What is the nature of your company's business?" Bic asked.

"Distribution of our company's products in this region."

"What type of products?"

"Various industrial products," was Mikhail's vague reply.

"How about neighboring countries? Do you have offices in those countries?"

"No offices. I travel very often. I handle the business of those countries myself."

"I see," Bic responded. "You must be a very busy man, *Bwana* Smirnoff. I like your name—it's so Russian. All I know about Russia is that it's very cold there in winter. One of my cousins spent some time in Warsaw last winter and he complained about the cold."

"Warsaw is in Poland, not Russia," Mikhail clarified with a sigh.

Bic shook his head. "That's so confusing—Moscow, Warsaw, both similar-sounding names and still you say they're in different countries?" He decided to get back to more familiar territory. "*Bwana* Smirnoff, you say you don't know the man who was found lying outside?"

"No."

"And the yellow car? Do you know whom it belongs to?"

"No. I've never seen it before."

Bic took a more direct approach. "The car was parked outside your house and a seriously wounded man was lying near the car. Can you please explain how they ended up near your house if you say you were not involved?"

Mikhail remained unruffled. "Anyone can drive on the road outside my house and leave a car and an injured man out there. I know nothing of what happened. When I came home and saw the car and the man, I reported it to your department."

"Hmm. Okay," said Bic. "I have no further questions for now, but I might come back as we gather more information."

He rose to leave. He looked around, toward the dining room area and the back of the house, taking in the details. They stepped out through the front door and Bic glanced at Mikhail's vehicle parked outside. It was the workhorse of Africa, the Peugeot 504 from France.

"So, you are driving a French vehicle. You are not driving the Russian Skoda?" he queried, with a grin on his face that revealed his perfect set of milky white teeth.

Mikhail shook his head. "Skoda used to be made in Czechoslovakia, not in Russia."

"Oh, Czechoslovakia, is it?" said Bic. "But I read somewhere that Skoda was a popular car in Russia."

"That must have been some time back, since the Skoda is no longer being produced."

"Where?" asked Bic. "In Czechoslovakia?"

"Yes. And for your information, the country of Czechoslovakia no longer exists."

Bic realized he had little to gain by attempting to impress the Russian with his knowledge of that region. He was about to blurt out the inevitable request of a job in Mikhail's company for his cousin, who has just finished her secretarial course. But he held back—he didn't want to place himself under any obligation to a person with whom he was not comfortable.

Bic surveyed the house from the outside and at the compound wall surrounding the house. They bade goodbye and Mikhail shut the front door, relieved that, as far as he was concerned, this was the end of the previous night's incident.

\*\*\*

Police Inspector Bono Njoroge stepped out of his vehicle near Richard Collin's gate, in the neighborhood where the police had confronted the thugs. Oldest among his peers and portly in stature with a bulging waistline, Bono had been an inspector for several years, with slim prospects for promotion. Boisterous by temperament, he was prone to breaking into a guffaw with his mouth wide open, which accentuated his large, bulbous nose.

He started to question the *askaris* of the adjoining houses, hoping they might provide vital clues, but he soon realized it was a waste of time. In response to his query, "Did any of the night *askaris* whom you'd have met this morning report seeing a briefcase being handed over, dropped, or picked up?" he received bewildering replies, like, "The night shift guy admitted he was shit scared when the gunshots went off. I'm sure he wouldn't have recognized a briefcase, even if it were dropped right in front of him."

Bono realized he would need to come back late in the evening and question the night shift *askaris* who were on duty when the incident occurred. Unfortunately, due to a shortage of vehicles, Deputy Commissioner Gideon Odhiambo might not make one available to Bono for another visit. As he headed back to the office, Bono silently cursed the deputy commissioner for the plethora of procedural protocols he had recently introduced.

\*\*\*

Early that evening, Jay and Heidi were shopping at Uchumi, a chain of department stores.

"That's some serious shopping," Jay heard a familiar voice behind him while he was in the wine section. It was their good friend, Ravi Karnik, accompanied by his wife, Meena.

"Checking out the new booze that lands on these shelves, Jay?" asked Ravi in jest.

"Would hate to be the last one to try out something new—got to keep up with my peers," answered Jay.

"Keeping up with Ravi won't be easy," said Meena, "particularly when it comes to Scotch and vodka."

"I think Jay knows he's no match for Ravi," added Heidi, her mood brightening at the sight of her friends. "And I do my best to keep up with the wines— particularly the local ones."

Ravi, Meena, and Jay shared the same Indian ethnicity and had been close friends since Jay arrived in Kenya. Ravi was a lawyer by profession.

Turning to Heidi, Meena asked, "Have the kids left for their holidays to Germany?"

"Yah," replied Heidi. "The grandparents are taking good care of them."

"Which means you two lovebirds must now be enjoying your second honeymoon," Ravi looked mischievously at Heidi. "Do I notice a glow in Heidi's face that I'd never seen before?"

"Stop teasing her," admonished Meena. "Ravi, why don't we ask them to join us tomorrow?"

"We have a visitor from India. Bomy Daruwala— also a lawyer," said Ravi. "He's on a short business trip and we're making a day trip tomorrow with him to Lake Nakuru. If you're free, why don't you join us?"

"I guess that should be okay, right Heidi?" asked Jay, pleased at the prospect of having something to divert their attention over the weekend. Heidi nodded.

"We can all fit into my SUV, so there's no need for two vehicles," said Ravi. He again smiled at Heidi. "Well, Meena and I'll do our best to keep you entertained during the day. Now don't do something I wouldn't do, once we leave the two of you alone in the evening."

"What the heck do you think we're up to?" laughed Jay. "Anyway, thanks for inviting us. You know we always enjoy a day trip to the lake. What time do we leave?"

"We should be at your place around eight-fifteen."

"We'll stop at Naivasha for breakfast," said Meena. "We'll carry sandwiches for lunch."

As they bade farewell, Jay took a parting shot. "Ravi, I guess you'll want your friend Bomy to watch *The Ghost and the Darkness* while he's here."

Meena and Heidi broke into laughter, as Ravi merely nodded and smiled.

The Hollywood box office hit movie, starring Michael Douglas and Val Kilmer, had recently been released in local theaters. The movie's plot was based on true events that took place while the British were constructing the railroad from the port of Mombasa in Kenya to the shores of Lake Victoria in neighboring Uganda, toward the end of the nineteenth century. The explorer John Speke had established that the source of the river Nile was Lake Victoria, and the British wanted control of the source.

Vast stretches of land along the railroad route were uninhabited and wild animals roamed freely. The work progressed smoothly until they were roughly halfway between Mombasa and Nairobi, near a settlement called Tsavo. Unbeknownst to the crew, their presence had attracted the attention of two male lions. On waking up one morning in their tents, the workers, largely unskilled laborers brought in from India, realized one of their colleagues was missing. A handful more disappeared over the next few nights, and it was only when the half-eaten remains of one of them were discovered that they realized with horror what was going on.

Ravi's father had joined Kenya Railways as an accounts assistant during its formative years and was a member of the staff that had worked alongside the construction crew.

"As kids, we listened in awe as my father described the terrifying experience they went through," Ravi delighted in narrating this experience after the movie was released. "There was a virtual state of panic in the workers' camp. To make matters worse, those workmen who stayed awake at night on guard claimed they never saw or heard any lions, and yet men continued to disappear. It wasn't long before the hapless workmen believed that the man-eaters were ghosts."

His father's status as a staff member entitled him to camp in relatively better conditions, but like everyone else camping out in the wilderness, he spent stressful nights, fearful of the fate that could befall them. The British Railway Engineers eventually sought the services of an American hunter, Charles Remington, to hunt down the two beasts.

With Ravi's penchant for extracting maximum mileage from any situation, he left listeners with the subtle impression that his father had played an important role in making arrangements for Charles Remington to visit the camp and stake out at night until the two lions were killed.

After bidding their friends goodbye, Heidi remarked, "Yes, I'm sure Ravi would want their guest to watch the movie. But one must admire the extent of Ravi's contacts. I wouldn't be surprised if he has business interests with this lawyer from India."

"Yet one more pie that he has his finger in—is that what you're suggesting, *liebchen?*"

"And the size of the pie keeps growing," she nodded.

After completing schooling in Nairobi, where his family had settled, Ravi traveled to the UK to study law and started to practice it on his return. Later, when Kenya gained independence, he quickly built up a successful, high-profile law practice. Shrewd and full of confidence, his list of clients was impressive, and he did not shirk from taking up the defense of controversial politicians and officials. Those in power did not wish to antagonize a lawyer whose services they might well need when their days of glory were over.

"Yes, that's our good old friend Ravi," said Jay, as they drove home.

***

Later, on the evening news on the local TV channels, Jay noted there were no reports of any major robberies. Refraining from discussing the subject weighing on their minds, the two watched a few TV shows before retiring.

As they lay in bed, Jay felt compelled to reassure Heidi before turning out the lights. Putting his arm around her, he said, "I'll find a way out of this mess, I promise. Once we have some information from my police friend, we'll decide what should be done next. Please don't lose any precious sleep—you know me, I'll find a way out."

She merely nodded and remained quiet; he kissed her goodnight and turned off the lights. Both lay restless for a long time before he heard her steady breathing. He turned on his side toward her and, in the soft glow of the night lamp, gazed at her beautiful face. His thoughts drifted back to when it all started.

Eighteen years earlier, Jay had first set eyes on her, shortly after he had arrived in Germany from India in the late 1970s. His full name was Vijay Gupté, later shortened to Jay at Heidi's behest. He had been accepted as a trainee engineer in a machine tool manufacturing company in Bielefeld, a mid-sized town between Dusseldorf and Hannover in what was then West Germany.

Shortly after his arrival, he was summoned to the technical director's office. Walking along the office passageway, he glanced at the secretaries and assistants behind their desks, until his eyes settled on the one he considered most beautiful. She was the sales director's secretary and had given him a curious look. That did not surprise him, since that was the way Germans looked at the few Indians who lived then in Germany. He continued to stare awkwardly at her bright blue eyes while her wary gaze lingered on as he walked past. They greeted each other in a soft tone, and he realized that his voice was stuck in his throat—he could never have started a conversation, even if he wanted to!

A few weeks later, the company hosted its annual party at a dance hall. He had fervently hoped that she would be there and, even more important, that she would be without a male companion. His spirits rose when he spotted her in a corner with a female colleague, though he wondered if he would have the chance to dance with her and get to know her. She was one of the most attractive girls in the hall, and young men would be making a beeline for her once the dance floor was thrown open. Besides, would he be able to muster the courage to ask her for a dance? He was, after all, a foreigner and his German was patchy. But Jay was not the type to give up—this was just one more challenge for him—and he loved challenges!

When the band resumed with dance music, Jay took a deep breath and bravely began the journey toward her table. Inexplicably, with every step he took forward, he had the sinking feeling that she appeared to recede a step farther away from him! He was barely six feet away when a swifter young man beat him to it.

Jay was not sure if she had seen him approach, but the girl sitting next to her had. To avoid embarrassing himself and the girl in front of those nearby, he walked up to her and with a polite bow, asked, *"Darf ich bitte* (May I please)?"

On the dance floor, she introduced herself. "I'm Renate. I'm an apprentice in the Tool Design Department."

"And my name is Vijay, an engineering trainee in—"

"Oh, I know which department you work in."

"You do?"

"Sure, everyone knows about the trainee from India."

"Interesting," said Jay. "I don't recall having seen you before. But I do recall having seen your friend in the office."

"Oh, Heidi? Yes, she told me she's seen you before."

"She did? Well then, I certainly need to check with her and introduce myself," Jay said with enthusiasm.

"Uh, oh!" grunted Renate, probably sensing where that introduction would lead to.

And that was exactly what happened. When the music stopped, Jay led Renate back to her table and thanked her for the dance; he then mustered the courage to strike up a conversation with Heidi. Apparently, his tall, well-proportioned physique, sharp features, dark eyes, and a head full of dark hair impressed Heidi. She also appeared to be amused by Jay's stuttering along in his broken German. Renate watched with mixed feelings as he and Heidi merrily chatted and danced together for most of the evening.

They agreed to meet again, but Heidi insisted that they not spend time together at work. So their meetings were limited to the weekends, when they danced at the *Tanzhalle* (dance halls) or watched movies, or dined in cozy places of Heidi's choice.

A few months later, Heidi invited Jay to her house to meet her family over dinner. He recalled being angst-ridden when entering the house, despite Heidi's assurances that her parents were easy to get along with. And sure enough, her father, Wolfgang Schlemming, and mother, Gisela, put him at ease. Heidi's older brother, Kurt, did not appear too excited about her boyfriend from India, but her parents kept him out of the conversations most of the time. After an enjoyable evening with the Schlemmings, Jay left their house in high spirits.

"I told you you'd have no problem getting along with them," Heidi had chuckled. "And they seem to like you, too."

As the two developed a steady relationship, he visited the Schlemmings more often. And Heidi was pleased that Jay appeared to have been well accepted by her parents. They both knew how hopelessly Heidi had fallen in love with Jay.

It was not too long before they decided to marry. Jay continued his training while Heidi held on to her job with the same firm. In the evenings, he attended technical classes, while she studied English.

Three years later, they left Germany for India.

As he lay awake that night, Jay felt flustered about the perilous situation that he and his family were in. He thought about their two children, Raj and Anita, and felt a sense of relief that they were not home. Then his thoughts strayed to Heidi's parents and wondered how they would react if they knew about his deed that had placed their daughter and grandchildren in danger. He recalled the promise he had made to them many years earlier, that he would take good care of their daughter as he ventured with her to lands far, far away. As those memories flashed through Jay's mind, he spoke almost aloud, "Wolfgang and Gisela Schlemming, your daughter, and your grandchildren will come to no harm—of that, I swear by my Lord Ganesh."

He prayed in silence for a few moments. As the stress ebbed away, he fell fast asleep.

# Chapter 4

## *Sunday*

Heidi woke to the soft chirping of birds in her garden—it was the crack of dawn and she sensed there was at least an hour before the alarm was set to go off. But the unsettling memories returned and drove her sleep away. Turning over, she wished she could relax and be as carefree as the birds outside, but that was not to be; it was now her turn to lie awake and fret about what could happen. *"Jay,* mein schatz, *what have you gotten us into?"*

She opened her eyes and watched him, lightly snoring in deep sleep, as the first rays of dawn streamed through the window curtains. She knew she could sleep no longer and decided to take a long, hot shower. Sitting up, she turned toward Jay, whispering *"Dummkopf* (Dumbhead)," while shaking her head.

As she brushed her teeth and then stepped into the shower, her thoughts drifted to the early years she had spent with Jay in Germany and India, before moving to Kenya.

She recalled the curiosity with which she had first eyed him when he joined her company. He looked different from the other foreigners who worked there, mainly Italians and Spaniards employed as *Gastarbeiter* (guest workers), who took up unskilled jobs that were hard to fill with Germans. Unlike them, the Indian was a qualified engineer.

She had just come out of a relationship with Dieter. He was well-mannered and had a pleasant demeanor, but he was a bit too scholarly and serious for her—she realized she was not enjoying his company. It was thus with mixed feelings that she reacted when he announced that he had been accepted to a technical university for a five-year course in engineering.

Jay was refreshingly different—and good-looking, too. After he overcame his initial inhibitions, when they first met at the company's annual party, she realized he was fun-loving, with a great sense of humor. Besides, as she discovered on more than one occasion, he loved to take on challenges. Not everyone may have been pleased with his occasional brashness, but it almost always impressed her. Yes, she thought as she showered; that was what she had found so attractive in him—and the fact that she could trust him and he would be faithful to her. She knew she couldn't say the same of her previous suitors, starting from Klaus to Helmut to Dieter.

As their relationship turned serious, Jay told her about his family in India and what life would be like there. He had said that getting his parents, particularly his mother, to accept a Westerner as his bride could be a bit of a challenge—one more, he was confident, he would overcome.

Three years after they wed in Germany, she left with him for India, with nagging doubts in her mind about what to expect. A German company had recently opened an office in Bombay (now Mumbai), and Jay was to be in charge of technical sales.

They spent the first two weeks in his ancestral home in the western Indian town of Baroda (now Vadodara). His parents, his younger sister, and other family members who shared the property warmly welcomed her and did all they could to make her feel at home. She was excited about the Indian culture and lifestyle, particularly when she donned the Indian "sari."

"The crowds, the weather, and the dust can be overwhelming," she'd written home. "And I'm lucky my stomach has been holding up to the spicy and, at times, oily Indian cooking! I think I've been well accepted by Jay's folks. His mother is not at all like what he had made her out to be—you know how he loves to tease! And his father is such great fun—it's difficult to get him to stop talking once he touches on the time he spent in England during his younger years."

But most of all, it was Jay's always being there for her that mattered. He often went out of his way to make sure she was comfortable, and Heidi knew he was the man for her.

After two hectic weeks in Baroda, meeting several of his extended family members and old friends, Jay and Heidi moved to Bombay, where Jay would start his new assignment. After settling down in this large metropolis, Heidi started to enjoy life as her social circle expanded. A few years later, she was the doting mother of two delightful kids, Raj and Anita.

Jay and Heidi had often talked about the benefits of working as an expatriate in several countries that needed the services of professionals with his experience. At a social gathering, they met a British executive whose company had operations in various countries. He mentioned a possible job opening in Kenya, a former British colony. Jay showed interest and within three months, he and Heidi were packing their bags and heading for Nairobi.

***

Heidi was not the only one to have risen early that Sunday morning. A few miles away, the Minister had also lain awake since he heard the cock crowing. Now, at nine o'clock, after downing two cups of hot *chai*, he paced up and down the office in his residence like a caged lion.

Some fifteen minutes earlier, he had called the Police Commissioner's residence and left a message for him to call back. When the phone finally rang, he snatched it on the first ring and heard the commissioner's voice at the other end.

"Yes, Karanja, what's the latest?" the Minister said, coming straight to the point.

"My men are spread everywhere—they should soon come up with something," came the optimistic response.

The Minister was obviously not impressed. "Are you saying we still have no idea who snatched the briefcase and where the scoundrels are hiding? I thought you had contacts with people in the underworld."

"Yes, we do. But we still have no information about these goods."

"What information did you get from the man in the hospital?"

"He died," Karanja quietly replied. "He had been badly beaten up and was in critical condition by the time we got him to the hospital. Despite our attempts, we couldn't get him to say much before he passed away. We're still trying to establish his identity."

"And what did he say?"

"That he was hired by 'Tusker' John to snatch the briefcase from *Ndovu* Don. That information is correct, I assume."

The Minister remained quiet. The Commissioner waited before continuing, "He also said something about a *Mzungu* (European). We believe he's referring to the Russian, who lives near the place where the thugs abandoned the car. My man has met the Russian and questioned him, and we are continuing our investigation of his possible involvement with the theft."

"Yes, take a look from that angle. Maybe he was involved in some way."

Karanja paused before delivering the bad news. "But the thief did mention something that doesn't make sense to us. He said the briefcase is now missing."

The Minister felt a heavy thump on his chest. Gasping for breath, he wheezed, "Missing? What do you mean, missing?"

"Well, we're unable to establish what he meant — our focus is on recovering the goods."

The Minister virtually moaned, "That can't be possible, can it? Why would they steal the briefcase and then report it missing?"

"No one has reported the briefcase missing," Karanja replied, wishing to keep the record straight. "But this complicates our investigations."

"What's going on? Is someone else behind the whole thing? You have to investigate from all angles." The Minister paused before continuing, "Now, about the yellow car. What information do we have? Was the owner involved?"

"The owner is expected to come tomorrow to collect the car; some Japanese guy. We'll question him then, but we believe the thugs stole the car to get away."

"We need to find the briefcase very quickly, Karanja."

"Yes, sir. But we also need more information about what was stolen. My men find it odd that all we are looking for is a briefcase."

"How can your people be so dumb?" the Minister retorted. "No one goes around carrying an empty briefcase. There is always something valuable in it."

"Yes, but we need to know what was in it."

"Are you saying your department can't catch the thugs who stole a briefcase that night?" the Minister asked, adding sarcastically, "we don't need the services of Scotland Yard for this investigation, do we?"

The Minister had touched a raw nerve and held his breath as he heard what he believed to be the grinding of teeth at the other end. Realizing he couldn't push the Commissioner any further, he decided to back off. "Okay, I know you and your men are capable of catching the thugs on your own. Let me know as soon as you have something."

The Minister hung up abruptly, as Karanja slowly placed the telephone back in its cradle.

He was at home in his small study and had been sipping a cup of tea. He closed his eyes and rubbed them with his fingers, as he brooded about this case. There were no reports of anyone splurging with large amounts of money. Whoever was in possession of the stolen money was sitting on it and biding his time. That person was also not turning it over to the police or any other authority. There's something different about this case, Karanja intuited, that would demand all the skills and resources that he and his team could come up with.

\*\*\*

Driving a Mitsubishi Pajero, a popular SUV model in East Africa, Ravi Karnik arrived at Jay's house at the appointed time. Jay and Heidi climbed into the vehicle to join Ravi's wife, Meena, and their visitor from India, Bomy Daruwala, a stocky gentleman in his mid-fifties with a jovial disposition.

As they drove off, Bomy said, "What flower is that?" pointing to one of the many flowers that Heidi had worked hard to grow in the small garden patch.

It was one of Heidi's proud brood. "The Bird of Paradise," she replied.

Meena explained, "A plant native to this continent and so named because of its resemblance to a brightly colored bird in flight."

"Beautiful," commented Bomy. "I've never seen one before."

As they drove off, Ravi mentioned to Jay and Heidi, "I was telling Bomy about the sights we'll be viewing along the way."

"Ravi is good at it. I can still recall his narration when we traveled with him the first time," said Jay.

"He's done that dozens of times—and still does it with passion," added Meena.

"And I still need you to help me out when I get stuck somewhere," Ravi smiled at his wife. He continued, "Bomy, as I mentioned earlier, the interior of this country rises over eight thousand feet. Those are the Highlands, a region of rolling uplands with rich volcanic soil, cool weather, and abundant rainfall."

They'd reached the outskirts of Nairobi and started to ascend the Highlands that Ravi had described. The hundred-mile drive between Nairobi and Lake Nakuru is one of the most scenic, with several viewpoints along the route offering spectacular views of the Rift Valley.

The morning air was cold and the trees were still wet from dew. They traveled past the small towns of Kikuyu and Limuru, nestled among the sloping fir tree-covered hills. Large stretches along this section of the highway were covered by dense fog and Ravi drove cautiously, as visibility was barely fifty feet. He continued with his narration to the visitor. "We're approaching the Great Rift Valley. It's believed to have formed some thirty million years ago by violent subterranean forces that tore apart the Earth's crust."

"What's a rift?" asked Bomy.

"A deep fissure or a fault in the Earth's surface. This process called 'rifting' is still in progress. There are a few active and semi-active volcanoes along the rifts."

"In simple terms, Bomy," Jay butted in, "it's pretty much like a rift between family members—husband and wife or two brothers. In this case, two sections of the Earth decided to part ways."

"Ho, ho," laughed Bomy. "I like the comparison, *dikra* (son), I like it."

Heidi smiled as she glanced at Jay and said, "Jay has a knack of making goofy remarks, doesn't he?"

Ravi ignored the interruption. "Getting back to its formation, it was earlier believed that the Great Rift Valley traversed in a north-south direction all the way from Syria in Middle East Asia, down to Mozambique in southern Africa, a distance of nearly four thousand miles. But subsequently, it was established that there are several separate rifts that collectively form what was thought to be one Great Rift Valley."

As they emerged from the fog, Ravi pulled up the vehicle and said, "We're now at the most dramatic section of the East African Rift, where it slices through East Africa, dividing Kenya into two segments. We'll step out to get one of the best views of the rift."

They stepped out of the Pajero onto a viewpoint perched on the edge of a hill. It offered a panoramic view of the valley as it plunged down more than a thousand feet and beyond it, the rift, a few miles wide. Several lakes, some of them alkaline, lie within the rift, as well as one semi-active volcano a short distance ahead.

As Bomy clicked his camera, taking pictures of the magnificent view, Ravi explained some of its unique features and added, "You know, Bomy, the Great Rift Valley is discernible from outer space. Astronauts in orbiting spaceships have reported sighting this formation."

"I don't know why we are trying to reach up to the heavens—the place up there is reserved for our gods. I tell you, Ravi, we humans are going to regret it if we continue messing around in the Almighty's territory," Bomy concluded in his typical Parsee accent.

The Parsees, who had fled from Persia to India more than a thousand years earlier, are followers of Zoroastrian, a religion that prevailed in that part of the world long before the birth of Islam. Facing religious persecution in later years with the spread of Islam, boatloads of them left Persia by sea and landed on the west coast of India. They sought shelter from the local Hindu ruler, who allowed them to settle on the condition that they not convert any locals to their religion. They were also required to speak only the local language, which was Gujarati. The settlers accepted his terms and learned the local language—which they speak, but with a delightful twist. With their unique accent and interspersed with a few words concocted from some of the many Indian languages, they speak Gujarati and English in their own inimitable "Parsee" style.

Hard-working, illustrious, and enterprising, they have remained a small, tightly knit community numbering barely a hundred thousand. Like most of his kinsmen, Bomy was jovial, loud, and gregarious. And like them, his spoken English was sprinkled with a fair amount of swear words from the local language, even in the presence of women. But no offense was ever taken, because by and large the Parsees are considered warm-hearted and good-natured.

At the Rift Valley, Bomy took several pictures, after which the group continued their journey. A few miles ahead, their next stop was to view Mount Longonot, with its distinctive conical shape ending with a concave tip with the crater.

"As you can see, it's a relatively small mountain and it had a major eruption some twenty-seven thousand years ago," said Ravi. "Occasionally, smoke is seen rising from the crater. A hiker's trail takes one from the base to the top of the crater. We've all climbed up to the edge on top and peeked down into the crater."

They continued their journey and stopped for breakfast in the town of Naivasha, where they helped themselves to freshly baked croissants and buns with coffee at a popular bakery. And then they moved on, driving past Lake Elmenteita, an alkaline lake in the Rift

Valley and home to some flamingos. But it was the spectacle a few miles ahead that Bomy found truly tantalizing.

They were approaching their destination, Lake Nakuru, one of the larger lakes in the Rift Valley. For a first-time visitor like Bomy, the lake would appear to be one vast pink blanket, waving in the wind. A closer look would reveal that the pink color comes from the flamingos that are attracted by the abundance of algae in the alkaline lake. In the shallow lake, the constantly shifting mass of pink from more than a million flamingos is truly a sight to behold.

They entered the Lake Nakuru National Park, a large reserve that attracts other birds, such as pelicans, cormorants, and Goliath herons, and within which roam rhinos, giraffes, gazelles, and a few leopards. Ravi parked his vehicle on a shady patch overlooking the lake. They opened up the lunch hampers as they relaxed over beer and sandwiches.

Like Ravi, Bomy was a lawyer by profession. He made this trip on behalf of his corporate client from India, who was setting up investments in Kenya. He had approached Ravi to advise him on Kenyan legalities.

"So is it company law that you've specialized in, Bomy?" asked Jay.

"*Arre Dikra* (My dear fellow), as you know in India, you must be a jack of all trades if you want to be successful."

Jay nodded, though he wasn't quite sure what Bomy meant.

Bomy continued, "As a lawyer, you have to have experience in all fields. I started off by defending all those *charso bees* (420s)," he cackled.

The Section 420 of the Indian Penal Code deals with punishment for offenses relating to cheating and dishonestly inducing delivery of properties. The term "420" is widely used to describe a cheat or a confidence trickster. At least two popular Indian movies have been produced using this number as part of their titles.

With his penchant for using a mixture of English, Indian, and Parsee words, Bomy said, "I tell you, *dikra*, there are so many *charso bees* on our streets that no bloody lawyer worth his salt can be successful unless he has at least tried defending those *sala chors* (crooks). *Arre,* a person like me would be *ek dam* (totally) useless unless he's had experience in defending these guys in court."

"There must have been plenty of drama in the court during those trials," said Heidi.

"I tell you, my dear," Bomy said, addressing Heidi. "I know you've lived for several years in India, but some of those bandicoots that I've defended—I tell you they've no bloody shame. It's just as well I also specialized in Section 411."

"That's the one that deals with possession of stolen goods, right?" asked Ravi.

Jay had just popped open a beer can and his hand jerked several inches when he heard Ravi's question, spilling half the beer on the ground.

"Don't be so clumsy, Jay," admonished Heidi, whose own hand shook as she took a bite of her sandwich.

"That's right," responded Bomy to Ravi's query. "I can understand the normal human tendency. If you find some goods that you suspect are stolen, but about which no one knows, then you might be tempted to hold on to them, hoping no one finds out."

"But in the eyes of the law, possession of stolen goods is considered a felony or a misdemeanor and is punishable accordingly," said Ravi as he stood up to put away his plate. "Heidi, the grilled chicken was delicious—I'm so glad you could join us."

"It was indeed our pleasure. Thanks for inviting us."

After finishing lunch, the men headed for the bushes to relieve themselves, while the two ladies packed the hampers.

Before Ravi could return, Jay cornered Bomy and peppered him with questions. "About the possession of stolen goods, what's the punishment for such offenses?"

"It can be up to seven years in prison."

"Have there been cases where the culprits have been treated leniently?"

"If the stolen goods are returned to the owner by a person who can prove that he was not aware that the goods were stolen, then the court might not take any action. But if one has kept the stolen goods for his own use, then he would be punished."

"In India, could you trust the police to return the goods to the rightful owner if you handed over the goods to them?"

"That's a good point," Bomy admitted. "But you cannot be the judge. One could pity the person from whom the goods were stolen if the police didn't return them to him. My friend, you are asking so many questions; are you speaking from personal experience?"

Jay replied, "No, but someone I know is in a similar situation."

As Ravi walked back, Bomy suggested to Jay, "You should ask your friend to take the help of someone like

Ravi. He might be able to help return the goods to the rightful owner and your friend could be spared any punishment."

Ravi shrugged his shoulders and said, "It's unfortunate, but true, that in many countries, one can never be certain if the authorities will return all the stolen goods to the rightful owners. That does not, however, mean that one can just hold on to them."

He gestured to the others that it was time to board the vehicle for the return journey.

\*\*\*

In an occupation where taking off on Sundays was deemed a privilege, Tusker was an exception—he had reached that status when he could travel to his village over the weekends. But this Sunday was different—not only did he have to abandon his plans to travel, but it was also a day that found him in a foul mood. There had been no news about the missing cash—his contact in Don's camp had just confirmed that—and he feared it was only a matter of time before the Minister would send his henchmen after him.

Late afternoon, his cell phone rang; at the other end was his contact in the police department, Inspector Boniface "Bono" Njoroge.

"*Habari?*" Tusker answered in as soft a tone as his guttural voice could muster.

"We have information that you arranged the theft of the cash," came the terse response.

"I don't know what you're talking about," was Tusker's defiant reply.

"Where did you get hold of that guy in the fancy jacket? Why did you have to finish him off?"

After a brief pause, Tusker said, "We lost the stolen goods because of him."

"What do you mean. 'lost'?"

"He got nervous when he saw the police cars and threw the bag out."

"You want me to believe that? You used him to snatch the goods and then beat him to death so he wouldn't talk."

"No, chief, that's not what happened."

"Then what happened?"

"The idiot threw the briefcase away. After that, I beat him up and left him."

"If you know where he threw it, why didn't you go back for it?"

"We looked all over, but there was no sign of it."

"Where did this happen?"

"In Lavington, where your police car cornered us."

"So what are you doing to get it back?"

"Everything that can be done. If someone told me where that bag is lying, I'd go and get it, no matter what. You know how it is in this business. Those guys will finish me off if I don't produce the money."

"Who are these guys?"

Tusker hesitated. "Someone big. I can't name him."

There was silence at the other end before Bono responded, "I was wondering—in case I come to know where the stuff is, should I tell you about it?"

"Yes, chief. If you find out, please tell me."

"What will you then do?"

"I'll somehow get it and return it to the owner."

"How do I know for sure?"

"I've had enough trouble. I'll return the stuff and forget about all this."

"Why did you arrange to steal the money in the first place?"

Tusker hesitated, "I wanted the Big Boss to give me back my business."

"Let me think about it and, if I find out anything, I'll give you a call."

Tusker kept staring at the phone for some time after Bono hung up. His left eye started to twitch as he wondered what his rival Don was doing right now.

\*\*\*

A few miles away, his adversary was also spending a miserable Sunday, away from his family. He was sitting outside a kiosk, drinking *chai* and munching a *mandazi,* the local version of a doughnut made from corn flour, when his phone rang. He noted it was his contact in the police department, Inspector Wycliffe "Bic" Okello. Apparently, late Sunday afternoon was the preferred time for police officials to touch base with their contacts in the underworld.

"Yes," Don quietly hissed into the phone.

He recognized Bic Okello's high-pitched voice at the other end. "Were you thinking of your wife's sister when that man in the colorful jacket snatched the briefcase from you?"

Don gulped hard before he came up with a standard response. "I don't know what you're talking about."

"Don't waste my time—do you think I'm a fool?" Bic's high-pitched voice sounded positively shrill.

Don gulped some more—he knew he had better admit his failure. "I got distracted, chief—I was taking a good look at the briefcase."

"But why was it with you?"

"I... I was asked to carry it... I mean, I was only carrying it to give it to someone... honest, I don't know what was in it."

"For whom were you carrying it?"

"I'll get my head chopped off if I mention any names."

"Did you recognize the thief who snatched it from you?"

"No, I never saw him before."

"How did he manage to get away?"

"A car was waiting near the road. He just snatched the bag and jumped into the car, which drove away very fast before I could do anything."

"Describe the briefcase—what was its color?"

"I'm not very sure. I couldn't see because it was dark, but I think it was light."

"Stop confusing me. It can't be both dark and light. What color was it?"

"I think it was light."

After a pause, Bic asked, "Was it bhayish?"

Don was confused. "Chief, are you asking me the color? What you just said sounded like a new type of hashish."

"Well, never mind. What else can you tell me about the briefcase?"

"It looked very expensive. I have never seen such a nice-looking one before. There was a metal tag on it that said it was made in Italy. There was one more tag that I was trying to read when that man came quietly like a leopard and snatched it away."

"That thief died the next day and we still don't know who he is. Do you think he was working for Tusker?"

"Yes, I'm sure that black *Mamba* (a poisonous snake) is behind the whole thing."

"The last words of that man in the jacket were that the briefcase is missing."

"Missing?"

"Yes, it's lost. Now, do you know any Russian?"

"No, chief, the only foreign language I know is English."

"No, no. I mean, do you know a Russian man?"

"No, I don't."

"What are you doing to get back the money?"

"I'm desperately looking for it, since if I don't hand it over to the Big Boss, he has sworn he will feed me alive to the hyenas."

There was silence at the other end as Bic paused briefly before continuing, "The goods might be lying someplace important. It might be risky, but would you go and get it back?"

Don gulped thrice before replying, "I'll do anything to find the cash."

"You'll do anything?"

"Yes, tell me where it is and I'll go and get it."

"What will you do when you get it?"

"Give it immediately to the Big Boss, of course."

"When I have some information, I'll give you a call," said Bic as he hung up.

\*\*\*

Before retiring that night, Jay said to Heidi, "The discussion with Bomy about possession of stolen goods wasn't very reassuring, was it?"

"No, it wasn't. But we know the consequences, don't we? What do you think—should we turn the money in to the police?"

"Yeah, I think we should."

"You sounded very brave when you picked up the briefcase and decided to keep it until you found out who it belongs to."

"Yes, *liebchen*, but now I'm not too sure."

Heidi was silent for a moment. "I don't know what to say, Jay—you've got us into such a mess. You should've driven straight to the police station that night. But there are now times when I wonder if the money should be returned to the owner if it's being used for something illegal."

She turned off her bedside light, and said, "I'm tired—it's been a long day."

As he pulled up a blanket, Jay wondered what Heidi meant by her last comment. Like the previous nights, it would be a long time before he would fall asleep.

# Chapter 5

## *Monday*

The sun had barely peeped over the horizon when Nicholas Cunningham's British Airways flight from London landed at the Jomo Kenyatta International Airport in Nairobi. As the burly detective from Scotland Yard disembarked and stepped into the terminal, an impeccably dressed gentleman approached him. "Mr. Cunningham? I'm Inspector Peter Otieno from the Kenya police. Welcome to Kenya. I hope you had a pleasant flight."

Cunningham was surprised someone was there to receive him, long before immigration and customs clearance. *Well, this is Kenya,* he thought, as he responded, "Thank you, Mr. Otieno. The flight wasn't too bad, though I must admit I can't sleep too well on an airplane."

The Kenyan official conveyed that he was assigned the task of providing assistance to the detective with his investigation. Since this meant they would be spending a considerable amount of time together, Cunningham suggested they address each other by their first names. "Call me Nick—and your first name is Peter?"

"Yes, but I'd feel more comfortable addressing you as Mr. Nick—that's customary in our society," the host explained.

Peter whisked them through the immigration and customs counters, much to Nick's relief, and when they stepped out of the airport terminal, he remarked about the pleasant weather.

"That's normally how it is over here," said Peter. "What was the weather like in London last night? No, let me guess—wet and cold?"

"Yes, I suppose you could safely place your bets on that one."

They climbed into the waiting police vehicle and headed for Nick's hotel. There were no discussions on the Mary Wilson case, since Peter said they were scheduled for later in the day with the Police Commissioner.

Given the case history and the nature of his assignment, Nick anticipated encountering hurdles at virtually every stage of his investigation. He had met Mary's father, Barry Wilson, over lunch two days prior in London, who cautioned him that the Kenyan officials would make all possible attempts to ensure he uncovered nothing to discredit their findings. Barry had spent several days in Kenya soon after he received the devastating news about his daughter. Those days had been frustrating, he complained bitterly, and urged Nick to be vigilant during his visit.

At a personal level, Nick looked forward to this visit that would take him to the famed game reserve of Maasai Mara, which, along with the Serengeti in neighboring Tanzania, formed one of the world's most renowned wildlife game parks.

As Nick soon discovered, Peter turned out to be loquacious and spoke fluent English. "Mr. Nick, there are many followers of the British premier soccer league out here. Manchester United is the team that I follow. How about you?"

"Well, I'm a Chelsea fan. How's your national soccer team doing right now?"

The sports conversation continued until they reached the Serena Hotel, located a short distance from the downtown area. "I'm sure you'd like to relax for a while," said Peter. "May I suggest our vehicle pick you up after lunch? Our commissioner has planned to spend some time with you in the afternoon."

At the hotel front desk, a message awaited Nick. A meeting with the British High Commissioner was scheduled for later that afternoon.

***

Heidi took a late shower and started to dress up for the school meeting later that morning. Jay had left for work and the housemaid was busy in the kitchen downstairs.

Heidi taught German and European History at the Nairobi Expatriate School that catered mainly to children of diplomats and expatriates living in Kenya and the neighboring countries. Her school, like the others in the country, was closed during August for the winter holidays, but she had a special assignment over the next ten days. The local business community was hosting their Annual Summer Fair the following week on her school's premises. This event was a platform for all international companies that had a presence in Kenya to set up stalls and booths to display their products and services. The organizers had enlisted the services of a few staff members from the school to perform some of the tasks for the event. Heidi had signed up for arranging the sale of raf-

89

fle tickets and soliciting items from various corporations and well-wishers for distribution as prizes to the raffle winners.

"Mama, I need some Omo," the maid called out from below, referring to a washing detergent.

"Yes, Beatrice, wait till I come down."

*Oh, it was so easy to get spoiled with all the household help in these countries,* thought Heidi. Beatrice took care of most of the household chores. All upscale homes were built with small living quarters at the back of the house, where one or two servants could board. They were not allowed to bring in their families (an edict introduced by the British colonialists, but continuing to be conveniently practiced even now) and they lived alone. Beatrice was a single mother with three children, who were being raised by her mother in their village up country.

*Life here is wonderful,* thought Heidi, and she certainly did not wish to move back to India or Germany. They had been making plans to settle down here permanently. The children also loved the place and that was what mattered most to her. She loved Jay so much more for having taken the bold step to leave his country and move here.

His impetuous act a few nights before weighed heavily on her mind; this morning she had reluctantly agreed to Jay's arguments in favor of holding on to the money for now. They somehow had to resolve this mess, she said to herself, as she made her way down the stairs. Nothing would be allowed to come in the way of the life that she and Jay had been planning so carefully over the years.

\*\*\*

"I've some great news for you, Jay. The tea factory in Kericho, with whom I've been following up the last four months, has finally confirmed their order. So gear up, my dear fellow, for a busy period ahead! Meanwhile, meet me with Zach in the next ten minutes to go over the details."

"That's wonderful news, Mr. Jennings. Sure, we'll be there shortly," said Jay, placing down the intercom.

Jay's gloomy mood quickly evaporated at this piece of information from his chief executive. He reached for his coffee as he settled down in his private office and opened a folder with the previous day's reports. There were more reasons for him to cheer; production figures were impressive, and they were making good progress on various orders on hand, including the all-important one from the Tea Authority.

"All that's fine," he muttered. "In spite of all this, I wonder how long I need to keep looking over my shoulder."

Casting a glance around, he quietly opened the secret drawer in his desk and peeked in to make sure his precious package lay safe and secure. Earlier that morning, his thinking had been more philosophical—the other night, was he destined to be at that particular place at that particular time and been granted custody of the briefcase with its contents for a specific purpose?

"Bullshit!" he said to himself and recalled his discussion with Heidi in the morning, when he had persuaded her that they hold on to the cash for now. In his mind, he was convinced that there were several players involved in the heist and that, sooner rather than later, one of them would blurt out information that the police would pick up. He would keep in touch with his contact in the police department and continue to lie low and put up a normal appearance.

Pushing those thoughts away, he glanced at his watch. With a sense of relief, he noted it was time to meet his boss—the meeting would keep him engaged until lunchtime.

\*\*\*

Shortly after ten in the morning, a well-dressed Japanese gentleman walked up to the front desk at the Nairobi Central Police Station. Shinzo Okamoto had come to take possession of his stolen Nissan sedan. He filled out several forms and patiently answered the questions asked by the clerk at the front desk. He explained he had had dinner at the Kentmere Club on the outskirts of Nairobi the previous Friday evening. Subsequently, he found his vehicle missing when he returned to the parking lot and had promptly reported the theft to the police. He received a call from them the next day that the vehicle had been recovered and was asked to come to their headquarters on Monday, with required documents and a duplicate car key.

The clerk made subtle attempts to hustle the Japanese into parting with a hefty tip, but Okamoto remained steadfast. "You drive a very good car," the clerk finally remarked. "Our vehicles couldn't catch up with the thieves as they drove away in your car."

"Yes, Nissan is a good Japanese car," Okamoto remarked.

The clerk picked up his phone and spoke briefly before directing the visitor to the office of the Deputy Police Commissioner, Mr. Gideon Odhiambo.

\*\*\*

The Deputy Commissioner rose to greet the Japanese visitor and offered him a seat. He went through the documents in detail; they appeared in order, but the vehicle was involved in a crime and he had to investigate further. He said, "Where do you work, sir?"

"Our company has an office here and I am the country manager," Okamoto replied, handing over his business card.

"What is the nature of your business—cars, televisions, video recorders?"

"I'm so sorry," Okamoto replied, bowing his head slightly. "Our company does not make those products. We produce only big machinery. And we make large ships," he clarified, stretching both his hands to emphasize the size.

"So you supply ships to Mombasa?" the deputy asked, referring to the Kenyan port.

"No, they need only small boats. Our ships are too big for Mombasa."

"Then do you supply machinery to Kenyan factories?"

"No, but we hope to get orders from the steel industry. Our machines are too big for many Kenyan companies," Okamoto replied with a slight smirk.

"If your company doesn't have business in Kenya, then why have an office?"

"We have set up an office here because we expect to develop business with some potential customers."

"Can I please see your work permit?" the officer asked.

Okamoto pulled out his passport, opened to the page where his two-year work-cum-residence permit was stamped and handed it over. Gideon appeared to find everything in order until he scanned the visa sheets and a frown appeared on his face. "Why do you need to travel to South Africa?" he asked.

Despite the recent cessation of the apartheid regime in that nation, suspicion lingered among several African nations, including Kenya.

"There are quite a few large plants in South Africa that require our machinery. We do good business in that country," the Japanese replied.

There was not much for Gideon to pursue down this road, so he decided to get on with the next line of questioning. "Do you have any business dealings with Russians here in Nairobi?"

"No," Okamoto shook his head. "We have nothing to do with them."

"Your car was found in Lower Kabete near the house of a Russian businessman. Do you know him and do you have any business dealings with him or his company?"

"No, no," he shook his head twice. "My car was stolen and I don't know why it was there."

Raising his tone, the police official said, "Mr. Okamoto, the car was involved in a major robbery and the stolen goods have not yet been recovered. The vehicle was parked near the house of the Russian. We are investigating if he was involved in the theft and wonder if there's a reason why your car, and no other car, was used for the robbery."

He watched as Mr. Okamoto shook his head three times, with an accompanying "No" each time.

Gideon deliberated for a while. "All right, I have no more questions." Attempting to lighten the mood, he added, "We hope thieves will not use your car again for a quick getaway."

Mr. Okamoto paused before asking, "I think your department has only Land Rovers?"

"Yes, that's right."

In a light-hearted tone, Okamoto said, "British vehicles not good for chasing car thieves, who like to use Japanese cars to get away. See, your Land Rovers could not catch up with my Nissan."

A sharp cracking sound ripped through the room. Gideon had been fiddling with a pencil, which snapped under his sudden thrust. *Do I need to put up with such rebukes, when I'm the one who's been pleading with the department for several years to acquire turbocharged vehicles?* He remained silent while his visitor anxiously stared at him.

"I'm so sorry," Okamoto bowed his head slightly. "Can I leave now?"

"Yes—our man at the front desk will arrange to release the vehicle to you."

Okamoto rose to leave. As he reached the door, he turned around and said, "Do you know what business that Russian deals in?"

"No, I don't."

Okamoto's face broke into a smile as he continued. "We always do research on other foreign companies operating in this market. The Russian or his client might be needing getaway cars for their business."

"I don't understand. What business are you talking about?"

Lowering his voice, Okamoto replied, "Not good for me to talk about other people's business, but the Russian is not in good business. I'm not surprised my car was found near his house."

With that, Mr. Okamoto bowed and stepped out, as a perplexed Gideon Odhiambo kept staring at the door, long after it had closed.

***

Fresh and relaxed after a nap in his comfortable hotel room, Nicholas Cunningham walked into Police Commissioner Michael Karanja's office. A lunch of deep-fried shrimp with French fries and a salad helped perk him up, and he was now ready for a meeting with the Kenyan police officials.

"*Karibu sana*, (Hearty welcome) *Bwana* Cunningham," greeted Karanja warmly, with a firm handshake. "I hope you had a comfortable flight. Is this your first trip to Kenya?"

"Yes, it is. And I do look forward, during the course of my investigations, to spending some time at one of the wonderful game parks that your country is famous for."

"I'm sure that will be a great experience. We'll soon start planning your trip."

"Sure." After a pause, Nick said, "I've been keen on visiting Kenya ever since, as a child, I learned that our Queen unexpectedly ascended the throne while on a trip to this country."

Nick was referring to one of the momentous events in the British monarchy. Crown Princess Elizabeth, as she then was, visited Kenya on a holiday with her husband in 1952. They spent a night at the Treetops Lodge in the Aberdare National Park. Built literally on treetops, the lodge overlooks floodlit watering holes and visitors can view the animals that visit the holes at night. During the course of that night, her father, King George VI, passed away in England. There was no way to communicate this information to the Princess. Besides, the main entrance to the lodge was locked at night for the safety of its guests. The news was conveyed to her the next morning when she descended from the lodge.

Accompanying the royal couple was the legendary big-game hunter, Jim Corbett, and the historic turn of events that night was best captured in the now-famous lines that he entered in the logbook: "For the first time in history of the world, a young girl climbed into a tree one day a Princess, and after having what she described as her most thrilling experience, she climbed down from the tree next day a Queen. God bless her!"

"Oh yes," said Karanja. "I can appreciate you folks being fascinated by that event. Perhaps we could squeeze in a visit to the Treetops, depending on your schedule."

He called in his team of officers that had been working on Mary Wilson's case. They went through their investigation and their findings. Nick did not wish to go into details at this stage and he suggested they plan his itinerary. They agreed that he would visit the forensic laboratory later that afternoon. The next morning, he would travel to the Maasai Mara, the scene of the alleged crime.

"We have arranged for one of our sturdiest vehicles to take you and drive you around within the game park. We have assigned our best driver for the entire trip and Inspector Peter Otieno will be accompanying you," the Commissioner told Nick at the end of the meeting.

"Thanks," said Nick. "How far away is the game park?"

"It will be a good six-hour drive—plan on leaving as early as possible."

The Commissioner arranged for Nick to spend some time at the laboratory. Late in the afternoon, he proceeded to his meeting with the British High Commissioner.

***

"We shouldn't be spending so much time discussing the theft of just a briefcase," a visibly agitated Police Commissioner glared at the officers seated around his table. "The thief who stole it is dead and we still don't know his identity. The only confirmation we have so far, in this case, is that the stolen vehicle belonged to a Japanese executive, whom we have no reason to suspect."

Deputy Commissioner Gideon Odhiambo and Inspectors Julius Wachira, Bono Njoroge, and Bic Okello sat in silence as the boss continued, "Any developments to report—any of you?"

Bic cleared his throat and said, "I'm not sure if I can give the Russian a clean chit. As discussed, I went over and met him on Saturday." He briefed them about his meeting with Mikhail Smirnoff and continued, "I've made inquiries about his company. He mentioned they imported Russian equipment to Kenya and neighboring countries. My investigations do not support his claim—

all their supplies have been to neighboring countries and I believe they're involved in supplying arms and ammunitions. Boss, I think this man is up to no good."

With an appreciative look, the Commissioner remarked, "Good job, Bic, *vzuri sana* (very good)." He nodded his head several times as he looked around and said to the others, "See, this is the type of investigation that can lead us to the stolen goods. Yes, I think we should keep him under observation. Who knows—we might well uncover the supply source of illegal weapons to the drug dealers, poachers, and criminals in our country."

Gideon added, "Even the Japanese had some unfavorable things to say about the Russian—that the man is not in good business. So you probably have a point, Bic."

His boss nodded in approval. "Keep a watchful eye on this guy; it's possible that he's involved in the theft with the intent to use the cash for *magendo* (illegal) business. Now," he said, turning to Bono Njoroge, "what have you come up with?"

Bono briefed them about his conversations with the security guards at the spot where the two vehicles had encountered each other. "I couldn't meet the guards who were on duty that night. I'll have to go there in the evening when they're on duty. But I'll need a vehicle at that time."

The Commissioner turned serious. "In the evenings, it becomes difficult to provide a vehicle for routine questioning. But I see your point. Fill out the blue form and Odhiambo will see when he can spare a vehicle." The bureaucracy involved in getting a government vehicle could be formidable.

Turning to Julius Wachira, the Commissioner continued, "Wachira, how about you?"

"No, none of my contacts know of this theft. And they haven't heard of anyone spending money in a big way. Whoever has the money is sitting tight on it."

"I have the same information as Wachira," commented Gideon.

The Commissioner turned to Bic Okello. "Did you get in touch with your contacts?"

"Yes. The thief snatched the goods from Don. But he doesn't know what happened to the briefcase later. He's desperate to get it back."

The Commissioner turned to Bono, who replied, "Yes, Tusker arranged to have the briefcase snatched from Don, but then the thief tossed it away. Tusker hasn't been able to recover it and he too is desperate."

After a prolonged silence, the Commissioner turned to his deputy. "Gideon, I believe you have something to add."

"So as of now, we are looking for a briefcase with two tags that read 'Made in Italy' and 'Limited Edition.' And its color is—bheyish."

"No, be-ish," Karanja corrected him.

Pulling out a piece of paper, Gideon said, "I checked out this strange-sounding word in a dictionary and it means light brown in color. The spelling is b-e-i-g-e and is pronounced beyzh." He looked around before proceeding, "The pronunciation is beyzh and it's a French word."

He put down his glasses and looked around with his right eyebrow raised. But no one appeared ready to accept his challenge to pronounce the word. And to them, it didn't matter if the word was French or Italian.

"In fact," Gideon continued, looking at the Commissioner, "may I suggest that in our records we state the color as light brown, instead of beige? It would make it easier for our filing clerk—I'm told she has a hard time pulling out the correct file because of the confusing pronunciation."

Gideon took pride in following the correct procedures and protocol, which was why the irrepressible Peter Otieno had nicknamed him the "Proud Protocol Practitioner."

"No, I'm told the color is important and we keep it the way it is," Karanja emphasized.

Gideon looked disappointed as his boss continued, "We seem to be forgetting that what is important are the contents and not the briefcase. Let's stop paying attention to its description—somehow, everyone seems fascinated by it." Raising his voice, he continued, "It's been three days since the theft occurred, and we've still no clue. This reflects very poorly on us. Let's get on with the job and find that damned briefcase."

After his team left the room, Karanja picked up a note he'd scribbled earlier. The influential father of Toto Kilonzo had called to request that the Commissioner put the young man on more rigorous assignments, with a view to toughening him up. His family members felt Toto whiled away much of his time daydreaming; some even complained about his ogling at the womenfolk.

Karanja buzzed the intercom. "Ask Toto Kilonzo to come here in half an hour," he instructed his secretary.

\*\*\*

Inspector Peter Otieno, the official assigned to work with Nick Cunningham, was by far the most colorful and garrulous personality in the department. Reared in a wealthy family with large business interests, he attended private schools in Kenya and graduated from a college in the UK, specializing in public relations. Armed with this degree, he received a prompt offer from the Kenya police, who required the services of a well-heeled professional to help them polish their public image.

They could scarcely have found a better-groomed candidate—and, for that matter, one with a smoother tongue, qualities that enabled him to circulate effortlessly among influential business and political circles. He spoke fluent English and occasionally switched to a clipped British accent, much to the amusement of those around him. His department dumped tasks on him that his peers shirked, particularly those that fell in the "none of the above" category. Thus, when the services of a detective from Scotland Yard to reopen a particularly sensitive investigation were thrust upon the department, Peter was an obvious choice to be assigned the task of liaising with the sleuth.

Walking toward his office, Peter decided to swing by the Commissioner's office to check for any last-minute instructions before the next morning's departure with Nick Cunningham. On entering the outer office, he greeted the secretary, Elizabeth. She told him the Commissioner was in an important meeting with the top brass and she would call him when the boss was free.

"All the top brass, eh? Must be something really important, right, Your Highness?" Peter teased the secretary, who shared her first name with the most famous royal personality. He was aware that his flattery pleased her ego and helped him pry valuable information out of her.

"Everything that reaches the Commissioner's desk is important," she parried.

But Peter was intrigued by what he had heard was going on for the previous three days—something big, involving someone important. "It's not often all three of our vehicles are pressed into service for one crime. And I think I perceive the seldom-seen harassed look on the boss's face. Your Highness, what were the stolen goods— a truckload of gold involving someone big?"

"You'll soon come to know. Don't worry, you'll soon come to know," was Elizabeth's reply, trying to keep him at bay.

"There've been no reports of a big burglary. This makes the case all the more intriguing."

Elizabeth knew she had to part with some tidbit. After all, she occasionally needed his help. Through him, her niece recently had been employed in one of his rich uncle's companies.

"You are way off the mark." She lowered her voice. "It's just a briefcase."

"Ah, so!" exclaimed Peter. "Now, isn't that interesting—the top brass involved in recovering an ordinary briefcase? I think we can call this 'The Baffling Case of the Missing Briefcase'."

And that was how this case was known from then on within their department.

\*\*\*

Bic Okello put through a call to the Immigration Department at the Nairobi Airport. "Hello, this is Joseph Karema," said the official at the other end.

"Yes, hello, *Bwana* Karema. This is Inspector Wycliffe Okello from the Kenya police, *"Habari Gani, Mzee?* (How are you, sir?)"

After the pleasantries, Bic came to the point. "We have doubts about the activities of one Russian national living here. He travels often to neighboring countries on business that we believe is shady. Could you please inform us when he next leaves the country? His name is Mikhail Smirnoff."

"The same name as the famous vodka?"

"Yes, but he deals with something else—nothing to do with alcohol."

"Okay, so how can I help you?"

"I would appreciate if you could be on the lookout for a passenger with that name leaving the country," said Bic. "Please get back to me with details of his travel— date and time of departure, flight details, and how long he is planning to be away."

All departing travelers were required to fill out a form at the immigration counter, with the information that Bic had asked for. These forms remained in the department files and any officer could glean through them. Karema noted the details and agreed to inform Bic.

***

An abysmal scowl, stubbornly refusing to relinquish its perch the last three days, continued to adorn Tusker's face, as he helped himself to a bowl of *githeri,* a mix of corn and red beans, at the kiosk near Lavington

He listened one more time to the message on his cell phone. It was his cousin, Mwangi, who had introduced the luckless Fred. "Hi, brother, how is everything, and how is Nairobi? Fred's uncle has been calling me to inquire about him. He says there has been no news from

Fred for three days and he is concerned and sounds very upset."

Tusker was in no hurry to speak with his cousin. What he needed was to find out where the money was. But his assistants hinted to him that he was becoming a nuisance to the owner of the kiosk and the regular clients. His demeanor and appearance did not help.

He asked a few more questions of the *askaris* in the kiosk, but realized he was not making any progress. The clock was ticking and he had to find the money before the Minister ran out of patience. If only he could lay his hands on the neck of whoever was holding on to what was his. With a menacing look, he cast one more glance around before leaving.

***

Elizabeth gestured to Toto that he could step into the Commissioner's office, which he did with some trepidation. It was the first time he was entering the distinguished chamber and, despite being impressed by its size and trappings, he was more concerned about why he had been summoned.

"Yes, Toto, come sit down," the Commissioner said. "So, it's been three months since you joined us. How do you find working here?"

"*Asante sana, Mzee* (Thank you, sir)," Toto responded. "I find it very interesting and challenging."

"What are you working on now?"

"I'm assisting Inspector Wachira on the Mombasa fraud case."

Karanja nodded. "That one's interesting. You'll learn several aspects of our methods of investigation.

Now, were you not also working with Inspector Bic Okello on the case of the stolen briefcase on Saturday?"

"Sir, I was only told to keep an eye on the injured thief in the hospital, until such time the inspector arrived."

There was an interruption as Karanja's secretary Elizabeth walked in and placed a file marked "Urgent and Confidential" on top of a heap of files on Karanja's desk. He squinted at the file as Elizabeth picked up the files from his outbox and walked away.

Toto's gaze followed her as she trod carefully around the table and came close to where he sat. She turned to open a filing cabinet and bent over to place one of the files in the bottom drawer. Almost instinctively, Toto stared at her ample posterior and couldn't take his eyes off the outline of her panties that showed through her stretched skirt.

He heard a voice in the distance and, with a jolt, realized the Commissioner had been addressing him. "I... I beg your pardon, sir," he managed to mumble.

"What I was saying, this case is very interesting... and important. We might involve you in some way. I will speak to Mr. Odhiambo about it," the Commissioner said, referring to his deputy, who supervised Toto's training. "You will soon hear from him, and I expect you to take up the assignment seriously and put in all your efforts."

"Yes, of course, I shall do my best," Toto replied, as he rose to leave.

*****

Shortly after sunset, Inspector Bono Njoroge reached the Lavington neighborhood. Following the same routine that he went through two days previously when he had questioned the daytime *askaris*, he now started to question the nighttime *askaris* who had just reported to work.

The events of three nights earlier were fresh in their minds. They vividly described the dramatic confrontation between the police and the yellow car. And when the police opened fire, they admitted they had ducked for cover and remained cowered behind the gate for several minutes after the vehicles had driven away.

"What else happened out there?" asked Bono. "Did any of those vehicles come back?"

There was a brief silence before they said that one of the *askaris* told them that he saw another vehicle drive away shortly after the shootout.

"There was one more vehicle? And it drove off after those two had left?" asked Bono.

"Yes."

"Who is that, *askari*?"

"Mwaniki. He has his day off today and will report to work tomorrow evening."

"And which house does he guard?"

The *askaris* pointed out the house. Bono walked over and spoke with the substitute guard, but he was of little help. Bono realized he would need to make another trip the next evening to question Mwaniki. And that meant putting in one more request to Gideon Odhimabo for making a vehicle available the next evening.

\*\*\*

Jay struggled to keep the conversation going at the dinner table, confined mainly to Heidi's involvement in the upcoming Annual Summer Fair at her school.

"We need to have a serious discussion," she said shortly after dinner. They moved to the living room and Jay sat down, unsure of what to expect.

"Whatever happened to the second honeymoon that you were so excited about, before the kids left, uh?" came Heidi's salvo in a mocking tone. "I was expecting to have your hands all over me the moment they left. But you seem to be having more fun with the stuff that you picked up that night."

Stung by her attack, Jay stammered, "Now, now, *liebchen*, you know that's not true."

But she continued, "I keep believing in you, and have supported you in all that you've done over the years. But we've never found ourselves in as dangerous a situation as we're now in. For God's sake, do whatever needs to be done and find a way to get rid of that stuff."

"Heidi, please..."

It was of no use. She walked out of the room and made her way up to the bedroom. Jay sat staring at the blank TV screen, distressed and helpless.

His first thoughts were about Raj and Anita, and if he had failed in his parental responsibilities by his impetuous act. All that he could hope for now was that whatever the consequences were, they would be all over before the children returned.

But meanwhile, he had to deal with his dilemma with Heidi. Over the years, she had been tolerant of what were obviously his misdeeds—any other woman would surely have been less sympathetic. *But that was Heidi— my dearest, sweetest Heidi! What could I have done without her?* he wondered. Could he have been happier with anyone else—the few girls he had flirted with while in India, or any of the other German girls he'd met? He also doubted his parents would have found a more suitable match for him in the traditional Indian way. He had often admitted that he could not imagine what life would have been like with anyone else.

His thoughts drifted to their courting days in Bielefeld, the weekends that were made up of watching movies, dining out in the evenings, and dancing away till late at a *tanzhalle* (dance hall). He recalled his cherished moments with her—the long afternoon walks in the low-forested mountains in the *Teutoburger Wald* (Teutoburg Forest) and the sheer delight, during fall, of romping over a carpet of leaves that lay on the forest floor in a riot of colors.

Yes, Heidi was very, very special. She had never wavered in her love for him and had jealously protected him whenever the need arose. And she continued to be just as protective of their two children.

He realized he had been sitting there brooding a long time and stood up and prepared to retire. After cleaning up and changing, he quietly slipped into the bed and lay beside Heidi, who was fast asleep. Gazing at her profile in the soft glow, he thought, *Mein liebchen, you don't deserve to have to go through this harrowing experience after all that you've done for me. No, I must do something to bring the sparkle back into your life.*

They shouldn't be cooped up at home every evening, should they? He needed to plan an evening out with her; to offer respite from the persistent problem that weighed on their minds. The question was, when? The next evening was doubtful, but he would plan on one of the following two evenings. Yes, that's what they'd do—spend a cozy evening at one of her favorite restaurants, and then dance away till late, like they did in the old days.

Memories of the times they spent together kept flashing through his mind until he drifted to sleep.

# Chapter 6

## *Tuesday Morning*

When Commissioner Karanja entered the Minister's office, he found him awkwardly slumped in his chair. With some effort, the seated official turned his head and looked up at the visitor. As Karanja strode to grip the proffered hand, he noted a glazed look in the Minister's eyes. For one startling moment, he wondered if that could be the result of excessive sugar deposits in the Minister's system. He noticed that, even though it was still mid-morning, an empty teacup and a half-eaten large *mandazi* (a doughnut made from corn flour), generously sprinkled with powdered sugar, lay on the table— signs that he attributed to the Minister suffering from stress-related sugar cravings.

"Any news about the stolen goods?" asked the Minister.

Karanja had not quite settled in his chair when the secretary walked in and asked, "Would the Commissioner like tea or coffee?"

"Tea, please."

He cleared his throat and responded to the Minister, "We don't have any leads so far, sir. Our contacts haven't come up with any information, and whoever has the money is staying quiet."

"How can this be, Karanja?" the Minister raised his voice. "No, you'll have to step up all efforts to recover the goods. I'll repeat—the person who is affected is very close to me."

"Yes, you've mentioned it earlier."

"Then who the hell has the money?" the Minister hollered. "My friend is under tremendous pressure, since his transaction must soon be completed. The briefcase had... had stuff that was meant to settle dues to several people and he will be in one big shit if the goods are not recovered. Do you understand, Karanja?"

The Commissioner nodded while he listened to the Minister breathe heavily. Before he could respond, the door opened and the secretary walked in with a tray. She served tea to the men, added some milk, and asked about sugar.

"Two spoons, please," said Karanja.

She poured two spoonsful in his cup, three in the Minister's, and retreated.

Karanja stirred the tea and, after sipping it, spoke to the Minister in a measured tone. "We have very little to work on, *Bwana* Minister. I haven't been told why Tusker thought it necessary to engage a petty thief to snatch a briefcase from Don. Perhaps there's a dispute between you and those two, but that does not involve the *wananchi* (public). And then Tusker's men claim the briefcase is missing. As I mentioned, we are investigating the possible connection between a Russian and Tusker. He lives near the place where the car was abandoned, but we don't have any specific leads so far."

"There might be someone else involved."

"Unlikely," responded Karanja. "The briefcase has probably been picked up by someone along the route that the thieves traveled, which my men are investigating. If an *askari* or an ordinary passerby had picked it up, we would expect them to have started spending the money by now and we would've known about it. It appears to have been picked up by someone who's just holding on to it. And that makes our job difficult."

"Wouldn't that person come to your department to hand it over?"

"Yes, but no one has come so far. Do you suspect someone has plotted this against you?"

"No, I'm quite sure about that." Raising his voice, the Minister continued, "But Karanja, we can't go along at this pace. Get your men out in large numbers. By now you should have found some clues. Why don't you start with the third-degree treatment to the gangs or criminals that you suspect might be involved?"

"We have enough other crimes to deal with and do not have people to do what you've suggested, sir. We will carry out our investigations with whatever information you've provided us. It might take some more time, but we'll find out who the culprits are."

"We don't have the time. As I said earlier, we don't have that sort of time."

There was a moment of awkward silence, after which Karanja spoke up. "Is there anything else that you wish to discuss with me, sir?"

The Minister was quiet. As Karanja rose to leave, the Minister remarked, "So the Scotland Yard man is here. Any chance he'd come up with something different from your department's findings?"

"We have our reputation, sir, and we'll do whatever needs to be done to maintain it."

The Minister nodded. "Sounds very impressive. I hope you're right."

He looked up, but the Commissioner had already left. The Minister hadn't expected such a curt response from the police official. But he knew there was not much he could do, since he needed their help to recover the money. And the Commissioner was right—this matter was between him and Tusker and Don. The police needn't be involved in this dispute.

He picked up the *mandazi* lying on the table, took a large bite, and continued staring out the window.

\*\*\*

Mikhail Smirnoff stepped out of his car at the airport terminal and checked in for his early afternoon flight to Kigali, the capital of the central African country of Rwanda. As the burly Russian passed through immigration, he handed over his passport and a departure form to the officer, who looked through the papers and opened one of his desk's drawers. Tilting his head toward the drawer, the officer stared at a sheet of paper that lay inside, then turned to study the form, as Mikhail watched with slight apprehension at this unusual scrutiny.

"How long are you planning to be away, sir?" the official asked.

"Four days."

"And you're traveling to Kigali and Bujumbura?" he continued, as he read the information on Mikhail's form.

"Yes."

The official stamped the passport and waved Mikhail through with a friendly farewell. "Enjoy your trip, sir."

Over the years, on all the numerous occasions that Mikhail had passed through the immigration counter, the officials had never shown more than a passing interest in him. The unusual concern today in his travel plans was probably due to the Tourism Promotion Week that was advertised, he reckoned, as he proceeded to the departure gate for his flight.

Mikhail's travel within the East African region had increased significantly during the last year, following a steep increase in his company's business. On this trip, he was planning to meet a couple of warlords, who formed the bulk of his clientele. He had diversified his company's activities since arriving in Nairobi four years earlier as its country manager. Set up originally to import and trade in Russian engineering goods, the company struggled to sell their products of a questionable quality. Facing bleak business prospects, Mikhail decided to capitalize on the growing number of insurgency movements in the neighboring countries, which included Sudan, Somalia, Ethiopia, Uganda, Burundi, Rwanda, and the Congo. Arms and ammunitions were what the warlords in the region scouted for and Mikhail stepped in to meet their needs. Frequently traveling to meet them, he soon became their trusted supplier.

His was a dangerous mission and he stayed below the radar as best as he could. Kenya was a relatively stable country, with little if any rebel activity, and offered virtually no business opportunities for him. But Nairobi was a well-developed city and a convenient regional hub for him. He had been making a determined effort to avoid arousing any suspicion in Kenya and followed what he believed to be a relevant motto: "Don't shit where you eat."

Meanwhile, back at the immigration counter, Joseph Karema put a call through to Police Inspector Bic Okello. He left a voicemail message that the person of his interest was leaving the country on a four-day trip.

*** 

"Yes, Mwangi, why are you calling me?" Tusker spoke brusquely into his cell phone. His cousin had called three times in the last two days and left messages to urgently call back.

"How are you keeping, my dear cousin?" Mwangi asked in a customary polite tone.

But Tusker had no time for such niceties. "Fine. Why did you call me?"

"You know that guy Fred whom I introduced you to? What happened to him?"

"I don't know—why are you asking?"

"His uncle is very upset. He's going today to the city morgue to collect Fred's body. He died three days ago in the hospital after being badly beaten up."

Tusker felt his throat dry up and his left eye started to twitch. "That guy must have gotten into trouble after I dropped him. He was useless. So what is the uncle saying?"

"He was asking me where he could find you, since he firmly believes you got his nephew killed. I know he always carries a *panga* (machete) with him."

"Now, you don't tell him where I live, you understand? When is he coming here?"

"He's on his way today. I've been trying to reach you since yesterday. Please take care—the man can be vicious. He doesn't forgive and forget easily."

116

"I'm not to be blamed—Fred got himself into a mess," Tusker replied and hung up.

"That idiot has got us into trouble," Tusker seethed as he looked around at his three assistants. They had gathered at a quiet spot near Lavington, away from the kiosk where Tusker's presence had caused some nervous looks.

"What happened?" his trusted assistant Adam asked calmly.

Tusker glared at him. "You didn't take good care of the bag in the car that night, Adam. Why did you allow that idiot to throw it away?"

Adam maintained his calm—they had had this conversation several times over the last few days. "Tusker, I told you—it happened so fast. I didn't expect Fred to throw the briefcase away after expertly snatching it like a fox. But you're upset—what did your cousin tell you?"

Tusker looked down, his left eye now twitching rapidly. "Fred's uncle is coming after me with a *panga*. I have to be careful. See the mess we're in? We must find the money."

"We have to continue talking to as many people as possible in the neighborhood where that bag was dropped," said Daniel. "But we have to do it very quietly."

"The guys here are getting suspicious of us because they've been seeing you so often in the kiosk," added Jacob in a frank tone.

Tusker growled, "Who has the money? You fools lost the briefcase. I don't know when the Big Boss is going to send his hyenas after me. And now, Fred's uncle is out to get me."

His assistants were quiet. Tusker raised his hands and said, "Tell me who has the money—I want to grab that man's head in my hands and teach him a lesson."

*\*\*\**

Michael Karanja returned to his office and found the Director of the Pathological Department, Kenneth Wekesa, waiting for him.

"So how did the meeting go yesterday with Mr. Cunningham?" Karanja asked.

"I think it went well," Wekesa replied, as he leaned back in his chair. It was not often that he had the occasion to meet the Police Commissioner on a one-on-one basis and he felt he could take the liberty of indulging in light-hearted conversation. "But he's a shrewd guy. And cunning too—now we know how he got his name." Wekesa laughed awkwardly at what was meant to be funny. But Karanja did not appear amused.

In a disappointed tone, Wekesa continued, "He spent a great deal of time going through our reports. I answered all his questions, making sure he was left with no doubts in his mind."

"Questions like?"

"How long after the death did we conduct the autopsy, our testing procedures, the tests that we conducted to ascertain that there were no bullets or other wounds and if the burns had anything to do with her death." Wekesa paused as he looked up to ascertain the commissioner's reaction. He continued, "Now, we were expecting such questions, and they've been properly taken care of. I don't think he's an expert on laboratory matters. As we discussed, we've inserted the results of tests that were performed on another victim. But those reports look solid. I've made sure of it personally and the Brit won't be able to challenge any of the details."

"How can you be so certain?"

"The main thing is that her body is no longer available for him to carry out any tests. He did ask how we could establish that she died as a result of mauling by the animals. He also asked how we were certain that she was not shot or strangled. But I had managed to doctor all the test results to rule out such possibilities. It was tough, *Bwana* Commissioner, but I did it. He went through the reports, and I know he found nothing wrong."

"I'll make my comments only after the whole thing is over," Karanja responded.

"I believe he was to leave today for the Mara to visit the crime scene. He'll do a lot of snooping around there, which is what he's good at. I hope our guys there have properly covered their tracks, *Bwana* Commissioner. I've done as best as I could, but those guys at the crime scene, whoever they are, should be told that they did a terrible job."

Karanja nodded. "I know, Wekesa, I know what you mean. I too could make that out. I don't know them, but I do hope they handle him well."

After Wekesa left, Karanja buzzed the intercom and asked his secretary to get him a cup of tea. While he waited, he again had the sinking feeling that he had experienced two days earlier—this time around, things were not shaping out as well as he would have liked, which raised fears in his mind that his distinguished career with the Kenya police might come to an inglorious end.

***

Coming out of a meeting, Bic Okello checked his cell phone for messages. He knitted his eyebrows when he noted there was one from the immigration official at the airport. Replaying it twice, he nodded his head in delight, while he thought, *Now I need to convince Boss that we should go ahead with what I have in my mind.*

For a good five minutes, he deliberated on how best he should convey his unorthodox plan to his boss. Picking up the phone, he dialed the Commissioner's extension.

"Yes, Bic."

"I have something very important to discuss with you, sir. It's about the Russian; I have information that he's away. This would be a good time to check out if he is... he's hiding something that we're looking for."

"All right, come to my office right away."

After Bic outlined his proposal, the Commissioner said he found it outrageous and rejected it outright. But Bic persisted and reminded him that, on the previous day, he had considered conducting a brainstorming session, when each one in the group would be asked to present their ideas, no matter how irrational they might be. Bic had now put forth his idea—it was worth a discussion, he urged.

The Commissioner finally relented. He told his secretary to arrange for a meeting later that day with his deputies.

***

Nick Cunningham and Peter Otieno were on the road for nearly six hours, when Peter announced they were within a mile of the game park entrance. The Land Rover was designed to handle rugged roads, but a smooth ride and comfort were not its salient features. Nick had been relieved that the first half of the journey was relatively smooth but now, after covering some rough patches, he felt his bones were close to rattling.

The noise and dust made conversation difficult, leaving the two to their thoughts. Nick pondered the previous day's visit to the pathological laboratory and his discussions with Mr. Kenneth Wekesa. While he could not detect any glaring errors in the reports, he had doubts about their accuracy. He was not an expert in analyzing reports; if necessary, he would later take advice from his colleagues in the UK. For now, he would focus on investigations at the crime scene.

Meanwhile, Peter brooded on how best he could accomplish the task that he was entrusted with—keeping Nick distracted from his main mission.

They were now at one of the entrances of Maasai Mara Game Park, where Peter paid the park fees. As he climbed back into the vehicle, he said it would take them nearly an hour to reach their lodge, one of the several within the vast expanse of the reserve. But he pointed out that this would be a good time to view wildlife—it was late afternoon and the animals would be heading toward watering holes before nightfall.

And sure enough, they spotted a small herd of Thompson's gazelles—a small-sized species of deer named after the British explorer who first spotted them. The gazelles sprinted at the sound of their vehicle, some of them springing across the width of the dirt road in one incredible leap. Soon they came across a herd of zebras. Nick watched wide-eyed when Peter drew his attention to a pair of giraffes, who munched leaves from treetops. As Nick clicked away his camera, he realized that the vast savannah was full of diverse wildlife, with warthogs, guinea fowls, ostrich, and herds upon herds of zebras, giraffes, gazelles, and different types of deer.

"If we're lucky, we might spot some lions and chee-tahs or a leopard," Peter said. And lo and behold, in the distance, they spotted a small pride of lions relaxing un-der the shade of trees. The driver took the vehicle close to them while Nick hurriedly changed the roll of film in his camera. The beasts looked content after a heavy meal, while the cubs frisked and played around. A lion-ess approached their vehicle, head raised and sniffing as she followed the scent.

"*Bwana* Nick, I think she's taken a liking to you. She has picked up your scent—something very British and distinguished, and wants to come and cuddle up close to you." Peter poked fun at Nick, who gave him a dry smile.

"You guys sure have a sense of humor," he respond-ed. "The only stink that she would be picking up from my body is one filled with sweat and dust."

"She might have picked up whiffs of Scotch whiskey that must be circulating in your veins," Peter continued with his needling.

"Then she has some taste," came Nick's rejoinder. "A distinguished lioness would prefer the whiff of Scotch whiskey to that of Tusker Beer that probably circulates in your system."

Peter laughed. "White Cap, not Tusker. White Cap is my beer of choice." White Cap was the other popular lager from the same brewery.

The lioness had lost interest in them and their vehicle moved on. As they continued their drive, they passed a herd of wildebeest (a distant cousin of the American bison). Peter mentioned that the great migration of the wildebeest was a few weeks away, but Nick was doubtful he would be there that long. Some distance away were two elephants. And farther away, Nick spotted a wild buffalo that, he was told, was far more dangerous than his good-natured cousins, the Asian water buffalos.

"One needs to make a special tour in the early morning," Peter said, "to view even more wildlife and a chance to witness a kill by the cheetahs or the lions."

They were not too far from the lodge when they passed a strange-looking tree.

"The Baobab," explained Peter.

"Oh, yeah," said Nick. "Native to this region, right? Its funny shape must surely serve some purpose?"

"Yes, it does. Notice how large the trunk is. It can grow to be as wide as sixty feet and can store plenty of water so that it can endure severe drought. The tree has no leaves for most of the year and the scraggly upper branches stick up in the air and resemble tree roots. That's why some people call it the upside-down tree."

They reached their destination as their vehicle rounded a curve and the wooden lodge with a sloping roof, partially covered by Acacia trees, loomed ahead.

# Chapter 7

## *Late Tuesday*

The job of an *askari* (security guard) in Kenya is fraught with hazards, with little in terms of rewards. Their services are in demand—residential complexes, private homes, commercial and industrial establishments need them—but this requirement is more than adequately matched by the supply of unemployed men of all ages.

Those fortunate enough to be employed by the security companies are provided with uniforms, but little else in terms of training or benefits. Working hours are long and the guards are under the constant stress of being attacked, at times, unfortunately, with fatal consequences. By law, they are forbidden to carry firearms and all that their employers equip them with is a wooden baton and, at best, a flashlight. Thus equipped, they patrol the premises, keeping a vigilant eye out for any signs of danger.

A stool in the gatehouse, adjoining the entrance, normally provides the perch for the *askari,* from where he maintains his vigil. Holes provided in the steel gate allow him to peep through before opening it for visitors.

But woe befalls the poor *askari* should armed burglars mount an attack on their premises. Ill-equipped and outnumbered, he can at best put up a token resistance. But for these efforts, he would probably end up being beaten, brutally at times. On some occasions, the burglars might gag him and bind him up with a rope—a situation that many of his kin are content with. At least they were not beaten up and, more importantly, are lucky to be alive. This, alas, gives rise to the unfortunate quip that some guards discreetly bring their own rope and readily offer to be tied up when dangerous burglars strike.

This, then, is the public's perception of the travails of an *askari*. But there are exceptions.

One such exception now stood guard at one of the homes in the Lavington neighborhood of Nairobi. He always stood his ground and never wilted when in danger. One such experience occurred a few nights earlier, when a police vehicle confronted a yellow car outside. Despite several gunshots that were fired, this guard had stood firm—not one to be scared out of his wits, as indeed all the other guards in the neighboring houses were. Through the peepholes in the gate, he had witnessed the exchange between the two vehicles. And soon after they drove off, he observed another car drive away from one of the neighboring gates.

He was told earlier in the day that a police inspector, investigating the incident, had visited the neighborhood the previous evening, when he was off duty, and that the officer would be back today, specifically to meet with him. He had completed his round of the premises when a vehicle pulled up at the gate.

\*\*\*

Police Inspector Bono Njoroge had waited nearly an hour for a vehicle to be made available to him. Along the way, he deliberated on how best he should proceed with the questioning. From experience, he was aware that witnesses often hesitated to divulge all the information they had, for fear of possible repercussions. He decided he would deal with this witness with tact and humor—this meeting was important, Bono reminded himself, and the guard could hold the key to unlocking the baffling mystery of the vanishing briefcase.

When his vehicle pulled up at the gate, it was promptly opened. Bono looked out eagerly for his first glimpse of Mwaniki—and he was not disappointed.

Tall and muscular, the *askari* looked striking in his uniform. Bono introduced himself and took longer than usual with the introductory greetings. He inquired about Mwaniki's and his family's well-being and decided to go the extra mile by inquiring about his grandparents. Unfortunately, it transpired that Mwaniki's parents and grandparents had suffered at the hands of Bono's tribe during clashes some years earlier, thus bringing the greetings process to an abrupt end.

It also turned out that Bono's concerns of Mwaniki being intimidated by the sight of the police uniform were unfounded, since he had served both in the Kenya police and in the para-military on short-term assignments. Those organizations had no permanent job openings for him and he was therefore compelled to take on the job of an *askari*. But he had maintained his fearless demeanor as a law enforcement person, which is what had impressed Bono. In fact, his trim, athletic physique could well have been a source of envy to many a police official, not the least to the corpulent Bono himself.

They got down to serious business, with Bono asking the first question. "Now Mwaniki, there was a shooting incident here last Friday night. What did you see?"

"Yes, *Bwana* Inspector," Mwaniki correctly interpreted the official's rank by the stripes on his shirtsleeve. "I saw a yellow car being chased by a police Land Rover. And then the police fired shots as the car escaped."

"Do you know the make of the yellow car?"

"No, sir."

Mwaniki gave a detailed narration of all that he had witnessed up until the yellow car sped away. When he paused, Bono asked him, "What happened after the car left? Did you see anything else?"

Mwaniki appeared to hesitate.

"What did you see, Mwaniki?" Bono repeated. "Anything being thrown out of the yellow car?"

"Thrown out? Like what, sir?"

"A bag or a briefcase?"

"No," responded Mwaniki. "I didn't see anything being thrown out. It was dark here. What was the color of the bag?"

"It was bheyish."

"I don't know what that means," Mwaniki replied. After a pause, he asked, "Did you mean a bashed-up briefcase?"

"No, it's okay," Bono gave up. "You say you saw nothing being thrown out of the car?"

"No."

"What else did you see?"

"I saw another car drive away. He slowed down over there," pointing to a spot on the road just outside their gate. "I'm not sure what he did, but I could see he opened the door on his side, and maybe picked up something that was lying on the road. He then drove away."

"Where did the car come from?"

"Me, I think it must be from one of those three houses," Mwaniki replied, pointing in the direction farther away from his gate.

"Have you seen that car before? What type of a car was it?"

"A dark-colored car. I think it was a Honda. I'm not sure, but I think I've seen the car before, visiting one of those three houses."

"Which house?"

"I don't know."

"Anything else, *rafiki* (my friend)?"

"No, sir."

"Thank you, I might come back for more information."

Mwaniki gave a smart salute, and Bono returned it—far clumsier than the one he'd received.

"Sir, can you help me get a job in your department?"

"There's no recruitment going on right now. I'll contact you when there are openings."

Mwaniki promptly pulled out a slip of paper with his name and telephone number and handed it to Bono.

Bono walked to the neighboring houses and, after establishing that the owner of the Honda visited the Collins house, he walked there and asked the *askari*, "So *rafiki*, you were on duty that night when the shooting took place?"

"Yes," came the cautious reply.

When Bono asked the guard to describe what he had witnessed that night, the guard stated that when he heard the gunshots, he had ducked behind the gate for cover. He came to the gate after the din had subsided.

"Did you see anything being thrown out of the yellow car?" Bono asked.

"No," the *askari* replied.

"How about another vehicle?" Bono wanted to know. No again. He was crouching behind the gate, wasn't he?

But Bono wasn't done yet and asked, "There were visitors here that evening, right?"

"Yes, sir."

"When did they leave?"

"Shortly before the shooting."

"So how did they manage to go through without being stopped by the two vehicles?"

The *askari* paused before replying, "They must have gone through, or else I think they would have come back. I closed the gate after their car left and I didn't see them again."

"Which car was it?"

"It's a dark-colored car."

"What's the make of the car? Is it a Honda?"

"That I cannot tell. But Joseph, the driver, would know."

"Where is he?"

"He left a short while ago."

"Oh no," moaned Bono, shaking his head in frustration.

But the *askari* obliged by suggesting, "He might still be at the kiosk on the main road. He normally goes there for *chai* and snacks."

Bono caught up with the driver and asked for the description of the visitors' vehicle.

"It's a Honda Accord," Joseph replied. He also gave the color and its description.

Now Bono pitched forth his crucial question. "The owners of that vehicle must be friends of your master who, I'm sure, must also visit their house. Do you know where they live?"

"Yes, in Westlands. I have driven Mama there several times."

"I see," Bono finally broke into a smile. "And where in Westlands do they live?"

Joseph gave the address and the location. Bono thanked him for the information and headed back to his office.

\*\*\*

Bono Njoroge hummed his favorite tune on his way back. The commissioner's secretary had informed him about a meeting within the next hour and he mused over the limelight he would bask in when he divulged the breakthrough information he had unraveled. On reaching the office, he proceeded to the commissioner's room, where he found Deputy Commissioner Gideon Odhiambo and Inspector Bic Okello already seated, with Inspector Julius Wachira expected to join them later. When the Commissioner started the proceedings, Bono was not too pleased when his archrival Bic was asked to brief the others on what he had to report.

"Through my contacts at the airport, I have information that the Russian left Nairobi today on a four-day visit to neighboring countries," Bic said in a low, conspiratorial tone.

"You must tell them what you propose doing while the Russian is away," the Commissioner gently nudged.

"I think this would be the best time to establish if the Russian is hiding the stolen goods."

Not wanting to delay parting with his latest information, Bono cut in. "Excuse me, sir, but I believe I have information on who has the briefcase."

All eyes turned toward Bono and Gideon addressed him. "Bono, you were to question the *askaris* in Lavington."

"Yes, and I've been able to speak to one of them who witnessed what happened when our vehicle chased the Nissan."

Bono basked momentarily in the rapt attention that he commanded from his colleagues. He heard a grunt from the Commissioner, which he took to mean he could proceed. Speaking in a measured pace, he continued, "After the two vehicles drove away, a visitor to one of the neighboring houses drove out in a Honda Accord. I spoke today to the *askari* who witnessed the car drive out and then stop to pick up something from the road; something that must have been thrown out of the Nissan."

His words produced the desired effect. The Deputy Commissioner now sat bolt upright, while the Commissioner pulled himself up from his familiar slouch and swiftly straightened up in his enormous chair. His eyes narrowed as he asked Bono in a hushed tone, "Are you saying someone witnessed the driver of the Honda pick up what was thrown out of the Nissan—that he saw a briefcase that was..." he paused as he picked up the worn-out piece of paper from his desk and adjusted his reading glasses to read out, "bhey-uh... bey-ish in color?"

Bono was pleased to see his boss so energized, but felt helpless that he had to disappoint him with a less-than-satisfying piece of information. "Actually, the *askari* who saw this—and I can assure you that this fellow is a very reliable witness; me, I could tell from the moment I saw him that he is very upright—that fellow has served short-time both in the police and in the armed forces, and I knew as soon as I met him..."

"What exactly did he see?" Gideon cut short Bono's ramblings.

"He actually could not make out what the Honda driver picked up. The car stopped in front of his gate and the driver opened the door to pick up something from the road."

Bic had been listening in silence, not too pleased that he was being upstaged in a meeting that he had expected to dominate. He now started to punch holes in his adversary's narration and claw back the advantage. Posturing in the style of a high-profile defense attorney, he asked Bono, "The *askari* didn't see anything being thrown from the Nissan, did he?"

"No, but why would the driver of the Honda have stopped?" Bono countered.

"How can you be sure that the driver picked up a briefcase or anything for that matter?" Karanja asked.

"Circumstantial evidence, boss, circumstantial evidence. The driver of the Honda must have waited when he heard the two cars approaching, followed by gunshots. He then witnessed the briefcase being tossed out. After the police drove off, he pulled up his car to pick up the briefcase before driving away." Bono folded his arms and leaned back in his chair to convey that he rested his case.

But Bic wasn't done yet. "Why would some innocent driver, who is passing by, get involved in stolen goods? Besides, why would any burglar have thrown out those goods, to begin with? You admit that this heroic *askari* did not see a briefcase being tossed out of the Nissan. On the other hand, we have a suspicious foreigner, involved in dealing with weapons in this region, and near whose house the burglars finally abandoned their vehicle. Something went wrong, and the thief is found badly beaten up near the car. You all haven't seen the Russian. He is mean-looking and reminds you of a bear. In school, we had pictures of Yeti, the Abominable Snowman, who is supposed to live in the Himalayas, and the Russian reminds me of him. No, the Russian has got to be involved and the stolen goods must be with him."

Karanja had heard these arguments from Bic earlier in the afternoon and wanted him to present his proposed line of action. "It is a possibility, Bic. So what do you suggest we do?"

"We need to check if the Russian has the stolen goods in his house."

Gideon was the first to respond. "What are you suggesting?"

Before Bic could respond, he was interrupted by Bono. "The house that we should be checking is of the owner of the Honda Accord."

Gideon weighed in. "My feeling is that the Russian is more likely to be involved. Even the Japanese guy expressed some doubts about his activities. Who was driving the Honda, Bono? What do we know about him?"

"He is a *Muhindi* (Indian) with a *Mzungu* (white) wife. I have details of where they live in Westlands."

"Do we know why he would get involved in any of this business?" asked Gideon.

"Not really, but as I said, he might have happened to be there and picked up the briefcase," contended Bono.

Karanja asked Bono, "So what are you saying? You can't just go up to him and ask him about the briefcase. He would deny knowing anything about it."

"The same thing would happen if we asked the Russian," said Gideon.

"The only way to find out would be to organize a break-in on the quiet," Bic coolly suggested.

"That's highly objectionable—we, in our official capacity, can't do that," Gideon, ever the stickler for rules, shot back.

Michael Karanja looked at Bic and gave him a knowing nod. He was keen to have Bic present his proposal as quickly as possible so that there would be enough time for the heated discussions that would surely ensue. But that would have to wait a little longer, as Inspector Julius Wachira walked into the office.

"Sorry for being late, I got delayed in the Kisumu case," he said, as he sat down. Turning to the Commissioner, he said with a touch of triumph, "The case has been solved."

"Good job, Julius," commented the Commissioner. "We'll talk about it later. In the meanwhile, let me brief you on the latest developments of the case on hand. Bic has information that the Russian, who he suspects of being in possession of the briefcase, will be away for four days. And Bono has talked to an *askari* in the Lavington neighborhood who says he saw a car drive away after our vehicle's confrontation with the yellow car. Bono asserts that the owner of that car, a *Muhindi*, might have picked up the briefcase, and should be our prime suspect."

"So we now have two suspects? We certainly are in far better shape than we were yesterday, when we had none," quipped Julius, who was in an uncharacteristically cheerful mood. "But who's the more likely suspect?"

"We should focus on the Yeti," asserted Bic.

"A Yeti?" asked Julius, looking around. "So now, we have three suspects? A Russian, an Indian, and a Yeti, whoever—or whatever—it is?"

"It's the Russian. He fits the image of a Yeti," clarified Bic.

"That's impressive, man! Likening a white dude to a rare creature you've never seen!" came Julius's jovial response. "Okay, we have some leads; what do we do now?"

For the third time, Karanja turned toward Bic and said, "Bic has an unusual proposal. Why don't you tell them about it?"

Bic cleared his throat and began. "As I said earlier, my strong feeling is that the Russian has the briefcase in his possession. We need to check that, and the only way to find out is to organize a break-in into his house." He paused briefly before announcing his momentous proposal. "We know that we would never have the authority to break into someone's house ourselves. My suggestion is that we outsource this job."

"What outsourcing are you talking about, man?" Gideon sounded incredulous as he pounced on Bic. "Now mind you, I've heard this term before—a new business term used by the Western countries to send away tedious, unwanted jobs to other countries with cheaper labor costs. My dear Bic, where do you want to outsource this investigation? To the Brits in Scotland Yard? Or to the Russians, now that you are checking out some Russian connection...?"

"Sir, sir, please allow me to explain," Bic hurriedly cut in. "What I'm saying is that we outsource this job to some guys here in Nairobi. Some crooks who know how to break into a house to find where the briefcase is hidden. They'll know where to find the briefcase—under the mattresses or deep inside some closet. They'd take all the risks and we will keep them under surveillance to make sure they don't get caught. We'll also make sure they return the briefcase with its contents to us."

A stunned silence enveloped the room, with all eyes on Bic. It was Bono who broke the silence. "Actually, I like your suggestion Bic."

Taken aback at having received support from an unexpected quarter, Bic listened with suspicion as Bono continued, "But I think we should carry out this operation at the house in Westlands."

"Now wait, wait, not so fast," the Commissioner cut in. "Bic, who did you have in mind for this job?"

"The same gang from whom the briefcase was stolen—they have good reason to want it back. They've seen the briefcase, so we don't need to waste time describing it. And as for the contents, they probably know more about what was inside than we do."

"How will you make sure they return the contents?" Karanja asked.

"Leave it to me, boss. They know their game is up if they don't return the goods."

"This is a most unconventional proposal, and we can't agree to it," a visibly upset Gideon commented.

"Let's hear the full plan," said Julius. "You said we should keep them under surveillance while they carry out the... the operation. What did you have in mind?"

"Sir, I propose using our trainee, Toto," said Bic. "He'll be patrolling near the Russian's house while our friends—I mean this gang—carries out the operation. When they're done, he'll inform us and we'll make sure the goods are returned."

"You are wasting everyone's time by focusing on the Russian," interjected Bono. "It's the house in Westlands that we should be breaking into." He paused before continuing, "I have another proposal. Why not use the gang that stole the briefcase? They are the ones who lost the briefcase after stealing it and are desperately looking for it."

"Bic and Bono," Julius said, looking at the two of them, "are you saying that you can get those gangs to carry out the jobs that each of you is proposing?"

"Those guys are desperate, and they have no choice but to carry out this job. That's why I made this proposal earlier today to the Commissioner," Bic said.

The boss remained quiet, while his deputy glared at him. All eyes turned to Bono.

"I haven't had much time to think about this plan, but yes, I can get them to do the job."

"This is totally unacceptable—I don't recommend it at all," said Gideon.

Julius came to the Commissioner's rescue. "We haven't uncovered much. And without much evidence of where the goods are, there isn't any chance of obtaining a search warrant. For that matter, we don't even have an official complaint about the theft. This suggestion might be very unconventional, but it's worth a try."

"Sir," Bic addressed the Commissioner, "you've been telling us to think outside the box. No one has ever done what I'm proposing, but I see no other choice."

"Aren't you thinking far too much outside the box, Bic?" asked Julius, with a grin on his face. He turned to address the uncompromising Deputy Commissioner in a serious tone. "Sir, Bic is right—we're not left with too many options. If Bic and Bono decide to go ahead, they do so at their own risk and bear all the consequences. We have no knowledge of what's going on—is that agreed upon?"

"But we need Toto's assistance," Bic reminded them.

"That guy," Julius smiled and shook his head. "Don't be too frank with him and do not tell him the real story. He seems to be in a world of his own—wonder what he's thinking about."

"He'll need a vehicle," Bono interjected.

"Let him borrow a vehicle from the Store Department for some procurement job. Please organize that, Gideon," Karanja ordered. After a moment's reflection, he weighed in on the more likely suspect. "I feel the same way as Gideon—I doubt the Indian could be involved. We know these Indians—they would be shit scared to stop their vehicle to pick up something after our people opened fire at the thugs. The Russian looks more suspicious; he is engaged in some dangerous activities, and Bic says he also looks intimidating. Now, let's not organize both operations at the same time; it might not be necessary. I think Bic can go ahead with his operation on the Russian. If the goods are not in his house, then Bono can plan his."

The two agreed.

"I still have one question," Wachira said. "If we knew all along who was involved in stealing the briefcase, then why is it taking so long to recover it?"

"Neither of them has it. They've confirmed it's missing—but they don't know where," said Bic.

"That is a mystery that has been baffling us all these days," Karanja said.

"The Baffling Case of the Missing Briefcase—as the folks here call it," Julius had the last word. But he had come in late and remained unaware that Bono was targeting Jay's house. No names were mentioned in the meeting, but if he had been present earlier, Julius would have known that an Indian with a European wife, driving a Honda Accord, had to be his acquaintance, Jay.

\*\*\*

*Ndovu* Don munched on a *mandazi* while sipping hot *chai*, sitting listlessly outside a roadside kiosk. His cell phone rang. "Yes?" he hissed.

"I have information for you," came the familiar voice of Inspector Bic Okello. "I think I know where the brief... ah, the stolen stuff is hidden. You told me you'd go and get it if you knew where it was. Start preparing to recover it tomorrow."

"Wh... what... tomorrow?" Don almost choked.

"You know we have to act fast on such matters," Bic reminded him.

"But...but I need more time to prepare..."

"The concerned man is away for only two days, so there isn't any time. My assistant will be near the house to make sure no one disturbs you, do you understand?"

Bic heard a shallow croak at the other end, which he took to be a yes.

"Tomorrow morning, go to Lower Kabete and check out this house." Bic gave directions to Mikhail Smirnoff's house. "I've visited the house—there isn't much security there; just the usual barbed wire fence at the back. My man will also be nearby and I'll keep in touch with both of you. Call me by nine o'clock so that we can finalize the next step."

***

Inspector Bono Njoroge didn't lose time getting in touch with his contact and heard Tusker's voice when he called on his cell phone. "Did you see a car nearby when you were cornered by our vehicle at Lavington that night?"

"No, chief."

"Someone said a vehicle drove by soon after you left. The driver was seen to have slowed down and it's possible he might have picked up something."

"Then it must be the briefcase!" Tusker sounded elated.

"We don't know—but we know the house where the owner of the vehicle lives."

"Chief, you all should go and question him." Tusker checked himself from adding, "*and after we have recovered the money, just hand over that man to me so that I can teach him a proper lesson—never to mess around with me.*"

"He's not going to admit it," responded Bono. "No, the only way is for you to go inside the house and find out."

"Chief, what are you saying?" The alarm in Tusker's tone was unmistakable. "I can't break into someone's house; I told you I'm not in that business."

"And I told you that if you don't produce the brief-case, your body will be found floating in the Nairobi River to be fed to the crocodiles," Bono reminded him. After a pause, he continued, "We'll have our man in plain clothes make sure no one comes near that house once you are in, understand? You get your team ready; I'll call you tomorrow afternoon with details. Make sure your phone is working when I call, is that clear?"

Bono heard a gulp at the other end—which was all that he'd expected, as he hung up.

***

"Mr. Nick, I guess you'd love to spend the night in five-star comfort after this strenuous drive," Peter Otieno posed the question to the detective as their lodge appeared in view. Deep in the Maasai Mara, all that Nick expected was a primitive lodge with basic amenities and there was nothing in its appearance for him to believe otherwise.

"A hot shower and a comfortable bed would be nice—but maybe I'm being a bit too optimistic," he replied.

He was not quite prepared for what the lodge had to offer. They were welcomed by courteous staff, dressed in smart uniforms, as they stepped into a well-designed reception area. The check-in process was swift and Nick found the welcome drink of fresh passion fruit juice refreshing enough to ask for a refill. More surprises awaited Nick as he followed the bellboy, who carried his bags and led the way to the guest rooms—or, to be precise, his tent.

On entering the living area, he sensed the word "tent" was a misnomer, since what this place offered deserved a different name. The large tent was made up of several living areas: a small sit-out at the front that led to a living area with two luxurious beds, side tables with reading lamps, an armchair, and a dressing cabinet. A canvas flap that served as a door led to the toilet, which had all the necessary facilities: a sink, toilet bowl, and a small shower, with cold and hot running water. He could hear the hum of large generators, installed some distance away, which ensured a steady supply of electric power. Nick looked around with awe as he experienced all the trappings of a luxurious tented safari. For the safety of the residents, barbed and razor-wire fences surrounded the complex.

After a long, hot shower, he donned a light sweater, as the evening temperatures started to fall, and made his way to the bar to join Peter Otieno. After cooling off with a couple of much-touted Tusker Lager beers, they moved to the dining room to partake in a large buffet spread, with a variety of barbecued game meat, including gazelle and zebra.

When they were done, Peter suggested they proceed to the evening's entertainment arranged by the lodge. Adjacent to the main building was a stadium-like structure where the two took their seats. Traditional folk dancers entertained the guests and soon the lights dimmed. An air of expectancy descended upon those seated in the arena.

All eyes turned toward a spotlight that was directed toward the top of a tree a few yards outside the lodge enclosure. Peter pointed out a large piece of freshly cut meat that dangled from a rope slung over a branch. As their eyes adjusted to the darkness, they witnessed the shadow of a creature stealthily crawling up the branch. The viewers whispered in hushed tones and watched in awe as the dark creature stopped and turned his head toward the crowd. Both its eyes glowed red, reflecting the dim lights in the enclosure.

"It's a leopard, Mr. Nick," whispered Peter.

The murmurs in the crowd died down while the beast continued to glower at them. And then, a blood-curdling roar—Nick heard some women gasp. The next moment, the leopard lunged to snatch the piece of meat and started to move away. As he moved into the spot-light, the crowd got a proper view of his size.

"It was a big one, wasn't it?" Peter asked.

"Yup, sure was big," agreed Nick. "I must admit I enjoyed the experience."

"It was a female leopard," said Peter. "Did you not notice the adoring look she gave you with her blazing eyes?"

Nick smirked as he wondered if this line of needling would continue for the rest of their trip. "Peter, you seem to have a strange theory that the felines in this country have a crush on me. Once of these days, I just might de-cide to chase a female cheetah, if she throws an inviting glance my way."

A Scandinavian couple next to them grinned at hearing Nick's comment. They joined him and Peter as the four headed back to the lodge. In the lounge, over a cup of coffee, Nick struck up a conversation with them and some of the other tourists. The majority had plans to start early the next morning on a tour in one of the lodge's rugged vehicles, to view wildlife in its natural habitats. With luck, they might even witness a kill by lions or cheetahs. The more affluent tourists had plans to take a hot-air balloon ride to view the wildlife, undisturbed from high up as the balloon glided gently over the savannah. Their trip would include a champagne breakfast.

Nick had no such plans. As he retired to his tent and crept into his comfortable bed, he realized wearily that his assignment of investigating Mary Wilson's death was about to begin.

***

"Man, how did you pull off that tremendous shot?" Jay's tennis partner Nikki asked him. The two had settled down in the lounge of the Parklands Sports Club and ordered beers after three brisk sets of tennis.

Jay knew Nikki was referring to a volley he had smashed when he leaped high in the air earlier on the court. "Oh, that one?" remarked Jay. "It was one helluva shot, wasn't it? You know, Nikki, I've been quite stressed the last few days. Today's game is just what I needed to release the adrenaline that had been built up. Sorry you were at the receiving end, my friend."

Nicola Vinkovic, a Croatian, continued shaking his head. "Adrenaline, you say? Or have you been taking that concoction from a rhino's horn that was in the news the other day?"

Jay laughed and, lowering his voice, responded, "More like a concoction from a rhino's testicles, if there is one!"

The two had been tennis buddies for three years and played twice a week at the club. Today's game was what Jay badly needed to unwind and he now felt a surge of energy as he sipped a cold beer. He was not in a particular hurry to head home, as Heidi would be coming in late, after her karate class.

"How about some snacks?" suggested Jay and ordered his favorite fish fingers, while Nikki decided on chicken spring rolls. Jay had been off food the last few days, and as the waiter brought the piping-hot snacks to their table, he realized his appetite was back with a vengeance. The fish used was Tilapia, fresh from the nearby Lake Naivasha, neither farm-raised nor frozen. The fish fingers were finger-licking good as Jay polished them off and ordered another plate that he also promptly wolfed down.

It was unfortunate that he could not discuss his dilemma with Nikki. They talked about various issues, but Jay could not resist making an oblique reference to gunshots being heard near their friend's house in Lavington and reports of a robbery. Nikki had no knowledge of any such incident. Jay asked Nikki if he knew of a Russian living in Lower Kabete, to which Nikki replied that he did not. Jay wasn't too sure if it was his imagination, but he felt Nikki gave him a strange look when they parted company.

Jay had a quick shower after returning home, by which time Heidi arrived and soon dinner was served. They made idle conversation at the dining table, but Jay knew he had to broach the topic. "Look, I'm the one who's responsible for the state we're in. I'm figuring out the best way for me to return the money."

"It's very distressing, Jay—it's so stressful that I feel we should turn the money over to the police," Heidi responded. "But there is still no news of a robbery, which probably means the money was to be used for something illegal. So I then feel we should hold on to it for now and let those guys sweat it out. I just don't know what would be the right thing to do."

He held her close. "I'm so sorry, *liebchen.*"

· After a long pause, she suggested they stop worrying and clean up so that they didn't miss their favorite TV shows. The local TV stations broadcast a few recorded shows from other countries that found their way into Kenya several years later.

Settling down in the living room, they watched one of the more popular American soaps, *The Bold and the Beautiful.* This was followed by the dubbed version of a German mystery serial, *Derrick,* on another channel.

# Chapter 8

## *Wednesday*

"*Mama, ukiangalia nzuri* (the dress looks so chic)!" Beatrice remarked as Heidi stepped out the door toward her car.

"*Asante sana* (thank you), Beatrice."

Heidi was pleased that at least her maid had noticed. She hoped the extra time and effort she'd put into her makeup, hair, and choosing the appropriate attire would be worthwhile. A meeting was scheduled later in the day with the participating organizations in the forthcoming Annual Summer Fair being held in her school. It would be up to her to persuade them to donate attractive items that she could distribute as prizes for the raffle that she would be conducting. After the meeting, she planned to visit a few other organizations and embassies to put in a similar request. The task of soliciting donations could be daunting, and it was important that she made a striking impression.

As she drove her Volkswagen Beetle to the school, Heidi's thoughts drifted back to the current dilemma. *Just turn the money over to the police and get done with it*—this option raced time and again through her mind. But moments later, she would wonder if they should— the money was surely being used for something illegal, with the police doing little to curb such activities. *No, she* decided, *if the police can't be trusted, then let's hold on to it and deny those criminals the use of it. Ah, Mensch—what a mess!*

Well, maybe she was worrying unnecessarily—Jay had proven to be just as adept at figuring a way out of any mess as he'd been in landing in one. At the breakfast table, he'd mentioned they would dine out the following evening. Heidi decided to stop worrying and focus her mind, instead, on the meetings later in the day.

***

"No, sir, *Bwana* Minister, I know, I know..." Commissioner Michael Karanja patiently held on to the phone while the Minister blasted him from the other end. After enduring the tirade, he said, "As I mentioned earlier, there have been no reports of anyone spending large amounts of cash. Nor have our contacts been able to provide any specific leads. That's why it's taking so long."

After another "Yes, sir," "No, sir," followed by "Goodbye, sir," Karanja hung up.

Wearily looking up at the assembled assistants, he asked, "Do we have any information? You heard me—anyone blowing up a large amount of money?"

"No, sir, whoever has the money is lying low like an envelope," Bic Okello replied.

There were smiles and smirks on the faces of those in the room; the simile had been used by a cabinet minister a few years earlier. During a period of ethnic tensions in the country, the powerful minister from the Maasai tribe called on all residents belonging to other tribes to leave the Maasai territory or lie low like an antelope.

The minister's detractors promptly accused him of fueling ethnic tension—they reasoned that an antelope might lie low when threatened by a predator like a leopard or a cheetah. But there is no escape for the antelope, since it's a matter of time before the predator hunts him down. Thus, they claimed, the minister had effectively warned all non-Maasai residents to leave that territory or risk being hunted down.

In response, the minister accused his detractors of playing politics and misquoting him. What he had said was that those people should lie low like an "envelope," not an "antelope." The critics were stumped—this expression, though out of the ordinary, could not be faulted for incorrect usage of the English language. It might have done little to restore the minister's credibility, but he deserved credit for its increasing colloquial usage.

"Yes, Bic, I agree that the person is lying low like an envelope. But that doesn't help us," commented Karanja.

Julius Wachira spoke up, "We can't wait for him to raise his head. We need to smoke him out from wherever he is hiding."

"That's why you people came up with a plan yesterday. Before we go ahead as discussed, does anyone feel we should proceed differently?" asked Karanja.

Bono Njoroge made an attempt to sum up the situation from his point of view. "Boss, I would like to state that the situation we find ourselves in is very unusual. What do we know about this case? First, that an unknown petty thief snatches a briefcase late at night from a pedestrian and jumps into a getaway car. No one, not even the man from whom the briefcase was stolen, is willing to come forward to lodge a written complaint. We don't have eyewitnesses who are willing to come forward. The getaway car manages to dodge us, we are not able to catch anyone, and the suspected thief is found wounded and then dies. But before that, the suspected thief conveniently manages to get rid of the briefcase and says it is missing. So all we are looking for is an expensive briefcase that has some funny color. No, sir, this one is not a routine case and we cannot follow routine procedures. If we suspect the briefcase is lying in someone's house, we must use someone we can trust to carry out the job for us."

Karanja said, "We can't get a search warrant—there is no ground for getting a search warrant—the Russian is not a suspect."

"So what we are proposing is that we seek the services of a professional burglar to break into someone's house to recover the stolen item and hand it over to us," said Julius.

"I don't agree with this line of action." Deputy Commissioner Gideon Odhiambo was quick to reiterate his position. "Such unorthodox methods could get us into serious trouble."

No one spoke while the Commissioner squirmed in his seat. Turning to Bic, he asked, "Are you going ahead with the plans for tomorrow's operation?"

"Yes, sir, those concerned are carrying out the preliminary work right now."

***

The concerned, heroic men were hovering around the Russian's house.

Posing as workers from the City Council, *Ndovu* Don and his assistant, Francis, were clearing the brush some distance away from the targeted house in Lower Kabete. Armed with machetes and long knives, they labored in the thick undergrowth, though their attention was focused on observing the house layout and its security arrangements.

Inspector Bic Okello had earlier conveyed that one of his assistants in plain clothes would be patrolling the neighborhood, but they should not be seen together. And indeed, across the dry riverbed, Don spotted a man with a boyish face dressed in a Power and Lighting Company's faded uniform. He appeared to be inspecting the power lines in the neighborhood—though a keen observer would have wondered what exactly he could be inspecting without any tools or equipment. Even more puzzling was the fact that he was wearing an obsolete uniform, since the Power Company had changed their monogram and uniform color several years back.

Earlier, Don had observed the *askari* at the Russian's house peeking out through the gate with a puzzled, but suspicious, look. Don reckoned the man had never in the past seen council workers clearing up the brush and he asked his assistant to speed up the clearing before the *askari* became too curious.

After surveying the surrounding grounds, Don noted that a concrete wall protected only the rear side of the property, while the rest had barbed-wire fencing. He found this surprising, since such independent homes in a secluded neighborhood were almost always fortified with secure concrete walls and razor wire or an electrified fence running over the top.

A lone housemaid appeared to be living in the servant's quarters at the back. Such maids were invariably away in the afternoons, making that the best time to stage his operation. Don called Bic to inform him of his observations. He laid out his plans, to which the officer agreed.

The die was now cast—Don would break into the Mikhail Smirnoff's house the following afternoon. Bic reminded him that he was to use all available tools, skills, and resources to recover the stolen goods. Don mumbled a faint agreement.

"Good," said Bic. "I'll call you tomorrow morning to give you the final green light."

His phone rang again almost immediately after he'd hung up. It was Don, who spoke in an unusually aggressive tone. "Can you please ask your assistant to go away? We are lucky there are not many people nearby. Someone might soon start wondering why that man has been touching the wooden poles and gazing at the sky for the last two hours."

\*\*\*

Later that afternoon, Don sat down with his three assistants, Paul, Francis, and Mike to finalize the next day's operation. Francis scratched his hands after having worked on the bushes in the morning, while Paul was lost in deep thought. Don briefed them on what he and Francis had observed and the others listened intently as he outlined his plan.

Francis wondered how they were so certain that the stolen money was with the Russian, to which Paul stated emphatically, "The Russian has the money. We know from our police contact that the Russian was alone when he went out that night and came back. So he must have had the briefcase when he came back."

"But we don't even know if the briefcase was with them when they abandoned the vehicle," countered Francis. "It could have been dropped off somewhere along the way."

Paul shook his head. "That's what those guys and the police want us to believe. That thief must have hidden the briefcase in the car somewhere and the Russian must have found out from the thief where it was."

"Paul, you've been seeing too many movies," said Mike. "I don't think this, what you're saying, really happened."

Ignoring the interruption, Paul continued, "The police report says the Russian dropped his wife off and got into his car alone. The *askari* told the police that he heard his master talking to that injured thief and spent nearly ten minutes outside. That's when he took the briefcase and drove back in his car, so that the *askari* could not have seen it. That man certainly has hidden the briefcase in his house, and we are going to get it back."

*** 

Mikhail Smirnoff had an early breakfast at his hotel in Kigali, the capital city of Rwanda. The land-locked East African country was now relatively stable after witnessing the continent's worst genocide, resulting from ethnic violence in 1994.

As he stepped out from the dining area and walked through the reception, the assistant at the front desk called out, "Enjoy your trip, Mr. Smirnoff, and have a good day!"

He thanked her as he walked past, avoiding any further conversation. It was difficult for someone with his physique not to be noticed, and he headed for the exit. As a matter of precaution, he cast a quick glance around to make sure he was not being watched and stepped out of the hotel. He headed straight for an SUV in the parking lot, climbing into the rear while the chauffeur held the door open. The car rental company had agreed to his demand that they send a different vehicle with a different chauffeur each time he required their services.

Less than a hundred miles from Kigali is the border with neighboring Congo, a large country with massive minerals and precious stones deposits, but unfortunately, also one that had been in a state of lawlessness for more than a decade. It was there that Mikhail was headed. They drove past Rwanda's lush, green countryside; the country was blessed with fertile soil that safeguarded the locals from starvation, despite the brutal wars.

"Sir, you must be driving a big car like a Mercedes back home. This Toyota would be too small for you," the driver said in jest, attempting to make conversation.

But nothing could break Mikhail's resolve to avoid indulging in frivolity. "I drive an ordinary Russian car. Now please, I need to catch up on my sleep. Don't disturb me," was his terse response. That brought the conversation to an end for the remainder of the trip.

At the Congolese border, Mikhail made sure his passport was not stamped—one of the precautions he took to avoid letting the Kenyan and other authorities know of his visits there. He did not wish to enter into any discussion on the nature of his business activities.

In a little over an hour, they drove through the town of Goma, and the vehicle turned off onto a dirt road to enter a densely wooded area. They were now in the territory of the warlord Mikhail was visiting. Armed men, some still in their teens, stopped the SUV at crude check posts. After being searched and vetted by the private militia, Mikhail's vehicle proceeded toward a wooden log cabin.

Mikhail spent the next two hours with the warlord, a tall stout Congolese sporting a cowboy hat and who greeted Mikhail with a Russian bear hug. He had spent a few years in the Soviet Union and looked forward to brushing up on his Russian with the visitor. Over lunch, the two finalized an arms deal comprising ammunition and equipment that the host required to ensure uninterrupted supplies of mined precious stones that funded his insurgency movement. Mikhail collected the down payment in US dollars cash.

By mid-afternoon, Mikhail was on his way back, with the currency notes spread among secret pockets in his leather jacket. At the border, some of the dollars changed hands with the border officials. It was dusk when the SUV dropped Mikhail off at his hotel in Kigali.

A message awaited Mikhail at the hotel desk; it was from his wife, Olga, asking him to call urgently. He put the call through from his room.

"Tanya has suffered a burst appendicitis," Olga told him, referring to their twelve-year-old daughter. "She had to be rushed to the hospital. The surgeon said he could not wait and has performed the surgery and she is recovering. When can you come back?"

Mikhail said he had planned on spending another day in Kigali, for a meeting with a government official. On the following day, he had planned a two-day trip to the neighboring country of Burundi.

"Please come back soon," pleaded Olga.

Mikhail said he would change his plans and try to catch the earliest flight back to Nairobi, which was the next morning. He expressed his concern for Tanya.

"I hope she spends a restful night. But I'm glad you're coming back tomorrow—I miss you, my dear Mishka," added Olga as she signed off, addressing him with the name she had fondly been calling her oversized husband since their courting days. Mishka was the name of the cuddly bear mascot for the 1980 Olympics in Moscow.

***

Should he call Ravi Karnik and confide in him? Was it time to contact his police contact, Julius Wachira, for any new information? Was there anyone else he should get in touch with? In a muddled state of mind, Jay stared at the design drawings of their new equipment without absorbing any of its impressive details.

How about the news media? Did the vibrant Kenyan news media have no clue what exactly happened that night? The money was stolen from somewhere—he thought it strange that there was not even a pip for the media to have picked up. But it probably confirmed his and Heidi's belief that the money was part of some illegal activity—leading them to harden their resolve to hold on to the money—and placing them in an increasingly compromising position. How long should this waiting game continue?

Jay tried to focus on the drawings when his cell phone rang. A familiar voice greeted him. *"Habari gani, Bwana Jay* (How are you, Mr. Jay)?" It was Julius Wachira! There had to be some sort of telepathy at work, thought Jay—how else could one explain Julius calling this very moment?

A sense of relief swept over Jay as he responded, *"Mzuri sana asante rafiki, na wewe?"* (Very well, thank you my friend, and you?).

Like other foreigners, Jay found it hard to follow the local tradition of greeting each other by spending a few minutes exchanging information about oneself, the family, the weather, workplace, and the current hot topics. He normally greeted the other party briefly and got to the point, even though such behavior might be deemed impolite in the local custom.

Today, however, Jay knew he had to get his act together by observing the entire gamut. By the time they were through, Jay was well informed about the problems being faced by Julius's family members. On his part, Jay conveyed that his children were away and he'd been busy at work.

The reference to Jay's workplace brought Julius to the reason he'd called. His nephew would soon be completing three months of temporary service at Jay's plant and would Jay please extend his tenure? Jay had already decided on extending it—there was enough work at the plant, the reports on the nephew's performance were positive and, more importantly, Jay could ill-afford to create any animosity with Julius at this crucial point in time.

He decided to seize this opportunity to pry some information out of Julius.

"Oh yes, your nephew, of course," Jay sounded authoritative and disinterested. "When does his temporary service expire?"

Julius mentioned the date, a few days away.

Now that he felt he had the upper hand, Jay waited for Julius to put in his plea.

"He's a good boy—he will do whatever work that's given to him. Please, *Bwana Jay,* his family is poor, he's the only earning member in the family."

"Hmm... let me see," Jay sounded condescending. "I'll talk to the personnel officer. I shall let you know of our decision," leaving the option open to reach out to him if necessary. But he was desperate for some information right now. "What else is going on, Julius? Any news on the abandoned Nissan car that we talked about—what were those guys up to?"

"Obviously not anything good. They had stolen a briefcase and then tried to get away in the Nissan. I think I mentioned to you that our vehicles chased them, but they managed to get away. The briefcase has still not been recovered."

*Oh, I can tell you where the briefcase is*—is what Jay would have responded under any other circumstances. Instead, he casually asked, "Not yet? There was obviously some money in it. But I'm sure your department has some clues where it could be."

"No, but we suspect a Russian, who lives near the place where the Nissan was abandoned. He might have something to do with it."

*You bet he does. Keep pestering that Ruskie as long as you need to*—how Jay would have loved to convey that!

But his response was, "A Russian, eh? And you people have reason to suspect him?"

"Yes," replied Julius. "We'll know the results of our investigation shortly."

"And from whom did the gang steal the money?"

"That I can't tell you. Actually, even I don't know, since our boss has been told not to divulge to whom the briefcase belonged to," was Julius's candid response.

"That's interesting. But I'd like to know to whom the goods belonged to—just curious, that's all." A sense of elation perked up Jay, as he realized that the police were barking up the wrong tree.

"I understand."

"Maybe you'll have more information when I call you about your nephew."

"Yes, *Bwana* Jay. But please do something for him."

"I'll definitely try."

"Oh, I almost forgot. Did I mention that the gun-shots your friends in Lavington heard were fired by our men when they had cornered the burglars in their vehicle?"

"Yes, you did," Jay was getting impatient—what was Wachira going on about?

"There have been reports of a dark-colored car that was parked somewhere on the dirt road, which drove off soon after the two vehicles left. We've been trying to locate the vehicle since the occupants might provide some information..."

Jay barely heard Julius complete the sentence as the loud thumping of his heart drowned out all other sounds.

"Were you near that place when the shooting took place?"

This unexpected question rattled Jay, but he managed to quickly compose himself and reply, "Of course not—why do you say that? And the police don't know who was there?"

"I'm not sure—someone else is investigating," replied Julius, not wishing to divulge too much information. At the same time, since he came in late for the previous day's meeting, he was unaware that it was Jay who was in that particular vehicle.

"Well, *Bwana* Jay, please do something for my nephew, and give me a call. *Kwaheri.*"

Jay hung up and closed his eyes. His hands trembled and beads of perspiration formed on his forehead. *Who could have seen him that night?* he wondered. Must be one of the *askaris* from the neighboring houses. So, not all of them had chickened out, as he had assumed.

And what happens next? A knock on the door as the police come investigating? They would ask him if he was at that spot that night and what he had seen. He pulled himself together and took a large sip of water as he pondered how he would respond.

It would be in his best interest to admit that he was in that car and to tell them exactly what he'd witnessed: the police vehicle confronting the yellow vehicle and the thugs managing to get away; gunshots being fired from the police vehicle at the escaping vehicle while he and Heidi ducked for cover. And he then came up with what he considered to be an appropriate response to their obvious question—if he'd seen any object being thrown out of the yellow vehicle? To which he would reply, "Are you guys kidding me? With gunshots flying around us, do you expect us to be watching the fun from the ringside? Or ducking for cover?"

He would deny any knowledge about the briefcase—surely there were no witnesses to *that*. Yes, that's what he would tell the police. He was there in his car that night, had witnessed the entire confrontation and then left, badly shaken. He knew nothing about the briefcase.

Or was he missing something? Should he have turned the money over to the police? In his confused state of mind, he felt he needed to speak with Ravi Karnik. He sat contemplating how he would approach the sensitive topic when his chief executive called him for a meeting; his call to Ravi would have to wait.

\*\*\*

Wary of a long hot day ahead, Nick Cunningham took his time relishing a sumptuous breakfast. His companion, Peter Otieno, did full justice as well, while describing to Nick the variety of fruits grown in Kenya—passion fruits, mangoes, pineapples, papayas—the list went on. Nick brought an end to this conversation by reminding Peter it was time to leave.

They climbed into the Land Rover, and it didn't take long for Nick to be captivated by the wildlife all around. They had missed out on the rhino the previous afternoon, but there it was, standing in the distance, staring at a herd of zebras.

"There must be a good reason he's been given poor eyesight," commented Peter philosophically. "Things could've been ugly for us otherwise. As a kid growing up in my village, I've unwittingly walked close to rhinos on a few occasions. I tell you, Mr. Nick, if the rhinos had good eyesight, I would've had a horn from one of them right here," pointing to his abdomen.

"And I'm glad they have a poor vision, my friend, or else I probably would've had your commissioner accompany me on this trip."

They both laughed. "He's a good man," Peter said. "He takes good care of us."

The vehicle slowed down. The driver craned his neck and said, "*Simba.*"

"Look, Mr. Nick," Peter exclaimed, "A lion—alone by himself."

Some distance away, a lion sat half-crouched in an open patch. "Is something wrong with him?" Nick asked.

"He's old and looks sick. Probably injured as well and obviously abandoned by his pride. Looks too weak to survive for long."

The driver was now pointing in another direction.

"It's the hyenas. They've picked up the scent and they know that he's weak. Mr. Nick, the poor lion won't last another hour."

Nick could not help feeling sorry for the poor beast. Hailed as the "King of the Jungle," the one that Nick now beheld was far from that majestic state. His day of reckoning had arrived and the old order had to make way for the new. But did his life have to end in such an inglorious way— literally being left to the hyenas to devour him?

But that was what nature intended—some creature had to fall prey to the hungry hyenas. With this somber thought, Nick realized that he was observing life in its raw, natural state, where only the fittest survive.

They drove on in silence for a while. They had planned to head straight to the campsite where Mary Wilson had spent her last night. After consulting the driver, Peter said, "Mr. Nick, we are not too far from the

Maasai River, where there are plenty of crocodiles and hippos. I suggest we visit it now—there's no better place for viewing those creatures."

"If it's on the way to where we're headed, then I guess it's okay."

It was not actually on the way and it took a good hour to reach. But Peter had been right—the experience was astounding. The hippos lazed in the shallow waters of the river and grunted as they moved around. They occasionally came out of the water and Nick was amazed by their enormous size. Peter pointed to a spot farther down the river where he saw a few crocodiles. Their huge snouts could barely be seen sticking out of the water. One of them stealthily crawled out of the river, probably looking for food ashore. Nick estimated him to be more than fifteen feet long. Woe to any poor human being within the beast's range!

"I know what you're thinking, Mr. Nick," Peter commented. "Many villagers get killed by crocodiles every year, though even more are killed by hippos."

Nick shuddered at the thought of what the victims must have gone through.

They finally moved on. A short distance later, they drove into a cluster of trees. A tourist vehicle was parked in the shade and the tourists had opened their lunch baskets. The spot was shady, cool, and inviting and obviously a place where tourist vehicles took a break.

"Should we have an early lunch?" Peter suggested. "I've packed a few bottles of cold beer. This is a good spot."

Nick could not resist. This was getting to be more of a holiday. While sipping beer, Nick struck up a conversation with tourists in the other vehicles. Soon after lunch, they were getting ready to move, when there was an excited chatter among the tourists. Nick spotted a few odd-looking animals a short distance away.

"Meerkats," pointed out Peter. "Ha, don't they look funny?"

And funny-looking they indeed were, admitted Nick. Standing on their hind legs, these small mammals from the mongoose family cast cautious glances around with curious expressions on their faces. They were blocking the way of the vehicles, but the tourists did not appear to be in any hurry to leave, and the Meerkats stayed put in their place.

While they were waiting, dark clouds gathered overhead. By the time the Meerkats moved away, it started to rain—or, to be precise, to pour.

"We'll wait for the rain to stop," Peter said. "You can see the road right ahead has become very slushy."

A few vehicles drove away cautiously, but the roads were slippery and most of the vehicles stayed put. For a good half hour, the downpour continued. By the time the rain subsided, the roads were in a treacherous state.

"We'll have to wait for some time, Mr. Nick," Peter said. "The driver says our vehicle will get stuck in the mud."

And so they waited, along with the other vehicles. It was late afternoon by the time the roads looked safe enough. Peter said it was now too late to travel to the campsite, and that they needed to head back to the lodge so that they could make it before dark. They would visit the campsite the next morning.

While Nick chafed at the thought of having lost one working day, Peter Otieno gloated at the thought that he had won round one in his task of frustrating Nick's investigations.

***

Elizabeth, the police commissioner's secretary, was occupied in completing a report on her word processor.

"I've never seen our bosses so busy—and frustrated."

Behind her stood Lucas, a self-styled analyst in the Crimes Department. Continuing to focus on the screen, she responded, "I would agree on the busy part. But why do you think they look frustrated, Lucas?"

"It's so obvious—whatever case they're working on seems tougher than a macadamia nut to crack."

Elizabeth was not surprised to see him hovering around. He had been hired recently in this position, which was specially created to accommodate his all-powerful older brother. She wasn't sure if anyone kept track of the cases he'd analyzed, but he had ample time to indulge in gossip and rumor-mongering.

"Not all cases get solved quickly, Lucas," she countered.

"And not many cases take so long to resolve when so many of the top brass are involved. So what's gone missing—lots of money from some big shot?"

"You can analyze all that once the case is resolved."

"But this one seems more exciting. I've never seen that kiddo, Toto, getting so involved without appearing to have a clue about what's going on. And I hear that a special file has been opened—even the filing clerk has a hard time pronouncing its name."

"Good, at least our folks have some exciting work on hand—they've been complaining it's pure drudgery," she said.

A buzz on her extension interrupted their conversation and, noting that she had been summoned by her boss, Lucas knew it was time for him to move on.

***

Inspector Bono Njoroge made the phone call late that afternoon. He asked Tusker to plan on surveying the house, which he might be required to break into the following day. He gave directions to Jay's house and asked him to check out the layout of the house, its surroundings, and the security systems. One of Bono's assistants would be in the neighborhood to keep an eye on Tusker, but they were not to talk to each other. Tusker was to call Bono when he reached the designated place the next morning at nine o'clock.

Tusker was keen to know more about the person who was suspected to be in possession of the briefcase. But Bono did not part with any further information. He knew Tusker long enough to be aware of the very short fuse that he worked on and the complications that could arise if he indulged in anything more than just recovering the missing goods.

***

Jay called Ravi Karnik later that afternoon and broached the purpose of his call. "Ravi, remember the discussion we had the other day with your friend Bomy Daruwala regarding Section 411 in India? We talked about the options one can resort to in that situation. Someone I know was recently involved in an incident and I'd like to discuss the options with you."

"Wait, wait," interrupted Ravi. "What incident are you talking about? And should we be discussing this on the phone?"

"No, we shouldn't—we need to discuss this in person and I'll call later to fix a time. Meanwhile, I need to ascertain if you'll be in town or traveling this week."

"No, I'm not going anywhere. Give me a call when we should meet."

They signed off and Jay's mood lit up. It was reassuring to know Ravi would be available on short notice to help out should the police pay him a visit as he feared. If they insisted on him accompanying them to the police station for questioning, Jay could take comfort in knowing that he could summon Ravi to ensure he was not unduly harassed.

An air of confidence, which he'd experienced earlier, returned. He wouldn't bother turning the money over to the police. He would hold on to it for now and work out later on donating it to a worthy cause. A mischievous grin swept over his face as he reflected on the turmoil he'd caused within the police and the gangs involved. All the drama that was being played out was his creation! A thought flashed across his mind—*maybe he could spend some of the money?*—but he promptly brushed that thought aside, even though it kept popping up the rest of the afternoon.

When he stood up, he felt almost giddy with delight. He was alone in his private office and he started singing one of his favorite songs—one that gave him a sense of relief after experiencing a stressful situation. Unable to resist any further, he belted out, "I Whistle a Happy Tune" from Rodgers and Hammerstein's musical *The King And I*:

> *Whenever I feel afraid,*
> *I hold my head erect,*
> *And whistle a happy tune,*
> *So no one will suspect,*
> *I'm afraid.*

> *While shivering in my shoes,*
> *I strike a careless pose,*
> *And whistle a happy tune,*
> *And no one ever knows,*
> *I'm afraid.*

While heading home that evening, Jay wondered how Heidi would react to the information that Julius Wachira had passed on to him.

***

Richard Collins felt something didn't quite add up. His *askari* had updated him on the latest developments, which set Richard thinking.

Soon after Jay and Heidi had left their house that night, he heard gunshots in the neighborhood. His *askari* later described the confrontation with the thugs and the shots fired by the police. Jay had called soon after and said they were close to the scene of the shooting, but assured him they were fine.

Two days later, Richard gathered that the police were inquiring about a vehicle that was seen driving away after the incident. They sought details about that vehicle and he started to wonder if there was a contradiction between Jay's account and what the police stated. He wondered if there was enough time for Jay to have driven onto the main road before the other vehicles entered the dirt road.

Richard did not give it any further thought until earlier that day, when his *askari* came with the latest information. One of the neighbor's *askari* had informed the police about a vehicle that was waiting outside one of the neighbor's gate during the shoot-out, but later drove off. The description matched Jay's Honda and police were attempting to locate the vehicle and its owner.

"My God!" exclaimed Richard. "I hope you guys didn't give them any details about Jay."

"Of course not," lied the *askari*.

But Richard knew that he had to alert Jay right away.

\*\*\*

"How are the preparations for next week's event progressing?" Jay asked Heidi at the dinner table.

"Hmm... *gar nicht so schlecht* (not at all bad). I've been meeting several interesting people from well-known organizations and from a few embassies. I'm doing my best to persuade them to donate prizes for our raffle."

"I'm sure they would—in fact, they must be considering themselves lucky they are getting to meet someone as charming as you."

"Flatterer!" she said, reaching out to ruffle his hair.

After a moment, Jay said, "I think, *liebchen,* that we're stuck with the loot."

"*Wie so, mein schatz?*" she asked, wanting to know why.

"No one seems to be missing the money—it's been five days and there is no report of any burglary. The amount may be small change for the guys who lost it."

"Trying to justify your dumb act, aren't you?"

They had barely finished dinner when the phone rang and Jay answered.

"Jay, old chap, how have you been doing?" It was Richard Collins.

"Thanks, Richard, I'm fine. Hope all's well with you and Anne."

"We're doing fine—but hey, listen. I called because I thought I should tell you something our *askari* told me today. A police chappie was here asking the guards what they had witnessed that night of the shooting. Seems one of them reported seeing your car drive away after the shooting. My *askari* thinks that the other guy is confused, since you said you'd already driven away, right? I don't know which car he's talking about, but I thought I should let you know. Did you see any other car that night?"

"No, only the yellow Nissan and the police Land Rover," Jay said and quieted his conscience by reasoning—*you can't see your own car, can you?* "But Richard, thanks for briefing me on what's going on. Say hi to Anne—oh, I almost forgot. You guys are coming next week for the Annual Summer Fair at Heidi's school, aren't you?"

"Yup, we should be there. See you then." Richard hung up.

"So, what did he have to say?" Heidi asked.

"Someone spotted our car that night." Jay paused for a moment before continuing, "While we waited outside the gate, one of the *askaris* saw our car. He's reported that to the officer who's been investigating. My friend in the police department gave me much the same info today."

"But do the police know it was our car?" Heidi asked.

"Julius said they're still investigating. While Richard says the *askari* did not know the car belonged to us."

"The police would've been here by now if they'd traced the car to us."

"I agree. But it's a matter of time before they come to question us. I'm getting very concerned for our safety if we hold on to the money."

"I hate turning the money in—those crooks will merrily continue with their activities," said Heidi. "It could be drug smuggling, gun-running, or poaching. We have a chance to make a small difference and it'd be a shame if we just gave it up."

"I had no idea my stupid act would have such an impact, *liebchen*," Jay looked at her with admiration. "And initially, you were the one pushing me to turn the money in. Anyway, I've been thinking: all we know is that an *askari* saw our car parked outside a gate during the confrontation. Okay, we'll admit that part. But I'm quite sure no one saw me pick up the briefcase. So, we maintain that we witnessed the gunshots being fired and were so shaken up that we didn't see anything being dropped off from that vehicle. We drove off when all was clear."

Heidi looked pleased. "Yes," she said. "That's what we'll tell them. Can you think of any reason why they shouldn't accept our story?"

"No, I can't. Ah, well," Jay sighed. "It's just that I'm so stressed out having the stash lying here—and all this is of my making."

"Come; let's not talk about it. We'll be late for our TV shows."

But Jay continued to fret. Once again he stayed awake late into the night, while Heidi slept peacefully by his side. Looking back, he couldn't believe that he'd been in such high spirits earlier in the day that he'd sung "I Whistle a Happy Tune."

At this time, he reflected, his soul felt about as tormented as that of Hamlet, when he delivered his soliloquy, *To be or not to be.*

# Chapter 9

## *Thursday Morning*

A light, wintry mist hung over the lodge as Nick Cunningham and Peter Otieno climbed into the Land Rover. A somber expression on the detective's face left his companion with no doubt that a day of serious business lay ahead.

A wildlife game park does not offer an appropriate business setting—certainly not the Maasai Mara. It teems with wildlife at all times and it was difficult for a first-time visitor like Nick not to get distracted whenever he sighted a new animal species. His companion continued with his protracted comments. Nick attempted to maintain his composure, but when Peter rambled about the mating habits of guinea fowls, he snapped, "Peter, for God's sake, let's get on with our business—can't we talk about this later?"

Peter looked hurt and remained silent. As they drove on, Nick regretted having lost his cool, but he had to get on with the job—he couldn't fill his daily reports with his discussions with Peter on wildlife.

They'd driven in silence for barely ten minutes when Peter pointed out to his right and said in a hushed tone, "Mr. Nick, look—two cheetahs!"

Nick glanced in that direction and, without realizing it, asked the driver to slow down.

"I think they're getting ready for a kill," said Peter.

Nick peered through his field glasses: a herd of Thompson gazelles grazed in the open savannah, while two cheetahs stealthily approached them. One of the predators started to skirt around the herd, moving farther away from his mate. A few gazelles looked up, sensing danger, but the rest continued to graze. The wily cheetahs remained downwind while stalking their prey, thus minimizing the chances of their scent being picked up.

"The cheetahs are clever," whispered Peter. "Look at the way they're walking; the poor gazelles would assume the two are taking a walk in the park." Even the dour Nick could not suppress a smile.

As the cheetahs kept moving away from each other while encircling the herd, the gazelles started to disperse in different directions.

"See the way they are cornering the gazelles from opposite ends?" asked the insuppressible Peter. "Perfect teamwork—how often do you see two humans work that way?"

Without realizing, Nick found himself nodding in agreement as he continued to watch with anticipation at the unfolding of what he hoped would be an unforgettable experience. One of the cheetahs started to gallop toward the gazelles, which ran in different directions, while it zigzagged to drive them to a chosen corner. The gazelles sprinted in the direction of the second cheetah, that waited hidden behind a shrub, his dark spots providing a perfect camouflage.

"They are falling into the trap, Mr. Nick," Peter kept up his commentary in a hushed tone. "Now watch closely for some real action."

And sure enough, there was plenty of it: the second cheetah sprang from behind the shrub, catching the gazelles by surprise. They now started to sprint away from him, but with an astonishing burst of speed, the cheetah leaped forward and focused on chasing one of the gazelles.

"That must be the weakest one of the herd," Peter explained. "The cheetahs know which one to pick."

Nick couldn't help admiring the power and grace of the cheetah's strides as it sped at about sixty miles an hour. The gazelle could not keep pace, but as the cheetah was set to close in, the nimble-footed gazelle swerved and started to run in the opposite direction. The cheetah could not stop and swerve fast enough and he slowed down and gave up the chase.

But now it was the turn of the first cheetah to take over from where his mate had left off. As the gazelle once again picked up speed, the first cheetah, that had lain low and watched its mate's failed attempt, sprang forward to take up the chase.

"I told you, Mr. Nick," came Peter's comment, "this is perfect teamwork."

Once again Nick smiled and nodded as he watched in awe the cheetah racing across the open savannah to reach his peak speed and close the gap between him and his hapless quarry. The exhausted gazelle slowed down as the cheetah grabbed his neck and brought him down. They slithered to a stop on the grass with the cheetah's jaws, now locked in position, holding the gazelle's neck in a vice-like grip.

"It's over," Peter commented. "The cheetah will hold on to the gazelle's neck until it can breathe no more."

A few gazelles moved closer to ascertain the fate of their fallen mate, but there was nothing they could do. The second cheetah, meanwhile, strode to his mate and slumped down, panting heavily after the exhaustive sprint. It would take a full quarter of an hour for the two to recover, before settling down to feast on their prey.

Nick looked through his field glasses at the other gazelles—and focused on their eyes. He felt sorry for them as they shuffled around in anguish. They were among the gentlest of animals, not known for being aggressive. Nimble and light-footed, one would expect them to sprint away and escape from any predator. And yet, in nature's grand scheme of things, they formed a vital link in the food chain.

Nick looked once again at the cheetahs—endowed with an anatomy befitting the fastest animal on this planet: long, muscular limbs on a supple, slender body with a flexible spine that allowed it to bend and maneuver with ease; retractable claws to provide improved traction; broad nasal passages for easier breathing; and endowed with an enlarged heart to enable it cope up with the burst of oxygen fuelled into its system at the time of its explosive start.

The carnivorous cheetah, being smaller in size and weight than its larger cousins—the lions, tigers, and leopards—can only feed on a small herbivore. The gazelle is of ideal size and weight for its meal. But it is swift on its feet and the cheetah had to evolve to be even faster.

Once again, Nick mused, he was witnessing nature in its starkest form. The poor, aging lion yesterday, the hapless gazelle today...

*What the heck?* thought Nick. *When would I ever have the opportunity again to be part of such an astonish-*

*ing experience? Why am I being such a stickler for work schedules when life here follows its own pace?* Yes, he had to accomplish his task while he was here, but he'd be damned if he were not able to take some time to admire nature operating in this incredible setting. Thousands would give anything to trade places with him. As for witnessing a kill, the assistant at the British High Commission said he had not been lucky enough to witness one during his two visits. His ex-boss at Scotland Yard had told him he was fortunate that this assignment would take him to the famed Maasai Mara.

So why did he feel pangs of guilt for not having started his assigned task two days earlier? Was it because he was wired to think this way after working as a sleuth all these years? He would have missed this experience and, to add insult to injury, be ridiculed by his wife, his ex-boss, and his friends. Why, would they ask, did he rush through the Mara, past some of the most exotic wildlife? Merely to look for clues in a suspected crime case that was several weeks old?

*No,* he said to himself, *this time, I'm done with all the hustling—even if it means taking a day or two longer. Fate ordained that I be at the right place at the right time—how foolish would it have been if I had missed out on what has surely been a once-in-a-lifetime experience?*

As they continued their journey, Nick broke the silence. "Let's take a break, Peter. I could do with some coffee."

"I beg your pardon?" asked Peter, not sure if he heard right.

"I know you're wondering why I'm not pushing like crazy to get to work, as I've been doing all morning,"

Nick replied with a smile. "I'm sorry I was a bit rough on you earlier."

"That's all right," Peter replied in good spirit.

Nick was relieved to get that off his chest. As they sipped coffee, he looked around and said, "This whole place is so different; it's a whole new experience for people like me. When I saw the cheetahs with their majestic strides, chasing the poor gazelle, using sheer power and stamina, I felt so humble—all that we puny humans have is a larger brain. We need to acknowledge that other creatures are endowed with features that in many ways are superior to ours. When will we appreciate these facts and accept our limitations?"

He sounded philosophical and appeared somber. Peter decided to lighten up the mood. "Nice to hear that. Perhaps that's why people from all over the world travel thousands of miles to see what our game parks have to offer."

"It's a pity I'm not here on holiday, but on an official assignment," said Nick. "For us, loss of one human life is a serious matter and that's why I'm here."

After pausing to sip coffee, he continued, "It's a bit of an irony, isn't it, spending so much time, money, and effort investigating the loss of one human life in a surrounding where thousands from other species perish every day? Does anyone even think about them? I could sense the anguish in the eyes of the gazelles as they mourned the death of one of their mates."

Peter looked up and noticed that Nick's eyes had moistened. He had never seen this side of Nick's character before and was lost for a response. After a moment's deliberation, he said, "Yes, Mr. Nick, we too have spent a great deal of time and money and we do value human life. But perhaps Mary Wilson underestimated the dangers of stepping out of the vehicle into the open in the midst of wildlife."

By the time they finished their coffee and resumed their journey, Nick was more relaxed and didn't appear to be in a particular rush to meet any deadlines.

*\*\*\**

Despite a nip in the morning air, Tusker had broken into a sweat as he and one of his lackeys, Jacob, toiled on a vacant plot next to Jay's townhome complex. They wore old, ill-fitting uniforms from the telephone company and appeared to be digging a trench for laying a telephone cable. From his vantage point, Tusker could observe Jay's house and the surrounding area, while Jacob toiled at the bulk of what little digging was being done. Fortuitously, there had been no passersby, since even a layman would have wondered where the telephone cable they were laying was coming from or leading to.

Farther away, near another complex, Tusker sighted a young man, donned in the uniform of what appeared to be a security firm. He was carrying a toolbox while he moved around, checking the perimeter walls of the complex. Tusker suspected he must be the assistant that Inspector Bono Njoroge had arranged for.

Satisfied he'd completed surveying Jay's house and its complex, Tusker phoned Bono to let him know he was done and was departing.

"Good," said Bono. "I'll call you later to confirm your plans for the operation tomorrow."

"Yes. And, chief, tell your assistant to leave. People may start wondering what a security firm technician is doing moving around with an auto repair toolbox in his hand."

The only toolbox that Toto Kilonzo could arrange on such short notice was from a police truck—loaded with a jack, hammer, and complete toolkit.

***

Late in the morning, Mikhail Smirnoff's flight from Kigali landed at Nairobi. He climbed into the company vehicle that was at the airport to receive him and proceeded to the hospital, where his daughter Tanya was recovering from surgery. She had been admitted to Nairobi Hospital, a privately run institution and one of the best in the region. In terms of quality of hospital care, it lay at the other end of the spectrum to the Kenyatta National Hospital, where the briefcase snatcher, Fred, had succumbed to his injuries less than a week earlier.

As Mikhail entered the private room, his wife, Olga, greeted him and said Tanya appeared to be recovering well. The doctors were pleased with her progress and said she could be discharged the following day. After spending an hour with them, Mikhail said he would make a trip home to unpack, shower and change, and would come back later. Along the way, he dropped the driver off at the office.

***

"'Morning, Jay, good seeing you," greeted James Maina, Managing Director of the Tea Authority, as Jay walked into his office.

Jay's company had long been the suppliers of tea machinery to this corporation. After he took over, Jay had worked hard to remove the kinks in delivery commitments and quality issues that the client had complained about. Mr. Maina had been appreciative of the improved performance, which he attributed to Jay's capabilities. Today's meeting was scheduled to review the progress made in the execution of a large pending order. Jay had arrived with his engineer, but was told the Managing Director wished to see him in private and he now sat alone with the Director.

James Maina lost no time in broaching the subject. "My niece is the principal of a school in my hometown and they need to construct additional classrooms. They are collecting funds and a *Harambee* has been organized this Sunday, where I will be the Chief Guest. You know how it works—I am expected to announce a generous donation. My friends have pitched in, but I'm still short. Now, my dear Jay, the kids in that school and my niece would be grateful if you would make a nice contribution."

This widely prevalent practice of collecting funds was originally conceived for worthy causes. The country's first president, Jomo Kenyatta, coined the word *Harambee,* which was later adopted as the fledging nation's slogan and whose literal meaning in Kiswahili is "All pull together." While the objective is to pitch in funds to pull up the community together, this practice was soon overused and, unfortunately, too often abused.

The organizing of *Harambees* became widely prevalent, with an influential person being invited to be the Chief Guest. He would be expected to kick off the collection drive with a large contribution, after which he would turn to his friends, business partners and, as expected, his suppliers to pitch in. Such contributions were a norm that executives like Jay had grown accustomed to and his company maintained a separate account for this purpose. He always carried an envelope, filled with large-currency bills, drawn from this account.

Opening that particular envelope, Jay pulled out a five-hundred-shilling bill and handed it over to Maina. While Jay started to fill in the donation form, Maina kept ruffling the bill in his hand with a not-too-pleasing look on his face. Casting a glance at the envelope in Jay's hand, he said, "You have a two-hundred-shilling bill in there. Come on, *Bwana,* you don't need to hold back that one."

Jay found it difficult to refuse when approached in such a brazen manner and he pulled out the bill and handed it over. Beaming a broad smile, Maina said, "That's better. Here's the invitation for you and your family to attend the event this Sunday. Now, let's start the meeting."

As Jay watched Maina reach for the phone, a thought flashed through his mind. He cut in, "Wait, *Bwana* James, I have something personal to discuss."

"Yes, Jay?"

"This is confidential and I'll make it brief." Jay paused as he attempted to put his thoughts together. "You move around in influential circles and are privy to certain information that others like us are not."

Maina's expression turned serious as he listened with full attention to Jay, who continued, "A few nights ago, our close friends stumbled upon a bag with large amounts of cash. They witnessed a car, apparently driven by thugs, being chased by the police and they believe the bag fell out for reasons unknown. My friends are hesitant to turn the money over to the police since they fear they would be suspected of being involved in the crime. They're also not sure if the police would return all the money to the owner. They are in a dilemma."

"I understand their predicament, but what do you expect me to do, Jay?"

"Perhaps, it might be possible for you to find out if someone important has lost a large amount of cash. My friends would like to return the money directly to the owner by using the good offices of some trusted person, like an attorney."

Maina weighed in on what he heard before responding. "Quite an interesting situation, but not one I'd like to be in. There must be additional information that might be of help."

Jay briefly narrated the incident on Friday night, after which Maina responded, "I'm not sure if I could be of much help, Jay."

Undeterred, Jay asked, "How well do you know the Police Commissioner, Michael Karanja?"

"Quite well."

Jay made his final pitch. "Then would it be possible for you to talk to him and get him to agree to our proposal—that someone has the money and is willing to return it directly to the owner? But no questions are to be asked."

Maina leaned back and stared at Jay for a long time. He then shrugged his shoulders, glanced at his watch, and said, "I'll give this some thought. Look, we are running late for our meeting. I'll talk to you later if I need more information."

\*\*\*

*"The poor, aging lion yesterday, the hapless gazelle to-day..." "The old order had to make way for the new." "... in its raw, natural state, where only the fittest survive." "Perhaps Mary Wilson underestimated the dangers of stepping out of her vehicle into the open."* Nagging doubts troubled Nick Cunningham for the rest of the trip. Shortly before noon, their Land Rover pulled up at the campsite, where Mary Wilson had spent her last days.

They walked into a log cabin office where a tall, slim gentleman with sharp features and elongated, pointed ears greeted them. He was the manager, Paul Oloitokitok, and Peter asked him to narrate all the events relating to Mary Wilson's stay at the camp.

Paul showed them the spot where Mary had pitched her tent and camped for a week. In a rented vehicle, she had driven around alone in the vast game park that stretched into the even larger Serengeti in neighboring Tanzania. In Paul's opinion, Mary was unlike the other tourists: apart from her keen interest in wildlife, she displayed greater curiosity in the lifestyles of the local Maasai people. Of particular interest to her was how they interacted with the wildlife around them and came to terms with sharing the natural resources. She had expressed disappointment about the lack of concern among the local authorities on matters of deforestation, conservation, and poaching.

Toward the end of her stay, she made friends with a male British tourist. They traveled together in his vehicle on his last day. He left early the next morning for Nairobi. A half hour later, Mary drove out of the camp in her vehicle, never to return.

"What do you think was the cause of her death?" Nick asked Paul.

Paul appeared to hesitate, as Peter Otieno glared at him. "The police have investigated and given their report," he finally answered.

"Do you believe wild animals could have mauled her to death? Or was she killed in a brush fire? Have there been deaths as a result of such causes?"

After a moment's reflection, Paul answered, "We've had accidents when overconfident visitors step out of their vehicles. They seem to forget how dangerous it is out there."

"... *underestimated the dangers of stepping out...*" Nick muttered to himself. He asked, "Could humans be responsible for her death?"

"I can't say."

"Were the Maasais upset with her for being too inquisitive?"

"Even if they were unhappy, they would never harm a woman," Paul defended his tribesmen.

Nick had no more questions. He thanked Paul and said he might come back after visiting the site where her body had been discovered.

As they walked toward the vehicle, Paul stopped and said, "That lady: she was very curious and wanted to know so many things. On the last day, I told her to be more careful and not ask too many awkward questions; some people might get upset and she could get into trouble. To this day, I wonder if my warning was too late."

"Which people could she have upset, and on what issues?" Nick wanted to know.

Paul offered no reply, but turned toward Peter and said, "I told her this is Kenya."

Nick looked toward Peter, who merely shrugged his shoulders. Nick knew Paul's lips were sealed as long as Peter was around. He climbed into the Land Rover and they headed toward their next stop.

\*\*\*

Deputy Inspector Toto Kilonzo pulled up his vehicle in a small clearing on a dirt road, from where he could view the gate to Mikhail Smirnoff's house. He was driving a white Toyota sedan, assigned to him especially for this mission.

He heaved a sigh of relief that the most arduous assignments of the last two days were behind him. He had not been fully briefed on how exactly he fitted into his department's elaborate plan of which, he was told, he was a vital link. His bosses played it up as though they were undertaking a covert operation. But others in the department were not fooled—they knew it was part of the rapidly unfolding drama of "The Baffling Case of the Missing Briefcase."

For his part, Toto was to strictly carry out whatever he was instructed by whoever might be his supervisor. His problem was that the supervisors came up with schemes that were hare-brained at best, with vague instructions for him to follow.

The two tasks so far had been challenging. He was told the previous morning to pose as a technician of the Power and Lighting Company in a hastily arranged, shoddy uniform. The site was close to where his vehicle was now parked and he had been told to keep an eye on two other men who would be working nearby. He had to figure out what was required of him as a technician. He did as best he could, which his boss later on said was not good enough. Besides, he was lucky not to have been bitten by a small vicious dog in the neighborhood.

This morning, he was required to pose as a technician from a security firm. He was told to carry a toolkit and the only kit he could lay his hands on was an auto toolbox: his arms still ached from carrying the heavy box around. To add to his woes, he had stumbled upon an anthill of red ants. The swollen marks on his legs bore grim testimony to his sufferings. He had managed to dash home for a quick shower and change before he proceeded to the Stores Department to pick up the vehicle. It was an old white Toyota and there was nothing to distinguish it from the hundreds of other similar Toyotas on the streets of Nairobi.

Before he branched off from the main road onto the dirt road, he had noticed an old Mazda sedan parked along the main road. Toto was told that a getaway vehicle for the gang would be parked along the main road and that he should stay away from it.

His cell phone rang. His supervisor for this assignment, Bic Okello, informed him that the "operation" would soon commence. He reminded Toto to be vigilant for the next hour so that there was no unwanted intrusion from the security firm or any visitors.

There was little else to do but wait, and Toto turned on the car radio. His thoughts drifted to the attractive assistant named Jane in the Stores Department whom he'd met while picking up the car. They shook hands when they introduced themselves and her skin felt so soft and sensual that he continued holding her hand until she quietly withdrew it.

They made small talk and when she turned away, Toto could barely take his eyes off her well-formed hips as they swayed as she walked. When she turned sideways, he could view her profile and his eyes feasted on all the well-developed parts of her anatomy. With little happening outside to keep his mind occupied and with heady music from the radio for company, Toto mused over his romantic tryst earlier that afternoon. Visions of Jane appeared before him as he drifted into his world of fantasy.

*** 

A few miles from the campsite, Nick and Peter made their next stop—the site where Mary Wilson's body had been discovered.

Nick stepped out of the vehicle and started to inspect the surrounding area. Investigators from more than one department had already trampled upon the site and Nick was aware there would be little, if any, undisturbed evidence that might be of use to him. But he patiently went around, looking for clues while taking pictures, collecting samples, and making notes in his diary. Peter hung around nearby and, at Nick's request, allowed him to continue the investigation undisturbed.

A short distance from where Mary's remains were found, Nick came across a patch of dry undergrowth. He bent down to examine the ground—there were unmistakable signs of shoe prints. He surmised that it had probably rained when someone had stepped on that patch, and the shoe prints had remained intact after the patch dried up. He noted that the prints led to a shrub, but found no further clues when he walked to the shrub and inspected the area around it. A short distance away was a small rock, but nothing of interest showed up.

Nick looked around. *What exactly happened here seven weeks ago?* he wondered. *Who could have wanted Mary Wilson dead? Would the local people really have been upset with her for being too inquisitive?* From what little information he could gather from the forensic reports, it was highly improbable that she died of gunshot wounds. A more probable cause was strangulation. But how could he prove anything, when there was virtually nothing for him to work with?

He had been speculating that Mary had been dragged out of her vehicle, against her will, by her assailants. But if the shoe prints belonged to her, it meant that she had stepped out of her car and walked. Doubts raced through his mind; "... *perhaps Mary Wilson underestimated the dangers of stepping out of her vehicle into the open.*"

The sun was disappearing over the horizon when Peter reminded Nick that it was time to head back to their lodge.

# Chapter 10

## *Late Thursday*

With mounting trepidation, Don approached Mikhail Smirnoff's house, his forehead glistening with beads of perspiration. He was on a mission he had never carried out before—breaking into a private home. The more dangerous operations like ivory poaching and drug running were his areas of expertise; not mundane ones like house break-ins. But there was no one else he could blame—he had not been vigilant enough the night when the thief snatched the briefcase.

For today's mission, Don had to depend on his deputy, Paul, who touted his experience of having burgled several homes before he teamed up with Don. Picking open the most secure locks was no problem for him, he claimed, but that was not enough to satisfy Don. Had he burgled only the homes of *Muhindis* (Indians), who were softer targets than *Mzungus* (Europeans), one of whose homes they were about to break into?

Don had positioned one of his assistants, Mike, near the front gate, with instructions to alert them by phone in the event he sighted anyone suspicious. One more assistant, Francis, was with him and Paul as they stood outside the compound wall and surveyed the rear of the house. Each one carried a gun on his person and a backpack with tools and ropes. With no one in sight, they clambered up the rear wall and slid down inside. They were now at the back of Mikhail's single-story house.

Paul gestured that one of the windows was not bolted—not entirely surprising, since daytime burglaries were uncommon. After pulling open the window, Paul whispered it would be easier to break through the security grills on the window than break open the rear kitchen door and deal with the drop bolts on it. Don nodded in approval.

From his bag, Paul pulled out a pair of heavy-duty metal shears that he handed over to Francis, while he donned a pair of industrial gloves. While Francis cut through one of the metal grills, Paul firmly gripped the rod with both hands to dampen the sound. Working silently, they cut through all metal grills and bent them outward. There was now an opening large enough for one person to enter. Don gestured to Paul to enter first. Squeezing himself through the opening, he peered around and beckoned the others to follow.

\*\*\*

Reaching home after leaving the hospital, Mikhail took a shower and was dressing when he heard a thumping sound. He paused for a moment before he resumed buttoning up his shirt when he heard the sound again and wondered if the maid had returned. But this sound was different and when he heard it for the third time, he suspected he had unwanted visitors.

Stealthily tiptoeing into the bedroom, he found it puzzling that burglars would attempt to break in while he was at home. They were probably not expecting anyone inside at this time and had been unable to sight his car parked in the front porch.

He stuck his head outside the bedroom and listened. From the rustling sounds, he sensed that at least one of the intruders was in the dining room area. Slinking back in, he opened the dresser and pulled out a Makarov 9mm pistol. From the closet, he picked up a powerful Kalashnikov automatic pistol, making sure they both were loaded. Thus armed with one weapon in each of his powerful hands, he made his way toward the door and leaned against it. He heard the whispering of at least two men and heard their footsteps approaching the bedrooms.

While in the Soviet Army, Mikhail had fought on several battlefronts, with a few close encounters. Proficient in handling powerful weapons, he had inflicted heavy casualties on his enemies. But the setting today was different—his house was no battlefield and it had been years since he had handled a weapon. Besides, this would be his first encounter in Kenya, where he would be facing armed burglars.

Taking a deep breath and firmly gripping both weapons, Mikhail stepped out of the room. Pointing the guns at the intruders, he roared, "Stop! Throw your weapons down or I'll shoot!"

The effect was electrifying. The man closest to him almost jumped and shrieked in fright. He dropped his pistol to the ground, prompting Mikhail to step back for fear of it going off. Another man stood farther back and he lowered his gun. A third intruder near the dining room window did not hold a weapon.

Don's assistant, Paul, was the man in the forefront of this confrontation, something he was ill prepared for.

No one was expected inside the house and the sight of a big, brawny, white man with menacing looks and even more menacing-looking guns in both hands was too much for him. His shriek was accompanied by a puffing sound that escaped uncontrollably through an orifice in another part of his body. Despite this setback, he managed, with remarkable self-control, to gather his wits and, raising his hands up, pleaded, "Oh, *Mzee* (sir), please, we mean no harm. Don't use the gun."

"Get the hell out of here or I'll shoot," thundered Mikhail.

"Please tell us where you've kept the money that was in the car outside your house last week," Paul calmly countered.

Mikhail was astounded by the man's ability to maintain his cool. He had expected the intruder to be scared out of his wits on seeing the powerful weapons and yet, here he was, carrying out a conversation, visibly unperturbed. Somewhat unsettled, Mikhail sought clarification to Paul's remark. "Money, what money?"

Before Paul could respond, a peculiar stench pervaded the atmosphere. Waving one of his arms to and fro in front of his nose to clear the air, Mikhail growled, "You bastards also had to fart and mess up my house!"

Francis, the third member, who stood by the window, could not suppress a titter.

"Stop laughing and get the hell out of here," Mikhail barked.

Emboldened by Paul's responses, Francis said, "Sorry, *Mzee,* but my colleague had too much *maragwe* (red beans) for lunch. But we mean no harm; please keep your guns away."

Don was not entirely pleased with the manner in which this encounter was proceeding. He too had been taken by surprise at the sight of a heavily armed man. He held on to his gun, even though it made a pathetic contrast to Mikhail's sophisticated weapons. And unknown to Don, Paul's pistol sometimes jammed, while Francis's revolver was not even working. He heard Paul ignoring the Russian's threats and continuing with his request. "There was a briefcase with money in that car—it's been missing."

Don scolded Paul in Kiswahili, "You fool, why are you telling him all this?"

But Francis called from behind, "It was an expensive Italian briefcase."

Paul continued, "We'll be in real trouble if we don't find the money—please, *Mzee*, just hand over the money and we'll go away."

"And how about the briefcase?" asked Francis. "It was a gift from the Somali to the *Bwana Kubwa* (Big Boss). I was going to ask him for it."

Don hollered, "Shut up!"

Paul said, "But last time, the boss said he would give something to me."

"No," said Don, "he told me he would give it to me."

"See," said Francis. "You always get the best stuff."

"That's right," said Paul. "Whether it's the Rolex wristwatch or the Pierre Cardin sunglasses from the Gulf guy."

"One of the lenses had a crack. It was of no use," said Don. He turned to a bewildered Mikhail and said in a commanding voice, "Quick, brother, we need the money."

"There was no briefcase in the car and no money," retorted Mikhail. "Now, I want you guys out!"

Francis was the first to respond. "Sir, you can keep the briefcase, but give us the money. We'll understand; after all, you might not be getting Italian leather goods in your country—Germany right?"

"I'm not a German—I'm Russian," shouted Mikhail, "and we get plenty of Italian goods in Russia."

Paul cut in, "What my colleague is saying, *Mzee*, is that please, we need some money. So please give us what you have and we will leave without anyone getting hurt."

Paul's cool demeanor might have unsettled Mikhail, but it made Don even more impatient.

"*Haraka, haraka* (hurry), *Mzee*," Don said to Mikhail.

Paul interrupted Don. "No, take your time, *Mzee*," he said, "We'll put away our guns and you can take your time in bringing us the cash and we'll then go away."

Mikhail sounded even more exasperated. "Look, guys, I don't know what money you are talking about— I'll repeat, there was no money in the car, just one badly wounded guy near the car, who later died in the hospital. Why didn't you guys meet him before he died—he might have been able to help you."

Don looked puzzled. "How could he have helped us?"

"Maybe he would have told you where he kept the briefcase. There was nothing on him," Mikhail replied.

Paul said, "Nothing on him? Now, this is very confusing, Don. I told you our man in the police department is not giving you all the information. Maybe the police found the money in the car and are keeping quiet."

Before Don could respond, there were footsteps outside the front door and all conversation ceased as the doorbell rang.

***

While Mikhail and the intruders were engaged in this stimulating conversation, the *askari* at the gate needed to relieve himself. His master, who had unexpectedly driven in an hour earlier, had said he'd soon be leaving. While he was still in, the guard decided to go for a quick pee.

He walked toward the toilet in the maid's quarters at the back of the house. As he passed the house, he heard voices within and paused to listen. He assumed the master was on the phone, but he heard more than one person's voice. Unsure of what was going on, he decided to check and walked toward the front door to ring the doorbell.

***

"Who's it?" Don whispered to Francis.

"The *askari*."

"Why did you call him?" Don asked Mikhail.

"I didn't—how could I have?" Mikhail responded.

"Francis," commanded Don, "you have to tackle the *askari*—we need him to open the gate for us. Paul, phone Mike and tell him to pull the car up to the gate." Turning to Mikhail, he said, "We don't want any bloodshed—so please listen. Let us go away and don't call the police. No one will get hurt—neither you nor the *askari*."

196

Mikhail moved toward the front door, still holding on to the weapons. Meanwhile, Francis moved to the front door and flung it open, catching the *askari* by surprise. Grabbing him by the neck, Francis held the gun against his head and ordered, "Move to the gate."

Don and Paul made their way to the front door, but when they attempted to step out, they found Francis and the *askari* blocking the way.

"He says he must go for a piss—his bladder is about to burst," Francis explained to Don.

"Why didn't you go for a piss earlier?" a vexed Don asked the *askari*.

"I go to piss only when I need to, not otherwise," came the stoic response. "I came here to piss in the toilet at the back."

"What—you came here? Why don't you piss near the gate in the open?" Don sounded irritated.

"I can't do it today when the boss is at home," explained the *askari*. "He'd skin me alive if he caught me pissing near his house. I've seen him skin chickens with his bare hands and he wouldn't hesitate to do the same to me if he saw me messing around inside the compound."

A quick glance at the Russian's hands dispelled any doubts Don might have entertained about the *askari's* explanation. "Okay, okay, go quickly—and don't try anything funny—even I can skin chickens."

The *askari* walked toward the toilet. Meanwhile, Mikhail called out as he approached the door, "What's holding you guys up?"

"The *askari* had to piss," replied Paul.

"Hurry up—my daughter's in the hospital and I've got to get back," said Mikhail.

"Hospital?" Francis could not resist asking. "Is it the same hospital where you admitted the injured man last week?"

"I don't know where that man was admitted by the police," came the gruff response from the Russian as he slammed the front door.

A few minutes later, a physically and visibly relieved *askari* watched as the three intruders left in the car that had just pulled up at the front gate.

***

Partially hidden behind a shrub near Mikhail's gate, in a parked Toyota, Toto Kilonzo was adrift in a fantasy revolving around his encounter with the Stores Department's assistant, Jane. Swaying her hips, she approached him with a seductive gait and leaned forward, placing her elbows on the counter while she dangled the car keys in front of him. His heart started to pound as he eyed her ample bosom, exposed especially for him, over her low-cut blouse. He lifted his hand to grasp the car keys when she giggled and dropped them into her blouse. He stretched out his hand to grope her breasts when the sound of an oncoming vehicle brought him out of his fantasy. Reluctantly, he forced himself to part with the vision of Jane and attempted to focus on what was happening around him.

A car was rushing down the dirt road. It was the same Mazda that had been parked on the main road. Toto glanced toward the gate and observed three men rush to the approaching vehicle; after they jumped in, it sped away.

Apparently, the planned operation was over, Toto surmised, and checked the time. Barely twenty minutes, nowhere near the hour his boss had mentioned. He felt cheated that his reverie of the rendezvous with Jane had to end so abruptly. The men—whoever they were—appeared to have done a very efficient job.

Toto called Bic Okello to let him know that three men had left—his supervisor sounded surprised and asked him to await further instructions. In a few minutes, he called back to say the mission had not been accomplished and Toto should head back.

\*\*\*

Don gave vent to his frustrations the moment the Mazda took off. He blamed his assistants for indulging in frivolous arguments that led to the debacle. The accusation didn't help: it resulted in finger-pointing. Hot words were exchanged before Don lamented, "We would not have been in this mess if you guys had been alert that night and warned me when that fox snatched the briefcase."

"Don, there's no use blaming anyone," Paul said. "We've been in one mess after another, right from the time you took down the elephants. And your police friend gave you the wrong information. He told you that bear-like man was not in town, but there he was, sitting and waiting for us with his big guns. We had no chance. Now your friend must give us correct information so that we can finish the job."

But Don was inconsolable. "I'm ruined," he shook his head. "I'm ruined."

\*\*\*

Mikhail headed for the liquor cabinet and took a large swig of vodka—a well-deserved treat, he reasoned, after this harrowing experience with the burglars. He called Olga at the hospital to give her a brief account of the encounter and said he'd drive to the hospital after he'd lodged a complaint with the police.

After one more swig of the vodka, he decided to seek the advice of the Russian Embassy. He put through a call to his good acquaintance, Boris Karpov, the Deputy Ambassador. He briefed him about the incident and said he planned on putting in an insurance claim for the damage to his property. The official said it would be necessary to lodge a complaint with the police before filing the claim. A personal visit to the police station would be essential and, to speed things up, Karpov agreed to accompany him. As an added precaution, he would ask a lawyer from a law firm they worked with to accompany them.

Before hanging up, the official asked, "Did you say not a single shot was fired, no one was injured, and the burglars walked away without any goods?"

"Yes," replied Mikhail.

"Strange—very strange," was the response.

They met at the police station, where Mikhail was introduced to the Kenyan lawyer, James Kariuki. At the front desk, they approached the officer on duty, who took down details of the incident. After reading his notes, he asked with a puzzled expression, "Since nothing has been stolen and the burglars ran away, why do you wish to report this incident to us?"

"We demand the thugs be brought to justice for breaking into my client's residence," said Kariuki, adding a new dimension to the purpose of their visit.

The officer shrugged his shoulders. "I'll see how my boss can help."

When he returned, he ushered them into the office of Gideon Odhiambo, the Deputy Police Commissioner. *Yes,* thought Mikhail, *having the Deputy Ambassador and a lawyer accompany you does open doors to a senior official.*

The Deputy Commissioner greeted them and asked his secretary to organize tea and coffee for the visitors. He addressed Mikhail. "My assistant tells me you had a very dangerous situation in your house?"

"Yes, *Bwana* Commissioner," Kariuki interjected. "I think it's best you hear from my client his traumatic experience and his daring in fighting off the thugs single-handedly."

Mikhail narrated his experience, concluding with, "They kept asking me for money that was supposed to be in the car that had been abandoned near my house."

"Oh yes, the Nissan. I remember that well. So, that was what they were after," Odhiambo nodded. "Did you give them the money?"

"Of course not."

"You mean you have the money and didn't give it to them?" Odhiambo clarified.

"I don't have any money," Mikhail responded in exasperation.

Boris Karpov turned to Mikhail and remarked, "I wasn't aware of the abandoned Nissan near your house. Whose car was it and do we know where the money is?"

Mikhail grated his teeth and muttered, "No."

"Please continue," Kariuki suggested to Mikhail.

"I threatened to shoot them if they didn't leave and they backed off," said Mikhail. "But they kept repeating they'd be in trouble with their *Bwana Kubwa* (Big Boss) if they failed to bring the money."

Odhiambo looked at Karpov. "Who's the *Bwana Kubwa?*"

Karpov turned to Mikhail. "I don't know—who is he?"

"I don't know—I'll repeat, I know nothing about what they were asking," said Mikhail, "not even the Italian leather briefcase that they kept talking about."

"I've seen you carry a stylish briefcase," Karpov said to Mikhail. "Is that what they were looking for?"

"Mine is an imitation piece from Taiwan—it's not genuine leather. And why would anyone break into my house to steal a cheap briefcase?"

"It's important that we establish the motive behind the attempted burglary," Kariuki said in a somber tone, adding, "a totally uncalled-for and senseless act that has subjected my client to enormous stress and trauma."

Odhiambo asked Mikhail, "So, those thugs wanted money and an expensive briefcase? Did they say the color of the briefcase was bhey... well, never mind. It's obvious they were after some big stuff. And you say you have nothing?"

"That's what I've been saying all along—I don't have anything and I've no idea what they wanted," Mikhail replied. "I'm glad the *askari* came at that time, since he had to pee. The thugs were able to get away after that."

"Does the *askari* come to your house to pee?" Odhiambo asked.

"Of course not," replied Mikhail. "He was on his way to the toilet at the back when he heard our voices and came to the front door to check. The thugs held him at gunpoint and made their way to the gate, from where they drove off."

"And that was all there was to it?" Odhiambo asked, adding with a smirk, "it was indeed fortunate that the *askari* had to go for a pee and passed by before anything serious happened."

The Deputy Ambassador remarked, "This could be one instance when attending nature's call turned out to be a blessing in disguise."

He appeared pleased with his comment and looked around, but Mikhail wasn't amused. He sat dour-faced and reflected that he would gladly have forgone lodging an insurance claim if he had any forewarning about the ordeal that he was going to be put through.

"We're happy that all's well, but the thugs mustn't get away scot-free," said Kariuki

Odhiambo addressed Mikhail. "You say you chased the thugs away and they did no harm, nor did they take anything from you?"

"Yes."

"And not a single shot was fired; the thugs walked away without causing any injury?" Odhiambo continued.

This time, Mikhail grunted, as he silently suffered the indignity of being subjected to the same line of questioning.

Odhiambo was quiet for a moment. Turning to Kariuki, he said, "I don't believe such a case has ever been reported where the house owner chases the thieves away and there is no injury or theft. What do you expect us to do?"

The lawyer responded, "My client can provide a description of the thugs—you should be able to pick them up for questioning."

Odhiambo summoned his assistant for taking down notes while Mikhail was asked to narrate the events. Of particular importance was the dialogue about the Somali and the expensive Italian briefcase for the *Bwana Kubwa*. After the notes were transcribed, Odhiambo asked the officer, "Did you get them to fill in the correct form?"

"I was not sure which form to use," he responded.

"My dear fellow," Odhiambo chided him, as he opened a drawer in his desk. "I have told you guys about the new form that I've designed for such occasions—when thieves break in but are unable to burgle anything and no one's hurt."

With a flourish, he pulled out a ream of brown-colored forms. Moistening his middle finger and thumb, he peeled off a crisp new form and said, "See, this is the form that they need to fill in." Handing it over to Kariuki, he said, "Please make sure all details of the incident and description of the burglars are filled in. My men will work on the clues and attempt to identify the thugs."

As they rose to leave, Odhiambo said to Mikhail, "*Bwana* Smirnoff, you did a great job of scaring the thugs away. I hope these *Muhindis* (the Indians and Asians) would take some tips from you. They are the guys who get robbed the most."

Mikhail and his colleagues filled in the form, thanked the police officials and left, with Mikhail heading for the hospital.

***

Despite the late hour, the Police Commissioner called a meeting to conduct a postmortem of the afternoon's debacle. With him were his deputy, Gideon Odhiambo, and Inspectors Bono Njoroge and Bic Okello. The Commissioner kicked off the meeting by targeting his hapless officer. "Well, Bic, your man sprinted away with his tail between his legs."

Bic was prepared with his response. "Sir, the Russian was armed to the teeth with some of the most modern weaponry available. This confirms my view that he's an arms dealer and must be involved in the theft."

"But the men you sent did not even put up a fight," pitched in Bono, ridiculing Bic. "Were they carrying toy guns or water pistols?" His big face, with its bulbous nose, opened up in a wide smile, as Bic squirmed uncomfortably.

Gideon Odhiambo came to Bic's rescue. "I met the Russian when he was here to lodge a complaint. He's big in size and is obviously well armed. But, Bic, how did you plan for them to break into his house when he was there?"

"He left the country two days ago and was not expected to be at home," replied Bic.

"That means your information about his being away was incorrect," commented Karanja.

"No, sir, it's a fact that he left two days ago, but he returned unexpectedly today. My contact at the airport wasn't on duty, or else I'd have known."

Karanja felt gentle vibrations on the large conference table and on his chair. He glanced in the direction of Bono Njoroge, seated alone in a corner. The little finger of his left hand was inserted into his ear and he vigorously jiggled his arm around the ear, obviously to relieve an itch. Conversation at the table ceased, as all eyes turned to establish the cause of the vibrations. Sensing all eyes on him, Bono looked up in embarrassment and lowered his arm.

Karanja resumed. "Bic, do you still maintain that the Russian is involved?"

"I'll keep that bear—that Yeti—under my watch. I know he's in some *magendo* (illegal) business, and I'm sure he'll lead us to something," Bic persisted.

"What do we do we in the meantime?" Odhiambo asked.

A squeaky sound and gentle vibrations from Bono's corner once again distracted them. They turned to see him jiggling the eraser tip on a pencil in his belligerent ear, his eyes shut and an expression of blissful relief on his large face. He opened his eyes upon realizing the conversation again had ceased.

"While we continue to check out the Russian, maybe we should go ahead with Bono's plans with the Indian," Karanja proposed.

Bono looked up with rapt attention, despite the persistent itch in his ear. "Yes, sir."

"How far are you in getting ready with that operation, Bono?" Karanja asked.

"Sir, I'm ready. The men carried out the survey today and we can go ahead with the plans tomorrow."

"Now, is there a lesson to be learned from what happened today?" Karanja asked. "Let's hope your guys don't make a mess of it."

"The men involved have far more experience than the ones who were there today," bragged Bono. "These men are ruthless and will do what is expected of them."

"We need to put this behind us quickly," Karanja appeared tired as he closed the meeting.

His assistants had barely left the room when his phone rang. It was Peter Otieno, calling from the lodge in the Maasai Mara. He gave the Commissioner a report on the last two days' activities with Nick Cunningham— which, he proudly announced, was not much. He described how his maneuvers the previous day had resulted in Nick wasting a full day without uncovering any fresh clues or evidence. Peter also felt that Nick was beginning to accept the police version that Mary Wilson's death could have been caused by her stepping out of her vehicle into the wild. To reinforce that possibility, Peter had passed on to Nick a wildlife magazine that highlighted the dangers of overzealous tourists stepping out of the safety of their vehicles into the open.

"We shall be meeting the game park rangers tomorrow," said Peter. "I hope they are well briefed on what their responses should be."

"Yes, they've been briefed that they should stick to the same version. Keep me informed."

Karanja sat staring at the portrait of the President mounted on the wall in front of him. Nothing had gone right today; would tomorrow's planned operation swing the tide in his favor?

***

Built atop a wooden platform, the Toona Tree restaurant and the surrounding complex straddles a hillock and overlooks the city's main arterial road, *Uhuru* (Independence) Highway. A large toona tree (a type of mahogany), after which the restaurant is named, covers the complex. The two open sides of the restaurant offer a panoramic view of the jacaranda tree-lined avenue below.

Jay had reserved a corner table offering the best view, where he and Heidi took their seats. She remarked that their favorite local band was in attendance, accompanied by the female crooner with a silken voice. The live music, the excellent Italian cuisine, and the ambiance always made dining at the Toona Tree a delightful experience, and Jay hoped tonight would be no different. The two had agreed there would be no conversation on the events of the past week.

Jay ordered a South African cabernet sauvignon, while Heidi selected a white wine from the vineyards at Naivasha. As they clicked their glasses, Jay toasted to their eighteen years. *"Zu unserem achtzehn jahren, liebchen."* He took her hands and raised them to his lips.

Not forthcoming from Heidi was the warm smile that Jay had hoped for. Instead, all she said was, "Eighteen years, yah? But it's not quite our anniversary."

"Eighteen years ago, to this day, we went out on our first date," he smiled. He had tweaked the days a bit, but he could think of no better reason to give her to celebrate.

She didn't bother to dispute as she sipped the wine and turned her attention toward the band playing "Staying Alive" from the Bee Gees. It was one of her favorite tunes and she gradually began to sway to the beat. Sensing a change in her mood, Jay leaned forward and said, "I still recall how I felt about you that evening, eighteen years ago, and nothing has changed my feelings ever since."

She turned to face him and picked up her glass for one more sip. Continuing to sway to the rhythm, she broke into a smile. "You know you can say the same about me. We've spent some pretty wild times together, haven't we?"

"Oh, yeah. I don't think I've ever missed out a chance on that, have I?"

She shook her head. "Probably not. Let's see—when was the first time that you did something—shall we say a bit wild?"

Jay paused for a moment before responding. "That's got to be the time when we spent a weekend in West Berlin without your parents' approval. Oh, it made your brother so mad—you should have seen the way he glared at me when we got back."

"Yah, I know how mean Kurt could be. And he wasn't that way just with you. But that was quite cheeky of us, wasn't it?"

Their conversation was interrupted as the waiter served dinner. Jay had ordered his favorite *Wiener Schnitzel*, while Heidi ordered grilled red snapper. She loved the variety of fresh seafood that was readily available from the Indian Ocean. Both their entrees were served with generous portions of sautéed fresh vegetables, also available in abundant variety from the nearby farms in the Highlands.

While they enjoyed their meal, the band played a local hit, "Jambo, Jambo Bwana." This was another of Heidi's favorite tunes and, as she sipped her wine, she reminisced, "Some of the things that you did were downright stupid—but... but, it seemed like fun later on."

Jay looked up to see her fluttering her long eyelashes with a mischievous smile on her face. He realized she had been sipping wine faster than she normally did and the effect showed. But he was not complaining and he queried, "Now, now, aren't you thinking of something silly? Tell me, what is it?"

"I was thinking of what you were up to at the Amboseli Game Park when the cheetah jumped on our van."

Jay leaned back and chuckled as he recalled the incident. Two years earlier, they had traveled to the game park with friends in a minivan with a retractable roof. Their driver spotted a cheetah striding across the savannah; he looked content, obviously just having had a meal and posed no danger. Their van stopped as the beast continued to stride toward them, but instead of crossing the track, he disappeared from their view, only to suddenly appear at the rear of the vehicle and leap up to the roof, part of which was retracted! While those in the vehicle crouched in fear, the cheetah casually looked around and settled down on the front of the roof. Thrilled by this unusual spectacle, other tourist vehicles approached them, but the beast showed little interest in them. Instead, he settled down comfortably for what appeared to be a snooze! The ordeal of those in the vehicle lasted a few minutes, as they continued to sit in hushed silence. But soon, the sounds from the increasing number of tourist vehicles around them disturbed the cheetah and it stood up on the roof and looked around. Leaning forward on its haunches, it raised its tail and stayed in that position for what seemed to Jay like one full minute. He knew he had to act and had whispered, "He's going to do his business and it's going to land right in here! I'll have to push him over," and had started to reach for the beast's tail. Heidi used all her strength to hold Jay back as the cheetah turned around toward Jay and snarled before jumping off the vehicle.

Recalling that incident, Jay couldn't resist chuckling. "What an experience! Just imagine if he'd pissed or pooped right on us!"

"And just imagine what he would've done if you'd caught him by his tail!"

The mood was much lighter by the time they finished their desserts. "Let's dance," said Jay; they both loved to dance the blues—way back from their days in Germany.

"It's something in the way you hold me that's so special," Heidi had mentioned during their courting days. "It's different from the way others hold me."

"You've been dancing with too many Germans—with stiff and frigid arms," he had teased her. "See how different it is when you dance with someone from the land of *Kama Sutra* (the famed Indian treatise on love-making, complete with illustrations)?"

She now recalled their conversation many years earlier and said, "The *Kama Sutra* hasn't been of much help in the last week, has it?"

"I guess the author could never have imagined a scenario where his readers needed advice on how to go about making love while they have stolen cash stashed away in their closet."

"*Schatz,* see how much our life has been affected? And the stash is just sitting there."

"And we can't practice any of the stuff given in that book while we are supposed to be on our second honeymoon," Jay added with remorse.

*Time to change the subject and the mood,* he thought, as he looked her in the eye and said, "Now that you've reminded me of the cheetah incident, you've also reminded me of something else."

"Of what?"

"The thing that happened to you when the cheetah was sitting on our van also happened last week during the shootout: both times you peed in your pants!"

She pinched his back while he held her tightly as they danced, with the female crooner belting away their favorite number, "I'm in the Mood for Love."

As she cuddled up close to him, they were the only couple left on the floor and some diners looked up in surprise at the love-smitten couple; such a public display of affection was rare in the modest Kenyan society—but Jay and Heidi could not have cared less.

# Chapter 11

## Week 2—Friday

"It's there in the newspaper! Boss, we'd decided we didn't want these incidents to be reported by the press." A visibly agitated Inspector Julius Wachira thrust a copy of the local daily toward the Commissioner.

"What are you talking about, Julius?" Karanja asked as he reached for the newspaper. After reading the offending news item, he sighed. "Now, who could have passed on this information to the press?"

The item was brief, but in bold print on the front page: **"Russian Executive Chases Away Armed Intruders."**

The report described the break-in by armed burglars during the daytime into the house of a Russian company executive in Lower Kabete. He had returned home early from a business trip and had surprised the burglars as they broke into his house, apparently unaware of his presence. They were reportedly looking for a briefcase with money that had gone missing and took flight after he brandished a gun. The report went on to add that a vehicle had been found abandoned late at night near the executive's house about a week earlier. The police were reported to be on the lookout for the intruders.

Karanja picked up the phone and dialed his deputy. "Gideon, who passed on the information about yesterday's burglary to the press?"

"That's exactly what I am checking on right now, sir," came the crisp reply. "I shall report to you within the hour."

"You're right," Karanja admitted to Julius after he hung up. "We don't want anyone to know what happened yesterday—we need to make sure that today's operation is kept secret."

After the inspector had left his office, Karanja called the Minister to convey the depressing news of the previous day. The Minister was furious. "What's going on, Karanja? Who are these idiots who break into a house when the owner is inside?"

"No one was supposed to be at home. The family members and the maid were all away. But the Russian guy returned home from his trip ahead of schedule— what were our guys supposed to do? They were caught unawares and chased away by the Russian, who was armed with modern, powerful weapons."

"Why are you people running around like a chicken without its head? You assured me this plan would work and the briefcase would be recovered. But it failed miserably."

"We've planned a similar operation today on the house of a *Muhindi*," Karanja responded in a calm voice. "As I mentioned, he was seen by some *askaris* near the place where our vehicle confronted the getaway car. We're confident the briefcase will be in his house."

"Are you using the same bunch of idiots?"

"No, sir, the guys today are more experienced."

"Karanja, do you realize almost a week has gone by? I expected you to recover it *mara moja* (promptly). This is not at all good, *Bwana* Commissioner. The President will not be pleased."

"Mr. Minister, today's operation will be successful."

"I hope you're right. And keep this information away from the press."

"Yes, Mr. Minister."

***

Tusker was in a restless mood, fretting on what lay in store for him later in the day. Like Don, he planned to break into a house in the afternoon, when no one was expected to be home. And he too faced similar logistics problems like Don had—he had never been involved in breaking into homes and would need to depend on one of his assistants to do the actual job.

But there had been a startling development on the eve of his planned operation. One of his contacts brought him information about his rival's abortive burglary attempt. Don had broken into a house near the spot where Tusker has abandoned the getaway vehicle—he was also told Don and his men were chased away by the occupant, who was at home when they broke in.

"Ha!" exclaimed Tusker. "Only an idiot like Don would believe the money would be in that house. I hope he also got beaten up in the process." He turned to his assistants. "Now, no messing up like Don, do you understand? If any of you don't do your job properly, you'll get beaten up like Fred was."

He paused to glare at them and his left eye started to twitch. "And if the person who took our briefcase is in the house, I'll hand down a beating he'll never forget."

Adam, his long-time lieutenant, knew it would take several minutes for Tusker's rage to subside. "Let's go and have some *chai*," he suggested, as they broke up.

\*\*\*

After a hectic morning work schedule, Jay settled down for a cup of coffee and reflected on the time spent with Heidi the previous evening. Taking her out had helped, and she appeared to be in a better mood this morning. He opened the newspaper to read in detail a news item whose headline had caught his attention.

The report related to the attempted burglary at a Russian's house the previous day. *Could this be the same person Julius Wachira had spoken about two days ago?* Jay wondered. He had been elated on learning that the police suspected someone else, but now he felt a twinge of guilt that the wrong man had been attacked. He managed to calm his conscience when he read that the Russian could fend for himself and was not seriously injured. But who were the thugs that had broken in in such a brazen manner?

Jay started to wonder if the police had made any progress in tracing the mysterious car to him. They still had not visited to interrogate him, as he had feared. Should he call Julius to find out what was going on? *No,* he thought—he had decided to lie low and not do anything to arouse suspicion. *Just sit tight, for now,* he decided.

He looked at the news item once more. *Was it possible,* the thought occurred to him, *that someone from the police had passed on information about the Russian to those thugs? And if it could happen to the Russian, it could happen to...*

\*\*\*

The rumor mill in the police department whirred at a feverish pitch. A major breakthrough had been expected the previous day, but from all accounts, the highly anticipated mission in "The Baffling Case of the Missing Briefcase" was a resounding failure.

The bosses remained tight-lipped, but the rest of the staff were hard at work—patching together snippets of information garnered from overheard telephone conversations and scribbled notes. Some of the more curious ones stood by the meeting rooms, their ears glued to the walls.

Lucas, the illustrious analyst, had chanced to glimpse the brown form that was filled in the previous evening by Mikhail Smirnoff.

"It appears the fancy Italian briefcase was a gift from the Somali," he whispered to Phyllis, an administrative assistant with a voluptuous figure. Lucas had been casting lustful glances at her, which she ignored.

"Who's the Somali?" she asked.

Attempting to sound mysterious, Lucas responded, "Oh, he's involved with poaching. It's complicated, but I can explain—why don't we meet this evening at the coffee shop?"

She looked away, uninterested, as Toto Kilonzo walked into the general office. Aware of Toto's myriad roles in the grand scheme of things and of his fixation with the female anatomy, Lucas had earlier hinted to Phyllis that she put to use her irresistible physical assets to seductively coax some information out of him. Seeing Toto, Lucas whispered to Phyllis that this was her chance and tactfully walked out of the office, leaving the two alone.

Phyllis stood and moved close to Toto as he pulled a file from a cabinet. He turned around to find Phyllis standing a few inches away. She was adjusting the strap of her bra, and he found himself peering down her low-cut blouse, which offered a tantalizing view of her ample cleavage. He felt his heart begin to throb when he heard her purr, "Hi, Toto. You seem to be very busy these days. Wouldn't you like to share some of your burden with us?"

His head starting to spin, Toto lost his balance and bumped his chest on her upright breasts. The feeling was exhilarating and he stammered, "Thanks, um... but no, I'm fine."

"How about today?" she persisted. "Anything interesting planned for the day?"

But Toto remained steadfast and, even though he wished this close encounter could last indefinitely, he did not succumb. Phyllis observed him turning red behind his ears before he mumbled some excuse and left the room.

Then someone brought in the breaking news: another high-profile operation was slated for later that afternoon. There were some wild speculations on what that operation could be. But one of the superstitious gossip-mongers expressed her view that planning an important operation on a Friday, falling on the thirteenth day of the month, might not be such a good idea.

\*\*\*

Shortly before noon, Nick Cunningham and Peter Otieno reached the Chief Warden's office in the game reserve. Peter had earlier informed the official about the visit and thus the rangers involved with the investigation were available to meet with the detective. Nick spent time with each ranger, asking them to provide details following the discovery of Mary's body. He noted down their responses, but there was nothing he was not already aware of. He asked them if they suspected foul play—no, they responded, and talked about the consequences of tourists stepping out of their vehicles into the wild. And they stressed the fact that Mary's body was found lying outside her vehicle, which suggested she had stepped out. Their response to his next question was no different: the Maasais would never harm an unarmed woman, even if she had been making awkward inquiries about their lifestyle.

Nick stated that the general public did not believe the victim was mauled to death by a wild animal and later succumbed to a forest fire. He pointedly asked them if a senior official could be involved in covering up the real cause of her death. Though all denied any knowledge, one of them didn't seem convincing and appeared to empathize with Nick. A few questions later, Nick realized he was not making any progress—there was little else for him to do but wind up and head back to the lodge.

Nick was pensive on the trip back and Peter opted to leave Nick to himself. The troubling thoughts returned: *Mary underestimated the dangers of being alone in the wild. Where only the fittest survive.*

As the Land Rover rumbled on its journey, Nick's mind was in a state of conflict. *How is it really possible to find any important clues now? Why did Mary get out of her vehicle? Yes, getting out in the wild can be dangerous. What prompted her to do that?*

\*\*\*

It was early afternoon when Tusker and his men approached Jay's house. His thoughts and strategy mirrored those of his archrival, whose mission had ended in a miserable failure. Tusker realized he was more comfortable poaching elephants than breaking into a civilian's house, even an empty one at that. He had positioned one of his assistants, Jacob, to maintain a vigil on the approach road, while Adam and Daniel accompanied him.

It was time to move on. He had sighted a car near the main road that he knew belonged to the police assistant who was assigned to ensure there were no visitors. He checked yet again to ensure they were fully equipped—tools in the backpacks and guns in their pockets.

Thus armed, the task force comprising of "Tusker" John and his trusted lieutenants ventured forth on their assignment, blissfully unaware that virtually one and all at the police headquarters in Nairobi awaited the outcome of their mission with bated breath.

\*\*\*

At the fork where the approach road to Jay's house branched off from the main road was a white Toyota with a listless Toto behind the wheel. As on the previous day, he had picked up the vehicle from the Stores Department. Hoping to strike up a conversation with Jane, the assistant, he had even rehearsed his lines, but to his ill luck, she was busy with her boss. He lingered around, but all that he was rewarded with was a distance glimpse of her well-rounded "booty."

He had noticed a Mitsubishi sedan parked some distance away. A young man in a red cap stepped out and sauntered up to a kiosk that stood farther down. Toto reckoned he must be Tusker's accomplice with the getaway vehicle. He turned to face Toto and nodded. His presence near the gate suggested his mates were within the complex and had embarked on their mission. Inspector Bono Njoroge was directing today's operation and Toto was in communication with him over the cell phone.

Toto pushed his car seat back and felt optimistic that today's mission would be successful, despite not being aware of what the mission was. Hearing the sound of an approaching vehicle, he looked in that direction and saw a VW Beetle slow down and turn onto the approach road. His eyes fell on the driver—a European lady with an attractive face that made him wonder what the rest of her body would look like.

Toto watched idly as cars drove by and people walked past. His thoughts drifted to the encounter earlier today with Phyllis in the office. The thought of her breasts brushing his chest aroused tingling sensations across his body.

He turned on the car radio, rolled down the car window for fresh air, pushed his seat all the way back, and relaxed as he maintained his vigil.

*** 

Back at the lodge by late afternoon, Nick Cunningham relaxed in the lounge over a cup of tea and a plate of finger sandwiches. Peter Otieno left for the manager's office to make a radio call to his department in Nairobi. Noting that the assistant at the front desk was the one he'd spoken with the previous day, Nick walked up to him and said, "Hello, David. Has it been a busy day?"

"Oh hello, Mr. Cunningham. I'm fine. I hope you're enjoying viewing our wildlife."

"Yes, sure. Wouldn't miss it for anything in the world. David, I need a little information. Do senior government officials or ministers often visit this lodge?"

"Well, not too many. A lodge farther down is more popular with them. After all, it is owned by someone influential."

"Do you know this for sure?"

"Yes. My cousin works there."

Nick thought for a moment before continuing, "I think I'll visit that lodge tomorrow. Now, would you be kind enough to call your cousin and find out if he could provide me with some information?"

"What information?"

"Information like who were the ministers or officials who stayed at the lodge during the last two months."

"No harm asking Ben. I'll give him a call and let him know about your request."

"Oh, that would be great. We'll probably have lunch there. Now, please write down for me the name of the lodge and your cousin's name."

Nick had returned to his table for one more cup of tea by the time Peter finished his phone call.

***

It was early afternoon by the time Heidi could head home. The last three days had been strenuous, with visits to embassies and corporate offices to secure pledges for raffle prizes. She felt it was time well spent, since she hoped to achieve the distinction of being able to distribute the highest number of prizes. This was her first afternoon off since schools had closed for vacations, and she looked forward to spending a quiet afternoon at home.

As she drove home, her thoughts were centered on Raj and Anita and she hoped they were enjoying their vacation with her parents. When she drove off the main road onto the approach road, she did not notice a decrepit white vehicle parked alongside the road. Nor did she take any particular note of a young man with a red cap at the roadside kiosk. He eyed her VW Beetle with a disinterested look, but she had no way of knowing that he had instructions to be on the lookout for the Honda Accord that Jay drove.

Heidi slowed down as she approached the gate that led to a dozen townhomes, including theirs. When the *askari* opened the gate and greeted her, she called out, "Ngugi, I have some *chakula* (food) for you. Why don't you come by to pick it up?"

"Yes, Mama, I'll come when I'm a bit free."

Heidi drove into the portico in front of her house and alighted. Opening the front door, she stepped in.

\*\*\*

Nick spent an uneventful evening with Peter, opting to stay in his room as long as possible. For the second time, he read the magazine article Peter had given to him—fatality figures were high for visitors who exited their vehicles while driving in the game parks.

Nick had trouble falling asleep that night. There was nothing that he had uncovered to disprove the official version of Mary's death. Like several others, Mary's father was firm in his belief that there was a cover-up by the authorities on the cause of her death. They trusted him to unravel the truth. And here he was, still without a clue as to what other forces were at play.

As he tossed and turned in his bed, he started to doubt his mind was as sharp as it used to be. Was he getting old? Should this investigation be taken up by someone younger? As he suffered through fitful spells of sleep, images from the previous day returned to haunt him: *The poor aging lion yesterday, the hapless gazelle today. The old order had to make way for the new.*

\*\*\*

As Heidi entered the house and turned to bolt the door, a pair of powerful hands grabbed her from behind, pulling her firmly toward the intruder's body. One hand covered her mouth, while a gun was held to her head. Heidi dropped the bag in her hand and tried to scream, but the only sound she could muster was a muffled groan.

"Shh…" hissed a voice in her ear. "Don't make a sound, or you'll get hurt. Do you understand?"

The voice was guttural and sounded mean and menacing. Heart pounding, Heidi realized her worst nightmare was now a reality. She nodded her head to convey her agreement. Her captor forced her to slowly turn around and face him. He was big in size, with a hideous face that was adorned with large protruding eyes and a round, balding head. And he had foul breath—in fact, all of his body reeked. Two other men stood some distance away; one of them pointed a gun at her.

"We know your car was near the place where the briefcase was dropped off and you people have picked it," said Tusker, who was holding her. "Give us the goods now."

Heidi gestured that she wished to speak, and the man released the pressure on her mouth. She took a deep breath. *Ruhig bleiben* (remain calm), she told herself. *Stay calm and talk your way out of this nightmare.*

"I said, where is the money?" her captor addressed her in a rough tone.

"What money?" she asked defiantly.

"The money was in a briefcase," said Daniel, one of the accomplices. "Please hand over the money, and we'll leave you."

"I don't know what you're talking about," Heidi replied as she looked around, assessing the situation.

"Look, Mama, the money was in a briefcase—made from Italian leather," said Daniel.

"A 'Limited Edition' briefcase," added the third man, Adam.

"Shut up, shut up, you fools," Tusker roared. He looked at Heidi and said, "Quick, Mama, hand it over to us or tell us where it is."

"As I said, I haven't seen your beautiful briefcase."

Heidi might not have spoken the whole truth, but she was not lying. That night, she never got to see the briefcase after Jay had swiftly picked it up from the road and deposited in the rear seat; she had also not seen it when he later took it into the house. Regaining her composure, she did some quick thinking. She noted that only the man gripping her was still holding on to his gun, while the other man had put his away. But the money was in the house and that meant trouble. She had to find a way out—and the best way would be to keep talking.

Meanwhile, Adam decided to take a reasonable approach. "Mama, we know that you were in that neighborhood and you stopped to pick up the briefcase. All we're asking is that you give us back the money."

"Which neighborhood are you talking about?" she asked.

"In Lavington last Friday. We were in a yellow Nissan; it was such a beautiful car to drive." It was Daniel—he could not stop reminiscing about the pleasure of being in the driver's seat.

*Oh, Scheisse* (Oh shit), thought Heidi, *so these are the guys—but how did they find us?*

"Lavington is a large neighborhood. How can you be certain we were there?" she asked.

"There are witnesses who saw you, Mama," Adam spoke in a benevolent tone. "As our chief said, we'll not harm you if you give us the money."

"Your chief doesn't know what he's doing," Heidi decided to change tack and be more aggressive. "He's wasting everyone's time by breaking into our house and looking for money."

It didn't quite turn out the way she had intended. A remark as innocuous as this one was enough to enrage Tusker. Grabbing her around her waist, he spun her around and yanked her toward him, pressing her against his body with his left hand. Wrapping his right palm over her mouth, he snarled into her ear, "Don't act too smart, do you understand?"

He glared at her with such intensity that Heidi turned her head away and meekly shook her head. His left arm moved up at an angle as his forearm now pressed against her breasts. She could feel him breathe faster as he lowered his right hand from her mouth and circled it around her waist to hold her firmly with both hands.

Heidi had braced herself for being smacked by her captor and held her breath for his next move. She glanced down to see his left forearm slide up and down her breast, gently stroking it in the process, while she could sense him gently rubbing his big, round nose in her hair, sniffing the fragrance. *Oh, Mein Gott,* she wondered, *what's going on?*

Her doubts about what was happening were dispelled when she felt the stiffening of his groin against her butt. *Oh no,* she thought, *this beast is getting aroused with me firmly in his clutches!* She glanced toward his face and could see his right protruding eye peering with lust down her blouse at her bosom. His breathing became heavier and faster.

The two accomplices were equally unprepared for the sudden change in their chief's behavior. They had never seen him in such a state before—holding a woman in his arms, fondling her breasts, rubbing his nose in her hair, while peering down at her cleavage. From where they stood, they could hear his heavy breathing and were aghast at the sight of the huge bulge in his crotch. They stood watching this spectacle in awe as Daniel whispered, "Chief has been spending too much time with the elephants."

Heidi was deliberating on her next move when the chimes of the front door bell hushed the conversation.

Daniel tiptoed to the window near the front door and peeked out. "It's the *askari*."

"What does he want?" Tusker hissed to Heidi.

"I had called him to give some food."

"Don't do anything—he'll go away," said Tusker, still breathing heavily.

"No, he won't. I'll have to meet him," said Heidi.

"Daniel, take care of him," ordered Tusker, relaxing his grip on Heidi while displaying irritation on being disturbed while in a sensual state. Daniel cautiously opened the front door.

Heidi decided it was time to act. She heaved herself up against her captor and swung to kick Daniel straight on his butt with her right foot, which jettisoned him out of the house through the door. He landed in the arms of the *askari* outside, who grabbed him and held on tight.

Straightening up, Heidi swung her head back so that it landed with full impact on Tusker's nose, temporarily stunning him. His grip on her slackened and he used one hand to check if his nose was bleeding. Putting months of karate training to good use, Heidi executed some moves in a blinding flash. Exhaling with a shrieking "*Hutch,*" she pummeled her right elbow squarely into Tusker's crotch. The impact was doubly painful, considering the condition that part of his anatomy was in, and she heard a deep whoosh of air as he gasped in pain. In a split second, she lifted her right foot up and, flexing her knee backward, she landed her heel right on his testicles. She was now free from his grip, as he bent forward to clutch his crotch.

Daniel had just been thrown out of the front door and thus missed witnessing a rare spectacle, but his mate Adam did not. A moment earlier, Adam had seen, for the first time, his boss in a highly aroused state, fondling a woman in his arms. The next moment, an astounded Adam watched his indomitable boss being felled by the same woman. But that was not all—Adam now witnessed a phenomenon that no others in the room did.

As various parts of Tusker's body started to register the full impact of the blows meted out by Heidi, his facial responses startled Adam. A smug expression reflecting the sensual state he had been in, until a moment earlier, lingered on one side of Tusker's face. The expression on the other side of Tusker's face though was, by now, contorted with the sheer agony of the blows that had landed on the most sensitive parts of his body. Adam watched, bewildered at these contrasting expressions on two sides of the same face as Tusker sank to the floor.

Heidi next readied herself for the final kill. She swiftly turned around to face a confused Adam, who was holding a pathetic-looking gun. Tusker's gun lay next to him while he writhed in pain on the floor.

Heidi was aware that Jay had placed an iron crowbar behind a table near the front door, to be used for defense in such situations. Snarling like a ferocious feline, she sprang toward the table and, in one swift movement, snatched the crowbar and pointed it at Adam. She lunged with it at Adam's right hand, screaming, "*Du Schweinhund* (you dirty swine)". The crowbar connected to Adam's wrist, knocking out his gun. Heidi swiftly used the crowbar to push both guns farther down the room, away from the two men. She swung the crowbar up and, holding it with a firm grip, she pointed it toward Adam again, who stood his ground, transfixed.

***

Spellbound, Adam watched this woman executing swift maneuvers, accompanied by shrieks and screams in a foreign tongue. From where did she muster all this strength, despite the way Tusker had handled her? Her blond hair was ruffled, her face appeared flushed and strewn with patches of bruises, while blotches of crimson and blue were beginning to appear around her neck. It was a sight far too overwhelming for Adam who, by now, was convinced that the woman in front of him was evil— casting spells on Tusker and anyone else who threatened her. She had bewitched Tusker—how else could one ex- plain his sexual arousal as he held this... this vixen? Their chief, who had the temperament of a raging bull, had behaved as though his libido had increased exponen- tially, panting like a young colt experiencing his first heat? Their chief, who never flinched into retreating while confronting an enraged elephant, being rendered *hors de combat* by a single blow from this... from this Medusa?

And poor Daniel—she had disposed him off with one swift kick in his ass. Adam had to save his chief from further suffering. "Chief, this woman is evil—we must get away before she casts any more spells on us," he cried, offering to help Tusker from where he lay.

His groin in agony and a confused look on his face, Tusker struggled to rise to his feet. The two men clumsily managed to stand up as Heidi hovered over them with the crowbar. They bolted out through the open door, grabbed Daniel from the *askari* who was holding on to him, and hobbled along as fast as they could toward the gate. Their fourth companion at the gate picked them up in their vehicle and they fled.

\*\*\*

Toto Kilonzo had been making good progress with Phyllis. He had steered her toward a quiet corner in the office and was taking his time, exploring the sensual parts of her anatomy. But what were the sounds that distracted him? It had been quiet and peaceful—why could he, at this crucial moment, not be left in peace?

The flurry of activities around him persisted and he focused his eyes as he reluctantly came out of his reverie. The man with the red cap was on his cell phone while he walked rapidly toward the Mitsubishi, parked a short distance away. Toto sat up in a confused state. *Oh, man!* he thought. Just when he felt certain he was going to make it with Phyllis. *Why didn't those guys take more time? How long had the operation lasted, anyway?* He looked at his watch. *Only twenty-five minutes!* he almost exclaimed aloud. *Why didn't these guys take the full hour that was given them?*

Meanwhile, the man with the red cap had driven his vehicle down the dirt road toward the gate of the townhomes, obviously to pick up his accomplices. From a distance, Toto saw the *askari* open the gate to allow three men to step out. All the three appeared to have suffered some injuries, but one of the men, the biggest of them, hobbled along as though in great pain. He kept touching his hand to his crotch, where he had obviously suffered a severe injury. His condition reminded Toto of his experience some years earlier in his village. A young farmer had received a kick to his groin from a zebra that had strayed onto his farm. The poor man had suffered in agony for several days. Rumors circulated that his young bride was distressed her husband could not "service" her for a long time. Toto recalled how much he had desired each night that he could "service" the well-endowed bride, if only...

He brushed these thoughts aside as he gazed at the spectacle of the injured men helping each other into the getaway car. He wondered who could have meted out such a severe thrashing to all three.

As the car sped away, Toto pulled out his cell phone and conveyed to Bono Njoroge what he had just witnessed. After listening to Toto, an astonished Bono asked Toto to wait until he called back. And in a repeat of what his colleague Bic Okello had done the previous day, Bono called back and asked Toto to report back to the office.

***

Gasping for breath, Heidi locked the front door and sank into a chair. As the rush of adrenaline ebbed, her hands started to tremble and she broke into a sweat. She called Jay and was able to maintain her cool as she delivered the news in brief. Shattered by what he heard, he was at a loss for words, but assured her he was heading home right away.

Heidi stood up to look at herself in the mirror—it was not a pretty sight, but she was relieved there was no bleeding. While she started to place cold compresses on the blue blotches on her neck and face, the *askari* rang the doorbell.

"*Pole sana* (So sorry), Mama," sympathized the *askari*. He had failed in his duties and knew he would face rough interrogation by the police and his boss.

"That's okay, Ngugi," replied Heidi. "It wasn't your fault. You did your best."

"Is Mama badly hurt?" he asked in an anxious tone. "Did they harm you, Mama?"

"Not much. But we did well, didn't we, Ngugi? We chased those thugs away."

"Yes, but I'm so sorry, Mama."

He continued with his apologies, while she tried to assure him he was not to be blamed. As he turned to leave, he lingered at the door and she knew he wasn't done yet. "Yes, Ngugi, was there something else?"

"My duty ends soon and I'll then leave," he responded with hesitation. "But Mama said she wants to give me some *chakula* (food)."

"Oh, of course. I'm so glad you reminded me—just wait."

From the kitchen, Heidi brought leftover portions of a casserole and *Kartoffelsalat* (potato salad). "Here you go. You do like my potato salad, don't you, Ngugi?"

"Yes, Mama," he said as he thanked her and left. For Ngugi, the taste of the salad was not what mattered. With an extended family to feed, he would gladly have accepted even Heidi's *sauerkraut*.

The maid soon returned and, while they waited for Jay, she nursed Heidi's bruises and massaged the sore spots.

***

Jay had a difficult situation on hand when he reached home. Blaming himself for having picked up the briefcase and not turning it over to the police, he consoled Heidi as best as he could. It took a long time before she calmed down.

Jay now had to take care of the formalities. He called the police and was told it would take some time for an officer to come over; they said it would be quicker if he were to visit them to lodge the complaint. Jay decided to call his friend Julius Wachira on his cell phone.

***

Julius was at his desk when his cell phone rang and Jay came on the line. He assumed Jay had called to confirm the extension of his nephew's employment. But his face took on a strange hue when he was told the purpose of the call. Jay informed him that the police were unable to depute an officer to his house and wondered if Julius could visit him soon to investigate. He gave his address.

Julius remained seated in stunned silence after the phone call. His heart started to beat as the consequences of the day's events began to sink in. *The house that Bono had targeted in Westlands was Jay's house? And the outcome was the same as the previous day? How would his boss and Bono react when he divulged his relationship with Jay?* He could now recall that he had come in late for Tuesday's meeting and had not realized that Jay was the Indian who Bono targeted. Now what was he to do?

He walked to the front desk and inquired if there had been a call about an attempted burglary in Westlands. When told there was, he offered to take up the case and proceeded to the Commissioner's office.

As expected, a crestfallen Bono sat slumped, facing the boss's wrath. The Commissioner looked up when Julius walked in; Julius said he gathered that the planned operation had been a failure. It would be more appropriate, he felt, for the police to visit the scene than having the victim visit the police station to lodge the complaint. He reminded the Commissioner of the previous day's incident and the resulting undesirable publicity. He offered to undertake the assignment, to which the Commissioner agreed, though he suggested that Toto Kilonzo accompany him.

\*\*\*

Jay opened the front door when Julius arrived with Toto in tow. He gave his visitor a stern look, but decided to remain silent in Toto's presence. The two officers moved around the house, examining the window through which the burglars had gained entry and the signs of the struggle with the intruders. Julius picked up the two guns lying on the floor and placed them in a plastic bag.

Toto, meanwhile, surveyed the scene with considerable curiosity and was keen to find out who had handed down such a thrashing to the three intruders. When Heidi entered the room, he stared at her in surprise as he realized that she was the same woman who drove up in the VW Beetle earlier that afternoon. He reckoned she must have entered the house while the "operation" was in progress and she must have had an encounter with the three intruders. He just couldn't comprehend, though, why she wasn't the one to have been beaten up instead of the other way around. He stared at Heidi in awe and looked away only when he realized Jay was glaring at him.

Julius said he needed to record statements and the first one was from the *askari*. Heidi's turn was next, and Julius asked her for a detailed description of the encounter. When she reached the part where Tusker started to fondle her, Julius sought clarification. "So, Mama, you said the big man had you firmly in his arms, and then he... he started to behave funnily with you?"

"Yes," replied Heidi. "He pulled me toward him and I thought he was going to hit me. But then he suddenly changed. His hands moved all over me and I felt he had bad intentions."

"What did he do?" asked Jay anxiously.

"He started to feel my..." She paused and, modestly averting their gazes, said, "he started to feel my boobies."

Toto whispered "boobies" without realizing it. He had a habit of repeating any word or expression that tickled his senses. He had never before heard this word being used to refer to a woman's breasts, but it sounded so delightful—right out of a children's storybook! It had such an innocent ring to it that he repeated it and fantasized about how delightful it would be if he could caress Heidi's boo—

*No, stop it,* he thought, forcing himself to focus on what was being discussed. Julius was seeking more clarification. "Now, Mama, the big man had his grip around you and the second man went to the front door when the bell rang. And you say that is when you attacked the big man? Where did you hit him?"

"I kicked him in his... in his nuts," came her response.

Once again Toto could not help repeating "nuts?" while marveling at Heidi's impeccable choice of words to describe one of the most disgusting parts of the thug's anatomy.

"I kicked him hard in his balls," Heidi said, leaving no room for any ambiguity. She cast a glance at Toto as she would to a third grader, to make sure he understood it this time. Toto not only understood, but he also grimaced as the memory of the hobbling Tusker appeared before him.

"And that knocked him down completely?" asked Julius.

"Yes, I think I did a good job of making sure that *Schweinhund* wouldn't be able to satisfy any woman for some time," said Heidi, using a German swear word for added satisfaction.

*Oh yeah? And how about the agony that we are going through?... is how Tusker's nuts would respond to Heidi,* thought Toto. *But hush.* Once again he brushed these thoughts aside.

"And the other two men?" asked Julius.

Heidi described how she tackled the other two. When she completed her narration, the three men now in the room—Jay, Julius, and Toto—were reluctant to accept that three armed intruders were beaten up and thrown out of the house by one unarmed woman. Julius wondered if any of those intruders would readily accept Heidi's account.

Julius went back to his notes and continued, "You said, Mama, that they were asking for the money... and an expensive briefcase?"

"Yes, and in fact, I found it strange they were keen to describe the briefcase with all the details," responded Heidi. "They said it was a genuine Italian leather briefcase with a tag that read 'Limited Edition.' Must be some special briefcase."

Julius agreed without uttering a word. He had been briefed on what took place the previous day at the Russian's house and the equally fervent obsession of those burglars with the briefcase. He asked Heidi, "Mama, you say you have no idea about the money and the briefcase that they were looking for?"

"No, I haven't seen anything," replied Heidi once again with a straight face. What was she to do now? Admit to the cops where the money really was? Once again, she satisfied her conscience by reminding herself that she had not laid her eyes on this fascinating piece of baggage or the money.

Julius turned to look at Jay. Jay turned his eyes away from Julius to look at Heidi. Heidi turned to look at Jay. And Toto continued to stare at Heidi.

"Do you have any idea who the burglars are?" Jay asked Julius.

"We are investigating," replied Julius. "We've got to check the fingerprints and the weapons. We'll contact you as soon as we have more details."

He stood up and bowed to Heidi. "You were very brave, Mama. I don't know how many women could have done what you did to those thugs."

He turned to Jay. "We'll have a patrol outside your house for the next few days. But please be careful."

He and Toto stepped out as the door shut behind them.

After dinner, Heidi took a long, hot bath—she felt drained and exhausted and soon dropped off to sleep.

For Jay, it was yet another miserable night as he lay tossing in bed, pondering in despair his next move.

# Chapter 12

## *Week 2—Saturday*

Struggling to pull himself out of bed when the alarm went off, Jay felt his body complaining about what was becoming routine—a restless night of disturbed sleep. He was relieved to find Heidi still asleep; the poor girl needed all the rest she could get. After a hot shower, he went downstairs for a stimulating cup of hot tea. He had not eaten very well the previous night and he asked the maid for an extra fried egg while helping himself to an extra piece of toast, as well.

After breakfast, he went back upstairs to find Heidi sitting up in bed, rubbing her eyes. She had a groggy look on her face and he sat beside her, holding her close. She said she felt better than expected and what she needed was a full day's rest. Jay worked half a day on Saturdays and he said he'd get back early.

During the coffee break at work, Jay called Julius Wachira and told him they need to have a face-to-face talk. They agreed to meet at the Thorn Tree Café in the afternoon. Next, Jay called Ravi Karnik, putting in a similar request. Ravi said he had a luncheon meeting at his club, but could meet him later. Jay agreed to link up with him at the Norfolk Hotel, the venue of Ravi's earlier meeting. The timing of the two back-to-back meetings worked out well for Jay.

Around noon, as he prepared to leave for the weekend, Jay opened his office desk and reached for the hidden drawer at the bottom. The package lay there, safe and secure, and he carefully pulled it out. For one fleeting moment, he was overwhelmed with the desire to open the paper wrapping to get one last glimpse of the briefcase—but he resisted. He headed for the parking lot where, after placing the bag in the boot of his car, he drove home.

***

Despondent and grim-faced, they filed into the Police Commissioner's office—the four officers who had spent long, fruitless hours trying to recover the missing briefcase. Peering over his reading glasses, Karanja eyed each one as they walked in, noting the somber expressions on their faces. Even the normally flippant Bono did not sport his usual grin, aware that it was his turn today to be in the hot seat.

Commencing the meeting on a sardonic note, the Commissioner said, "My dear brethren, for the past week, I have been listening patiently to your views and following your suggestions. So let us continue the same way—you all continue to speak up and I will listen. So pray, Bono, would you do us the honor of enlightening us on the outcome of your brilliantly planned operation of yore?"

Despite his reputation for being thick-skinned, Bono visibly wilted under the heavy dose of sarcasm and cut short his rehearsed, lengthy explanation, coming up instead with a terse response. "Someone tipped off those people. Why else would Mama come back home so early? And she had come well prepared."

"I see," said Karanja. "Two days ago, we had a bungled burglary attempt at the house of a Russian. And yesterday we had another burglary attempt on a *Muhindi's* house with a *Mzungu* wife and that too failed. In both cases, the gangs were forced to run away. Have we ever had such a situation before?"

He looked around at his team as they sat in hushed silence.

"No, sir," spoke up Julius. "And in the second case, it was a woman, all by herself, who beat up the three men."

"That woman behaved as though she was possessed by something evil," said Bono. "She's made him *kaput*. He probably still has problems pissing."

"That man..." the Commissioner raised his voice, "... that man should be the last one to complain about pissing. He probably started pissing in his pants the moment the woman entered the house."

Bono remained quiet as the Commissioner continued, "We've failed miserably and I might soon be summoned by the President. Do you know what it's like to face him in such situations, Bono?" He glared at Bono and then at Bic. "Some of those who've been through the experience said it's like facing a firing squad."

The two inspectors squirmed in their seats before Bono mustered the courage to pitch his rehearsed rebuttal. "Sir, this is a big conspiracy. Me, I think it's an international conspiracy. Look how many foreigners we are chasing and how many are involved. The stolen money is in an Italian briefcase, the getaway car belonged to a Japanese executive, and it was abandoned near a Russian's house. And an Indian man and his German wife were doing something suspicious that night near the place where the briefcase went missing. The thief—just some petty thief—was beaten to death. Now *Bwana*, is this not an international conspiracy? Those guys are too smart for us and have too many sophisticated weapons. They are not spending the stolen money and are doing so many things to fool us. We also have a British detective carrying out an investigation. Maybe we need to involve someone to solve this case."

They were interrupted by the Commissioner's secretary, who called out, "Sir, the American Embassy is on the line."

"Maybe that's what we need, right, Bono?" the Commissioner asked in a caustic tone. "To involve the Yanks in the mess we're in."

He swiveled away in his chair and took the call. Meanwhile, Gideon Odhiambo took over the conduct of the meeting and remarked, "So your plans, Bic and Bono, to 'outsource' the recovery process have failed. From the beginning, I said we shouldn't try something like that."

"We had to think outside the box and try something different, particularly in a case like this which is so, so..." Bic replied, struggling to find the right word.

"... so unconventional," finished Julius, who continued, "we were provided very few details on this case, *Bwana* Odhiambo, but I think we've made good progress."

"Before we proceed, I notice that you didn't fill in the correct form for yesterday's burglary attempt at the *Muhindi's* house, Julius," said Gideon. "Remember, you do not use the yellow form when no goods have been burgled. In such situations, you should use the brown form that I've designed."

He pulled out a blank form, which he passed on to Julius with a proud chuckle. "Can you believe it? We've used up two of these forms in the last two days."

Michael Karanja swiveled back to his desk. "The Americans are calling again about the latest intel on Somalia—it appears we'll be having problems on our northern border for a long time. Now, what were you all discussing?"

His deputy said, "Sir, our strategy has been a complete failure. I've been against it all along and I say we give it up *kabisa* (completely)."

Karanja did not respond. After a moment's silence, Julius asked, "Are we still convinced the money is either with the Russian or the Indian?"

"I still strongly suspect that Yeti," said Bic. "He's involved in many suspicious activities for which the transactions are made in cash. That's where he must have used up the cash—he's not going to spend it on women or in bars as you suggest, *Bwana* Odhiambo."

All eyes turned to Bono. "That Indian with the German wife—I don't know what business they're in— maybe they are using cash for their business. But I'm sure they picked up the briefcase that night. Somehow, we've got to get it from them."

"Bono and Bic, if you're so certain, then you must find a way to recover it. Not leave it to a bunch of thugs we don't trust," Gideon glared at the two.

Julius turned to the Commissioner. "Is there any way we could get a search warrant?"

"No," responded Karanja. "I don't think we need to spend time discussing that option."

"Some more information, I think, would help," said Julius. "Not just a fancy briefcase in some fancy color."

"That's all the information we have to work with. Which is why I agreed to your suggestions to think outside the box and outsource the operations," said Karanja.

"And me, I wonder why everyone is so much interested in the briefcase," said Bono. "There is something fishy about it. I say, what's so special about it and what's all this talk about 'Limited Edition'? It's so confusing to me."

"Bono, I'll tell you what it means," Gideon started to explain in a condescending tone.

But the Commissioner cut him short. "Stop it! Stop all this talk about the briefcase!" He was uncharacteristically livid as he continued, "Even a small child wouldn't keep asking such stupid questions. Everyone knows that a briefcase is used for carrying cash. Now I don't know how much was in that briefcase, but that's not important right now. Between all of you here, you haven't been able to recover even one single shilling."

He glared around at them all until Gideon broke the silence. "We do what has worked for us in the past. We keep in close touch with our contacts for possible tips. Our friends in the banks will alert us of any major transactions. All thieves make some mistake somewhere—we have to be very alert—they'll make a mistake at some time and then we..." He snapped the palms of both his hands to mimic the snapping of a crocodile's mouth.

There were no other suggestions and Karanja called the meeting to an end.

He started to browse through his papers when the phone buzzed. Phyllis, the office assistant who was on the switchboard for the day, said Mr. James Maina, the

Managing Director of the Tea Authority, was on the line. Karanja and Maina had been schoolmates and had maintained contact ever since.

"Michael, this is James Maina. How've you been keeping? And how's the family?"

"Oh, we're all fine, James. How are you and your family? It's a pleasant surprise to hear from you on a Saturday morning. Tell me, how are things at the Tea Authority?"

"Not too bad. Luckily, a large number of people, mainly the Brits and the Indians, are hooked on tea. They keep buying whatever we produce. But Michael, you shouldn't be working so hard on Saturdays. Take some time off, man!"

Karanja sighed. "James, do you need someone like me in the Tea Authority? At least I could relax over the weekends."

"No, no, you stay right there where you are, my friend. We *wananchi* (the people) need you to protect us. Now, I was going to call you yesterday, but got busy," Maina paused. "Michael, I've been requested by a good friend of mine to have a word with you. But his story sounds a bit awkward to me and you tell me frankly what you think about it."

"Okay, James, what is it?"

"Tell me, did a briefcase containing cash go missing in the Lavington area last weekend?"

Karanja sat bolt upright in his chair and responded, "I'm listening. Tell me more."

"This friend says someone he knows was in that neighborhood last Friday night when he saw a briefcase lying on a side road and picked it up. That man thinks he's in trouble and is looking for ways to return it to the owner. Has any such incident taken place?"

Karanja cautiously replied, "James, some such thing did happen. But your friend or that other person, like everyone else, should come to our department for us to deal with it."

"That's what I told him, Michael, but he says his friend is... you know, a bit scared. He's worried the police might accuse him of stealing the money and lock him up or something."

"Do you know him and trust his story?"

"Yes, I can vouch for my friend—I don't know the other person."

"In that case, James, ask your friend to come with his friend and meet me directly and mention your name. I'll make sure that the matter is settled to everyone's satisfaction."

Karanja hung up and sat back, the deep furrows on his forehead rapidly disappearing. So the money was neither with the Russian nor the *Muhundi,* but with someone else? His first reaction was to convey this to the Minister. But as he deliberated, he felt it prudent to keep quiet for now. It's too early, he reasoned, to share this information with anyone, the Minister included. Not even his deputy, Gideon. So much had gone wrong along this investigation's tortuous journey that until Maina's friend showed up with the cash, he would take nothing for granted.

Meanwhile, James Maina conveyed to Jay his conversation with Karanja. Jay thanked him and said he would pass on the information to his friend.

\*\*\*

When Gideon Odhiambo walked out of the Commission-er's office after the meeting, he gestured for Bic and Bono to follow him. In the privacy of his office, he addressed them in a stern tone, "Your strategies failed miserably. Do you have a Plan B?"

The two inspectors looked at each other before Bic responded, "I've said it before—I strongly suspect the Russian. I'm not going to give up until I recover the goods."

"Whose help are you going to take?" Gideon asked.

Bic was quiet for a moment before responding, "Don's."

Gideon didn't appear pleased, but Bic asserted, "At this stage, I have no choice but to continue with him."

"Do so at your risk. And you, Bono?"

"I'll continue pursuing the Indian. But Tusker will be out of commission for a few days and I'm not sure if I can work with anyone else."

"Tusker's assistants should be available," Gideon reminded Bono. "Get to work fast with them—we shouldn't lose the trail. And this time, both of you have to take personal charge."

***

Nick Cunningham and Peter Otieno were on their way to visit the other lodge that David, the clerk, had men-tioned. Nick's mood remained downcast, as increasing doubts about his own capabilities plagued his mind. Pe-ter could scarcely conceal his glee at Nick's plight and was beginning to relax about the need to hover around the detective.

Upon reaching the lodge, Nick asked for David's cousin, Ben. He worked in the accounts office and came to the front desk to greet the visitors. They settled down in the lounge and, during the course of the conversation, Nick inquired if the lodge attracted a large number of local tourists.

"Yes," replied Ben. "We also attract a large number of senior government officials and their families and friends."

"Is this lodge owned by a senior government official?" asked Nick, to which Ben nodded. He agreed with the suggestion that this could be the reason why government officials frequented the lodge. While Peter was briefly distracted greeting an old acquaintance, Nick conveyed to Ben that he would pass by alone to his office after lunch. Ben excused himself to get back to work, while Nick and Peter proceeded toward the dining hall.

After lunch, Peter said he needed to make a radio call and walked toward the manager's office, while Nick proceeded to Ben's office. He told Ben that he had heard this particular lodge was considered one of the best in the game reserve and asked him who owned the lodge. Ben obliged by giving the name; he also added that the official frequently visited the lodge and had made several visits during the last two months.

Nick thanked Ben, returned to the lounge, and was soon joined by Peter.

"So, how are things in Nairobi?" asked Nick.

"Busy as usual. In a country prone to crime, the police force is one department that doesn't enjoy the luxury of having a day off."

"Sounds familiar. Do you think our chaps in the UK have time for a holiday?"

"I know, I know, but we are always so understaffed. Though, right now there is a mysterious case that my colleagues are trying to unravel."

"Want to talk about it?"

Peter lowered his voice before continuing, "A gang stole a briefcase a week ago from another gang, but somehow the briefcase went missing. Both gangs have been desperately looking for it and have broken into two homes hoping to recover it, but no dice. Some senior official is involved and that's why the police have been kept busy."

"A week now and still nothing?"

"That's right," said Peter. "The curious aspect is that everyone involved talks more about the briefcase than about what's in it. It's an Italian one made of genuine leather."

"Wow, I've seen some of them. They sure are exquisite," agreed Nick.

"And this one has a tag that says 'Limited Edition'."

"That makes it even more exclusive. So what's happening?"

"Well, it certainly is keeping many a tongue wagging. That's the first thing that Phyllis—the girl on our switchboard—told me when I was connected. You know, Mr. Nick, if our department is unable to resolve this mystery, I might suggest that they engage your services."

"I guess I could consider taking up that assignment if I get to keep the briefcase."

"Could well be worth it. And Phyllis said she'd heard some Somali guy involved with poaching had arranged to present this briefcase to some top shot. But it never got that far—in fact, it seems to have done the vanishing trick."

"An expensive briefcase... poaching... a Somali..." Nick was lost in thought. While Peter settled the bill, he felt something click into place.

"I reckon the manager at the campsite, Paul Oloi-tokitok, should be there at this time. Let's pay him a visit."

"The campsite?" Peter looked surprised. "Okay, as you wish."

They rode in silence to their destination, with Nick feeling energized for the first time on this trip, his brain analyzing and processing at a frenetic pace the information he'd just received.

\*\*\*

"The Big Boss will send a few women to finish you off once he finds out that one woman could knock you down senseless with a kick to your balls," mocked Bono on the phone.

He heard a gasp at the other end, as Tusker struggled to respond. Finally, "Ah... I'm okay, no problem. But he shouldn't come to know of what you just said."

"So what do you want to do now? Are you able to face up to that *Mzungu* woman?"

"We need to tackle her husband, that *Muhindi*. He's the one sitting on the money."

"How will you tackle him—can you even walk?"

"I'll send my men—they'll do it," answered Tusker.

"Do what? They can't do anything on their own. Ask them to meet me at five in the afternoon at the Nyayo Monument in the Uhuru Park."

"I need Adam to be with me today. I'll send Daniel and Jacob to meet you."

"Very well," said Bono as he signed off.

\*\*\*

Located in the central business district of Nairobi, the Thorn Tree Café had opened several decades earlier as a small cafeteria around a solitary Acacia tree. Its convenient location at the crossroads in a busy section of the city made it a popular meeting place for travelers. The city itself had, for long, been a major gateway for travelers venturing on a safari and for climbers destined to Mount Kenya or Mount Kilimanjaro. Sometime following the era of pigeon couriers and before the dawn of the internet age, an intrepid traveler set up an innovative messaging system for his fellow travelers—pinning paper notes with messages for their friends on the trunk of the Acacia tree, while they continued with their travels.

Over the years, the Thorn Tree Café flourished, as it became a popular meeting point for travelers and locals alike. The tree itself has become a landmark in its own right, as travelers continued to pin notes even in the internet age, perhaps for the romantic experience of posting notes the old-fashioned way. Colorful sun umbrellas cover the tables placed alongside the roadside pavement, under the shade of the aging tree.

Seated at one of the tables, Jay watched tourists and locals strolling alongside the busy road. Periodically, a tourist would walk up to the landmark tree, checking for pinned notes or posting one on the tree. A cool breeze wafted through the open-air bistro as Jay waited for Julius Wachira to join him. He looked at the people sitting around him, relaxed in a weekend mood, enjoying the beautiful weather, and here he was among them—*an asshole wallowing in misery, suffering from self-inflicted stress and spending sleepless nights.* Would his police friend, on whom he'd pinned his hopes, be able to put an end to his despair?

The café was within walking distance of Julius's office and Jay waved to him when he appeared. He approached the table, looking tired and with a serious expression on his unshaven face. They greeted each other without the usual warmth and Julius inquired about Heidi. "How's Mama feeling?"

"Surprisingly not too bad, considering what she went through."

"She's a very brave lady. We've never had a similar case."

After ordering beers and a plate of macadamia nuts, Jay turned to Julius. "Have you been able to identify who those guys were? You must have picked up fingerprints from their guns."

"Our men will be working on the prints. It may take a day or two."

"I read in the press about a burglary attempt at a Russian's house. Any clues on the culprits?"

"Not yet— our investigations are ongoing."

It was always a problem for Jay to maintain his cool while under stress, but he was determined not to lose control today and had even rehearsed his lines. The waiter brought their orders and retreated. After taking a large sip of beer, Jay said, "The other day you mentioned you were investigating some Russian's possible involvement with the stolen briefcase. Was it the same Russian whose house was broken into yesterday? I can't imagine two Russians in this town being involved in the same incident."

"It can't be ruled out. But we're looking at it from all angles."

"I'll take that as a yes," Jay shrugged his shoulders and decided to fire his first salvo. "Did you folks really bother to investigate if the Russian had the stolen goods or did you ask those thugs to check that out for you?"

A look of concern was all that Jay could discern on the normally unflappable officer. He remained quiet and stared at his beer glass.

"Well, Julius, I must thank you for coming personally to my house last night when I called. I do appreciate that—you saved us the hassle of making a trip to the police station."

Julius merely nodded, but continued to sit dour-faced.

"Heck!" Jay sounded exasperated. "I've been in touch with you since last week about this incident and have inquired if there were any developments. And what happens? The thugs break into my house. Was it too much to expect at least some warning from your side?"

Julius sipped his beer and helped himself to macadamia nuts before responding, "Several police officers are involved in this investigation. I do get some information, but the other guys do a lot of stuff without my knowledge. Believe me, I had no idea that there was any plan for yesterday's attack."

"You told me three days ago you were investigating the presence of a vehicle that night in Lavington. So do I assume that has something to do with the attack on my house?"

Jay continued to glare at Julius. Despite his low tone, the intensity of his emotions could scarcely be concealed. The oncoming waiter veered away, picking up the unmistakable signals.

Jay realized he needed to back off. Two attractive female tourists strolling along the pavement offered a welcome distraction to them both. They continued sipping their beers before Julius spoke up. "Let's go back to the beginning. Can you tell me why you approached me in the first place?"

"I had mentioned at the outset that our good friends, who live in Lavington, heard gunshots that night. They spoke to us and said they were concerned about the shooting. When I spoke with you last week, I asked you to let me know if you were aware of this incident."

"But why did they call you? Were you with them that night?"

"There were several other people there, as well." Jay had expected this question and was following his script.

"Were you in the car that left the area after the thugs escaped?"

There was a deliberate pause from Jay. "Julius, I honestly appreciate your help, but obviously some decisions are being made without your involvement. After yesterday's attack, I have to be careful and don't wish to say anything that could put my family in danger."

"Why are you putting yourselves at risk by holding on to the money?"

"I didn't say we picked up the briefcase—it could be anyone else who happened to be there that night."

"And you know who has the money?"

"And do you expect me to let you know where it is? So that a third operation could be carried out by your department?"

Julius looked hurt by that response. Even though Jay felt an apology was not necessary, he did not wish to upset his friend any further. He quickly added, "I'm sorry, please don't take it personally—it's nothing against you. But let me put this straight across. Do your colleagues wish to continue chasing around town for the stolen money and arranging to break into more homes? Or would you rather have the money returned to the rightful owner?"

"Are you assuring me that the money is in a safe place?"

Jay merely nodded his head.

"Then hand it over to us and we'll make sure the owner gets it back."

"And you expect me to allow your department to take credit for its return? The same folks that placed my wife in a life-threatening situation yesterday?"

The atmosphere turned tense once again and Jay decided to cut his friend some slack. He watched a minivan unload a group of newly arrived tourists at the hotel entrance before continuing, "Julius, be reasonable. How can your department expect people like us to trust you when we strongly suspect your department's hand in arranging the two attacks? Would you blame us if we had doubts that the attacks were arranged to get the money back for the owner or to be split up and shared between a number of people?"

"So, what are you suggesting?"

"One thing is certain. The money will not be handed over to your department. The money will be returned only to the owner."

"That's not acceptable. Our department has that responsibility."

"Julius, please don't make me repeat what I just said. It must be possible to find a way."

He watched Julius ponder before querying, "What exactly are you worried about? Don't forget—the owner himself might insist the money be returned through us."

"But you guys might lock us up, accusing us of the theft or of being accomplices."

"Off the record, I can say that our bosses would be careful if you or your friend were accompanied by a good lawyer. He should first meet the police chief and come to an understanding before you accompany him to hand over the cash. It could work—it might be worthwhile for you to talk to a good lawyer."

"Ravi Karnik is my good friend. He should be a good lawyer for this purpose."

"Yes, Ravi Karnik would be a very good lawyer to work this out."

Jay knew he had to push until the end was in sight. "But Ravi, or any other lawyer, would want the money to be returned directly to the owner."

Julius was silent.

"Why don't you tell me who it is?" Jay asked.

"I honestly don't know," Julius replied as he finished his beer and rose to leave.

"If you'd tell us who the owner is, we'd return the money to him," Jay persisted.

Julius waited as he stood by the table. Jay got up, leaned over to Julius. "The owner must be spending many sleepless nights. Tell me who it is and the money will be returned in good faith and in strict confidence. You and everyone else in your department can also get a good night's sleep," Jay concluded as he tapped Julius on his shoulder.

The officer had a faraway look in his eyes as he deliberated on this proposal. Turning to look at Jay straight in the eye, he gave a nod and left the café without uttering a word.

\*\*\*

"So what are you going to do now?" Bic spoke in a caustic tone on his cell phone. "Wait for the henchmen to finish you off?"

"Chief, please help me," replied Don. "I must find the money—tell me what I should do."

"Keep an eye on the Russian—one of your guys should follow him to see what he's up to. Keep in touch with me—we'll have to come up with a plan," Bic commanded.

\*\*\*

Built near what was then the city's main railway terminal, the Norfolk Hotel was one of the first hotels built in Nairobi during the British colonial period. The terminal was later moved elsewhere, but that did not diminish the hotel's popularity and its hallowed reputation.

Over its nearly hundred years of existence, the esteemed institution had witnessed a fair share of the colorful colonial history. Unfortunately, not all of it was pleasant. On New Year's Eve in 1980, a bomb explosion destroyed a portion of the hotel and claimed the lives of thirteen people. The perpetrators were never apprehended, but were suspected to be terrorists acting in vengeance against the Jewish owners. The hotel was restored to its former glory and has been a popular meeting place, particularly with the British settlers.

Jay met Ravi at the Lord Delamere Terrace, a verandah restaurant, accessible from the street. The ambiance could not be more British and they ordered the very English "cuppa tea," served in a bone china tea set. And true to the English tradition, they were served scones with cream and jam, finger sandwiches, and dainty cakes from the food trolley.

"It's been more than a year since I last visited this place, but it continues to be just as popular," said Ravi as he eyed the uppity clientele that the place attracted. "And thank heavens the British have stuck to some of their age-old traditions. Nothing beats the 'high tea' experience," he concluded, as he helped himself to a scone, which he topped off with a dollop of fresh cream.

Turning to Jay, he said, "So my friend Bomy Daruwala's reference to Section 411 of the Indian Penal Code appears to have struck a raw nerve. Does our meeting today have something to do with it? You did sound mysterious when you phoned me the other day."

Deciding to come straight to the point, Jay leaned closer to Ravi and said, "I've something I need to discuss in strict confidence. Someone very close to me has stumbled upon a bundle of cash that he suspects was stolen. He doesn't trust the police and fears they might not return all of it to the owner. Is there a way he can hand it over to the authorities without being implicated in the theft?"

"As they say, 'possession is nine tenths of the law,' so there could be questions about how he gained possession of these items. What does your friend have to say about that?" Ravi asked.

"They came in its possession in a very bizarre manner—which is why they're in a bit of a pickle." Jay narrated the incident in brief and the dilemma of his friends on discovering the bag contained some fifteen million shillings in cash.

"He should hand it over to the police without delay; he would then not be accused of having broken any law."

Jay was prepared for this and countered, "And risk that some of the money would disappear? This obviously is stolen money, being used for something illegal. Where is the guarantee that the police wouldn't siphon some of it away? Would justice be served in such a situation? My friend has put himself at considerable risk, hoping to return the money to the owner without going through the police channels."

"Some swashbuckling friend you have! Looks like he's been watching too many superhero movies. As a legal expert, I wouldn't advise your friend to put himself at such considerable risk. But on moral grounds, I can't but help appreciate what he's doing. Now, what is it that you were expecting me to do?"

"If the owner of the stolen money is identified, could you help us ensure that the money is discreetly returned to the owner and that my friend isn't in any way punished?"

"I cannot offer any guarantees," Ravi answered, "but you know I'll do the best under the circumstances—I guess that's all I can say at the moment."

They both ate their sandwiches and sipped tea in silence. Ravi put his cup down and said, "I'm not sure whether to believe all this bullshit about a friend. You've been so stressed of late—not surprising if you've been sleeping with fifteen million shillings under your pillow."

With a remorseful look on his face, Jay responded, "I did something rash on the spur of the moment and then didn't know how to get out of the mess. And then, by coincidence, two days later, your friend Bomy talked about the legalities of a similar situation in India. Since then, I'd decided I would need you to provide me with legal protection and also help in returning the cash. I'm working with a police contact to find out from whom the money was stolen; I do hope to have that information in a day or two."

"I doubt it. But even if he does, what do you expect me to do?"

"Ravi, we must arrange to meet the owner and hand over the money to him on the understanding that he is discreet about it and this matter remains confidential. And, of course, that the incident is forgotten and closed."

"And what makes you think the exercise would be that simple?"

"No, it won't be easy, but that man and some thugs are desperate to recover the money," Jay paused for a bit before he decided to go ahead and let Ravi know the latest developments. "I haven't told you yet, but some thugs broke into our house yesterday afternoon. To make matters worse, Heidi returned home while they were inside and they grabbed her, asking for the money. But you wouldn't believe it—she fought them all and, with the *askari's* help, managed to chase them all away."

"What are you talking about, Jay? You make it sound so casual—is she badly hurt?"

"No, thank heavens, she is fine; just badly shaken. We'll talk about that later." Jay did not wish to get distracted from the purpose of the meeting.

But Ravi cut in, "Poor Heidi. Don't you feel remorseful about what you put her through?"

"Of course I do, but then after what she's been through, it'd be a shame to just hand over the money to the police and probably be grilled by them."

"I could accompany you and make sure they don't harass you as you fear," offered Ravi.

"I don't trust them, Ravi. I think they're the ones who tipped off the thugs to pay a visit to my house. And you think I should hand over the cash to the police and let them take the credit for recovering it? No, sir, they don't deserve any such credit. We've got to make sure the money is returned directly to the owner."

"Now again, what makes you so sure that you'd get to choose how to go about returning the money? I wish I could share your optimism."

"Well, I certainly am in no rush to hand it over to the police," Jay asserted. "After the hiding that Heidi belted out to those guys, I doubt anyone would venture to send another team to our place. Let's wait a day or two—at least until next Monday."

"I'm not sure whether to praise you for being some sort of a superhero or blast you for being a bloody fool," said Ravi. "But you've got yourself into some real trouble, my friend. Not only do I have to get involved in getting you out of the mess, but I also risk becoming a target for these hoodlums."

"No, Ravi, I'll make sure you are never at any risk. You have a great reputation and there's no reason why anyone would not be willing to work with you discretely." Ravi rose to leave. "Let's leave it at that for now. And you and Heidi better be careful and stay safe over the weekend."

Jay sat down and poured himself another cup of tea while taking stock of his discussions. Could he have pushed Julius or Ravi any further? Probably not. But how long could he wait until Julius divulged the owner? He was not concerned about putting Ravi at risk—he was too smart for that and had surely survived riskier situations. But Jay had concerns about Julius—would he be able to convince his boss to divulge the owner? It wouldn't be easy to convince any police boss to forego the credit of recovering the stolen cash. Jay signaled to the waiter for the check and was soon heading home.

As he neared his house, he passed the kiosk on the approach road. A young man in a red cap stood near the kiosk, munching on a roasted corn on the cob. As Jay drove past, he realized that the man had his eyes glued on to him. Jay didn't give it a second thought, being unaware that the man was assigned to look out for an Indian driving a dark-colored Honda.

*** 

Jay was right about Julius' ability to persuade his boss. The Commissioner had left for the weekend by the time Julius returned to his office. He called him on the cell phone and briefly explained Jay's proposal. But the Commissioner was unrelenting—the money should be turned over to the police and there should be no direct contact with the owner.

But Julius persuaded his boss to reconsider. Finally, the only concession he made was to think about it over the weekend and they would discuss it on Monday.

\*\*\*

*What am I missing, what am I missing?* Nick racked his brain while on the way to the campsite. Did it have to do with something that Mary's father, Barry Wilson, had mentioned to him in London? Or was it something the manager at the camp had mentioned about Mary's concerns? And in what way was it connected with the Nairobi incident mentioned by Peter?

They reached the campsite and met the manager, Paul Oloitokitok. "I'm back for some clarification," Nick told him. "When Mary Wilson's father met you, I believe there was reference to a conversation Mary had with you on an issue with which she had some concerns. Can you recall what it was?"

"I'm not sure which one you're referring to."

"Perhaps something to do with a briefcase?" suggested Nick. Peter looked up as Nick followed up with, "Or perhaps something about poaching?"

Paul glanced at Peter, who glared at him. With some hesitation, Paul replied, "It was not Mary, but her male acquaintance."

"Her male acquaintance?"

"I did mention, didn't I, that she met a British journalist during her last two days? It was he who mentioned poaching."

"What did he say?"

"He had some information about poaching activities not far away from here. He asked me if I had any specific information about who was involved. I keep away from these activities and I told him as such. He must have mentioned this to Mary and that's what bothered her. On the last day, she told me before leaving the camp that she was keen to find out what was going on. I cautioned her to be careful, but I never saw her after that. To this day, I often agonize if I could have done more to prevent her from getting involved in those matters."

No further information was forthcoming and Nick said, "I think you did your best. Thanks so much for everything. Ifs there's anything else, I'll get back to you."

Nick gestured to Peter. "Let's get going. We need to reach the site where Mary's body was discovered."

They climbed into the Land Rover and, as the vehicle drove off, Nick caught a glimpse of the camp manager in the rearview mirror. He stood, crestfallen, before trudging back inside. *Does he, in some way, feel responsible for what befell Mary Wilson?* Nick wondered. *And is he disappointed in me for not having come up with anything?* Along the way, Peter made several attempts to find out from Nick what was going on, but the Brit maintained a studious silence.

Upon reaching the site they'd visited two days earlier, Nick followed the footprint tracks that led to a shrub near the crime scene and a rock nearby. Nick felt certain that the footprints were Mary's and she had walked up to this point after alighting from her vehicle.

*What was she doing here?* he wondered. *Did she see or hear something she was not supposed to?* He followed her footprints up to the rock and bent down to study them. From his briefcase, he pulled out his magnifying glass and studied the prints. The last two prints had formed a deeper impression than the others. She had obviously stepped onto the rock at this point. He climbed up, something he had not done on his last visit, and presto! a new vista opened up below. The ground dropped some forty feet beyond that point and, from the top of the rock, he surveyed the ground below. He peered through his binoculars and could discern that a large clearing below had been trampled upon. He decided to go down for a closer look.

As he started to descend, Nick noticed footprints on the ground leading up to the shrub. Farther away were more footprints, some leading up and others leading down. The sizes of these footprints were different from the ones near the first site. And the pattern of the prints suggested that more than one person had walked up to the shrub from the clearing below and then back down. Peter started to follow, but Nick asked him to stay clear and insisted that he wished to carry out the investigation alone, without being disturbed.

Reaching the clearing, he noted that the area had recently been the scene of intense activity. There were several dark stains on the ground, alongside bits and pieces of rope and metal. Nick brought out his kit and painstakingly began the investigation. He inspected the whole area methodically and collected all available evidence. It appeared undisturbed and obviously no one had been on this site.

For the better part of the afternoon, Nick closely inspected every square inch of the clearing, making sure nothing escaped his attention. Fully engrossed in the task at hand, he refused Peter's overtures to take a coffee break, pausing only to sip bottled water. Peter realized

Nick had stumbled upon something that had escaped the attention of the Kenyan authorities. And judging from Nick's intensity and sensing his mood, he realized there was nothing he could do to stop Nick from completing his task.

Nick walked back to the rock for one final inspection. A shiny object on the ground caught his attention. He leaned over and noticed that it was a plastic cap of a camera lens. It had to be Mary's, which suggested she had photographed something. No wonder the police evaded his questions about whether she was carrying a camera—it must have been destroyed. Nick slipped the lens cap in his pocket. He walked toward Peter and said he had completed inspecting the site—but that he wasn't yet done for the day. He had to meet the game warden and his rangers one more time.

By the time they reached the Chief Warden's office, it was late afternoon—on a Saturday—and only a few rangers were available. Peter arranged for them to assemble in the meeting room and Nick noted with satisfaction that the ranger, who had appeared sympathetic on his previous visit, was present.

Nick began by asking the rangers about their biggest challenges. Poaching of elephants and rhinos was their response. He commented, "I can well imagine that controlling poaching must be a challenging task. You are up against ruthless men with sophisticated weapons and for whom the stakes are very high. I commend you, gentlemen, for doing a splendid job under very difficult circumstances."

They looked pleased with what was obviously a very rare compliment.

"And like in many other places, some of these poachers would be enjoying the patronage of some influential people. This must hinder your efforts, right?"

They remained quiet, as he had anticipated. He moved on to his next query, which was about the mode of disposal of elephant and rhino carcasses that had been slaughtered.

"The carcasses are towed away by trucks if they are lying near the trails normally used by tourists," one of the rangers responded.

"Why is that?" asked Nick.

"The stench is unbearable," the ranger replied.

"Or perhaps," Nick suggested, "is it because the tourists should not see the slaughtered animals, which could give Kenya a bad name?"

"Oh, no, that's not at all the case," butted in Peter Otieno.

Nick glared at Peter. "Peter, we are discussing a serious issue that plagues your country's wildlife conservation efforts, as well as your tourism industry. Can we not have a serious discussion with these officials, who have been charged with supporting these efforts?"

The rebuke silenced Peter for the rest of the meeting.

Nick continued, "So, when was the last time you had to cart away the carcasses of elephants?"

"I think it was about ten days ago," one ranger replied.

"And I think I know when you had to cart one away before then," said Nick. "That was the time when Mary Wilson's dead body was found, not far from the place where the elephants were slaughtered. I could see the marks that were left behind when the elephants' carcasses were carried away."

While Peter looked up in surprise, Nick noted that the friendly ranger nodded and smiled. Nick did not expect any response from the rangers and, realizing that he was not likely to get any further information from them, he thanked them and rose to leave.

As the Land Rover lurched forward to commence the journey back to the lodge, Nick called out over the din of the vehicle to his astounded colleague, "Peter, I sure could do with some cold beer when we get back."

\*\*\*

After an early dinner, Heidi said she would prefer to watch a movie on the TV. Jay had mentioned he would be away for a short time on an errand. After Heidi made herself comfortable in front of the TV, Jay set out on his mission. From the boot of his car, he removed the briefcase that he had placed there earlier in the day and put it on the passenger seat.

He drove out of his complex, noting that the police patrol Julius had promised was parked near the gate. Reassured of Heidi's safety, he headed a few miles east toward Kariokor, a crowded Nairobi neighborhood. He knew there was a large open garbage dump, which the city administration could never empty fast enough and which was always filled with trash.

It was late in the evening and the streets in the neighborhood were deserted. Jay pulled up his car close to the dump and made sure no one was around. He sat for a moment in silence as he glanced at the package by his side. He started to mutter a few words, but ended up unwittingly delivering a soliloquy.

"It's time, you bewitching temptress, for us to bid farewell. Why did I have to succumb to your charms that dark night as you beckoned me with your glittering guise? An ordinary piece of baggage you certainly were not, that I would not hesitate to run over or to leave behind to bite the dirt and grime that lay on the track. Was I too much of a gentleman, who felt obliged to rescue an attractive object from an inglorious end? Or did you cast a spell that prompted me to snatch you from your dismal surroundings despite the hail of gunfire that rang out around me?

"But alas, you've heaped nothing but distress upon us, ever since I took you in my fold. For one long week, I resisted the wiser counsel that silently urged me to toss you away. Instead, I kept you safe and smug and yet, in return, all that I was bestowed with were even more travails. My beloved Heidi will never forgive me for yielding to your charms. She has suffered enough and it's now time for us to part. I need to make amends to Heidi and what better way to do so than to allow rats and cockroaches to feast upon you?"

He looked around, opened the car door and, with a mighty swing, flung the briefcase far away toward the dump. The stench was unbearable and he held his breath until he heard the object land in the heap. Swiftly shutting the door, he drove off.

From the dark shadows emerged a small figure that moved cautiously toward the dump.

# Chapter 13

## *Week 2—Sunday*

A loud thump on the tin roof startled Tusker out of his sleep. He sat up and squinted at the beam of light that shone through a hole in the roof.

"Don't worry, it's nothing," came the reassuring voice of his trusted deputy, Adam, who stood nearby.

"Are you sure?" asked Tusker, his heart still racing.

"Yes. Have a cup of tea—you'll feel better."

Tusker struggled to make himself comfortable on the sheet spread on the mud floor, as Adam handed over the cup. His bruised, swollen lips hurt as he sipped the hot beverage and he suffered in silence the numbing pain in his groin.

He had spent the first night at the hideout, along with Adam. After the botched attempt at Jay's house two days earlier, he felt there was virtually no hope for him to recover the stolen cash. Expecting the Minister to let loose his henchmen to hunt him down, he felt compelled to seek refuge.

Located a few miles from Nairobi's elegant city center, Kibera is the largest and poorest slum in Africa. One of the dwellers was Adam's nephew, and he agreed to let the two stay in his shack while he traveled upcountry for a week.

"No one will come looking for you here," Adam had sounded confident when they moved in the previous night. "Daniel and Jacob will alert us if they come to know of anything fishy, while they'll continue to hunt for the cash with the help of our police friend. But you have to lie really, really low. When you need to go out, we'll wrap this cloak around you like a woman."

Tusker merely grunted. What his bruised body longed for was a refreshing bath with clean water. But that was a luxury that he could now only dream of. Close to a million dwellers who call Kibera their home had no access to basic amenities like running water, electricity, and drainage.

Like most dwellings, this one was a one-room wooden shack with a mud floor and tin roof. Some dwellings had an enclosure of sorts that the occupants used as a toilet. This one luckily had one; a small luxury, Tusker conceded, as he visited the enclosure more than once during the night. But not all dwellers enjoyed this privilege—they had to manage as best as they could out in the open. Or, if even that was not an option, they made use of "flying toilets," a term used when dwellers are forced to do their business in a plastic bag, which they then toss far away, for it to land in the open or on some roof.

It was one such "flying toilet" that had landed on their roof that morning. The bag had dislodged the metal sheet that covered a hole in the roof and it was through this hole that the sun's rays shone directly on his face. Tusker was unaware of these "flying toilets" and had feared that a henchman had landed in his pursuit. But he need have no such fears, Adam reassured him over a cup of tea.

The hot cup of strong black tea did little to cheer Tusker's melancholy mood. He was resigned to suffering in silence in the days ahead. But Adam felt confident they could ride the week out in anonymity. He was familiar with the maze of alleyways that crisscrossed the hutments and assured his colleague that they would quietly slip away should the need arise.

***

A sumptuous breakfast was one luxury Police Commissioner Michael Karanja indulged in on a Sunday morning. After slurping down a bowl of cornflakes followed by an omelet, he was now sipping his second cup of tea, along with a slice of generously buttered toast. He lived in relative comfort in the government quarters near Eastleigh, a neighborhood with a predominantly African population. Browsing through the local dailies, he reckoned the previous day must have been uneventful, considering that both the newspapers had nothing sensational to report.

While his wife, Doris, was busy in the kitchen, Karanja heard his ten-year-old son, Johnny, enter the kitchen from the rear door. The young lad had obviously ventured out early and Karanja could hear his wife posing to Johnny some searching questions. Though he could pick up only snippets of their conversation, Karanja sensed that Johnny was working hard to satisfy his mother's concerns about his latest peccadillo. Finally, Karanja heard his wife say, "All right, Johnny, but you must promise you'll never do it again."

He heard them continue to converse in hushed tones, accompanied by the rustling of paper. By now,

Karanja was intrigued—what were mother and son up to?

Doris appeared at the kitchen door and said, "Michael, Johnny has a surprise for you."

"Oh, really? Johnny, let's see what it is."

"Uh, uh," Doris shook her head. "You need to close your eyes first."

"Now, this had better be good, Johnny." Karanja closed his eyes and laid the newspaper aside. He heard Doris move the tray away and Johnny place something on the table.

"Open your eyes, Daddy."

Michael opened his eyes and looked at the odd-shaped gift-wrapped item in front of him. Sporting a big smile, Johnny proceeded to remove the wrapping.

Karanja's jaw fell open as he gasped for breath. On the table, glistening in the morning sun, sat a briefcase.

It was, without a doubt, not just any ordinary briefcase.

Crafted from expensive Italian leather, the workmanship was exquisite and the light brown color had an unblemished finish. A metal tag on the top right read "Made in Italy." Another polished tag at the bottom left read "Limited Edition."

"Wh... where...?" Karanja barely managed to stutter.

"Don't you like it, Daddy?" Johnny sounded excited. "Isn't it something special? Wouldn't you like to take it to your office?"

Karanja sat transfixed, without uttering a word.

Doris looked at her husband and asked, "What's wrong with you? Why are you staring at it as though it's just landed from another planet?"

"Where did you get it?" Karanja asked his son, finally recovering his breath.

Johnny wasn't sure if his father was pleased or furious and he cowered while he shuffled toward his mother. She cut the chaff from Johnny's earlier explanations to her and said, "Johnny was able to retrieve this beautiful package just before it could be hauled away by a dump truck. I have warned him never to get involved in such stuff in the future."

Karanja continued staring at the briefcase while Doris continued, "It must be really expensive. I'm surprised someone threw it away. I've wiped it clean before bringing it in here."

Karanja looked at Johnny and asked him, "You found it in a garbage dump? Which one?"

"The one in Kariokor—toward Panagani—you know there is a big open dump, where trucks and cars and people come to dump the garbage?"

"Yes, of course, I know where that dump is," answered Karanja, fully aware of the city 's ineffectiveness in clearing the mounting garbage. And the officials acknowledged it as such; recently, the Provincial Commissioner proudly announced that the mounting, uncollected garbage suggested that the residents generated more garbage due to increased consumption—a testimony to their improved living standards!

Karanja continued, "And why did you go there to fetch this item?"

"Daddy, one of the kids there said he knew this must have been very special because he saw a man stepping out of a car last night and throwing something into the dump. It was dark, but that kid brought it out. When he found out what it was, he decided to give it to me since he knows me well."

"Why did he give it to you? You must have paid him something," Karanja knew there had to be more to the story.

"I paid him ten shillings," lied Johnny, since he had paid fifty shillings, most of which he had quietly picked from his dad's wallet.

"And why did you pay him and bring it to me?" his father persisted.

"Daddy, I thought you'd like it for yourself or to give it to someone. Isn't it a good item for the price?" Another lie—he was obliged to lift the item off the kid because of a lost wager.

His mother cut in, "Johnny, you shouldn't get involved in such things." Turning toward her husband, she said, "What's there not to like about this briefcase? It's made from pure leather, is beautifully crafted in Italy, and has an attractive beige color."

Karanja looked in surprise at Doris. "You mean to say you know this color—bheyish?"

"Why, of course, my dear. Doesn't the color suit this briefcase? It looks so chic."

"What word did you just use—schick?" asked her bewildered husband. "Where did you learn to speak all these foreign words?"

"Chic, my dear. Don't tell me you've forgotten this word. But I can understand. When would you get a chance to speak good English when you spend most of your time with thugs, pimps, and prostitutes?"

"Those fancy French and Latin words are so confusing," lamented Karanja. "And now we have this Italian briefcase...."

"Now stop making such a fuss; Johnny meant well for you. And do take it to the office and start using it—it's so much smarter than the crappy piece of baggage you've been lugging around all these years," she admonished him before retreating to the kitchen.

Karanja continued staring at the briefcase before shaking his head and addressing his son. "You wouldn't know it, Johnny, but this briefcase is probably stolen. It's not right for me to use stolen items. Anyway, don't do such a thing again, do you understand?"

His son meekly nodded.

"Okay, now wrap it up properly, the way you found it. I'll take it to the office—we'll need to carry out some investigations."

\*\*\*

Nick Cunningham awoke to the trumpeting sound of an elephant and blinked his eyes as the early morning rays streamed through the blinds. Unsure if it was a dream, he stumbled out of his bed and pulled back the flap of the tent to squint in the direction of the sound. He was not dreaming—a herd of elephants ambled some hundred yards outside the lodge fencing and he retreated inside to grab his field glasses. Peering through them, he felt goosebumps on his back when he spotted a tusker in their midst. He zoomed the lenses and marveled at the sight of the magnificent tusks, though with a touch of helplessness—nature's gift could turn out to be a curse for some of these creatures. *Was there something ominous about sighting a tusker at the start of the day?* he wondered, stepping back into the tent.

It was still early morning and he considered going back to sleep. He had stayed up late the previous night, jotting down in his diary his observations and the discussions of the previous day. Earlier, on the way back to the lodge, Peter Otieno had resorted to every possible trick to uncover what Nick had determined at the site. While divulging nothing, Nick had managed to keep him in good humor.

He recalled his state of despair barely twelve hours earlier, while now he sensed the thrill of being hot on the trail of solving a baffling crime. Something had provided a spark to his moribund brain the previous afternoon after Peter conveyed his conversation with the girl in Nairobi.

Realizing the futility of attempting to snatch more sleep, he decided to take a long, hot shower. After dressing, he headed for the breakfast room. Along the way, he stopped at the front desk, where he found the assistant, David, alone.

"Good morning, David. I appreciate your help yesterday; can I ask you for one more favor before I begin my long journey back home?"

"Morning, Mr. Cunningham. Sure, I'll gladly help however I can."

Nick leaned over and whispered, "You're aware that I'm here on an investigation. I suspect one or more gangs of ivory poachers have been active in the park where Mary Wilson's body was discovered. Could you please get me the names of the most active gangs? Surely, you or Ben would have access to that information. As soon as I have it, I'll be on my way."

The smile on David's face disappeared. Casting a nervous glance around, he said, "I don't know, but I can try."

Nick was the first guest to reach the breakfast room. He had considerable time on his hands and decided to enjoy the large spread on offer. He worked his way through fresh fruit juices, a platter of fresh fruit, a small bowl of cereal, and finally ordered a Spanish omelet. He was halfway through this course when Peter Otieno ambled in. He said he had sat up late the previous night at the bar with some acquaintances and it showed in his unkempt appearance.

Nick was in no particular mood to chat with Peter and, after breakfast, he excused himself and headed toward the restrooms. Along the way, he passed the front desk, where David calmly handed over an envelope. There was no one else in the restroom and Nick opened the envelope to find two names written on a piece of paper. He smiled; *getting that information wasn't too difficult, was it? Everyone here seems to know what's going on—it's just that they can't talk about it.*

While relieving himself in a restroom in a luxury lodge, deep in the Maasai Mara Game Reserve, Nick deliberated his next move. He was now at the crossroads of his investigation and needed to take stock. He was satisfied that he had uncovered the circumstances under which Mary Wilson met her death. She had stopped her vehicle when she witnessed an operation being conducted at the behest of a senior official. She had photographed the act, but her camera had been destroyed—he had chanced to find the lens cover lying at the crime scene.

He had been able to reconstruct the events that she had witnessed and for which she had paid the ultimate price. He now had the names of two possible perpetrators. Under normal circumstances, he would have continued with his investigations until he had identified the real culprit. But the state of affairs here was not normal and offered little scope for him to uncover further evidence.

The odds were stacked heavily against him: all evidence at the crime scene had been tampered with or even removed; forensic reports were obviously doctored; and the officials were determined to prevent him from unearthing the real cause of death. How could he be expected to come up with any further information, no matter how much longer he continued?

Nick's thoughts were interrupted when a tourist walked in. He cleaned up and returned to the breakfast room. He told Peter that his investigations were complete and they could head back to Nairobi right away.

Within the hour, Nick and Peter began their long journey back to Nairobi. After they exited the game reserve, they passed through a small town and Nick asked Peter to stop at a public phone booth. He put through a call to the attaché at the British High Commission whom he had met. He put in a request for a meeting with the High Commissioner the following day. He also conveyed to the official that following the meeting he hoped the report could be presented to the President of Kenya at his earliest convenience.

Nick checked in at the Serena Hotel in Nairobi late that evening.

***

## Week 2—Monday Morning

"The Commissioner needs you to come immediately to his office." Elizabeth, the secretary, could barely conceal her excitement as she summoned the officials over the intercom. "Something important seems to have come up."

With an air of expectancy, they walked in—and weren't disappointed. Nods of approval and appreciative looks were exchanged as they glimpsed the shining exhibit perched in the middle of the large table.

"The Italian briefcase!" exclaimed Julius Wachira.

"Made from genuine leather," added Gideon Odhiambo.

"With a 'Limited Edition' tag," said Bic Okello.

"So this is what bheyish color looks like," concluded Bono Njoroge.

Commissioner Michael Karanja watched them in silence as they took their seats.

"Congratulations, sir, on recovering such a vital piece of evidence," remarked Gideon. "I'm sure there's a lot we can learn about the techniques you employed in its recovery."

"Do we also have the goods—I mean, the cash?" asked Wachira.

"No," replied Karanja.

"So we found only the briefcase without the money? But that by itself is a major step forward. I knew all along you'd be able to crack the problem. You must tell us about the problems you undoubtedly encountered," said Gideon.

"In fact, it was my son who recovered it," the Commissioner responded, a sheepish expression on his face.

"Your son, boss? That's a smart kid—a chip off the old block, as they say," beamed Bic. "We now have a major piece of evidence. This could lead us to important clues; how about dusting it for fingerprints?"

"Yes, of course," said Gideon. "As I've been saying, we have to depend on our own resources to solve this case and not outsource the investigation. Where did your son find the briefcase?"

"The thieves must have thrown it away after removing the money, as they always do."

"But where did he find it?" persisted Julius. "If your son tells us where, we can take over from there. That's the least we can do to show our appreciation for the lad's initiative." He looked around at his colleagues, who nodded in approval.

"Some kid found it in the garbage dump at Kariokor. My son took it from him and brought it home." Karanja's response was barely audible.

There was silence all around as the initial excitement ebbed away.

"But we could at least check for fingerprints," said Gideon.

Karanja shook his head. "The briefcase was thoroughly wiped after it was brought home—naturally, no one was aware of its importance. There's no need to waste time checking for fingerprints."

They continued standing in silence until the Commissioner spoke. "Look, I don't believe finding this piece will be of much help. I called you to take a look, since it's become the center of attraction. We can close the meeting for now—Gideon, you might wish to carry out further analysis of the briefcase." After a pause, he added, "We could've had a photo shoot with us around this piece if we'd recovered the money. But no pictures for now."

They rose from their chairs to take a closer look at the briefcase. Bono shook his head and remarked, "How can anyone throw away something as expensive as this in the garbage dump? Is other expensive stuff also thrown away by people in the dump?"

Julius sniggered, "Bono, I hope you aren't getting crazy ideas. Don't go crawling into some filthy garbage dump in the hope of finding fancy, expensive stuff!"

Before others could take a swipe at Bono, Toto Kilonzo walked in.

"Come in, Toto," Karanja said. "I called you to take a look at the briefcase, which has been recovered."

Like his colleagues, Toto stood in awe, admiring the object on the table.

"Just making sure you didn't see either of those two gangs walking away with this piece last week?" Karanja asked.

"No, sir, I could never have missed such an exquisite item."

"It looks good, doesn't it?" Bic asked.

Toto nodded his head.

"But it has a flat bottom," said Bono. "Toto only likes objects with nice round bottoms." He gestured a well-rounded female figure using both his hands. His large mouth opened up in a wide grin with his bulbous nose bulging to its limit. Breaking into laughter, the officers left the room—all except the Deputy Commissioner Odhiambo.

He remained seated and said, "I've just received information from our boys. Tusker has gone into hiding—in Kibera."

"Why?" asked Karanja. "To hide from the Minister?"

"Must be. He probably believes the Minister's threats that he'll send his men to finish him. That's what the Minister does—makes those who carry out jobs for him believe that he has men who use strong-arm tactics."

"Are you sure the Minister hasn't taken on more men for such jobs?"

"No," his deputy confidently answered. "Maybe one or two bodyguards, but no one who can overpower someone like Tusker."

Karanja didn't doubt his deputy's contention. He was aware that Gideon's informant was his relative, an ex-police constable who had now joined the Minister's force. He said, "Are we sure Tusker hasn't found the money?"

"He would certainly hand it over to the Minister if he had recovered it."

"Yes, I guess you're right," agreed Karanja. "And what's Don doing?"

"Still sulking and feeling guilty about losing the briefcase. But he's not being threatened by anyone and he's keeping quiet. And he too doesn't have the cash."

"So we're still looking for it—but where on Earth is it?"

Gideon was pensive for a moment before replying, "At first, I suspected the Russian, but when he came to the police station, I knew he couldn't have had the money. But I haven't yet met the Indian, so I can't say."

"Or it could be with someone else."

"Bic and Bono haven't delivered on what they promised. If they're so sure the money is with either of these two men, then they must be told we expect them to deliver," Gideon sounded firm and unrelenting.

"But what can they do now, Gideon? We can't have any more break-ins in private homes." Karanja stopped himself from letting his deputy in on the information he'd received from James Maina of the Tea Authority. He continued, "Okay, Gideon, I've got stuff to take care of. Make sure our boys continue to keep a close watch on Tusker and Don."

*Damn it,* thought Karanja, as soon as Gideon left the room. *Who the heck is holding on to the cash and inflicting misery on so many people?* Maybe it was time to go along with Julius Wachira's proposal. He reached for his phone.

***

Julius Wachira proceeded to the Commissioner's office after being summoned. Along the way, he wondered why the Deputy Commissioner was engaged in an animated conversation with Bic and Bono outside his office.

The Commissioner got to the point after Julius settled down. "You called me Saturday afternoon with a proposal—let's hear it."

"I'm glad you were able to retrieve the briefcase—unfortunately, the contents are still missing. It's now time we acknowledged that the person holding the cash has the upper hand. If it's possible to facilitate an arrangement by which the cash is returned directly to the owner then, in my opinion, there should be no objection to it, as long as it's not known to anyone."

The Commissioner listened in silence as Wachira continued, "I know the money is with someone who doesn't wish to come forward to the police. He's afraid he might be detained or be treated roughly. And he's not sure that the money—or all of it—would be returned to the owner. In short, he doesn't trust us as custodians."

"Does the Indian have the cash?"

"I can't be sure. If not him, it could be his friend. But one thing he's made clear—he doesn't trust us after the two break-ins. He's convinced we were somehow involved with the burglars."

"Why is that? Did you tell him something?"

"No, sir. Honestly, I didn't even know it was his house that was to be attacked."

Karanja thought for a while. "So what are you suggesting, Julius?"

"These people would be more comfortable returning the goods to the owner through a trusted third person, like a good attorney."

"We can't allow that practice. However, if someone does it on his own, we can't stop him."

"That's correct, sir, but how can that person return the money to the owner without knowing who the owner is?"

"So if the owner's name is known, what would happen then?"

"These people would return the money through a third party. If this arrangement is kept confidential, I'm sure it would satisfy the owner."

"As the police chief, I shouldn't encourage this arrangement. But if it's the only way to close the case, then I'll give it due consideration."

"So, would you be telling me who the owner is?"

"I'll need to know who this person is before we let him know the name of the owner."

"Sir, these people will use a reliable third party, like the attorney Ravi Karnik. All we need now is for the owner to agree to this proposal. And to let Ravi Karnik know his name so that he can be contacted."

"I'll have to talk to him," said Karanja. "But I expect him to say the money should be returned to me."

"Why should it matter to him if all he wants is to get back his money?" Julius asked. "In our meetings, we've been talking about coming up with unconventional solutions. If this proposal is unconventional, then let it be considered so, but this way, at least, you have a quick solution to the problem. Isn't that more important?"

His boss took some time to respond. "Julius, you realize that we have to be very careful with what you're proposing. But I guess we might as well get done with it quickly."

Satisfied with the outcome, Julius rose to leave. He stopped briefly, as he recalled there was one puzzling aspect that he needed to clarify. But he decided to discuss it later. As he stepped out, he found Toto Kilonzo waiting outside.

"Oh, hello, Toto. Are you waiting to meet the Commissioner?"

"Yes, sir."

Julius stood outside the door, lost in deep thought, while Toto waited for him to move away. But Julius changed his mind, turned around, and headed back into Karanja's office. *So was this the missing piece of the puzzle?* he wondered.

"Yes, Julius?" the Commissioner looked up.

The inspector stood a few feet away, tapping his baton against his palm. "I've often wondered what our plans were if one of those attacks had succeeded. You certainly wouldn't have risked Tusker or Don running away with the money?"

Karanja remained silent, so Julius continued, "I would've been surprised if no one had been assigned to keep an eye on them, but I didn't expect it to be Toto Kilonzo. How was someone like him to know if they had the money?"

"From their expressions, their behavior—you know how they would have behaved if they had the money. But from the way Toto described the conditions of Don and Tusker, I knew they had failed—particularly Tusker. And they ran away empty-handed—no bags, no bulging pockets, nothing."

"And if one of them had succeeded, what was Toto supposed to do?"

Karanja was quiet for a moment. "All right, I might as well tell you. Toto's job was to alert me. Our three vehicles were on the ready nearby and would have blocked Don or Tusker if they'd tried to run away. This time, they were driving run-down cars, not stolen turbocharged vehicles. Besides, our men were itching for revenge. They were determined not to allow those guys to escape."

Julius stood in silence for a moment. "So you chose Bono and Bic to be on this team because of their contacts with Tusker and Don. What was the reason for choosing me?"

"You are a good man, Julius. And, as I said earlier, you have good judgment."

"Thank you, sir."

He turned to step out and was halfway out of the door when he heard his boss say, "And don't send too many cousins and nephews to the Indian for a job."

Julius smiled as he nodded in acknowledgment and stepped out.

Toto Kilonzo was still waiting. Julius walked up to him, straightened Toto's shirt collar and tie, patted him on his shoulder, and said, "You're doing good, Titus, you're doing real good. Keep up the good job!"

Julius sensed that being addressed to by one of his seniors by his correct name, and not Toto, would work wonders to boost Titus's ego and self-confidence.

\*\*\*

"So how has Her Highness been keeping?" Peter Otieno greeted the commissioner's secretary with his customary taunt.

"Back from a nice holiday, are we?" Elizabeth responded, making an impressive attempt to sound British.

"Phew, a holiday you say? I'm all beaten up and stressed out with the mission impossible that I was entrusted with," he responded, never missing an opportunity to unabashedly exaggerate his assignment. "I did my best to distract the Brit, but there's a limit to what I could come up with. I was like a walking encyclopedia on Kenyan wildlife, but I just couldn't go on and on." Lowering his voice, he continued, "I have this bad feeling that he's on to something—someone big is going to be in trouble."

Elizabeth merely smiled and Peter changed the topic and asked, "How are we progressing here on the briefcase saga?"

"I might as well let you know—only the briefcase has been recovered; it was empty."

"Well, that's some progress. But it probably doesn't amount to much."

The door to the commissioner's office opened and Titus Kilonzo walked out.

"Hey, lover boy, how have the ladies been treating you?" Peter spiced his greeting with ridicule.

Without a stutter and looking Peter in the eye, Toto responded, "Hello, Peter, I'm fine. You look much better after your well-deserved holiday at the Mara."

Taken aback by the tart response, Peter turned to Elizabeth and remarked, "Someone's getting smart— wonder who's been coaching him."

There was a buzz on Elizabeth's intercom and she told Peter he could go in. Elizabeth turned to Toto. "I notice boss has been spending time with you and putting you on various assignments. Are you enjoying them?"

"Oh, sure, I do. He has just given me an assignment with Bono—it sounds interesting. I finally have something to keep me busy. You know, it was difficult for me to remain attentive when I didn't have much to do. But from now on, I want to remain focused on the job at hand without getting distracted," Toto sounded confident.

"Good for you, To... I mean Titus, good for you." Elizabeth, who had not missed a word of the conversation between Julius and Toto a short while earlier, corrected herself.

Titus started to walk out of her office when Elizabeth heard a bump. She looked up to see him rubbing his forehead as a small swelling started to appear at the spot where he'd bumped his head against the doorframe.

"*Pole sana* (So sorry)," Elizabeth said as she clicked her tongue in sympathy. She turned to look at the frosted glass on the upper portion of her office partition, wondering what could have distracted him. She shook her head and smiled as she discerned the unmistakable profile of the well-endowed Phyllis walking by.

\*\*\*

"You said the detective has been able to dig out some awkward stuff?" Commissioner Karanja opened up, even before Peter Otieno could take his seat. "I told you to stick to him like a leech."

"Yes, sir. Not only did I stick to him like a leech, I also kept yapping like a rabid hyena. But those men in the game park did a lousy job. They didn't bother to clear up the area where they carried out their *magendo* (illegal) stuff, a short distance away from where the girl's body was found. This detective went through the whole place with a fine-tooth comb and a big magnifying glass. I'm sure he didn't miss anything—not even the places where those guys pissed in the bushes."

"You think he'll be able to find out what really happened?"

"Yes, sir, it's possible."

"Hmm... that's not good. You also told me on the phone he suspects that some senior official is behind these activities. You think he has any ideas who that might be?"

"I can't say for sure. He talked to quite a few rangers, the manager of the camp, and the staff at the lodges. He might have gotten some names from those guys."

"I knew those stupid guys wouldn't be able to hide everything," the Commissioner said. "Now, this detective is not required to discuss his report with me or any other official—only the President. So we just have to wait and see. All right, Peter, I think that's all for now."

"Sir, can I get a two-day vacation? I have been working all week."

"Working? I thought you just came back from a vacation at the Mara."

"Why does everyone believe I was there having a good time? Sir, it was stressful, constantly sticking to that Brit and trying to keep him busy. I don't think you need me for the next two days."

"All right, take two days off," said Karanja. "And stay away from that detective. He's still in town and he's probably tired of seeing you. I will send for you if I need you."

***

Before writing his final report, Nick Cunningham met the British High Commissioner in the morning and briefed him about his findings. He was told to go ahead and complete the report; in the meantime, the High Commissioner made an appointment to meet the President of Kenya the following afternoon, when Nick would present his report.

This had been the understanding with the President's office when the investigation with the help of Scotland Yard was arranged: the report would be presented directly to the President. There were to be no meetings or discussions with the Police Commissioner or any officials.

Working assiduously on his report, Nick reflected with satisfaction, on more than one occasion, that his fears of having become "the aging lion," and that "the old order had to make way for new" were unfounded. He had completed his mission, though he couldn't help feeling a tinge of sadness about how the victim's life had come to an end. Peter had been right—Mary Wilson had indeed erred by stepping out of her vehicle into the wild, but, alas, it was not at the hands of wild animals that she met her fate.

Uncharacteristically, he had been missing vital clues for two days, until... until what? All that happened on Saturday was that Peter mentioned the briefcase and the poaching. He had yet to come up with any plausible explanation, but hoped he could figure out this intriguing phenomenon sometime soon.

By the end of the day, Nick had his report typed and, after a brief discussion with the High Commissioner, could scarcely wait to present it to the President the next day.

# Chapter 14

## *Week 2—Late Monday*

"Yes, Karanja," the Minister greeted the Police Commissioner as he entered the office. "What information do we have?"

Glancing around the large office to ensure they were alone, Karanja settled down in a chair and responded in a hushed tone, "I believe the money is safe with someone."

The Minister sat bolt upright in his chair. "What? Where?"

"The people holding the money have come forward and want to hand it over. I've been assuring you, sir, we were on the right track and the attacks on the two homes have had some effect. The cash might not have been recovered, but the person is shaken up."

"Who is it?"

"He's not coming forward and is insisting on returning the cash to the person who lost it. He'll do it with the assistance of his attorney."

"Why doesn't he hand over the money to you?"

"He thinks that could complicate matters for him. Anyway, since news of this theft hasn't been reported, wouldn't this arrangement suit you?"

"But I don't want that person to know the money belonged to me. Tell me, why doesn't he want to hand it over to you? You are the Police Commissioner."

"Says he doesn't trust us. He fears that all the cash might not be returned to you."

"Has that happened before—the police holding on to some of it?"

The Commissioner remained silent, his head bent down.

"Well, never mind," the Minister said. "So what does the man want?"

"His attorney to accompany him when he comes to hand the stuff over."

"And who is the attorney?"

"Ravi Karnik."

"Oh, Ravi, is it? That name comes up all the time. What do you think?"

"He has a good reputation. I think he can be trusted for this transaction."

The Minister stared outside the window. Karanja felt this an opportune moment to bring up the other issue. "We found the briefcase—it was thrown away in a garbage dump."

"Really? So it's of no use?"

"It's in good condition."

"Where's it now?"

"With us; we're checking for any possible leads." Karanja continued, "I've also yet to mention about the Scotland Yard detective. He's ready to submit his report to the President. My man tells me he has found out something about Mary Wilson's death."

"What is it?"

"He hasn't mentioned anything specific, but it appears he's onto something. The guys at the park, I'm told, did a poor cover-up job."

"Those damned fools," the Minister muttered.

There was a long, uncomfortable silence before the Commissioner spoke. "*Bwana* Minister, this search for the stolen cash has gone on for too long. Now that we know it's safe, may I suggest you meet this man so that the case can be closed?"

"And what about the Mary Wilson case? I've been forced into this problem and now I could be in deep trouble. I wonder what the President would glean from the report?"

"I have one more suggestion. Ravi Karnik has a great reputation as a defense attorney."

"I know him well," the Minister retorted. "So, what's your suggestion?"

"If you're to meet him when the cash is being returned, perhaps you might consider discussing with him what you just told me about the Mary Wilson case."

The Minster was quiet, tapping a pencil on a writing pad. Karanja continued, "*Bwana* Minister, can I inform my officer that you're willing to meet that person?"

"No," said the Minister, "tell the man to get in touch with Karnik and to hand over the money to him. I shall call Karnik and ask him to see me. The man should never know I was in any way involved."

As the Commissioner rose to leave, the Minister continued, "The same thing goes for your department. My name should never be mentioned to anyone. Tell them the case is closed to the satisfaction of the complainant; that's all they need to know. Is this clearly understood?"

"Yes, sir."

Karanja called Julius Wachira and conveyed to him that his contact should hand over the money to Ravi Karnik. The concerned official would contact the attorney directly.

\*\*\*

While sipping a cup of tea after an exhausting day in the law courts, Ravi Karnik received a call from the Minister, George K. This was the first time the distinguished official had called and Ravi was cautious when he picked up the phone. "Good afternoon, Mr. Minister. Nice to hear from you; how has the day been so far?"

"Not bad, thank you, Ravi, and how has it been for you?"

"Very hectic. I just got back from the courts; as you're probably aware, I'm defending your ex-colleague against the charges leveled against him."

"Yes, I know—you are a very important person, Ravi." The attorney gave a modest response and the Minister continued, "I've been told you have a package for me."

"Sir, is this something my client has?" was Ravi's cautious response. Jay had alerted him earlier to expect a call from a senior official.

"Yes."

"I'll have to arrange to have him deliver the goods."

"To you, just so we are clear," emphasized the Minister.

"Yes, I understand."

"In that case, can you meet me in my office tomorrow morning at ten o'clock?"

"Yes. But I've to make sure I get the delivery before then. I'll call you to confirm."

"No, let's meet at ten. Tell your friend no delays. And Ravi, this whole thing is very confidential. My name must not be divulged to your client or anyone else."

"Yes, of course."

"We might need to sign a legal agreement. Bring a form with you tomorrow."

"For this transaction, signing an agreement is not necessary."

"There's some other business we need to discuss," said the Minister and hung up.

*So, it was this Minister who was involved with the briefcase that Jay stumbled upon,* thought Ravi. *Well, he was an important official and it's not surprising he's involved in various businesses. How did he manage to lose the money? And he now wants to sign an agreement with me? What problems is this very senior and influential minister in?* In his years of practice, no officials had ever sought Ravi's services unless they were in deep trouble.

He called Jay, who was at work, to let him know that the official had reached out. Jay was required to deliver the money to Ravi in his office forthwith.

***

On his way home, Jay called Heidi and gave her the update. She was relieved that their dilemma was to soon end and said she'd accompany him to meet Ravi.

"Is that a good idea?" he asked her.

"Why not? I haven't met him since the incident and would like to have a word with him."

Jay wondered what was on her mind, but didn't wish to enter into a discussion. Reaching home, he dashed upstairs to collect the backpack full of cash and the two drove off.

While driving along the approach road outside his house, he noted a gray Mitsubishi sedan parked on the side. In the passenger seat was a young man with a red cap. When his Honda entered the main road, Jay glanced in the rearview mirror to note that the Mitsubishi had started to move.

Despite the rush-hour traffic, Jay made good progress as he coasted along the Waiyaki Way and entered the Chiromo Road. From the rearview mirror, he noted the gray Mitsubishi speeding in the fast lane and catching up with him. He expected the car to pass him, but it switched lanes to stay behind him as they entered the Uhuru Highway. He wondered if they were being followed, but he refrained from mentioning it to Heidi.

The traffic slowed down when they approached the busy roundabout at the intersection of the Uhuru Highway and Kenyatta Avenue. Jay turned left into the avenue and noted that the Mitsubishi made a stop at the corner. He asked Heidi to keep an eye on the vehicle and, in the rearview mirror, she saw a stout man climb into the rear seat before the car began to move again. Traffic was heavy and both vehicles made slow progress. A few yards ahead, Jay noted in the rearview mirror, the Mitsubishi swerved left into a side street, cutting off traffic on the service road, as the driver deftly maneuvered his vehicle through the narrow back streets and by-lanes. Heidi looked anxiously at Jay, but he remained quiet and turned left at the next traffic light.

They were barely a block away from Ravi's office when the Mitsubishi emerged from a side street ahead of them and swerved to join the flow, two vehicles ahead of them.

"It's the same car!" Heidi gasped.

"Who the hell are these guys? The same ones who attacked you?" Jay asked.

"Not sure—can't see them."

When the traffic started to move, Jay made a quick decision—he turned left onto the same street from where the Mitsubishi had emerged. While turning into the street, he glanced toward the other vehicle, now stuck in traffic a short distance ahead, and got a proper view of the young man with a red cap. Jay could now recall—it was the same man he'd seen two days previously outside their house by the kiosk.

Jay sped down the street and turned right into a back alley. A car was pulling out from the curb ahead and he lost no time in parking in the empty spot. He looked around and realized they were three buildings away from the one housing Ravi's office.

"Come! Let's make a dash to Ravi's office," he said to Heidi, grabbing the backpack.

\*\*\*

Darkness had descended in the Lower Kabete neighborhood by the time Mikhail Smirnoff returned home from work and pulled up his car outside his house. The gate swung open and, as he drove by, he noted that it was not Njiru his *askari* who stood there, but someone unfamiliar. At first, he assumed that the security firm had sent a substitute guard, but something in the man's demeanor didn't seem right and Mikhail stopped. Turning his head around, he was surprised when two men approached him and stood alongside the car.

"Good evening, *Bwana* Smirnoff," greeted one of them.

Mikhail's eyes popped open as he recognized the two men, both armed with guns.

"What are you doing here, Mr. Officer?" Mikhail could not recall Bic's name.

"We're here to have a little chat. Remember this man?" the man said, pointing to his companion. Mikhail recognized him as the leader of the gang that had broken in the previous week. "He says you haven't returned the cash that was stolen from him ten days ago."

"Why are you guys wasting my time? And what have you done to my *askari*?" Mikhail asked when he noticed his guard lying in the gatehouse with his mouth gagged and hands and feet bound with rope.

The officer continued in a firm tone, "Let's go in and talk. I think Mama and your daughter would be keen for you to solve this man's problem."

"Mama and...? What have you guys done?" Mikhail hollered at them as he shifted the gear stick and drove the short distance to his house with the two men following him on foot at a brisk pace. In one swift movement, Mikhail slipped the revolver that he carried in his car into his hip pocket before stepping out. He rushed toward the front door, but the officer cautioned, "There's no need for any hasty action. Let's play it cool so that no one gets hurt."

Mikhail waited while the officer walked up to the front door and tapped on it thrice. An armed man, whom Mikhail recognized as one of the intruders, opened the door to allow them in. When he stepped in, his attention was immediately drawn toward the sight of his wife, Olga, and daughter, Tanya, each bound to a chair with rope and gags on their mouths. Another member of the gang stood near them, a gun pointed at Olga's head.

"*Moi suet*," he cried out to Olga and continued in Russian, "I'll get you two free, no matter what. I swear I'm going to kick the shit out of these bastards."

***

"Jacob, chase them! Don't lose sight of the car!" Inspector Bono ordered from the rear seat in the Mitsubishi. Dressed in plain clothes, he was directing today's mission. "Daniel, park the car and join us. I'm sure they're headed for one of these buildings. I'll join Jacob and will give you a call when we spot them."

Bono hauled himself out of the back seat. A half hour earlier, he had received a call from Daniel—the young man reported in an excited tone that the *Muhindi* had rushed home earlier than usual and, a few minutes later, had dashed back out, accompanied by his *Mzungu* wife. Bono suspected they were planning to deliver the cash to an accomplice or store it someplace safe. He had to act fast and had directed Daniel to follow the Honda and to pick him up at the designated place.

They were now in the commercial district. Their quarry was heading to one of the surrounding buildings and Bono wondered who were they meeting, He trotted as fast he could and saw Jacob wave and point to the parked Honda Accord. The couple had to be somewhere nearby. Two buildings away, Bono spotted a man carrying a backpack and a *Mzungu* woman by his side.

\*\*\*

Jay and Heidi ran down the back alley, past three buildings, heading toward the front of the one that housed Ravi's office. They were about to join the stream of pedestrians when Jay held Heidi back. Barely fifty feet away, the Mitsubishi was double-parked on the road and the driver stood by his vehicle, apparently waiting for a parking spot.

"My God!" exclaimed Heidi. "He was there that day they broke in the house."

"Is he the leader?"

"No, he's the guy I kicked out of the house."

"I see. Now, let's slip into the building as quietly as possible."

"Wait!" said Heidi. "He's gesturing to those guys there." She pointed to her right, where two men waved to the driver by his car. One of them was plump and portly, while the other wore a red cap.

"That man there—the one with the red cap," Jay exclaimed. "I'm sure I've seen him hanging around outside our house two days ago. Was he also there that day?"

"No, and neither was that stout man."

"Quick, *liebchen*, let's get moving." Grasping Heidi's hand, Jay stepped out and the two merged with the milling crowd around them. While stepping into the building entrance, Jay glanced sideways and could make out that the man beside the Mitsubishi had spotted them and was pointing them out to his accomplices.

Jay and Heidi made a dash for the two elevators, but both were in use. They turned and ran toward the door to the staircase. As he shut the door, Jay saw the plump man and Red Cap enter the building. Jay and Heidi bounded up the stairs—they had a long way to go to Ravi's office on the seventh floor. They had barely made it past the third floor when the staircase door on the first floor flung open and someone raced swiftly up the stairs. If he was one of their pursuers, his speed suggested it must be Red Cap, the Plump One probably having opted to take the elevator.

Reaching the landing on the fourth floor, Jay noticed a niche behind the fire hose mounted on the wall. He gestured to Heidi to sneak into the niche while he opened the staircase door and slammed it shut again to suggest to the pursuer they had exited the stairwell. After shutting the door, Jay turned back and slipped into the niche with Heidi. The two sat still as they heard Red Cap reach the landing on their floor. The ruse worked. Their pursuer opened the staircase door and entered the passageway, believing that the two were now on that floor.

They emerged from their hideout and resumed their climb up the stairs—three more levels to go. Halfway up, they heard the staircase door on the first floor open and, once again, they heard the footsteps of a man bounding up the stairs.

"Oh shit!" exclaimed Jay; he reckoned it must be the third man, the Driver. The two continued running up and were on the sixth-floor landing when the staircase door on the ninth floor above them opened and someone walked in. Jay and Heidi slipped into the hiding spot behind the hose reel on the sixth floor when the man on the ninth floor hollered down the stairwell, "Jacob!" It was the Plump One, who had taken the elevator to the topmost floor and was now working his way down. The man ascending the staircase below them cried out, "It's me, Daniel. Where's Jacob and where's that couple?"

Jay realized the niche wasn't large to conceal them both—he would be spotted by anyone passing them. He whispered to Heidi to remain crouched in the niche, no matter what happened. They heard the staircase door, two floors below them, being flung open and a man called out, "Daniel, are you down there?" It was the voice of Red Cap, who had obviously reentered the stairwell.

"Bono, Jacob is here. We're both coming up," Daniel called out to the Plump One.

Jay and Heidi held their breath as the three pursuers closed in on them from both directions. In the cramped niche, Heidi wrapped her arms firmly around Jay, while the thumping of the footsteps of the Plump One, now identified as Bono, turned louder as he descended the stairs. The younger, fitter men, meanwhile, made swift progress as they raced up.

Jay braced himself as Bono trotted past them and then attempted to stop after sighting his target behind the fire hose. Firmly gripping his backpack, Jay stepped out and watched Bono struggle to arrest the momentum of his enormous weight while swinging around at the same time to change direction. Retreating back, a few steps at a time, Jay kept his eyes focused on Bono as he lunged forward, attempting to snatch the backpack. Jay was ready—he swerved away, drawing Bono close to the landing of the stairs. This was the moment—in one aggressive movement, Jay sprung forward, raised the backpack and swung it at Bono, striking him on his cheek. The blow forced Bono to step back and he stood gasping, precariously close to the edge of the staircase landing. He looked down to see his accomplices climbing up the last flight of steps. "Quick," he wheezed, "this man is attacking me."

Sensing he now had the upper hand, Jay lunged forward with his arms raised, threatening to swing the backpack at his adversary, sending him teetering over the edge of the staircase. Unable to find his balance, Bono went into a free fall down the staircase. He yelled as he landed into the arms of the Jacob a few steps below. Both men tumbled down the staircase, knocking down Daniel, who was not far behind.

The sudden lunge left Jay with a torn foot ligament, but he pulled himself up and glanced down from the top of the landing. What he witnessed below was not a pretty sight—Bono, with a bloodied nose, lay in a heap on a landing along with the other two.

Jay called out to Heidi and they raced up one more floor and exited the staircase door, making a dash for Ravi's office. They pounded on his door and when an anxious Ravi opened it, they rushed in. Jay bolted the front door behind them, while Heidi collapsed in the nearest chair.

***

From the front door, Inspector Bic watched as Mikhail rushed toward his wife and daughter, but was stopped by Don, who stepped in, brandishing a gun.

"Easy, *Bwana* Smirnoff, easy," Bic addressed him. "Your wife was good enough to show us where you store your weapons. We have placed them in that corner and, since we would not like to have the sound of gunfire, the bullets have been removed and kept away. And just so you know, one more man is at the gate and his job is to make sure no one disturbs us while we resolve this issue, which, I need hardly add, should be done with a sense of urgency."

"Why are you after us?" the Russian retorted. "Haven't I told you we don't have the money?"

"I doubt Mama would agree with you," Bic continued in a calm tone. "She kindly showed us where you stack the dough. Twenty-five thousand US dollars in cash—there it is in that blue bag. That's too little. Where's the rest? Did you collect some more from a client on your way home? We might find it in your car."

"You guys tortured my wife? And someone has been following me?"

"Now, now—I'll repeat. We're not interested in the money that belongs to you. This man wants back the money that was stolen from him. Let's resolve this issue and get it done with; as I said earlier, we mean no harm."

Bic had methodically planned his unorthodox operation to recover the stolen cash and had conducted it with remarkable composure. He had anticipated tough resistance from the Russian and had taken precautions to deny him access to his formidable weaponry. Where he erred was in assuming that Mikhail had, at worst, the temperament of a Yeti. He was about to discover, to his misfortune, that he had unwittingly unleashed in the Russian an extreme mix of the Incredible Hulk and Bruce Lee, the two heroes Mikhail adored.

With his eyes shut, Mikhail brought all his senses to a sharp focus while triggering his enormous strength. When he opened them, there was little that Bic or Don or their minions could do. He sprang forward with the unexpected agility of a martial arts master and, leaping high in the air, swung in a full circle to land a stunning kick on Bic's jaw that knocked him down and smashed his dazzling teeth. Swinging around, Mikhail cartwheeled to Don and Paul, grasped their heads and banged them hard against each other, leaving them dazed and disoriented. As the two sank to the floor, Mikhail kicked their guns out of their hands and sprang toward a bewildered Jacob. Delivering a karate chop on his wrist to knock his gun down, Mikhail pulled his pistol out from his hip pocket. Pointing it toward the intruders, he ordered them to leave forthwith.

"I warned you to leave us alone," were his last words to Bic and Don as they were bundled out. He set Olga and Tanya free and, after ensuring his weapons, bullets, and the bag with money were safe, he headed for the bar, where he opened a bottle of vodka.

***

Ravi was alone in the office; his staff had left for the day when Jay and Heidi made their dramatic entry. After they'd settled down, he offered sodas and juices from his refrigerator and cold compresses for Jay's swollen ankle.

After listening to their harrowing experience, he phoned the building's security firm and asked their supervisor to come immediately with additional men to deal with the intruders. His next call was to the reception desk of the building, now manned by a guard. It took a while for him to respond, explaining he was busy with the commotion initiated by a few visitors. When asked to elaborate, he said three men with serious injuries had just tottered out of the building. They explained that while descending the staircase, one of them tripped and had unwittingly injured the other two. The *askari* described the nature of injuries: the plump one suffered a broken nose, the red-capped man hobbled on one foot, while the third one bemoaned that his driving skills might be permanently jeopardized, owing to a broken wrist.

When the supervisor from the security firm arrived, Ravi asked him to ensure there were no other intruders in the building and to keep an additional guard available to escort him, as well as his two visitors, to the car park.

After the supervisor took leave, Ravi said to Heidi, "Jay told me about the burglary last week—you truly are amazing, Heidi! You were not seriously hurt, were you?"

"I'm okay, Ravi, but as you can see, they haven't given up. We need to return the money quickly to the owner—can you arrange to deliver it today even though it's late? Only then would our minds be at peace."

Ravi picked up the phone and dialed a number. But there was no response: the Minister and his staff had left for the day. And Ravi did not have his house phone number.

"I guess that rules out handing it over today. Meanwhile, let's count the cash."

"The breakdown is here on this sheet," replied Jay, opening up the backpack. He pulled out the bundles of currency, and the three counted and checked the notes.

"Looks okay to me," said Ravi. "My problem would be to get it safely to the owner. I'll need to ask him to send his security personnel to accompany me."

He rose from his chair and walked to a corner of the room. Moving a corner table away to reveal a built-in safe, he deposited the backpack in it and said, "We'll have to trust the security firm to keep the intruders away tonight, particularly after my conversation with their supervisor."

Settling down in his seat, he said, "We need to leave soon, but can you guys tell me what the heck is going on?"

Avoiding Ravi's penetrating gaze, Jay replied, "It's all about my stupid act last week—these guys are dangerous and I had no idea we were being followed when we drove here."

"The amount is no small change, Jay, and don't forget, you are dealing with criminals."

"Jay did something stupid—that we know," said Heidi. "But we've got to decide about the money. You're planning on returning it to the owner, aren't you?"

"Isn't that what you wanted?"

Heidi didn't wait for Jay to respond. "Yes, that's what I said earlier. But I'm concerned that the money is being used for something illegal. By returning the money, it'll be business as usual for them."

Ravi looked confused. "Now, how on Earth am I supposed to take care of that?"

"Why not ask the owner to donate the money to a charity?" Heidi suggested.

Ravi rolled his eyes. "How is donating to a charity connected to illegal activities?"

"Heidi and I would have the satisfaction that, to some extent, by denying them access to funds, we would make it difficult for them to continue to freely conduct whatever business they are up to. She risked her life, you know—let that effort not have been in vain," Jay sounded emotional.

Ravi thought for a moment before replying, "Why don't you just hand over this cash to some charity instead of returning it?"

"I'm bound to be questioned about the source of this money and I could be in trouble. On the other hand, a rich, influential person would know how to go about making a donation, without too many questions being asked," said Jay.

Ravi stared at the two of them before addressing Heidi. "This is the first time I'm dealing with a German—you certainly are living up to the reputation of them being tough nuts to crack—you don't give in easily, do you?" He was silent for a moment before continuing, "Well, all I can say is that I'll give it a try. I'll let the owner know how strongly you feel about the donation. Let's see what he says."

Ravi phoned the reception desk and asked for a guard to escort the three of them to their vehicles.

"Now, no more of your smart moves, do you understand?" Ravi admonished Jay as they walked out of his office. "Let's pray this saga comes to a quick end."

# Chapter 15

## *Week 2—Tuesday*

The chirping of birds woke her up—but this time, Heidi felt fresh and relaxed after a full night's sleep, the first time in ten days. Despite the harrowing experience the previous evening, she felt confident their dilemma would soon end.

The details of last Friday's break-in were not known to many—she and Jay explained to their friends that she and her *askari* had surprised a burglar who had broken into the house when she reached home that afternoon. He had roughed her up while struggling to flee through the front door, which would explain the ugly bruises on her face.

Meanwhile, she had kept herself occupied with the upcoming event at her school, collecting several attractive prizes for the raffle. Apart from members of the business community, she expected many of her friends—including Anne and Richards Collins—to attend.

***

"*Jambo* Ravi. *Habari gani* (How are you)?" the Minister greeted Ravi Karnik as he was ushered into his office. While Ravi took his seat, the Minister instructed his secretary they were not to be disturbed. He turned to Ravi. "Do you have the money?"

"Yes," responded Ravi and pulled out two large envelopes from his briefcase.

"Do we need to check?" the Minister asked after opening the envelopes.

"There's fifteen million shillings. I have counted—you have my word."

"All right, then, make sure this stays between us. I don't need to know who gave you the money and that person doesn't need to know who received it, is that clear?"

Ravi nodded as the Minister continued, "For more than sixteen years, I've put in hard work for this government. During that period, I've made many friends, but there are others who are jealous of my success and would do anything to bring me down."

Ravi shrugged and commented that he guessed that's how things were for those in power.

The Minister continued, "On the one hand, I'm under pressure to oblige some people by doing things that I cannot refuse, while on the other hand, my enemies would stop at nothing and would accuse me falsely of doing things I haven't done. Can you imagine how difficult it can get for me at times?"

Ravi nodded and assured the Minister that he would be happy to provide any legal advice that might be of help.

"Of course, there is the issue of complete confidentiality," the Minster continued.

"Oh, absolutely. I'll be bound by our agreement."

"There was a transaction—well, actually an operation—that was forced upon me. Several things went wrong and I might be made the scapegoat. Not only would I be forced to resign or be kicked out by the President, but also my foes might try to bring legal action against me. That's where you come in."

One more nod from Ravi before the Minister continued, "You've been very successful as a defense attorney, Ravi. As my attorney, you will protect me from any civil or criminal suits that my enemies might file against me. I'll be depending on you to defend me, should those bandicoots from the sewers carry out their threats to finish me off."

"I'm honored, sir, by your trust in me. You would appreciate that each case I've worked on has been different and you would, no doubt, provide me with all the details."

"I am confident you would be able to work with me—I'm aware of the cases you've successfully defended. I'll provide all the details; but not now. At this stage, I need to be assured of your services since, when those crooks decide to move, things might happen swiftly."

Ravi cleared his throat. Almost all the past cases had begun with such intangible statements from his clients, but he had to make his requirements known. "Sir, this is the agreement I would need you to sign so that we have confirmation that I will be acting in the capacity of your attorney."

Ravi pulled out a few sheets of blank forms from his briefcase and placed them before the Minister as he continued, "Attached is a schedule of my fees, which needs your acceptance. There is also a requirement of a deposit that you would need to pay for the contract to be deemed valid. Undoubtedly, that deposit would be returned if the case does not materialize."

Both men knew the Minister had very few options if he was in the kind of trouble that called for such a meeting.

"The Scotland Yard detective is scheduled to meet the President this afternoon," said the Minister. "We'll know what the President decides to do next. We should plan to meet tomorrow morning around eleven o'clock. I'll give you a call to confirm the meeting."

Ravi thought for a moment before querying, "A Scotland Yard detective is meeting the President? Are your problems in some way connected to the Mary Wilson incident?"

"You'll have the information tomorrow when we meet."

"All right—I'll wait for your call, sir," Ravi said as he rose and left.

*How do these chaps get themselves in such a jam?* thought Ravi, as he headed for the law courts. But then, that was why he had maintained a dominant position in this business; a niche area in which no other lawyer had yet achieved any degree of success.

\*\*\*

Deputy Commissioner Gideon Odhiambo paced up and down his office, shoulders stooped, head hunched down and a grim expression on his face. Casting an impatient glance at the clock, he muttered, "What's holding up those fools?"

The door opened and Bono and Bic entered. They had reported late to work after calling in to say they both needed to visit the doctor for reasons they would not divulge. Gideon stared at them aghast and asked them to be seated.

Grimacing in pain, the two settled down as Gideon, without wasting a moment, embarked on his tirade. "How could you guys blow this job as well? Is this what you learned at the police academy—allowing yourself to be trashed by unarmed civilians? Now we're all knee-deep in elephant shit—all because you two failed to deliver and for which you'll pay the price."

Gideon realized no legible words could come forth from Bic's bruised mouth. He sat there in pain, his perfect set of milky white teeth brutally shattered and with grim prospects for any prosthodontist in the country to restore them to their former glory. He started to scribble on a notepad.

In relatively better shape was Bono, from whom Gideon expected some response. Heavy bandages covered the nasal area above his mouth, with the doctor delivering the grim news that his smashed bulbous nose would never regain its original shape. He did, however, provide a ray of hope to Bono's wife that it was possible that the reconstructed nose might bestow upon her husband a more amenable appearance. Despite his constraints, Bono could muster, "Those two assistants of Tusker's were useless. They could not catch the *Muhindi* and his wife. Those guys did not even warn me when I was attacked and pushed over the staircase by that evil couple."

"You took a beating from an Indian, of all people?" Gideon pounced on him. "You're lucky your balls were saved from being mauled by that German woman."

Bono looked away, while Gideon sat fretting in his chair before speaking up. "That thug, Tusker, seems to be having a nice vacation after creating a mess for us all."

Bic pushed his scribbled note toward him and Gideon turned to Bic after reading it. "And you say that Don was of no help? And that he should give up poaching and go back to being a nomadic Maasai herdsman?"

The two inspectors remained silent and Gideon continued, "What a mess! Both of you better stick to the stories you made up about how you suffered your injuries. If the Commissioner ever comes to know what really happened, the two of you would need to start looking for another job."

After a pause, he continued, "And some people might have to wait a long time for their promotion—starting with me."

***

There was a flurry of activity outside the State House of the President in Nairobi. Members of the press requested that the spokesman confirm if Mr. Cunningham, the Scotland Yard detective, was to meet the President to present his report. The spokesman, like his counterparts in other parts of the world, evaded giving a direct response, stating that the latest information he could share was that the detective's report was in the process of being finalized for presentation to His Excellency, the President, who would choose to receive it at his pleasure. He then clamped his mouth shut when a newsman reported that the British High Commissioner's limousine had pulled up into the main State House entrance a minute earlier.

The evening news on the television channels confirmed that the British High Commissioner, along with a Scotland Yard detective, had met with the President at the State House and submitted his findings. The President was reported to have thanked them for their efforts and said that he would study the report and take appropriate action. But none of the news channels had access to the contents of the report.

\*\*\*

After browsing through Nick Cunningham's report, the President passed it on to his Permanent Secretary for him to study and discuss the next day. The report remained in his office and a staff member gained access to it. After going through it, he put in a call to his good friend, the Police Commissioner. "The detective hasn't missed much, *Bwana* Commissioner. What Mary Wilson observed, how she met her death, and the name of the senior official—it's all covered."

"How about the names of the actual culprits?"

"He has given two names—he says with the available evidence, he cannot establish which one of the two is the culprit."

"From the outset, I knew we had a difficult situation on hand," the Commissioner said. "Too many players were involved and someone could be expected to slip up. We did our best—the rest is now up to the President."

\*\*\*

# Week 2—Wednesday Morning

Ravi Karnik sensed an air of helplessness surrounding the Minister when he walked into his office. From his desk, the official pulled out the agreement Ravi had given him the previous day and handed over a signed copy. He took out his checkbook and wrote a check toward the deposit.

After ascertaining the documents were in order, Ravi said, "Mr. Minister, we have formalized our relationship and I am now bound by the client-lawyer confidentiality clause. Would you like to provide me with more details?"

"As I mentioned yesterday, the last operation went terribly wrong. It's not just the money aspect that I am worried about, but, through no fault of mine, my name has been implicated in the Mary Wilson case. Of course, I have no direct connection with her death—it's just that the operation went wrong and the guy on the spot lost his cool and committed the heinous act. Unfortunately, the incident became a high-profile case and now the Scotland Yard detective has uncovered something and submitted his report to the President yesterday."

Ravi made notes at a brisk pace in his pad as the Minister continued, "I don't think I need to provide you with more details today. In the event a case is filed against me, you'll be given all the information. This morning, I've submitted my resignation to the President, which he has accepted; I'm retiring on health grounds."

Ravi looked up in surprise, but said nothing as the Minister continued, "That stupid woman—that Mary Wilson—why did she have to poke her nose everywhere? She started to take photographs of these guys with the elephants. They caught her and asked for the camera, but she refused and threatened to report the matter. That is when that fool went crazy and finished her off."

"Was this operation being carried out with your... your knowledge?" asked Ravi.

The Minister nodded. "As I mentioned, I was forced into some of these things to please important people. Personally, I'm totally against this business of poaching. Anyway, some of the guys at the Mara opened their mouths to the detective and my name was mentioned and he's put it in the report."

Ravi thought for a moment and decided not to dwell on this any further. But there was another issue that he needed to clarify. "And the money that I returned to you?"

"That money was for the ivory, but the briefcase with the money was stolen and then thrown away. Your friend... I mean your client, found it and now that has been taken care of. But a lot of damage has been done."

"You have submitted your resignation. But are you still concerned that there could be a legal case against you because of the money or due to involvement in the murder?"

"The gang leader who killed her will be picked up by the police and will be charged with the murder. That was the understanding with the President. About the money connected with the ivory—that could be a problem if my enemies come to know about it."

Ravi was silent as he recalled Heidi's and Jay's impassioned plea the previous evening. A surge of sympathy swept through him—yes, this money was being used for an activity that he strongly condemned, and he felt compelled to express his resentment the way Jay did.

That's the least he could do for Jay—or, more importantly, for Heidi. He addressed the Minister. "If I may suggest, you might consider donating the money to the Wildlife Conservation Fund. I'm sure the President would view this gesture favorably and it would certainly not harm your case if someone were to charge that you were involved in this business for monetary gains."

"But I have to make settlements with various people."

"Settlements for what?" asked Ravi, starting to sound passionate. "The money would only go to line people's pockets. The poor elephants that were slaughtered are the ones that have paid the price. At least the donation would go some way in preventing this evil practice, which you said you were reluctantly forced into."

The Minister seemed shaken by Ravi's response and sat in silence. His voice was meek when he spoke up. "So you think I should let the President know about the donation and seek his blessings before donating it?"

"Yes, sir, that is my humble suggestion."

"All right then, Ravi. I think I'll follow your suggestion. I'll let you know if there are any further developments."

"Yes, of course, Mr. Minister. I'm sorry the country is losing your services after all these years. But I'll do my best to ensure your reputation remains untarnished."

\*\*\*

Ravi Karnik had barely walked out of the Minister's office when the Police Commissioner was ushered in. The Minister was gazing out of the window and he gestured to Karanja to take a seat.

"It's all over, Karanja, *kwisha* (finished). I've just come back from a meeting with the *Mzee* (referring to the President). I've put in my papers for retirement. I did my best to accommodate many people, but in the end, it didn't work out. After some time, things get complicated and it's just not possible to please everyone; am I right, Karanja?"

Karanja nodded in agreement, though he had no clue what the Minister was talking about.

"Whatever I have done was to help someone else. I haven't done anything to help myself, as you know." Karanja once again nodded, though this time he didn't fully agree.

The Minister pushed aside some papers on his table and continued, "Now, let me tell you what needs to be done. I met Ravi Karnik and the cash has been returned. So you can call off the hunt for the cash."

Karanja heaved an audible sigh of relief even as the Minister continued, "The cash will be donated anonymously to a charity organization. So you see, I'll not be making any money in this *magendo* (illegal) operation."

Karanja was surprised to hear this announcement. But he held off from making any comments as he heard the Minister say, "As I'm sure you know, 'Tusker' John used to do some jobs for me. And when I say 'me,' I mean so many other people who have been forcing me to do this dirty work. But Tusker messed things up and then I started to use *Ndovu* Don. But he could not even hold on to a briefcase and has left me with this big problem. And this would not have come out, but that detective has found out what caused the British girl's death and submitted his report to the President."

"I haven't seen the report. Who does he blame for her death?"

"That stupid girl had no business snooping around. As a tourist, she should have stuck to her route. But no, she had to go out of the way to snoop around, just when these guys were handling the elephants. She threatened to report their activities to the authorities and that's when this brutal man could not control himself and finished her off."

Karanja could not see the connection, but he did not interrupt as the Minister continued, "Now that the President knows, there is no alternative but to arrest that guy and charge him with the murder of Mary Wilson. This was the agreement with the President."

Karanja cautiously asked, "So, should I go ahead and arrest Don?"

"Don? Not Don," snapped back the Minister. "It's Tusker."

"Tusker?" asked Karanja incredulously. "I thought Don was working for you..."

"Don has a quiet temperament and he wouldn't have done this stupid thing. It's Tusker who is hotheaded and lost his temper when he caught that girl spying on him. That idiot couldn't control himself and has landed us in this mess."

"Then what's the connection with the stolen money?"

"After the girl's body was found, there was so much publicity, as you know. There were many reporters moving around Maasai Mara making inquiries. Also, people from the British High Commission were there and then her father came here and made so much noise. The ivory just could not be moved out and we had to lie low. It had to be hidden for some time until things quieted down."

The Minister paused to take a breath before resuming. "But there was a contract for a set amount of ivory and we were falling short. The Somali, who takes the ivory out of the country and sells it, was after us to complete the contract. I was mad with Tusker and told him our relationship was over and decided Don would work for me. He carried out the operation two weeks ago to make up the total quantity of ivory for the contract."

The Minister took a sip of water. "The full quantity of ivory was handed over ten days ago to the Somali and it was arranged that he would hand over the money to Don, since I didn't wish to be seen with the Somali. But Tusker came to know of this transaction and wanted to take revenge by stealing the money and then maybe making a demand on me to take him back."

"So Tusker arranged to steal the briefcase. But then how did it go missing?"

"That's something that is puzzling. I don't know whether to believe the story that the thief who Tusker used became nervous when the police car cornered them. He threw the briefcase away before others could stop him. He was a petty thief, as you know. Again, Tusker was so mad that he beat him to death. That also was not necessary."

"So the briefcase was picked up by someone, and that person arranged to return the money to you through Ravi Karnik?"

"Which I have now donated and not kept for myself," completed the Minister.

"All right, sir. We'll arrange to pick up Tusker. Is there anything else?"

The Minister remained quiet as Karanja stood to leave. He had reached the door when he heard the Minister say, "You told me you've recovered the briefcase."

Karanja held his breath as he replied, "Yes."

"Please arrange to deliver it to me. And make sure it's properly wrapped up. No one should know what it is."

"Yes, sir," was the response from a visibly disappointed Police Commissioner.

\*\*\*

"We need to pick up Tusker and bring him in," Karanja instructed his deputy, Gideon Odhiambo, from his secure phone as he drove back from the Minister's office.

"For what? We haven't yet recovered the cash."

"It has been—it's been returned to the owner."

Karanja heard a gasp at the other end as Gideon queried, "How was it recovered? And where was it? You didn't tell us anything."

"It was highly confidential—we can't talk about it to anyone else."

"Sir, we've been frantically looking for it over a week. Why were we not informed?" Gideon sounded agitated.

"Gideon, I thought you would be happy to know our search is over—but you sound so upset. You see, the transaction has just been completed. We've been told to call off the search. Meanwhile, we have to bring Tusker in."

In an exasperated tone, Gideon asked, "Bring him in for what? For the robbery?"

"No, for the Mary Wilson case."

"For the Mary Wilson case? But what has that got to do with the stolen cash?" Now Gideon started to sound irritated.

"I'll explain to you later. His arrest is a result of the Scotland Yard investigation and is required by the President."

Gideon remained silent.

"You heard me, Gideon. Bring Tusker in."

With a gruff "Yes, sir," Gideon hung up.

\*\*\*

Tusker stretched his legs as he sat in the hut, brooding over his options. The pain in his groin had eased, helped by short spells out in the open in fresh air during the last two days. He would have felt better if Adam had not insisted he wear a cloak over his head as a matter of precaution. Adam's nephew was due back in two days, when Tusker expected to have recovered and be ready to move on.

The stillness was broken when Adam, looking out through the door, yelled, "*Polisi, polisi!* (Police, Police). Run!"

They rushed out of the hut, with Adam leading the way down one of the alleyways. Through a gap in the huts, Adam spied three men in plain clothes who, he was certain, were the police. He directed Tusker to turn into another alleyway and thought he'd gotten away when two uniformed policemen spotted them and gave chase. But Adam found an opening between the huts that led to yet another alleyway. They weaved their way through the crowds and Adam looked back to see Tusker breathless and finding it difficult to keep pace. Their pursuers were nowhere in sight and, a short distance ahead, Adam planned to turn into another alleyway that would lead them safely away from this neighborhood. He had stopped to wait for Tusker when he was almost blinded by a flash of metal in the bright sunlight. Freezing in his tracks, he yelled to Tusker, "Watch out!"

He heard a blood-curdling scream that was even louder and more threatening.

"Murderer! You killed poor Fred!"

A gray-haired man had swung his *panga* (machete) high up in the air. From where he stood, transfixed, there was little Adam could do as he watched the man's hand swiftly descend. Tusker raised his left arm to defend himself, but nothing could arrest the momentum of the firm unwavering hand as it continued its downward descent until the sharp blade of the machete made contact with the victim's jugular vein. Two women screamed and even a seasoned huntsman like Adam had to shut his eyes to avoid witnessing a sight he knew could haunt him the rest of his life.

# Chapter 16

## *Week 2—Wednesday Afternoon*

Rushing back from the cafeteria after grabbing a sandwich for lunch, Jay headed to his office to clear urgent papers before heading to the Annual Summer Fair. The event provided a great opportunity to view new products and services and to build networks. He hadn't missed attending it in the past and this year's event was of greater significance because of Heidi's involvement.

His cell phone rang—it was Ravi Karnik. "So how's it going today, Jay? Feeling better, now that the load is off your back—or, should I say, your mind?"

"Much, much better, thank you, Ravi. I'd almost forgotten how it feels like having eight solid hours of sound sleep. I really appreciate your pulling it off. So, how's it going with you?"

"Listen, I'm sure you'd want to know who's behind the stolen money and the break-in at your house. But I hope you'd appreciate that I'm required to keep some information confidential. I can't disclose too many details but, as your good friend, I'm taking the liberty of throwing around some clues and leave it to you to put the pieces together."

"I understand," said Jay. "And I sure am curious to know what that was all about."

"All right, let's see how good you are at connecting dots to complete the picture."

"Okay."

"Today's puzzle is obviously not exactly kids' stuff because you'll first need to pick out the dots and then connect them in order to put the picture together."

"Ravi, why have you chosen today of all the days to make things sound so mysterious?"

"Just trying to lighten things up, my friend, particularly after what you and Heidi have gone through. Anyway, tune into this afternoon's news on the local TV channel. I expect them to cover the events that are of interest to you. Which means that you need to sit through the entire broadcast. Now, I know that can be an ordeal normally, but you said you've had a good night's sleep, so you should be able to sit through it. You need to pick up the news that matters, then connect the dots, as I said, and get the whole picture."

"The stuff one is required to do to please a good old friend! Instead of putting me through this grueling exercise, why not make things a lot easier by quietly whispering something in Heidi's or my ears?"

"Can't do it, my friend, on a matter of principle. And, oh yes, don't bother checking with me if you've come up with the right answer. Once again, my lips are sealed."

"I understand, I understand," muttered Jay. "I'm now on my own. The afternoon TV news had better be good, but I guess I must thank you anyway."

"Oh, one more thing. Just remember: I did this for Heidi's sake. I felt I owed it to her."

They hung up and Jay was running late by the time he hopped into his car and headed to Heidi's school.

Along the way, he remembered that he hadn't spoken with Julius Wachira after the issue was resolved. He called on his cell. "Hello, Julius. How're you doing? I've been wanting to call you to thank you for all you've done for me."

"You are welcome, *Bwana* Jay."

"You're probably aware that Ravi Karnik has resolved the issue, as you suggested. Incidentally, you must have heard from your nephew—his services have been extended by three months."

"Oh yes, he did tell me about it. Thank you for your help."

Jay was about to hang up when Julius said, "I think I should let you know. We have instructions to pick up a notorious ivory poacher. He was the one who raided your house. Now you and your wife can relax."

With an unmistakably buoyant feeling, Jay stepped on the gas as he raced to Heidi's school.

*\*\*\**

Frantically putting finishing touches to the arrangements for the Annual Summer Fair at her school, Heidi noticed many of the stall owners were just as busy with last-minute chores. With a few minutes to go before the start time, Heidi made a trip to the restrooms to freshen up. Glancing in the mirror, she noted the few remaining traces of the bruises, while the swelling around her mouth and neck had receded. She appeared fresh and relaxed, with her maid, Beatrice, commenting in the morning that she looked positively radiant.

The gates soon opened and invitees and the general public started to stream in. She saw some of her friends arriving and went forward to greet them. One of them was her friend Karen, from the former East Germany, married to a Russian. Accompanying her was another Russian couple: the wife's name was Olga and she turned to introduce her husband to Heidi. He towered well over six feet and, when they shook hands, Heidi's dainty palm disappeared in his huge paw-like hands. His name was Mikhail Smirnoff and, despite his overbearing physique, Heidi found him warm and friendly. It struck her as odd, though, that the couple appeared to have suffered recent injuries—Olga had bruises around her neck and her wrists, while Mikhail had a swollen cheek and wore a bandage around his left wrist.

The halls started to fill up and attendees moved around the various stalls. Some of the exhibitors with a hospitality section offered snacks and beverages. One of the German companies served what they proudly announced as "authentic German bratwurst and sauerkraut."

Heidi watched senior government officials, diplomats, company executives, businessmen, and other well-known personalities streaming in and started to wonder why Jay hadn't shown up. But there he was, cheerful as always while greeting his friends, though he walked with a slight limp from the torn ligament.

***

Spotting Heidi, Jay went over and complimented her and the organizers on the impressive arrangements. She introduced him to her friend Karen and to Mikhail and Olga Smirnoff. Jay struck up a conversation with them and, when he learned they were Russians, asked where they lived. The smile vanished from Jay's face when Mikhail said they lived in Lower Kabete. *Could he be the Russian who was in the news?* Jay wondered. If that was true, then the encounter with the burglars nearly a week earlier must have been more violent than was reported—they both had visible bruises on their bodies. While Jay wondered if he might be able to dig out more information from the Russian, Heidi announced, "Oh look, the Collins are here."

Jay turned around to see Anne and Richard Collins approaching them, accompanied by a poker-faced, unmistakably British-looking gentleman.

"Hello, hello," beamed Richard as he and Anne hugged Heidi and gave her a peck on her cheek and then gripped Jay's hand for a warm handshake. "As you can see, I've been able to persuade our very special visitor from England to accompany us. I trust, Heidi, you'll see to it he won't regret spending his afternoon here."

Anne cut in before anyone could respond. "I'd like to introduce my cousin, Nicholas Cunningham, who has been deputed by Scotland Yard on a special assignment here. Nick, please meet our very dear friends, Heidi and Jay Gupté."

As they shook hands, Nicholas said, "Please, call me Nick. And even though Anne might have made it sound like a cloak-and-dagger mission, I believe anyone in this country who reads a newspaper would know why I'm here. And Heidi," he said, turning to her, "I sure am looking forward to spending a very interesting afternoon here. Thank so much for inviting me."

"You're most welcome. You'll get a good idea of the type of companies that do business here. And yes, I think almost everyone in this room would know why you're in Kenya."

"Wouldn't it add to the excitement if we were to announce we have a very special personality among us today?" Jay asked.

"Now that's definitely forbidden," Nick quickly put in. "And I can produce an order from the President to enforce that," he added as others smiled.

"Nick spent a few days at the Maasai Mara, not as a tourist, but as part of his assignment," said Richard. "And yet he witnessed virtually everything there was to see, including a kill by a pair of cheetahs. I've made three trips to the Mara over the years and I've yet to witness a kill. Can anyone explain that?"

"Peter Otieno, the police officer who accompanied me, had an interesting theory," said Nick. "A female leopard, who he felt took a fancy to me, must have done so because she sensed aristocratic blood in me. And then, about a lioness, his theory was that she probably picked up a whiff of Scotch whisky in my system. So, Richard, next time you visit a game park, keep these important tips in mind."

"There you go, Richard, you never wanted to believe me when I told you I have aristocratic blood in me—something that you do not," came Anne's rejoinder. "I'm afraid there's nothing you can do about it."

"Enough of this crap," Richard countered. "Nick, if you seriously start believing all that every Peter and every Otieno tells you, all I can say is you're in for a miserable time."

The group dispersed to move around and visit the stalls.

Jay looked at his watch—it was time for the afternoon news. He had called Heidi soon after speaking with Ravi and she mentioned their staff room was equipped with a TV set. She led him to the empty staff room and turned on the TV. She headed back to the main hall, while Jay tuned to the local channel that aired the afternoon news.

It began with the somber announcement that His Excellency the President had accepted the resignation of one of the senior-most ministers in the Cabinet, popularly known as George K. The honorable minister was retiring on health grounds and the next few minutes were spent paying tributes to his services. Jay wondered if this was one of the dots Ravi spoke about.

The next news item was far more interesting. Even the news announcer appeared animated as she announced the gruesome slaying by a machete-wielding man of the notorious poacher, Jonathan Kiilu, also known as "Tusker" John. The incident took place a little earlier in the crowded slums of Kibera, even as the police were closing in to arrest the poacher. They confirmed that the poacher was being arrested for the murder of the British tourist, Mary Wilson, the subject of a joint investigation by the Scotland Yard. Police were still to establish the identity and motive of the killer, who was arrested.

Jay stood riveted at attention with an air of certainty that this event was an important dot—even Julius Wachira had said a poacher was to be arrested. The ensuing news was of no interest until the end of the broadcast when his ears perked up—the Wildlife Conservation Fund had announced the receipt of a large donation from an anonymous donor. Though the amount was not mentioned, Jay felt certain this was another important dot. He stood in silence, absorbing these diverse news items and connecting the dots as Ravi had advised.

Turning the TV off, he walked out, deep in thought—unable to fit in one piece of information. Who was the man who had slain the poacher? Was it important to the puzzle he was working on? He decided to put that piece of information aside and to get back to the other bits. And then, in a flash, the dots started to connect and his face broke into a smile. Yes, he had figured out the whole picture.

Jay limped along to the main hall and noticed Heidi standing with her colleagues. He gingerly walked up and stood behind her, wrapped his arm around her waist, and smoothly led her away. She was overawed when he planted a kiss on her ear and whispered through her hair "It's all over, *liebchen,* it's all over. I'll explain it later."

It was Heidi's turn to be embarrassed by Jay's gestures. Such displays of affection in public were rare in the modest Kenyan society—but today, they both could not have cared less.

Leading her back to her friends, Jay sauntered around the stalls looking for Richard. He spotted Nick engrossed in serious discussions in one of the stalls, while Richard and Anne emerged from it—he walked toward them.

"He's run into an old colleague," said Anne, gesturing toward Nick. "That company specializes in security and surveillance systems and Nick is very much into that sort of stuff."

It was now their turn to be guided gently by Jay into a quiet corner, where he said, "I'm afraid, Richard, I wasn't quite frank with you the other day when we talked about the shooting near your house. I was actually caught bang in the middle of a crossfire between the cops and a gang in a getaway vehicle. I had to pull my car outside one of your neighbors gates to stay clear."

"I'm sorry to hear that, dear chap, but what happened and why didn't you let us know?"

"Neither of you was hurt, I trust?" an anxious Anne asked.

"Oh, we were fine. The thugs managed to dodge the cops and sped away with the police hot on their heels. After they left, I started to drive away when the headlights picked up something bright lying on the road. It was either thrown out or fell off accidentally from the thug's vehicle when it swerved."

"And—what was it?" Richard asked.

Lowering his voice, Jay said, "I was mesmerized right from the moment I laid my eyes on it. And mind you, this was just moments after several gunshots were fired barely fifty yards from where our car was parked."

Both Anne and Richard stood riveted in their positions, waiting for Jay to continue. "I shouldn't have succumbed to the temptation and should have known that picking it up could get me in trouble."

"That's right; I would have just driven away," said Richard. "*Hakuna matata* (No problems) with the authorities—that's what I believe in."

"But what was it, Jay?" asked an impatient Anne.

After ascertaining that no one was within earshot, Jay whispered, "It was a thing of beauty. An Italian leather briefcase; and it was beige in color…"

"Wow, those things are gorgeous!" Richard exclaimed.

"… and it was a limited-edition piece," added Jay.

"Now, that must have been a real piece of art. I've seen some of those items in Florence. Those Italians produce some amazing stuff from leather," said Richard, warming up.

"So you did pick it up, right Jay?" asked Anne.

"Of course he would—can't blame him for it," Richard felt he should rush to Jay's defense. "It's hard to resist that stuff. Remember, darling, how we ended up on a shopping spree while we were in Florence?" he asked looking at Anne. "We had planned on buying only a—"

"Jay," Anne interrupted in a commanding tone. "What did you find in the briefcase?"

Richard continued on his glorious Italian journey. "Those guys are masters at producing some exquisite stuff. My uncle was in Italy with the Occupation Troops during the Second World War. And boy, was he impressed with the stuff they had. Even today, he uses the leather suitcase he bought there."

Anne raised her voice. "Enough, Richard. Jay, what was in the briefcase?"

Jay gestured to them both to come closer as he whispered, "There was cash; plenty of it. Fifteen million shillings."

"Fifteen million shillings!" exclaimed Richard.

A few heads turned around as Anne gestured with her hands to keep their voices low. She asked, "Why're you guys spending so much time arguing about a briefcase that costs about two thousand shillings when there were fifteen million shillings in it?"

"You'd never get a piece like that for two thousand shillings," Richard interrupted. "Probably more like five thousand shillings."

"All right, five thousand," Anne sounded exasperated. "But what have you done with it?"

"I threw it away in a garbage dump," Jay replied.

"What, you threw away fifteen million shillings in a garbage dump?"

It was Anne who had now raised her voice. Jay could sense that the heads that had turned around a minute earlier found it hard to resist the temptation to do so again. One head remained half-turned, and Jay wondered if that person was attempting to swivel his eyeballs around backward in their sockets without turning his head. He responded, "Of course not, Anne. I dumped the briefcase in the garbage."

"Ooh, no," moaned Richard. "That's not pretty. Was there no—"

But Anne refused to be interrupted. "Jay, where are those fifteen million shillings?"

"I held on to them—I did not want to hand the money over to the police. One can't be too sure what those guys would do with it."

"You did the right thing, my dear fellow," commented Richard. "Those guys cannot be trusted. As I keep saying, the British government spent nearly half a million quid training the local police, but the guys have frittered all that away."

"Oh, stop your ranting, Richard," admonished Anne. Lowering her voice, she said, "So Jay, are you still holding on to the money?"

"Of course not," Jay replied. "I have been able to return it to the owner."

"So then all has ended well," Anne commented. "I'm glad you didn't end up having problems from what you did that night."

Jay cleared his throat and said, "Actually, we did. That night after the shootout, I think some *askari* in your neighborhood saw my car and mentioned it to the police."

"The darned fool did?" Richard asked. "I wonder which *askari* was it. I'm not sure if I could have done anything to stop them from talking to the police, Jay. So did the police pass by your house?"

"Now that's where things became messy. No, the police didn't visit us—but some armed burglars did. You know we mentioned a break-in last Friday. Well, it was far more serious than what Heidi and I have been telling you."

"What happened?" asked Anne.

"They had already broken into the house by the time Heidi came home early in the afternoon. There were three of them, all armed, and they surprised her as she walked in. But Heidi did something incredible that day— using her karate skills, she beat the crap out of all three and they ran away."

"You're kidding, right?" Richard asked.

"No, honestly, no kidding. Some other time, we'll tell you exactly what happened."

"Did they hurt her really badly?" Anne asked.

"Just a few bruises, "Jay answered.

"Oh, the poor thing," Anne said. "I must talk to her."

"Not now, please—she's busy. Later, perhaps."

Over Anne's shoulder, Jay could see Nick Cunningham walking toward them. Reluctant to discuss this subject in Nick's presence, Jay announced, "Anyway, the important thing is that the gang has been liquidated."

Jay noticed Mikhail Smirnoff walking toward the same stall from where Nick had emerged. Oblivious to what was going on behind his back, Richard asked Jay, "Who were those guys? They obviously had some taste; choosing an expensive Italian leather briefcase for this transaction."

"That sounds familiar," said Nick, as Richard and Anne turned around and smiled at him. "An Italian leather briefcase being involved in some dubious operation."

An astonished Jay asked, "Sounds familiar to you? Where did you hear about it?"

"Oh, deep in the Maasai Mara."

"Now that's not possible—unless there are two separate incidents," Jay responded. "The one that we were talking about took place in Nairobi more than a week ago."

"Then that's the same one. Well, I'm telling you this in confidence, but while in the Mara, a police officer told me that he'd spoken to his colleagues here in Nairobi and had gathered that several officers were working on the case of a missing briefcase full of cash. The briefcase sounded special and he even joked that recovering it could well be my next assignment. So, has it been found?"

"Yes, it has been, so I'm afraid you might have to forget about that assignment," replied Jay. "It's a long story, but all's ended well."

"Sorry for interrupting, but I overheard your discussion about an expensive briefcase," a deep voice with a heavy East European accent boomed behind them. They looked up at an oversized hulk of a man. Jay greeted him, "Oh hello, Mikhail. Yes, we were talking about a briefcase—you seem to have had some experience with it."

"Before I respond, I'm curious to know from you," Mikhail turned to face Nick, "did you say the burglars came after you in the Maasai Mara, demanding a briefcase?"

"Oh no, my dear chap, that's not what happened. One of my colleagues mentioned it while we were in the Mara."

"So, you were telling us about your experience?" Jay reminded Mikhail.

"I'm not sure if I should be discussing this, but, last week some burglars broke into my house, demanding a briefcase with cash. Of course, I didn't have it and I was able to chase them away."

"The encounter appears to have been pretty rough," said Nick, taking a closer look at his swollen cheek and the bandage on his wrist.

"So you didn't get to see the briefcase, did you?" asked Richard.

"No, I didn't. But from the way the burglars were talking about it, I suppose it was something very special."

"Oh, you can bet your sweet ass on that—uh, sorry, darling," Richard turned to apologize to his wife. "But to think I missed a great chance to at least get a glimpse of it while it landed just outside my gate." He stopped himself when he realized he'd said more than he should have.

"Has the briefcase been recovered?" Mikhail asked.

Jay replied, "Yes, but it's been thrown away in a garbage dump."

"A garbage dump? What a shame!" responded Nick.

"That's what I also felt—an inglorious end for something that deserved better," said Richard.

"But those burglars—they were after the cash until two days ago," Mikhail added.

"Two days ago?" Jay asked, with a puzzled look on his face. "I think we need to have a chat a little later."

Nick, meanwhile, was in a pensive mood. "There's something that has been baffling me. When I started working on this case, I struggled to find a single clue. Nothing worked and I was beginning to lose confidence in my capabilities. And then, *voila!* Come Saturday afternoon and a chance mention of... of the thing you guys have been talking about, sets my mind jingling and the same evening I had the case solved! It sure was an odd experience—one of those things that are hard to explain. Hopefully one fine day, the Lord, in all his wisdom, enlightens me on the role of that prized object so that I can be at peace."

Anne looked at the men around her, shook her head, and said, "And one fine day, I hope the same good Lord, in all his infinite wisdom, enlightens me on why four mature gentlemen are raving, not about any of the attractive women here, but about some mysterious briefcase."

The men exchanged sheepish glances and merely shrugged. Jay excused himself and moved away with Mikhail. Picking up a can of soda from a beverage stall, he led Mikhail to a quiet corner, where he explained, "I'll try and keep it short. The briefcase ended up in my house for reasons that are hard to explain, but it was to be returned to the rightful owner. Meanwhile, a gang of desperate burglars was somehow given the wrong information that it was with you, which is why they attacked you on Thursday. I'm glad you were able to chase them away."

Jay paused for a sip before continuing, "The next day they broke into our house, but didn't succeed. We've since been able to sort things out. The cash was returned to the owner and, an hour ago, I received confirmation that the gang leader was slain."

Mikhail didn't look satisfied. "I'm not too sure about all this. Have all the problems been solved—how can you be so sure?"

In a reassuring tone, Jay said, "I have access to a lot more information on this incident than you have. Let's just say, the bad guys made a mistake and the police messed things up. That's what probably caused the confusion to continue until two days ago. It really is unfortunate you were caught up in this intriguing mix-up, but it's all over. You need have no anxiety about them bothering you again."

With a reassuring smile, Jay turned his attention to the Russian's swollen cheek and the bandaged wrist. "Looks like the encounter was rougher than what was reported in the press."

Mikhail looked down at Jay's injured ankle. "Yeah, it has been a rough week for us all."

They shook hands and went their separate ways.

As the afternoon wore on, an announcement was made that it was time for the raffle drawing. The crowd moved toward a stage set at the corner of the large hall. Jay looked on in admiration at Heidi on the stage, in charge of this part of the program.

After welcoming the attendees, she thanked the donors of the prizes and read out their names. The Chief Guest was a cabinet minister and Heidi invited his wife to come up to the stage. She spun a small barrel that contained slips of papers with numbers and requested that the minister's wife pull out one slip at a time from the barrel. She called out the numbers and the Chief Guest's wife presented prizes to the winners as they came up to the stage.

The final prize was donated by the Italian Embassy. Their ambassador was invited to come up to the stage to pull out the lucky number and present the prize to the winner. He proudly announced that the prize was an exquisite product Italy was renowned for.

Many in the audience had expectant looks on their faces as the lucky number was drawn. When the winner proceeded to the stage, everyone watched in earnest as the winner opened the prize for all to see. The ambassador was right—the prize was an exquisite set of wine glasses with a decanter from Murano, famous for its glassware products.

Heidi thanked the Chief Guest and was about to move the barrel away when the official rose from his seat and walked to the microphone.

"I do not wish to prolong the proceedings or to spoil your pleasant afternoon, ladies and gentlemen. But may I take the liberty of announcing that there is a surprise prize to be given away? Would you allow me to proceed, madam?" he politely addressed Heidi.

"Why yes, of course, sir," Heidi responded with a surprised look on her face. "This is wonderful news for us. Please proceed."

"Thank you, madam," he said. "One of my good friends has donated a very attractive item for what he considers to be a good cause. May I request of the gracious lady that we proceed to draw the lucky number?"

He looked at Heidi, who rolled back the barrel with numbered slips.

"If you would do us the honor?" she asked the Chief Guest to pull out a slip. She called out the number.

"Here," called out the winner from the audience. It was Jay!

The crowd cheered, but those who knew Heidi and Jay jeered in jest and called out, "Rigged... rigged!"

The Chief Guest was pleased to learn that Heidi's husband was the winner. "Well deserved," he said. "I know she has worked hard to put together so many prizes and I'm pleased this prize stays in the family."

Heidi placed the wrapped prize on the table at the center of the stage. She once again thanked the Chief Guest for his generous donation and invited him to open it. Meanwhile, Jay walked up to the stage and stood next to Heidi. Carefully removing the gift-wrapping, the Chief Guest pushed aside the wrapping paper with a flourish to reveal the prize.

Jay's jaw dropped as he stared at the object. He was not the only one in the room—Mikhail Smirnoff, Richard and Anne Collins, and Nick Cunningham stared wide-eyed at the item.

Sitting atop the table—in the center of the stage and glistening under the spotlight—was a briefcase.

It was, without a doubt, not just any ordinary briefcase.

Crafted from expensive Italian leather...

...and the second metal tag read "Limited Edition."

The End

## Prakash Dighé

Prakash Dighé lived in India, Germany, and Kenya before settling in the US. Living in Africa for more than
two decades was, for him, a unique experience and it's
long been his desire to use Kenya—a country with a fascinating colonial history and from where the word "safari" originates—as a setting for a novel. *Limited Edition:
A Poacher's Endgame* represents the fulfillment of
that dream. Prakash lives with his family in Dallas,
Texas.

**Progressive Rising Phoenix Press** is an independent publisher. We offer wholesale discounts and multiple binding options with no minimum purchases for schools, libraries, book clubs, and retail vendors. We also offer rewards for libraries, schools, independent book stores, and book clubs. Please visit our website and wholesale discount page at:

## www.ProgressiveRisingPhoenix.com

**Progressive Rising Phoenix Press** is adding new titles from our award-winning authors on a regular basis and has books in the following genres: children's chapter books and picture books, middle grade, young adult, action adventure, mystery and suspense, contemporary fiction, romance, historical fiction, fantasy, science fiction, and non-fiction covering a variety of topics from military to inspirational to biographical. Visit our website to see our updated catalogue of titles.

CPSIA information can be obtained
at www.ICGtesting.com
USA
33291117
BV00007B/62/P